FROM THE *SECRET LIFE* BOOK SERIES

BECOMING MY OWN F-ING SOULMATE

FROM THE *SECRET LIFE* BOOK SERIES

BECOMING MY OWN F-ING SOULMATE

BRIANNE DAVIS

Printed in the United States of America

Edited by Colette Freedman
Copy Edited by Mollie Traver
Cover Design by Mark Gantt
Back Cover Photography by James Depietro
Formatting by Elaine York, Allusion Publishing (http://www.allusionpublishing.com)

First printing edition 2026
ISBN: 978-1-7361065-5-6 (paperback)
ISBN: 978-1-7361065-7-0 (ebook)
ISBN: 978-1-7361065-6-3 (hardback)

Published by Just B Productions

@secretlifenovel | secretlifenovel.com
@thebriannedavis | briannedavis.com
@secretlifepodcast | secretlifepodcast.com

To my readers—thank you for walking with me from book one to this next chapter. If the first book gave you comfort, hope, or the reminder that you are not alone, I pray this one carries you even further. You are the reason these words exist, and the reason I keep writing.

TABLE OF CONTENTS

Names have been changed to protect the shameless, the guilty, the drama queens, and anyone who'd rather set themselves on fire or take a chainsaw to their balls than get outed here.

Yes, this is a filthy rehash of the addiction and dating—equal parts trainwreck and dark comedy. But let's not kid ourselves: I'm dragging a deadly, rarely-talked-about disease out of the shadows and into your face.

So laugh, cringe, and try NOT to identify—then keep reading.

Buckle up, buttercup.

Enjoy!

PREFACE

FUCK ME! Another Ten Rules (Dating Edition)

I KNOW—I ALREADY handed you my Ten Commandments for getting sober from sex and love addiction. But here I am, deep in the wild, glitchy, chaotic world of modern *dating*, and guess what? This recovering addict needs another damn rulebook just to survive the pack of filtered wolves and emotionally unavailable man-babies. HELP ME, HIGHER POWER!

Turns out, recovery was just *Level One*. Level Two? It's navigating breadcrumbing, love bombing, ghosting, and the entire rollercoaster of toxic love *while* trying not to lose yourself again. I mean, can I go from a fearful avoidant—needy and anxious in the beginning, craving the dopamine hit of being love bombed, fantasizing about forever—only to turn cold and distant the second I "hook" them, ghosting them like they were never even there? Apparently, yes. And that's a problem.

And let's not forget the seductive trap of trauma bonding—where the emotional chaos feels so familiar, it tricks you into thinking it's love.

Now I'm wrestling with the real questions:

Can someone anxiously attached really learn to date securely?

Can I stop falling for emotionally unavailable men and calling it "chemistry"?

Can I recognize red flags before I'm ten orgasms deep and lost in a fantasy whirlwind?

Can I stop confusing chaos and passion with connection?

Can I let go of the fantasy and sit in the *reality* of a slow-burn, healthy love?

Can I even recognize what healthy love *is*?

So yeah, hold on tight to your private parts—we're going in deep again.This time, it's not just about getting sober. It's about healing the patterns that got us addicted in the first place. Because spoiler alert: Your soulmate? It's *YOU*.

Let's get to work.

A RECAP of the first set of rules from
Secret Life of a Hollywood Sex and Love Addict:

Rule 1: The key to getting better and becoming healthy is admitting you have a problem.

Rule 2: Believe in your own form of GOD, not anyone else's.

Rule 3: Walk through the fire and LET IT BURN!

Rule 4: To heal and move forward, look back at the WHY.

Rule 5: ADULT UP—Admit your mistakes.

Rule 6: Compare and Despair—Stop questioning your worth.

Rule 7: Let go of the people and things that trigger the SHIT out of you.

Rule 8: Be honest—Secrets keep you sick.

Rule 9: Help others without expecting anything in return.

Rule 10: We all die alone—Love yourself first.

INTRO

"WHERE THE FUCK IS MY SOULMATE?!" I declared loudly to a roomful of female sex and love addicts at my Sunday morning meeting in Brentwood, California. It was my turn to share—a full three minutes where I had the floor to spew my problems. This part of the Sex and Love Addicts Anonymous (SLAA) meeting was a brilliant solution for a room of self-obsessed addicts like me, who loved to hear their own bullshit. *Believe me—we needed a timer, a VERY loud one.*

It was a captive audience, and I was taking full advantage of my soapbox. "I'm tired, ladies. I hate dating in LA. I'm so over these horrible dates." A huge sigh as my head dramatically flung back in desperation. "Where is he already?" Insert an enormous whine after this statement. "Or maybe I'll just stay single and hire a male prostitute when I need a release?" Without me even realizing it, the timer had gone off—I was still so self-involved, I kept talking. *Obnoxious, I know! Sorry, not sorry.*

Grunting like a petulant child, I added, "I'm serious, I wonder if my sponsor, Alice, will allow that? I really don't want to go on any more of those stupid online dates. I mean, I asked a guy what his favorite flower was the other day at lunch. I don't. I just didn't know what else to talk about. Ugh, it's so hard to healthy sober date. It was a hundred times easier to use my old tricks to intrigue with a guy, then trap him in my web of deceit and use the shit out of him till he was a broken shell of a man." Insert a crazy chuckle and a twirl of my pretend bad-guy mustache.

The meeting's leader that evening had to cut off my tirade. "It's time, about two minutes ago, Roxanne."

I snapped back into the reality of the SLAA room, realizing everyone was staring at me in annoyance. "Sorry. I didn't hear the timer. Thanks for listening."

I closed my eyes and prayed that the eight other women didn't think I was a total nutjob. This was my life right now. Sober dating in Los Angeles was literally... *hell on earth*.

If you remember, I liked to visualize my life as if it were a scene in a television show or movie.

INT. RESTAURANT—HORROR DATING MONTAGE

ROXANNE sits at a table with a variety of men coming in and out of focus as she encounters a number of horrible dates. Taylor Swift's anthem "You Need to Calm Down" keeps the beat in the background of the unbearable interaction Roxanne has had to endure.

An actor type sits down across from Roxanne, wearing a beanie and scarf in hundred-degree weather.

ACTOR DUDE
I just did a scene, *Frankie and Johnny*, in class with my ex-girlfriend. Super method. We did so great, the teacher said we needed to travel the scene to the other classes. So, I'll be spending a lot of time rehearsing with her. Hope you're not another jealous psycho woman.

                    ROXIE
No, I—

                  ACTOR DUDE
Like, I'm talking Brando
method. She and I will be
having a lot of sex. Don't
worry, we're not getting
back together or anything—
it's just necessary for the
emotional honesty of the
scene work. You understand.

                    ROXIE
Actually, I don't—

                  ACTOR DUDE
I knew you were a jealous
psycho.

A pervert sound-mixer type
sits down across from Roxanne,
with a long leather trench
coat and awkward demeanor.

                  PERVERT DUDE
Sorry, I didn't mean to touch
the side of your boob when
we said hello. Please don't
report me. I can't get in
trouble again.

                   ROXANNE
Again?

                   PERVERT
It was just one time. Okay,
four, but it's so hard to be
a man after #MeToo. Know what
I mean?

                   ROXANNE
You mean it's difficult to be
a white, privileged man in
Hollywood?

                      7

PERVERT
You get me. You really get
me.

An old dude, fifty going on
seventy-five, sits across from
Roxanne. She double-checks
his profile picture.

OLD DUDE
I know my profile picture is a
little dated.

ROXANNE
A little?

OLD DUDE
But age is just a number,
right?

ROXANNE
No.

The no-show dude: It's just
Roxanne with her glass of wine,
looking like a sad, thirty-
something woman ditched on a
blind date.

ROXANNE
(To the camera) See? This
sucks! How's a girl supposed
to survive in this town?

We hear the Serenity Prayer
as it snaps Roxanne back into
the SLAA women's meeting.

SMASH TO BLACK

"Keep coming back. It works, if you work it and you're
worth it." Chanting signaled the closing of the SLAA meeting.
Once again, I was so lost in the replay of another fantasy that

I had missed everyone else's shares. *Good job, Roxanne! Way to stay present and in the moment.*

As I picked up my navy-blue Chanel Medium Filigree Vanity Case to hightail it out of that way-too-intimate candle-lit church, an old member of SLAA, Pinkie, reminded me very clearly, "Roxanne, don't block your own blessings. We are not allowed to be our needy, greedy, and seedy selves. As you've probably heard, nothing good in life is free. God bless you and have a great week."

I smiled at her treacly, goody-two-shoes advice, but I really wanted to scream, *Believe me, I know! I feel like I'm paying the price!*

CHAPTER ONE

The old identity must die for a new one to emerge—"What the Fuck, AGAIN?"

"WHY AM I NOT fixed yet? I did all this work and I'm still a hot mess."

Welcome to the shitstorm of my glitzy Hollywood world of recovery in sex and love addiction. Yep, that's right—I'm back! It's ME, your favorite Hollywood sex and love addict—nutjob, actress extraordinaire Roxanne. Named after the best Police song ever—*the street walker putting on her red light.*

I'm back and still sober in my program of sex and love addiction. I guess I'm one of the few willing to admit publicly that I'm actually a sex and love addict in this crazy industry of showbiz. I'm okay with that. I don't mind being the face of this disease. It's not like I'm Kendall Jenner approaching a police officer during a protest and handing him a can of Pepsi. I'm not appropriating Black Lives Matter protests. I'm just sharing my personal fuck-ups publicly. Especially as a woman. Look, I'm just your average working actress always putting on a show, but this time, I'm truly willing to be seen, especially since you know most of my dirty, dark secrets. It would be easier to keep myself locked in the anonymity that our twelve-step program suggests, but this is not the path I've chosen. I want to break all the stigma and shame of this deadly disease. So, I've decided to throw open the doors to my most horrible rock bottoms and show you the path to my recovery, official-ly becoming the only woman in showbiz willing to say, "Hi. I'm suffering from sex and love addiction." *You're welcome. Man, if you only knew who was really hanging with me in my meetings, it would blow your freaking mind.*

I definitely wouldn't be your first choice for the face of this disease. I accept this. If you knew who sat in these rooms, I'd probably be a distant eleventh or twelfth. There are much bigger celebrities than little old me. People who have graced the cover of... *PEOPLE*. At this point, I don't even feel like a celebrity. This sobriety has really humbled me. Saint Vincent de Paul's famous quote goes, "Humility is nothing but truth, and pride is nothing but lying." *And I was definitely humbled in my driveway two years ago.*

A quick recap of my fabulously messed up life that you might have missed on the first go-around. I hit my initial bottom in my driveway with two men I thought I loved. For your information—You actually can't love two people at once. And I couldn't love anybody because I didn't even know how to love myself.

Remember when boyfriend NYC was acting like a delu-sional pirate, waving around that Swiss Army Knife in boy-friend ATL's face, wanting to cut him? It's kind of funny to look back at the insanity of my life. It feels like it was just yesterday that the police were at my house breaking up my dual boyfriends' fight over whose dick was bigger *(NYC's, by a solid two inches)* and my neighbors were all watching like we were some bad TikTok clip. Now I'm so distant from that kind of drama, it feels like it happened to someone else. Instead, I imagine I was one of my neighbors watching and eating pop-corn, yelling, "Cut that lying, cheating son of a bitch!" *Yep—those sick, devilish fantasies still exist.*

Alice, my badass SLAA sponsor, who saved my life in more ways than one, blatantly loved to point out, "Your main character defect of wanting to escape and live in fantasy will always be present. So, watch that part of you, Roxie." *Blah, blah, blah!* Yes, I often dissolve into the screenplay of my fantasies, so I mentally block out most of her rants since I've heard them all before. I'm very aware of that disconnected part of me, but come on, don't most people not want to be present 24/7? Isn't that why we all have social media on our phones? Candy Crush for the ADHD-ers, Wordle for the intellectuals, Facebook for the over-40s, and Instagram for everyone else. Oh, and don't forget the ... TikTok or Snapchat for the Gen Alphas. *Jeez, I'm not the only one playing in a disconnected fantasy land over here.*

Anyway, I had finally changed for the better. I was way more present than I'd ever been. I didn't use people anymore. I was kinder and more patient. I truly loved myself. I had learned to love others. With all that internal growth, I realized it was time to take off my training wheels and join the big bad world of online dating. Honestly, I was a little reluctant but excited to bring back the sexual energy of being with another human being. I prepared myself to be rejected. I primed myself with my carefully cultivated dating plan that Alice helped me create. Logically, I understood it might take time to find someone I would be interested in, especially since I'd never healthy dated. Instead, I'd always been a professional unhealthy dater, as I repeatedly stumbled into relationships with my film costars while simultaneously attached to my high school boyfriend. *Classy, Roxie!*

I was anxious but determined to bring my type-A vigor to the transactions of profile dating. Jumping head-first into the shallow single pool of Hollywood, hoping for a fun, lustful outcome. Record scratch. Nope, that's right, folks, this year of sober dating became my next level of HELL. Because let's get real—dating in LA sucks!

Humor me, please—can you quickly close your eyes and imagine how much worse it is to date when you are completely your authentic self? Fully vulnerable and unapologetically real? Okay, yes, I know, I should have been myself the whole time, but give me a break. I'm a work in progress over here. And most people only show the best sides of themselves while dating, right? Think about it—you can't have an agenda when asking questions. You can't inflate your own ego to make yourself sound better than you actually are. You can't get too personal. You can't get too deep. The words of my therapist constantly scrolled across my brain like Wall Street ticker tape: "You have to keep it light and polite. No trauma bonding." Dr. Kath echoed this handy hint at every grueling session. She knows her stuff, especially since she specializes in dealing with addiction in the entertainment business.

Sounds really bad, right? *Well, it was.*

If you can recall, after I set my dating plan I was on my way to London to shoot that movie as the female lead. I truly felt like I "got this." That I had it all figured out, especially after Alice and I went for our official Echo Park swan-boat decompression ride. I was proud and confident that I had shed my addict self—*getting to the core by digging deeper with my personal growth.* I had peeled back the layers of my psyche to get to my real self. For the first time in a very long time, I felt alive. I felt like I could handle anything. My internal dialogue was something along the lines of, "Y'all, I'm good to go. Sign me up for a soul-stirring partnership."

News flash with the "y'all"— I must've been tired since my Southern was coming out. Time for my daily second espresso shot. My pink-clouded fantasy of being reborn and healed was obviously a BIG FAT NOPE!

Standing in my galley kitchen, knocking back my second— who am I kidding? —my fourth shot of espresso, I started to contemplate the sequences of my life. Reality hit me square in the face: I felt more lost than ever. How was that possible after all the work I'd done? The year I'd struggled through. The digging through my internal crap to get to my GOLD? *How the hell was that possible?*

Let's just say that things did not turn out the way I imagined they would. First of all, my this-is-going-to-make-me-a-bona-fide-star movie got pushed till the end of the year. I was supposed to start shooting six months ago, but production got pushed because of the instability of the entertainment industry. Dr. Kath repeatedly informed me that being an actress was the worst career choice for my addiction to fantasy and the desperate need for stability in my life. *Good times!* Here's the thing—productions get pushed all the time. That happens even when you are packed and ready to go with a ticket in hand. No idea why, that's just how it works in the business. One minute you have a job and the next you're back on unemployment, waiting for the magic-casting-fairy to hire you. *It's very empowering as a young woman! NOT!*

Secondly, with the postponement of shooting that part, I didn't qualify for my SAG health insurance. *No Vagina Gate trips to the ER this quarter!* Between career disappointments and navigating the whole dating world, I had hit a wall. Everything had come to a head. The biggest problem: I wasn't sure if I was coming or going with this whole online dating on Raya. Let me introduce you to this particular dating site. It's a super exclusive site that is far more elite than Match, less god-like than Hinge, less religious than JDate and Christian Mingle, and less horny than Tinder. It's a site where all the celebrities date each other with their cool, stylized music-picture montages. Where they act like they never stalk each other on Instagram or hit up each other's movie premieres. It's the site that *E! News* mentions every time a newly divorced star joins. Yep, that one! I was officially a member. *I know—I was kind of shocked that they let an old C-lister actress like me join their site. But I'm blonde, semi-hot, and under the age of forty, so I met their requirements.*

I told Alice while floating in our swan boat, "I don't want to date. I'm enjoying being single for the first time ever." AKA dating myself! But NOOO, she said dramatically, "I will not let you turn into an old maid. Get your ass out there. You are adulting up! You are learning to navigate your life in sober relationships, not sober singlehood. Humans are meant to be in relationships with other humans. Time to suit up and show up for your life, Roxie. Pronto." *I wanted to strangle her.* Don't get me wrong—I loved her very much and was grateful to her for saving my life three dozen times. All I was thinking when she demanded I get to my next level of sobriety was: where can I hide her body... after I kill her? I was over her psycho-cheerleader pep talk. I didn't want to go to her house after the swan boat ride from hell and eat our celebratory one-year sushi dinner. Instead, I wanted to go home to gorge on In-N-Out Double-Doubles by myself in my own bed. *No Protein Style lettuce wrap this time! I was eating that butter bun!*

The truth about my hesitation around dating that I had never shared: I was scared. I was scared to be seen. I mean, really *seen.* Plus, I was never good at dating in the first place. I hated small talk. I despised eating a side salad at dinner when what I really wanted was the hot wings with extra blue cheese! FYI—hell NO to ranch dressing. It makes me sick to my stomach. Too much garlic! Please tell that to the fired Vanderpump reality girl who had a deal with the Hidden Valley Ranch company! No judgment, but ranch is nasty! *Okay, maybe a little judgment.*

My major dating dilemma: I didn't do casual. I would normally move so fast with guys that you could never call it DATING. You know the joke, "What does a lesbian bring to a second date? A U-Haul." Well, I worked with the speed and commitment of a lesbian, albeit one who didn't like pussy. I loved dick, and I had my spiderweb of entrapment perfectly constructed. First, I was always that person who portrayed herself to be cooler than she was; I didn't need anything from anyone. That hooked them in. In the next breath, I would transform into the naïve, save-me girl who needed a man to take care of her, which men love. They love to save us. It was a 100% man-hook move. I would reel them in, portraying their "perfect girl," falsely advertising the manipulative message that I could never survive without them. I flirted, intrigued, and lied to get my fix of attention and validation. And when the HIGH started to wean, I would string them along while looking for a new victim. That was my pattern! *Hook, line, and sinker!* That method of scheming was designed for all the men in my life. I didn't know how to do that no-hidden-agenda first date thing. You know, where you try to get to know someone before you become intimate? You try to become their friend to see if you are both compatible with each other. Can this way of life sound any duller? *Nope, I don't think so.*

The only thing an addict like me is interested in is complete fantasy euphoria. Every other emotion is a problem. I loved being in a state of pure elation. I relished the predatory vibration my body felt while my mind drew up an unconscious plan to conquer and destroy anyone who entered my vicinity. *Dun dun duuun...* except one. My weakness, that toned and perfect-chiseled-dick West—THE EX. You remember that B-list CW actor who was the best-looking specimen I'd ever slept with? That ex-boyfriend of mine, who we both tortured each other? Playing those power-struggle games of being together? Acting like we were available and ready to commit, then someone would ghost? *Sounds like two fickle, attention-seeking actors, right?* Unfortunately, I had to give him up like he was a syringe of emotional heroin. Some nights, I still flashed back to my epic bottoming-out with him—that moment I looked in the mirror while on his toilet peeing out his semen! I saw the insanity of my behavior when he texted me and I went to his house, and screwed him up against the wall after my first meeting at SLAA. *Yep, the classic addict move!*

Hold up, record scratch, I just flat-out lied to you. Full transparency: That wasn't my biggest bottoming-out. I forgot my Hotel Bel-Air slip! Crap, my bad! Sometimes old habits die hard. Listen, I try my best to always tell the truth, not even a little white lie. If I don't, one lie leads to another lie, and then next thing you know, I'm sprawled out on my back or front, keeping secrets in all areas of my life. That's how this disease works. You have to be thoroughly and vigorously honest.

My ultimate shit-show-in-a-fuck-factory slip from my sobriety was the semi-threesome with Superstar and Cool-girl. Rewind—me throwing up on him, which led to Superstar throwing up on Coolgirl's naked breasts. Oh, and don't forget the follow-up of mistaken identity as a high-class call girl making $500 that night with the gorgeous Italian foreigner. I still don't know his name and never saw him again. Man, this disease is a tricky motherfucker.

After all that self-made sexual trauma, I was officially in the clear with my dating rules and red-flag lists. I dove right into the shallow dating pool on that ridiculous Raya dating app. It was bloody terrifying to see the available prospects in LA. Especially the semi-famous ones. How was I going to get through this without acting like someone else? Playing a role? Wearing the old facade mask? Come on, that was my jam back in the addict-self days. Instead, I had to sit in front of all these random dudes who were prettier than I was and be my *real self*? The ME I just met for the first time in years? Good god, I definitely needed my Higher Power on my side. *This kind of authenticity sucks a big fat nut.*

My apologies for jumping straight into my drama of dating. I was supposed to be the perfect poster girl of recovery from sex and love addiction. The pink-clouded recovery haven for all those unicorns, lollipops, and rainbows of sobriety. Yep, that's not what it was like at all. It was a constant upheaval to keep my spiritual sobriety—but there had been some major successes in my life. Other than the horrific dating experiences, things had been pretty great. I'd been doing dang good in other areas of my life. I'd been hitting the gym, getting ready for my role in the delayed movie. The production dates getting pushed was a true blessing for me to get back into top shape, since I had let myself go that last year, eating away my feelings, instead of trying to screw them away. Yes, I transferred my behavior to gorging on food, which included bagels, cakes, and those delicious Mother's Circus Animal Cookies. I had become a professional carb loader. Seriously, I could devour a whole bag of animal cookies in one sitting. *Not the mini 1 oz pack. I'm talking the 18 oz party size.*

Alice gave me a break on the emotional eating since I was doing all that hard work to get to the root of my addiction: fear of abandonment, fear of intimacy, fear of commitment, and the good old-fashioned low self-esteem. *You know, those pesky core issues that most humans suffer from.*

There I was—flaws and all. Trying to do better. I had officially been sober for a year and a half. But even with all my sobriety time and awareness, I was still a full-blown sex and love addict. Yes, we self-gratification monsters can change our ways, but we still have our addict selves trying to run the show. I mean, you just heard my share at that Sunday women's meeting. There I was at the precipice of my sobriety, wanting to take the next step in my vulnerability, but instead, I was starting to lose my zen-single-girl serenity and peace, dealing with the quirks of healthy dating. *Yep—all bets for emotional sobriety were off!* Emotional sobriety is the ultimate cornerstone of being free from attention, validation, and the high of finding love. Emotional sobriety is the primary goal for anyone addicted to drama and intent on riding the 100-mph super rollercoaster of emotions that life throws at us. I wanted that freedom from self. I knew it would take time to reach that level of awareness and self-control. Sometimes, even after this year and half, that anxiety and fear could be completely overwhelming. Who knows—I might start eating McConnell's Sea Salt Cream & Cookies ice cream for breakfast again. Not a pint. A quart. As I've established, I'm a professional at self-destruction. I love a good behavioral-process addiction. Anything with food, money, or love... give it to me! I will numb out those feelings.

After that embarrassing, rambling share at my women's meeting, I headed over to the fancy zip code, Beverly Hills 90210, for some much-needed self-care. *Always better than the cake and ice cream.* I was meeting my turbo trainer to kick my ass. I had started seeing him about a month before. Much-needed information: He was Coolgirl's brother! *I know, you don't have to tell me!* But I needed him, believe me—this slacker was jiggly all over. Belly, boobs, and butt—my body was experiencing equal-opportunity flab. And he was the best of the best at helping actors tone up and trim down. I'm going to give him a nickname, so you can never figure out who Coolgirl actually was. I think that's the best option for not getting sued, don't you agree? Let's just call him Trainer.

Trainer was a Madonna type! Not the is-a-virgin Madonna, the like-a-virgin Madonna. A sexy, naturally brown-skinned, sculpted specimen who would not take any of my crap. I'm telling you, this guy was no joke. He would fire your ass if you didn't give your workout all you had. I mean—he was a cancel-your-appointments-and-keep-your-money kind of badass dude. Makes sense, especially knowing that Trainer was one of the biggest commodities in Hollywood. He got all the Jennifers (Hudson, Garner, Lawrence, Aniston, Lopez) and Chrises (Hemsworth, Pine, Evans, Pratt, Rock) back into shape. Another much-needed update—Coolgirl and I were still not talking after her forced threesome. But who cares, I needed help, so I hired her brother to get my flabby butt kicked hard. *Glutton for punishment much?*

I felt totally out of place at the super fabulous modelFIT gym. I quickly overshared to Trainer about my holiday vacation, which I'd spent alone at a bougie silent retreat. I know, I should not have revealed so much, but a part of me wanted Trainer to tell his sister how spiritually evolved I'd become. How emotionally healed I was. How manipulative was that crap? *At least I'm aware of my bad behavior.*

I kept blabbering to him while lunging and lifting eight-pound weights strapped to my ankles. *Hey, don't you dare give me that look—eight pounds is a lot. That gets heavy fast.* I was barely breathing while describing the resort. "It's in Napa Valley, called the Silent Stay Retreat Center. It was absolutely stunning. We were high up on the mountain with rolling hills underneath us. The air was clear and crisp. I felt like I was on top of the world and connected to all living things. I did it for over ten days instead of going back home to see my parents."

I dropped the weights since I was having trouble getting my words out. I continued to overshare my reasons. "I needed a break from my father. He wasn't respecting my boundaries as his adult daughter."

Trainer gave me an odd look. I realize this wasn't the time or place to have a discussion about emotional incest with my dear old dad. *What is emotional incest, you ask?* Emotional incest is where a parent treats you like their significant other and wants you to fill their emotional needs, which is definitely not a very healthy parent-to-child relationship. I learned this during my numerous sessions with Dr. Kath. I thought that explanation might be a little too intense for this gym session with Trainer. One of the rules of my sobriety was not getting too personal while dating, but that included pretty much everyone in my life. *No "trauma bonding," we like to call it.* I was Trainer's client. Sure, I was overpaying for his services, but it was not his responsibility to listen to my shitty past. *Keep your side of the street clean, Roxie. NO EMOTIONAL DUMPING!*

Standing there breathing heavily so Trainer would take some pity on me, especially with my calves starting to cramp, I pressed on. "The retreat changed my life. In the silence, I got to hear all those crazy voices in my head. I learned how to quiet them with breathing and stillness. It's funny, I'm so used to talking out my problems with people that the first three days were like nails on a chalkboard. But by the fifth day, I started to enjoy being with myself. You should try it. It's worth it for $230 a night, including food and activities."

I grabbed the weights off the ground as he sneered that ultimate look of disgust, which translated to *NOW*. Trainer took a huge swig of his matcha latte. "Sounds fascinating. I can't stay quiet for even ten minutes, but I will check it out. You know Coolgirl is still seeing Superstar, right? I don't know what she's thinking, but she has always been like that. Even when she was a teenager. Did she ever tell you about her sophomore homeroom teacher?" *Oh man, if I weren't sober, I would jump to get into the gossip of Coolgirl's sordid past.*

I knew a little bit of her backstory but not the whole enchilada. Questions swirled in my mind—what happened with her teacher? Who did what? Was it against the law? Rather than ask my loud inner questions, I silently held back from the unnecessary gossip and returned to start a set of lat pulldowns. Dreading the final minutes of our session, I begrudgingly revealed, "Trainer, you know Coolgirl and I aren't really talking, right? I don't think it's a good idea for you to tell me her business. I don't want you in the middle of our shit. Plus, I can't fire you. I need you before my shoot." To prove my point, I shook my jelly-like underarms.

Trainer nodded in agreement with my mature decision. "I respect that. I get it. But you guys were thick as thieves, always together, and now nothing from both of you. What happened?"

I shook my head after the tenth repetition as the timer went off on his fluorescent-pink Apple Watch. Triumphantly raising my arms like a winner, I shouted, "Time's up! I guess you'll have to ask her." *Hell yes, saved by the bell!* "Damn, I need to get going. I have therapy. Thursday at seven a.m.?"

He wiped my nasty-ass sweat off the bench. "You have therapy on a Sunday? You must be all kinds of messed-up."

I gave him my Cheshire Cat bitch face. "You do what you have to do."

He grinned like the pure diva he was. "I hear ya. No more donuts! See you Thursday, chica!"

I jogged quickly to the ladies' locker room, forcing myself not to turn around and get sucked back into Coolgirl's drama. The entire way, I repeated to myself, Do not turn around and go back to Trainer. Her drama is none of your business. Stay in your own lane, lady! I was constantly having to talk myself off ledges to keep my boundaries. Why was I so addicted to drama and putting my nose where it didn't belong? Was it another way to avoid my own reality? Ugh... this much self-awareness sucks sometimes. No wonder gossiping was one of my major character defects. Hey, anything to take the focus off myself. It's better to look at others than do the inner work, right? Well, not anymore.

That was the deal I'd made with Alice. Deep down, all I wanted to do was some intense shit-talking behind my old friend's back, so I could continue to play the victim and be vindicated in her abandonment. You see, I loved being the victim. Victimhood and gossipmongering were both on my impressively long list of character defects—they were the nasty behaviors I turned to in order to not feel my feelings. Defects are our faults, failings, weaknesses, flaws, shortcomings, and inadequacies. Lovely, right? *Don't you dare judge me— we all have them!*

I made it out the door into my new black Range Rover Sport. No apologies, I'd bought it two months ago with my residuals from a TV show. I loved this car. This car was my external reward for all the internal hard work I'd done for my soul that first year. Black Stallion was my shiny prized possession. I know, it sounds nuts that I got a luxury car as a reward for finally being a better person. There I was not caring about my outside appearance, and I bought a freaking luxury car. *Kind of ironic!* Here's the thing—I needed a new car since my Prius was becoming unreliable. *Out with the old and in with the new.* The beauty of that purchase was that I'd made it very soberly. I looked at my accounts, and my monthly income. It wasn't an impulse buy. It was the most logical decision I'd ever made about a material item. Lastly, the car didn't give me a rush in any way. I didn't get HIGH from the purchase. If you took Black Stallion away from me tomorrow, I would be A-okay. That was the big difference for me—I knew it was *just a car*. It was a beautiful automobile. *Really—I could take it or leave it. And I could never say that about anything before.*

The same went for my new movie role in London. I was grateful I'd booked the job, because this mama has got to afford the gas and mortgage. Like I said—*no rich parents, sugar daddy, or backup plan.* Oh, what a nice life; to be a trust-fund baby and never have to worry about bills. Still, I know that in this lifetime, it would have been a death sentence for me. Can you imagine what a worse person I would've become if I'd never had to work for anything in my life? *TOTAL MONSTER!* I assure you; it wouldn't look pretty. There is a 100% chance I would be in a hospital or an institution, or have committed suicide from my addictive ways. How much worse it could've been if every wish I wanted... I GOT. One nasty, self-involved individual coming right up! So, let's just give a little shoutout to the big GOD for keeping me somewhat humble in this lifetime.

I was stuck on the 405 freeway in standstill traffic, headed to my bohemian-hippy therapist. You know the one? Dr. Kath! She loved to call me on all my crap with her Mother Earth aura and smile of wholeness. Yes, the therapist I paid $275 an hour.

After the last year of my oscillating, emotional bumper-car life, Dr. Kath deserved that money. Poor lady, she got the luxury of hearing all that stuff swirling in my head. *That sounds like pure torture to me—worse than waterboarding, I bet.*

While sitting in silence waiting for the car in front of me to move, I felt myself getting lost in the overcast LA morning. You know, the kind of morning you usually stay in bed with a lover? Or that gives you a migraine from those depressing gray skies? Pushing down those two scenarios, I settled on my disconnection from the world. Thoughts floated in my mind into those "what if" fantasies from another time period or even a different world. Please tell me I'm not the only one who does this? I found myself lost in my imagination—my go-to escape from the reality of horrendous traffic.

EXT. RENAISSANCE CASTLE — MORNING

Dark storm clouds hover over a castle that resembles the likes of *Frozen*, the Disney movie. Roxanne hangs her head out a high window. Obviously, she is stuck in the tower of her lonely castle. A modern-day Rapunzel.

> ROXANNE
> O Romeo, Romeo, wherefore art thou Romeo? (Thinks to herself.) *Wrong century. Plus, Juliet never wore a corset.*

INT. RENAISSANCE CASTLE—SAME

ROXANNE'S stunning long blonde hair cascades down the back of her beautiful, busty, beaded Renaissance dress. She has on a very tight corset. Roxanne looks into camera.

> ROXANNE
> This is so tight. How did a woman even eat a bite of bread?

I can't breathe. (Under her
breath) Crap, I'm ruining my
own fantasy. Shut it, Roxie.

EXT. RENAISSANCE GARDENS—A LITTLE LATER

ROXANNE dreams of her Prince Charming. Then
she sees him in the distance, an outline of
the perfect male specimen. She starts to run
through the lush gardens to her soulmate.
Struggling to breathe, she stops mid-stairwell.

ROXANNE
Seriously, I can't freaking
breathe in this corset. How
did our ancestors deal with
these fashions?

ROXANNE picks up since she is almost to him.
She is now jogging across the mile-long lawn.
Her face is bright red. Her breath is shallow.
Her eyes roll back in her head. She stops and
sways slightly, then turns to the camera one
last time.

ROXANNE
My BMI is thirty and I run
a twelve-minute mile. Screw
this fantasy.

ROXANNE falls face-first into the rosebush just
as we hear a horn honk.

BACK TO PRESENT TIME

My eyes snapped back into focus on the road. Hitting the
gas to catch up to the six car lengths ahead of me, I shouted,
"My bad!" as I waved to the angry driver behind me. Whoops!
Staying present has never been my strong suit. I grabbed
the cold espresso shot I brought from home. *Yes, this was me
trying to save money since I hadn't worked this past year,
even though I bought my expensive car.* My current healthier

breakfast option was a banana walnut RXBAR, since I had to give up my old-fashioned Krispy Kreme donuts and Noah's bagels—my out-of-work staples. That's the thing with being on camera—you are forever on a diet or gorging yourself when you aren't working. That's why when you see those paparazzi photos of a celebrity who isn't working, they are always about ten pounds heavier. You think to yourself, When did they get fat? They didn't! They're just not starving themselves for their job anymore. They are actually living their lives and eating that bread. *Man, I love a good bread basket.*

I walked up to the saddest-looking brick building on Ventura and Reseda made my way up to the third floor—only to have to wait on an extremely cramped loveseat beside another patient, always an odd scenario. Sometimes I played a game with myself and tried to guess who the lucky patron would be. Would it be my old friend, Hallmark Star, whom I haven't spoken to in years? She was the one who decided to unceremoniously unfriend me and talk poorly about me in an interview. Bitch. Could it be my lucky day to finally come face-to-face with her? Terrifyingly, it almost happened one Sunday! Months later, I still felt those aftershocks of an almost-run-in.

I had just pulled into the parking lot when I saw her walking out. My heart stopped! I ducked like the chickenshit I was and hid in my car till she got into hers. Luckily, I have tinted windows, so she couldn't see the absurdity going on. Not sure what I was afraid of, but the loss of that relationship was a hard one for me. It was before I entered the SLAA program, so I'm almost certain I had a hand in the demise of our friendship. No one ever told me when I was little that I would be heartbroken over friendships ending. It was always about fairytales and happily-ever-afters with a man. Friend break-ups can be just as heart-wrenching. Sometimes even more so.

Hallmark Star and I were great friends, then poof—she was gone, with no explanation. Making matters even worse, the only reason I found out she was over our relationship was through another friend. Ever since, I'd gotten mixed messages about why it ended. Her reasoning was a combination of issues—that I was too cool for her now that I had my own show, that I was selfish and never paid her back for Thanksgiving, that I couldn't afford to go to her wedding in Hawaii during the high season. I mean, come on, it was a couple grand a ticket, plus the hotel. I was poor and not the one marrying a rich man. *Give me a break. I know, sounds crazy to me too.* It wasn't the healthiest breakup, and I should've been able to confront her, but I still wasn't ready to come face-to-face.

I hopped out of the Stallion and walked confidently into the 1970s-style building. Would the Buddhist bells or water sounds be playing in the waiting room? What would Dr. Kath be wearing today? Did she get any new pillows? Did she put up a new dreamcatcher? These were some of the random thoughts I had while entering her office. I opened the door and turned on the little light switch, and guess who was there? Yep, that doppelgänger actress—Brittany! I've decided to officially call her Doppelgänger! It's more entertaining with the nickname. Ugh... and she had more audition sides sticking out of her stupid Louis Vuitton purse. I repeated over and over in my head, It's none of my business what other people are doing. I am not on her path, and she is not on mine. This was probably the sixth time I had run into her in this waiting room, plus once at an audition for another Ryan Murphy show, which she booked, and I did not. Yep, that sucked badly. One day you're hot and the next you're not! It's the shittiest part of this business. As my self-esteem was taking a hit, I smiled at her. She smiled back. And something happened. For the first time in my life, I said, "Hey, I saw you booked the Ryan Murphy part—congratulations! Did you shoot it yet?"

You should have seen Doppelgänger's face—she looked so proud. A huge smile broke out across her lips. "Thank you. Yes, I did. It was so much fun. My biggest role yet!"

"Well, it was a fun part to audition for. Glad you got it."
Am I actually happy for her? Who am I?

Her therapist opened the door to welcome her. Doppel-gänger turned back and said, "Thank you. I'm still pinching myself. Well, see you later."

WOW—this sober thing really works. For the first time ever, I'd congratulated another human being for beating me out of a job. I'd always hated when another woman succeeded, but in that moment, I meant it with all my heart. I felt her joy. It was like a warm bath flowed over me. I had changed. I wasn't selfish or self-seeking. *Holy crap, this serenity and connection is next level.*

I'm not sure you completely understand the enormity of that momentous occasion. Previously, I'd only wished ill will toward all my competition. The twelve-step saying "It works, if you work it" was NOT a lie. I had never felt so light and happy for another actress. Growth was no joke. *High five to ME!*

Dr. Kath picked that exact moment of revelation to open the door and surprise me with her new pink highlights. More of a champagne blush than a ballsy magenta. Still, I was in disbelief. I mean, I hadn't seen her in a couple weeks since she'd been out of town. Had she gone to a rave? Seriously, when did she become a teenage girl with her hair-color options? Personally, I didn't think it was a good look on a fifty-five-year-old woman. *Wow. See how fast I reverted back to my judgmental self?* This addict self was a tricky one. That was the dilemma I wanted to discuss with Dr. Kath. I was having trouble with the healthy dating and keeping my addict brain at bay. It flared up when I was least expecting it. *It was actually getting on my nerves! Like an annoying neighbor who won't move out.*

I shared my growth about Doppelgänger, and Dr. Kath nodded her head with very little fanfare. "Great, Roxanne. That's so lovely to hear." Switching gears like she always did, she added, "How have you been doing? How were the two weeks since we last spoke?"

I told her about my solo holiday vacation. "The silent retreat was so rewarding. Thank you for suggesting that option. I felt so much relief having a break from my father and not going home."

Proudly, like I was her little giraffe learning how to walk on my wobbly legs of sobriety, she stated, "So glad you did. Sometimes it's good to take a break from your family of origin to re-establish your boundaries. What can I help you with today?"

That's when I unloaded on her. It had been weeks since I'd gotten to talk my stuff out with someone other than Alice and the ladies in the SLAA rooms. *A much-needed massage for my soul.*

I explained my inner conflict. "I feel like I might just be as messed up today as I was a year and a half ago. Sobriety makes your head clearer, but the addict voices are still there. So how do I silence those negative thoughts so they're not the first things to jump into my head? How do I go on with this new life and stay sober when my first thoughts are always negative and I feel massive anxiety? How do I stay while I'm on these grueling dates, when every instinct in me wants to run for the hills? How do I feel the pain when all I want to feel is the euphoria? How do I be okay when I don't feel okay?" I paused dramatically for a second as the emotions started to rise up in my throat. The tears erupted and flowed down my cheeks. I realized that I'd been holding onto these fears for a while.

She handed me the notorious wooden box of Kleenex to blow my nose and wipe my eyes—of course, without messing up my warrior black eyeliner. As I calmed myself down, she asked quietly, "Are you feeling better?" I nodded. She pressed on. "All those thoughts are based on the unknown. I like to call that future tripping. Remember, anxiety is fear of the future. As an addict, you will always feel it rise up, but use your tools you learned from the program and the fear will subside."

I nodded my head in understanding, but I wasn't done dumping out my addictive internal inventory. "I'm really scared to know what a real relationship with a man looks like. I have no idea how to be authentic and true to myself without turning into someone he wants me to be. I love playing roles and can't help but transform myself when I find out the little details in a normal conversation on those dates. I can take that information and unconsciously mold myself into their perfect woman without even trying. It's not like I lose myself totally, it's just easier subconsciously not to be me. Does that make any sense at all?"

She jumped in abruptly, which fortunately gave me a chance to collect my breath. "Yes, it makes sense. Roxanne, dating is hard, especially when you are a recovered addict trying to be your authentic self. Here's the question you need to ask yourself: Is there any way to get to know someone other than being yourself? What would be the point of being anyone else? Did that ever make you happy?"

"No, I see that. But it kept me safe and comfortable, especially with the opposite sex. Now I don't know how to act. I feel like a thirteen-year-old girl all the time. I feel so disconnected on dates, like I want to crawl out of my skin. I make stupid jokes out of discomfort. Every single date has been a nightmare."

Dr. Kath looked me right in the eyes, which was a tad intense. "Roxanne, do you have any other choice? Do you want to be alone the rest of your life?" *Damn, this woman knows how to cut right to the chase!* She didn't mess around with those powerful neon-pink tips of hers.

I stared off into space as I thought about the alternative to dating. Alone, eating desserts, watching what I wanted to watch, and cuddling my Yorkie, Dog. *Not so bad!* Abruptly, there were flashes of a future romance fantasy hitting me square in the face—holding hands with a cute guy, late-night talks in bed, that moment, and first penetration.

I glanced up as Dr. Kath looked at me across the wood-plank coffee table. I saw her head doing that sideways tilt, like a dog's, when they're trying to understand what their owner is saying. No, I don't talk to my pup alone in my house like he's my best friend. I'm crazy but not that crazy! Why would you think that? I'm so much cooler than that. *Okay, I do!* So go and make fun of me. I'm like one of those cat ladies. I know. This is what my brain does when I'm looking at my real problems. It deflects.

Dr. Kath interrupted while I was mentally debating my life in a relationship with a human or just my dog. "It's a learned skill that you have not mastered yet. It takes time to practice these new behaviors. Dating is like an interview to see if you like the person. That's it. Try not to make it more complicated in your mind, Roxie."

"Right, I know that. It just feels like I'm a thirty-year-old who is still a juvenile. All the shame and guilt are still lingering from when I first acted out with cheating at such a young age. I feel like I'm behind on so many levels. I can't even connect to another person on a basic level. What's a healthy feeling, and what's not? It's so embarrassing to even admit to you—that I wasted a lot of time. I'm aware that if I get high off a guy on a date, I can't trust it. I get it, lust fades, and it means nothing. But I don't know what the correct feeling is anymore. I feel so ill-equipped for a healthy relationship in the real world." There, I said it. The truth about these feelings of shame and perfectionism was definitely not helping my Raya dates at all.

As the timer abruptly went off on her alarm, signaling that our session was over, she dropped words of wisdom that blew my mind. "Roxanne, people who live in shame come to believe they can't make mistakes. They imagine they should know what to do without having to learn it. But to make mistakes is to be human." *Drop the mic!*

Dr. Kath stood up suddenly, like the Buddhist baller that she was in her flowing floral skirt and beaded turquoise necklaces. Smiling her Mother Earth grin, she said, "See you next Sunday."

I walked out in a state of shock, wondering if she was going to high-five herself after the door shut. I waited a couple of seconds, my ear to the door to see if she did. *Nope, she was much humbler than I would have been.*

As I made my way down the dark corridor, I realized that, yes—I had been living in shame this whole time. That shame was making me believe that I should know all the skills to healthy date in this sick, twisted town. But I didn't. I was still finding my way. *So here I go—AGAIN. Learning to be my real self and to adult up. Time to suit up and show up for these dates.*

I'd had those first ten rules to get me out of my addiction; now I had another ten rules to survive dating without my addiction. Tools for the new ME! Good or bad, I was committed to living a healthy, authentic life as a recovering sex and love addict. I needed to surrender and not slip back into my old ways of being. They no longer worked for the life I wanted.

It was my mission to walk the walk, letting my sobriety speak for itself while proving to my thirteen-year-old inner child that I was worth knowing and open to being loved as the fully authentic weird me. Yes, I know, sounds like a tall order coming this recovered sex and love addict. I was ready.

Anything could happen next, so hold your breath. *I know I am!*

CHAPTER TWO

Rule II: Believe people when they show you who they are.

"THE TRUTH WILL SET you free. But first it will kick your ass."

This prophetic quote was once said by an unknown person who was one smart cookie. I find this quote to be painfully accurate, especially in the throes of healthy dating. The mapped-out plan in my head for dating—or anything for that matter—tended to blow up in my face. Even with that knowledge, I couldn't help my controlling ways. Come on, of course I had a list of requirements that my perfect partner needed to live up to. *Who doesn't?*

List of Partner Requirements for Healthy Dating

1. Financially wealthy—Fortune 500—but SELF MADE!
2. Very handsome, (AKA Oscar)
3. Makes me laugh so hard I almost pee my pants
4. Self-deprecating in a cute way, but also cocky at times
5. Self-employed, so he can travel freely with me
6. Sweet but has a bad-boy streak
7. Pays for everything
8. Available 24/7 for emotional support
9. Great communication skills, which he learned in therapy
10. Good at apologizing

11. Makes his bed every morning and has a clean home
12. Gives in to me even when I'm wrong

I know what you're thinking—she has twelve rules within the new ten rules, and don't forget about the original ten rules. That's thirty-two rules... that you even know about. Sue me, I am a list maker.

But even Alice thought I was taking this particular list overboard. "Okay, that might be a little unreasonable, don't you think? That kind of guy doesn't exist."

"Of course he does." I was adamant. I was determined to find my perfect online dating partner, who checked off every box on my list.

"You're setting unrealistic expectations." She was frustrated. "How can he be at your beck and call to take trips 24/7 when he is simultaneously running a Fortune 500 company? I'm sorry, that's logistically impossible."

I barked defensively, "Yeah, yeah, I hear you, but I'm putting it out there. I am asking for what I want. I believe I deserve it, and I am ready to receive what I think I truly deserve." Yes, I planned to "Secret" it into becoming true.

She sipped her chai latte at our weekly check-in at the Grove after the Tuesday-morning meeting. "When I started to date Charlie, I realized I was in a fantasy about what a real relationship looked like. I discovered that doing all this inner work on myself, I was constantly confronted with how little I truly know, and how tenuous my existence is." Yes, this was from a lady who was about to be married and not suffocating in the horrible Hollywood dating world. Who actually never even tried online dating! *Give me a break!*

I took a deep breath, smiling politely at Alice. "Here is the thing, online dating sucks a big fat dick!" *Okay, maybe not so polite.* I shoved the rest of my avocado egg-white omelet in my mouth, wishing it was a sprinkle donut. Or a jelly donut. Or an old-fashioned cruller. Hell, I wished it was all three. I took another deep breath, repeating *I love my job* in my head as I starved myself to be back at my fighting weight in a perfect size 2, while my witchy sponsor was enjoying her bacon-and-egg bagel sandwich and full-fat latte in front of me. Oh, to be an elementary schoolteacher and naturally slender! *The beauty of not caring about your pants size!*

Want to hear something even more annoying about dear old Alice? Once, while eating the most delicious-looking egg bread topped with cinnamon and powdered sugar AKA French toast from one of my favorite breakfast shops in the Valley, Bea Bea's, she told me, "I hate eating so much. I wish there was a pill that just made you full. Eating feels like a waste of time. I just hate doing it." Is that not the most insane thing you have ever heard? My mouth was agape when she said it too. Like, who the hell freaking hates eating mouthwatering, delectable food? There are two categories of eater: People who either eat to live or live to eat. Alice was absolutely the former, while I embraced the latter. Food gave me life. It was one of the main reasons I lived, so yes, I definitely dominated the "live to eat" category.

As I walked back to my car to accompany Alice to a ridiculously expensive wedding-dress shop, it hit me—man, I did have a long list of demands. Was I being impractical? Did I have magical thinking about the outcome of dating? Was that why I was struggling so much with all these dates? Was I the unavailable asshole when I met them at coffee shops, hiking trails, and restaurants all over LA?

I was more puzzled than ever. All I knew was that the handful of online dates were pure torture. Like poke-your-eyes-out-with-a-fork torture. Like become-a-nun torture—and not the hot-under-her-wimples Julie Andrews kind of nun, more like a frigid old Mother Superior kind of nun. Maybe I should just get offline? Maybe I should just hire a matchmaker to weed out the duds? I'd heard of the site Millionaire-Match for elite singles. But was I an elite single? And could I afford the fee? It was so much easier back in the *Fiddler on the Roof* days, when there was a yenta to set up everyone in the village. Only, I didn't live in a village, I wasn't the ideal marriageable age of seventeen, and, right, I wasn't Jewish. I was confused… and hungry. I could hear my stomach still gurgling after my $19 bland, calorie-friendly omelet with no cheese. I wanted that French toast. I wanted the double-stuffed pancakes. What I really didn't want was to go to Pilates after this shopping excursion. *Ughhh— "being of service" to Alice while hangry was too much… Could I possibly whine any more?*

Sitting in my car debating my future was never a good idea for this fantasy addict. I realized that the worst part of healthy dating in recovery was having to stay present. *Always!* It was beyond exhausting. Being available was hard work, especially for me. I was over it. I wanted to numb out so badly, with a mindless fling, scrolling through TikTok, or devouring a big slice of Joan's on Third coconut cake. Maybe opening a credit card and buying a used Hermès bag at The RealReal on Melrose. That's a sound investment, right? I could then sell it for more money in a few years. Look how financially savvy I was. Sorry, I digress… Stop it, Roxie. Stay focused on your dating goals!

I might add that I started this ridiculous journey of healthy dating at the ripe age of thirty. *Joke's on me!* I thought the bravest thing I'd ever done was get through my first year of sobriety in sex and love addiction, but no, that was just letting go of old behaviors. I now had to suit up and show up emotionally sober for complete strangers. *Kill me.*

I had never fathomed it could be more difficult to be available than unavailable. This was so hard. For example, really listening when they talked, not thinking of what I was going to say or what I was going to eat. On top of all that attention-giving, I was tired all the time. People exhausted me. Dr. Kath told me, "It will get easier. Your consciousness is getting used to being awake while staying vulnerable and more important-ly... available."

I remembered looking blankly at her when she set me straight in our last session, as I was bellyaching about the date I'd had with an unfunny comedy writer. He wrote on one of the top shows in town, yet he was a complete bore. It wasn't fair. I figured I'd at least get a laugh or two out of it, but clear-ly, he was one of those guys who was only funny on paper, because in person, he was a big fat dud. Incidentally, he was also dad-bod fat and ate a 3,000-calorie meal while I nibbled on a house salad, dressing on the side. Dr. Kath just rolled her eyes as I went on and on about how boring he was. She explained plainly, like I was a toddler, "Think about it like a muscle group you've never worked before in the gym. It takes time to build up your strength and stamina to staying open and building that muscle." All I could think about was that she had never slept with me—*I got all the stamina,lady!*

I knew that the SLAA program wasn't a quick fix for my addiction. I knew that I would not immediately meet my per-fect partner after doing the twelve steps. It wasn't a magical process. *I get it, there are no cash and prizes!* Here's the re-ality—I would always be a recovering sex and love addict. My mind would habitually have unrealistic expectations for my-self and others. The whole point of this journey was to find self-love and self-worth. Everything else is icing on the cake. Right? I mean, that was what Alice kept reminding me. But what did she know? She'd become engaged to Charlie and was knee-deep in planning her wedding. *Ugh, just saying that makes me nauseated.*

All I wanted to do was scream at her while we were in the Beverly Hills wedding-dress shop, down the street from the Erewhon. It's ironic how Japanese tourists scour Rodeo Drive for celebrity sightings, while Kendall Jenner, Brooklyn Beckham, and Kaia Gerber pick up their cold-pressed juices and non-GMO, biodynamic, sustainably sourced organic smoothies at the nearby supermarket. Man, I wanted a smoothie from Erewhon, but $21 for some blended-up fruit didn't sit right in my logical, recovered brain. Instead, I found myself practically drowning in the quicksand of thousands of white dresses, wanting to yell, "Where is the perfect guy I've been working so hard for?" Here was the gigantic irony—*I'd never wanted to be married!*

Obviously, I didn't say that to Alice. I wasn't as selfish as I used to be. I had evolved in my recovery. But the frustration was mounting. I'd been on multiple dates through that Raya dating app. The major kicker—I had never been matched with anyone close to the status of a Ben Affleck or a Channing Tatum. They were notorious users of the app. But did I ever match with them? Hell NO! What the actual f-? Clearly they were saying I wasn't famous enough for them. Was there a magic red-carpet list for the Raya profiles too? This was all very humbling! Instead of an A-list star, I'd gotten a handful of duds. Truly Milk Dud material—those caramel candies that get stuck in your teeth and aren't worth the calories. Yes, that was what ALL my dates were like: empty calories. Who wants to date an out-of-work writer or comedian? *I can't even count how many times I've been pitched a television show idea. Okay, nineteen.*

One of those horrific dates even wanted me to attach myself to his upcoming spec-project to help it get fully funded. *Oh, lucky me!* Let's name him Comedian, since I got a front-row seat to his comedy routine on our hour-long coffee date at Urth Caffé on Melrose, which was fifty-nine minutes too long. I spent the entire time staring at his bad hair transplant and listening to lackluster stories from his canceled long-running HBO series. *Excruciating!* I wanted to scream, "HELP! Save

Me!" to the barista when she walked by and heard him telling his sexist jokes. Something about the #MeToo movement being a witch hunt and how he desired a woman "who was bent but not broken. They're easier to manipulate." I simply stopped listening at that point.

As I looked at the menu, dreaming about their white-chocolate layer cake, my eyes glazed over, but of course, he was on a roll and never caught on to my disgust. He was on to the next self-obsessed subject—the high-profile project in which he was going to star. It sounded very similar to the plot of *Lost*, which had been redone about ten times. *Stop all the remakes, Hollywood! Please come up with some original ideas.* Plus, I was one of the actresses who had to go in for those bad remakes during pilot season every January to March. It was brutal learning nine pages of horribly written dialogue. Made you want to give up acting altogether.

The waitress caught my eyeroll and laughed out loud, which snapped me back into the moment of Comedian telling the cliffhanger of his "original" show. Note: There are basically seven plot types in storytelling, which can really be condensed to three—happy ending, unhappy ending, and tragedy. His original show was an amalgamation of all seven storylines, and this date could definitely be defined as a tragedy. Looking for any kind of distraction, I glanced over at the waitress and thought, *Damn, she is cool.* She was tattooed up with bright purple hair, so naturally, I nicknamed her Purple. I liked her vibe immediately and smiled at her. She returned my smile with a shake of her head in repugnance at the man-child in front of me, which included his cartoon T-shirt and cammo shorts. *Why did I say yes to going out with him?*

Okay, first, he said he was a writer. Not a comedian/Lyft driver living at home with his rich parents! Second, online he looked like a younger Brad Pitt with a more crooked nose. Very attractive in his profile pictures. I gave it a GO after Alice told me, "It's just one date, it won't kill you to try harder, Roxie." Except I felt like this date was indeed killing me, especially the fact that he looked nothing like his profile picture, which was clearly taken a minimum of five years and fifty pounds earlier. And I swear, Facetune was used on all his photos. Looking back, there was not a single wrinkle or pore. Tragically, I was never going to get back that hour of my life, and to be frank, Purple and I had a better shot at a second date. I wasn't into ladies, but I was getting to the point of such complete surrender that maybe lesbianism was the way to go.

INT. DARK BEDROOM—NIGHT

PURPLE sprawls out in the bed looking hot as hell, decked out from head to toe in La Perla black lace.

ROXANNE
You look hot.

PURPLE
Thanks.

Roxanne, still wearing all of her clothes, sits awkwardly on the bed.

ROXANNE
How can you afford La Perla on your salary? Don't answer. That was mean. Sorry. I'm nervous. I'm mean when I'm nervous. This is new for me. I'm a lesbian virgin. A newbie. I mean, I tried this once, like six years ago, and I threw up the second I saw her vagina.

Purple gives Roxie a look. *WTF?*

                    ROXANNE
          Not yours. Yours is beautiful
          and   clearly   defined   through
          the sheer material. I mean,
          a pair of La Perla panties
          costs more than my mortgage…
          Sorry, I'm doing it again.

                    PURPLE
          Just relax.

Purple puts her hand on Roxie's inner thigh.
She begins to glide her fingers slowly upwards,
underneath Roxie's miniskirt.

                    ROXANNE (Voiceover)
          Relax. I can relax. Can I
          relax and just lie back and
          let her eat me out? Is it rude
          if I don't reciprocate? I can
          close my eyes and think of
          dick. A nice thick dick.

                    PURPLE
          You okay?

                    ROXANNE
          Excellent. I am excellent.

Roxie doesn't move but closes her eyes tight,
like a kid trying to block out the monster
under the bed.

                    ROXANNE
          I can do this. It's just a
          pussy. How bad can a pussy
          be? It's kind of like a dick,
          but not hard. Or smooth.

                    PURPLE
          Hey, I just had a Brazilian.

                    ROXANNE
          Shhh, I'm in my *Rocky* moment.
          I'm Rocky, and I'm fighting

                       43

Apollo Creed, or Mr. T… No,
Dolph—

                    PURPLE
Whoa, you're comparing me to
Rocky IV?

                    ROXANNE
His best movie, and yes, I'm
pumping myself up. I need an
anthem.

Eyes still closed, she starts to gyrate to her
inner beat.

                    ROXANNE
We'd still worship this love.
We'd still worship this love.

                    PURPLE
Are you singing Taylor Swift?

Roxie, embarrassed, finally opens her eyes.

                    ROXANNE
She's kind of my go-to when I
need inspiration.

                    PURPLE
Hey, we don't have to do this.
I was only trying to help you
out.

                    ROXANNE
No, I can do this. I can
conquer THE PUSS.

                    PURPLE
Can you please stop calling
it THE PUSS?

Roxanne closes her eyes again, her fist pumping
the air as she chants her mantra.

                    ROXANNE
          You got this! Come on, don't
          puss out again.

     Purple gets up from the bed and leaves. Roxanne
     takes a deep breath and rips open her shirt.

                    ROXANNE
          Let's do this!

     Roxanne looks around. She's alone. Epic fail.

                    ROXANNE
          FUCK ME, ONCE AGAIN!

                                   SMASH TO BLACK

Yep, not going to happen. Even though I believe women are sexy as hell, I could never switch teams. That would be like an alcoholic switching from wine to beer. I might as well stop trying with all those unrealistic fantasies. Ironically, out of all my online dates, Purple and I had the best communication. We connected deeply over the pain of that self-involved Comedian. I mean, he didn't even look up to say thank you to her for clearing the table and taking away his trash. Where did basic manners go? You know this already, but I can't stand it when people are rude to the staff. That was when I knew I'd had enough.

I looked him straight in his eyes and loudly declared to the whole restaurant, "THANK YOU for picking up his trash, waitress!"

He glared at me as if I were the one with the social problem.

I stated clearly, "You are rude and selfish. I'm leaving. Goodbye!" I picked up my new green 3.1 Phillip Lim satchel that I'd just gotten on sale at Saks Fifth Avenue for 30% off. *Deal! Scored!*

Comedian apparently did not appreciate being publicly confronted on his bullshit, calling after me, "Well, I hate your work. And you have the smallest tits ever."

I stopped mid-stride in shock. I didn't know how to respond. He was welcome to criticize my work all day, but my tits? My tits were fantastic.

Luckily, Purple came up and told him, "Get out! You can't talk to a woman like that. And she's hot as hell."

He gruffly picked up his backpack. *Yep, that's right, a grown man with a salmon-colored JanSport backpack. Salmon!* He slung it over his shoulder and stomped out, telling us, "Both of you can go fuck yourselves!" *How poetic of him!*

I turned with gratitude to Purple. "What a dick. Thank you."

I pushed in my chair and grabbed my nonfat latte. Smiling, Purple wiped down the table for the next customer, who was standing right behind us, anxiously wanting to sit and finish her screenplay. *Note, nearly everyone in Hollywood has a screenplay. Your waiters, your Lyft drivers, your mailman. It's almost a rite of passage if you live in Hollywood.*

Purple stared at me. "Wait, I know you. Haven't we met before? Yeah, at the Wednesday-night meeting." *Which was code for the SLAA newcomer meeting!* She continued, "I heard you speak about your sobriety after you got your one-year chip. Yeah, I remember you talking about how you were just starting to healthy date." Purple looked at Comedian, getting into his cheesy Bronco, and grunted, "Wow, if that's all who's single after working in SLAA for a year! God help us all!" She spun back to me. "Your share really helped me get over my girlfriend. Just like you had to get over your old qualifier, West, or was it NYC? You were so inspiring. Thank you. And sorry about that guy. He doesn't know anything. Your work is great. I watched you on a crime show rerun the other night where you were a psycho white-supremacy killer."

Side note: I played a Neo-Nazi girlfriend opposite that actor who actually killed someone. That's right! I worked with a guy who turned into a real-life murderer. Talk about life imitating art. Kind of creepy and nerve-racking that I kissed him and then a year later he murdered an old woman in Los Feliz while high on PCP and Meth. Apparently, he strangled her and beat her cat to death before jumping off the roof to his own demise. Inside scoop—his famous singer girlfriend dumped him, and he spiraled out of control. See? Addiction to love really is deadly. The saddest thing with that situation, other than that poor woman dying and the cat being tortured, was that he was a nice guy when I worked with him. He was kind, sweet, and an all-around funny dude. Unfortunately, he let his demons destroy him. *Damn, he's a good reminder to stay on a healthy path.*

After the grueling date with Comedian, I had at least made a new friend. Purple and I exchanged numbers. I thanked her once more for the backup, and she insisted I take a free espresso to go. To this point, that was the best ending to all of my online dating experiences. *So, thank you, Purple! We might not be a romantic match but hopefully I will see you on Wednesday nights.* That's always a crapshoot, especially when people get back together with their exes—and she had just gotten back together with hers.

Purple filled me in on her relationship. "We moved back in together and are working on our communication skills in therapy."

Fact: If you walk into the rooms of SLAA, it's probably not about your current relationship, it's about ALL of your relationships. You've probably had problems in that arena your whole life. And now you are probably just using your current partner to fix your pain. Or increase your pain. Depends on what type of attachment style you have. Avoidant. Anxious. Disorganized. None of us in SLAA come in with a secure attachment style. That's why the program is so hard. It's tough to stick around and really look at all your relationships with a fine-tooth comb of honest reflection. It really is a revolving door in sex and love addiction! Listen, I hoped it would work out for Purple, but nine times out of ten—IT WON'T. *Sorry, girl! Come back when you're on your knees and ready to surrender. I know I will be there.*

So, you can imagine why it sucked even more to go wedding-dress shopping with Alice. I was in the back room being supportive of my sponsor, who was, at that moment, legitimately trying to bargain shop at the most expensive store in Beverly Hills. *Sometimes I just can't.* She tried to explain that she was only there to try on different shapes for her body type. *Hilarious—why torture yourself with a $10,000 dress when you can just go to David's Bridal in Burbank?*

Unfortunately, Alice was turning into the kind of bridezilla whom every bridesmaid fears. She was transforming right before my very eyes, with her glass of overpriced champagne and laced Swarovski-crystal Vera Wang dress. It was kind of cracking me up. Still, in a way, while I was being held hostage, so was she. So, I took advantage of the situation and continued to freely rant about my frustrations with dating on Raya. "The major problem is that I already kind of know a lot of the guys on that app. A friend has dated them, I've worked with them, they're in our program, or they're just plain losers. I already have the inside scoop on their baggage, which makes them deeply unattractive. It's a very shallow pool to choose from."

She continued to sip her champs with her pinkie finger in the air like she was a guest at a royal wedding. *Not kidding, I swear, people.* I wish I'd taken a picture to memorialize her in all her glory. Alice metamorphosed into a full-blown character with a faux British accent like Madonna. "Darling, you are simply too picky. Just go on a date. You need to practice. Get your feet wet again."

"My feet are soaked!" I grunted with annoyance. "Remember that coffee date with Comedian? And I went out with that sound-mixer guy with hair plugs. And I said yes to that director/producer with the lisp who just wanted to have sex in the Soho House bathroom against the huge glass window. And I even got stood up at Maestro by that married WME agent. Remember all of those horrible dates? Believe me, I have gotten my feet wet. They are so wet, they're submerged in the swamps of dating hell!"

Laughing at my anguish, Alice twirled away, glancing at her reflection in the full-length mirrors. "Oh my god, Roxie, they were not that bad. You are being so dramatic."

I rose to my feet, even with my legs half asleep from sitting on them. "Alice, cut the crap. They were horrible. All of them! And you remember that I saw West's profile on Raya too. That stung a little, not going to lie! On top of that, I went out with that guy, the one I slept with right when I got to LA? That douche music producer. The one I totally forgot about, and he called me out on it during our date at Umami Burger."

"Oh, yeah." She grimaced. "I forgot about that one."

"Yeah, that was a fun night. I was called a whore for not remembering him. Can you imagine? There I was, trying to eat my truffle burger, and he loses his shit. I was right in the middle of the room with truffle cheese dripping out of the corner of my mouth, and he started screaming about how he really liked me and thought we were a good match." While gurgling down my second glass of champagne, I recalled, "If that wasn't bad enough, he started crying and said I broke his heart when I ghosted him. REMEMBER???"

Feeling my pain, Alice drunkenly offered me a hug, which I took out of the desperate need to be touched by another human being, since I hadn't had any action in a year. Too much intimacy. I straightened my shoulders as I set down my glass of champagne and professed begrudgingly, "Crap, I should go.

I forgot I have another date tonight. I desperately want to cancel but can't, because my bridezilla sponsor made me put it on my bottom line for dating."

She smiled proudly. "Cheers to you and your hot date. Now I need to get out of this dress—I can't breathe."

Alice left the store empty-handed, since her teacher's salary wouldn't even come close to viably putting a down payment on one of those dreamy dresses. Alice and Charlie were paying for their wedding themselves, which I totally supported. I believe that at the age of thirty-seven, one should step up and pay for their own wedding. I mean, they were a little too old for Mommy and Daddy to foot the bill. That's my humble opinion, which we all know means absolutely nothing! On top of that, I think people spend way too much money on weddings. Come on, it's just a glamorized party that lasts a maximum of six hours! Why are you spending half a million dollars on that event? Morons! Even if I had that kind of money, which I don't, I would never pay that much. And while I have your undivided attention—every fancy wedding I've been to, celebrity or not, they are all now divorced. *The big fat D*. My theory on marriage and weddings: The more money you spend, the sooner you will be single. So, enjoy that $30,000 seven-tier wedding cake. You better freeze some of that decadence for the signing of your separation papers. Yes, I'm talking to you, KK, and your eight-foot, 600-pound chocolate-chip marble cake, which probably lasted a lot longer than your seventy-two-day marriage. Talk to me when you get to marriage number four—I'll make you a wedding cake for $200. You're welcome.

I jumped in my car, which had officially become my sound booth. One of my favorite ways to de-stress, especially in LA traffic, was singing my heart out. The particular song on repeat at that pissed-off juncture— "July," by Noah Cyrus— had recently become my new anthem. Every time I heard the lyrics, it took me right back to West's arms when things were good with us, even though I'd still been seeing NYC and ATL. That was the cheating addict in me—a man in every port. *ATL in Hotlanta, NYC in New York City, and West in Los Angeles!* Wow—that was a twisted triangle of lies and secrets to maintain. I'd definitely had my hands full. Sooner or later, listening to her beautiful lyrics, the memories would transform to when it all went downhill with West. It was a couple months before the dreaded bottoming-out-in-the-driveway standoff between NYC and ATL. *Ughh... major PTSD.*

Sometimes I still had nightmares where they started stabbing each other like Tybalt and Mercutio from Shakespeare's tragic love story, *Romeo and Juliet.* I guess that would make me Romeo—I would get in between them as NYC would be knifing ATL under my arm in iambic pentameter. *All very dramatic!* There should be a universal saying: "Love will kill you sooner or later." *At least for me!* My Shakespearean dream always had a very cinematic feel. A Quentin Tarantino vibe with bright colors and loud music. I felt truly alive during the fog of my subconscious haze. Until I woke up with an emotional hangover and realized I was still a mother-fucking addict, who loved drama and hurting people. Every time I enjoyed that morbid dream, the shame hit me full force. I would jump my ass out of bed, run into my bathroom, and look in the mirror, telling myself, "You are not a bad person. You do not want anyone to die over their obsession with you." *Huh, not so sure how truthful I'm being. Still sounds kind of dreamy to have that much attention, even if it's sick and twisted.* Looking in my brass-framed mirror, I'd breathe slowly. In for seven seconds, hold for seven seconds, then out for seven seconds. *Repeat!* I would do that until I was back in my body. Standing in my tiny, dark-gray bathroom, I'd brush my teeth and pee and get on with my day. *Back to reality. No dead bodies here!*

Those magical song lyrics, especially "July," brought me right back into my addict self. That was why I had to be very careful when and where I listened to music. On that ride after wedding-dress shopping with Alice, I should have known better, but as a fantasy addict, I still enjoyed my lyrical disconnection from my real world. As I mentioned, I went into full-blown memory recall of my relationship with West, which was a tad ironic, because I think we broke up in July. The lyrics started my daydream—*I've been holding my breath / I've been counting to ten / Over something you said / I've been holding back tears / While you're throwing back beers / I'm alone in bed / You know I, I'm afraid of change / Guess that's why we stay the same.*

I felt smacked right in my gut as I blasted that song. West and I were so messed up as a couple, and I was still fantasizing about our horrible relationship, so what exactly did that say about me? Especially when Noah Cyrus hit the high note—*While we're dying inside / I've done a lot of things wrong / Loving you being one / But I can't move on. WTF? Am I a glutton for punishment?* Maybe I would rather have something familiar but majorly toxic instead of a bunch of lukewarm dates on Raya. It was hard not to go back to the past when the future was looking so unknown. All those terrible prospects I had endured. Thinking back, I could see why I was stuck in the fantasy of the past. Dread was more like it. Could I swallow poison or stab myself instead of going on any more dates? *I know, I know, classic drama queen.*

I then headed to my Pilates class, which was brutal. It wasn't chill Pilates, where you work on getting longer and leaner without raising your heart rate too high. Instead, it was this turbo class where you had to run on a treadmill for the first thirty minutes of the session, then get on the Pilates Reformer machine for the last thirty minutes. The studio was called Fitmix. But the worst part of the whole hour was that for fifteen minutes, you had to run backwards on a 60° incline on the treadmill. *Pure torture!*

After my first class, in a complete exhausted daze, I'd hobbled down the sidewalk eating a hot dog while all the drivers on La Brea Avenue were probably laughing at me. It was the best hot dog I had ever eaten. Here's an idea for you—after your first class, head over to Pink's Hot Dogs right down the street to give some comfort to your sore buttocks. There is nothing in the world that a good hot wiener won't fix. *Forgive the pun.*

On this glorious day, as I jumped on my treadmill, guess who walked in the class? You would never guess by my description of him earlier. Literally the last person on the planet you would catch at a Pilates class. That douchebag, Comedian! Yep, the Raya date who Purple kicked out of Urth Caffé. He was all decked out in a white tank top with his obviously new fake tan. What's the likelihood of that? Out of all the Pilates classes in Los Angeles. My thoughts kept circling back to our horrible conversation—had I mentioned I went to this studio? Why else would he be here? Then, I kid you not, right behind him was a very young and very blonde girl. *WTF? The only thought ringing through my head: How was he able to find a new date already?*

Comedian looked over at me and gave me a smug smile. "Oh, nice to see you, Roxanne. I didn't know you worked out here. This is my girlfriend, Preteen!" *Obviously, she wasn't a teenager—I hope—but she looked like she had just graduated high school. Poor girl! I wanted to grab her and shake some sense into her.*

I was in shock as he blatantly lied. I had abso-fucking-lutely told him I worked out at Fitmix. And in what messed-up alternate universe does Comedian find a partner before I do? Well, that's LA for you—where awful assholes have their pick of young, fresh-off-the-bus females. Jeez, I hated this town sometimes. Comedian and Preteen started their machines for the warmup inclining walk. I said hello to her without rolling my eyes, which was a huge accomplishment for me. Dr. Kath would have been proud.

I was in exercise hell for the next hour, with that douche who chewed with his mouth open, told me I was a bad actress with too-small tits, and pitched me the most sexist television pilot ever. I glanced over and my stomach churned at the sight of them holding hands while working out. *Ughh!* God had a funny sense of humor—douchebag had a date, and I was all alone. The words from Dr. Kath rang in my head, "Life is truly not fair." With her words of wisdom reminding me of the ugly truth, I was a pissed-off bitch! *F- this shit!*

I aggressively threw off my T-shirt, revealing my newly sculpted two-pack abs. Yep, that was the most muscle I had ever developed on my stomach. All thanks to Trainer. Now I understood why Coolgirl had the best abs ever. I pumped up my treadmill and hit the ground hard. I was in the zone. I blocked out all my thoughts as I put in the best workout of my life. Bravo to me—I didn't look over at them once. I didn't care. All I focused on was my thighs burning and how hot I wanted to look on camera in my upcoming movie. Especially for that dreaded love scene with my pretend-husband actor, whom I prayed was not a dipshit, douchebag, or narcissistic asshole. I was determined to get back my eighteen-year-old butt, which was an impossible task, since my genetic DNA included cellulite. But my ego was not hearing that.

I blocked out any noise. Completely focused—I was in my kill zone! I upped the incline, I doubled my speed, I was a flawless machine of grit, muscle, and determination. Nothing could have stopped me, until... it happened. That dreaded fear since my first day at this studio. Yep, my clumsy ass fell off while running backwards on an 80° incline. Humiliation would be an understatement. Let me paint the picture for you—I tripped on the side of the machine and tumbled face-forward onto the ground. Instead of breaking my nose, I just bruised my elbow and jumped right back on like nothing had happened. Like I was an Olympic gymnast during a botched floor routine. Yes, I was channeling Simone Biles at her bravest. Only, the crowd wasn't supporting me; instead, Comedian was giggling hysterically while Preteen was taking a TikTok video in hopes of me going viral. The whole class stared at me as I reassured the instructor between audible grunts of pain, "I'm all right. I got this. Keep going. I'm all good over here."

Then, before I knew it, I heard the teacher call time. I was drenched in sweat. I looked around and Comedian was suddenly right next to me. Preteen was on the other side of me. I was literally flanked between sexist arrogance and naive idiocy. HUH? When did that happen? Did I miss something?

He looked at me. "Can you say clumsy?"

I stared at him blankly. "Excuse me, do I know you?" As I hobbled off my treadmill, I turned to Preteen with all the mocking sweet kindness I could muster. "Good luck with this one. He seems like a really great catch."

Ignoring both of them, I slid onto my Reformer and finished the best workout of my life. Screw that guy! And his new piece of ass with D tits! I knew when we sat down for coffee that the person sitting before me was showing me who he was within the first ten minutes.

Before getting healthy, I'd always tried to give people the benefit of the doubt. Maybe they'd had a bad day? Maybe they'd gotten stuck in traffic? Maybe someone in their life was sick? I had excuse after excuse for this human race. Just like I made excuse after excuse for myself. There was no accountability. I never wanted to see it or believe what they were telling me. Since becoming sober in SLAA, those rose-colored glasses had been ripped off and my bullshit detector was on high alert. I could see if someone was unavailable, lying, or putting on a front. I'd rather be single than date a guy like him.

I got home, kissed Dog, and jumped in the shower. This time, I gave myself proper time to clean my three Ps—my notorious saying for a quick body wipe-down. *The pussy, pits, and pooper.* I got ready quickly instead of my old ways of two hours of prep. Surprisingly, my character defect—MY perfectionism—was not as psychotic with my hair and makeup as it used to be. *Look at that growth! See, people can change! I'm living proof.* But I did put on my "war paint" eyeliner, nicknamed by Dr. Kath. I never left home without it on.

She repeatedly reminded me, "The eyes are the window to your soul, Roxanne. And wearing all that eyeliner circling your eyes is like war paint that the tribal people use. People can't really see the real you under all that black gunk."

Now, I wouldn't disagree with her very in-depth observation of my eyeliner usage. You would think that after all the hours I had spent in therapy, I would be much more evolved, but NOPE. I loved wearing my makeup mask. Truthfully, Dr. Kath and I discussed how it was very therapeutic for me to put on makeup. It was almost a form of active meditation. I zoned out and created different dimensions and angles on my skin. It was another form of creating art for me. But mostly, it was the only thing in my life that I had some sort of control over. Because everything else felt so raw and open, I couldn't let go of my eye-makeup crutch. Maybe one day it would be different, but right now, I NEEDED IT! Plus, I felt more powerful with it on, like I was a superhero or something. I hated Marvel, by the way. Really any superhero movies—I just wasn't a fan of those overly make-believe worlds! Hilarious, since I thrived in fantasy, but the superhero world seemed so false to me. Maybe my FALSE SELF felt too exposed? Who knows? *Okay, that's a lie. Gal Gadot is a perfect specimen of a human. So, I'll make an exception to my Marvel hatred. Although, Wonder Wom-*

an is technically DC Comics... Oh my god, am I having an inner monologue about comic worlds? Next thing you know, I'll start playing Dungeons & Dragons. Kill me now.

What was I getting ready for on that random Tuesday night? Oh yeah, date night! I had been hating all my Raya dates so ferociously that I joined a blind-date matchmaking service as well. I didn't want to, believe me, but she was the best service in LA. And desperate times call for desperate measures. More about that later, promise! This time, it was another dude from the Raya app, with a stupid name: Chad. Who wants to spend the rest of their life with a Chad? At least he picked a good restaurant—Pace, on Laurel Canyon Boulevard. Alice and I had met there many times for their famous cedar-wood-grilled salmon. Delicious and healthy! It should be, for $36! My question for you all: How does anyone in LA afford to live here? I don't get it at all. We pay ridiculous rent and exorbitant gas prices, and on top of that, dating? Now that I think about it, I feel bad for guys. They have to pay for most of the dates, or they look cheap. How do they manage? But when I really think about it, they do make more money than females, especially since the ERA has only passed in thirty-eight of the fifty states. Screw that bullshit! Here's a solution, guys—if you want to go Dutch, reach out to your senators to pass that through Congress, then you won't have to pay for every date! *My feminist side has officially emerged!*

I headed out my door that evening to drive up to Laurel Canyon—YES, I never let a date pick me up. I didn't know them, so why would I tell them where I lived? Duh, that was just a recipe for a Dateline special or the subject of a true crime podcast. I didn't even let my Lyft drivers know where I lived. I ALWAYS chose a neighborhood house down the street, then snuck into the bushes to hide till they pulled off.

Before any date, I of course said the Serenity Prayer, but most importantly, I opened my glove box and grabbed my golden-rules cheat sheet for dating—my laminated list of red flags and what I wanted in an ideal partner. Alice didn't fully approve of the dream partners list. Okay, so there might be a lot of requirements. Forty-eight qualities, to be exact! Yes, I have added on to the first twelve I told you about at the start of this chapter, but come on, they're important ones. For example, in no particular order of importance:

Roxanne's Ideal Partner List

1. Disease-free—tested regularly *(no dirty penis, please!)*

2. Good in bed

3. Big dick, but needs to know how to use it

4. Can cook gourmet meals

5. Travels the world on a whim

6. Makes sure I orgasm first

7. No children *(still didn't know if I wanted any! But it's a woman's prerogative to change her mind)*

8. No divorce

9. No actors

10. No debt

11. Creative-type job

12. A man's man *(no pussies allowed)*

13. Looks great clean-shaven or with facial hair

14. Can build things with his hands but then play gently with a puppy or kitten

15. Loves reading books

16. Will try anything once *(but no dare-devil bull-shit. I don't need him to die on me!)*

17. No baggage with exes

18. Nice to his parents

19. Drives a cool car (but no BMWs)

20. Has blue or green eyes

Actually, I'm going to stop reading this to you. I'm feeling quite vulnerable, like you're reading my diary, which is silly, but while I'm reading it, I feel like my inner thirteen-year-old is searching for the magical unicorn man who doesn't exist.

Frustratedly, I threw it back into my glove box and held my hands to the sky while closing my eyes. "Okay, you white-bearded spirit-man, I'll give it over to you!" I muttered my favorite prayer under my breath. "God, please align me with your will. Let me see that it comes from infinite love, caring, support, and protection. Good or bad in my eyes, I know you come from infinite love, caring, and support." This prayer always helped me with the *action of letting go,* while at the same time making me look like one of those crazed Bible-thumping do-gooders. *Both great options, I think.*

Laurel Canyon was stop-and-go with its notorious bumper-to-bumper traffic, but my mind was not fully present. All those future-tripping thoughts started to form in my head as the dreaded date with the aforementioned Chad loomed closer. This past year, my mantra had been "Self-love is my superpower." But at that juncture, I was wishing my super-power was seeing into my future. You know those thoughts, right? That magical future tripping, so that I could keep going through all these horrible dates and know that sooner or later, Prince Charming would show up to rescue me. Truly, if I could have one wish, I would wish for a crystal ball to let me know I'm always on the right path and that everything is going to be okay. You ever feel like that? You wish you could just see the future really quickly and know that it will all work out for you in the end? I did all the time.

According to Dr. Kath, it would be a bad idea for humanity as a whole. "We would all get too complacent. Which is dangerous for all of us humans, but it would be worse for someone like you, who is a control freak and addict." But it was hard not to go into that future-tripping fantasy. As I was contemplating my wishful thinking, an incoming message from the Raya app popped up on my Apple CarPlay. I kind of hoped Chad was canceling. Even though I'd just gotten ready for this date, a part of my sexual anorexia hated putting myself out there. That was the avoidant attachment in me. Such a strange juxtaposition! Of course, I wanted to find my partner, but I also wanted to stay at home in bed with my bag of Goldfish crackers. ALONE! Then, mouthwatering thoughts of that delicious cedar salmon permeated my tastebuds. Maybe I would just go to the restaurant by myself. Or get the salmon to go and eat it in bed watching *Forensic Files,* Episode 301. *Nothing like a bloody murder mystery while eating delicious fishy flesh.* It was a perfect plan! With my mind made up about my early evening, the car's monotone voice read the DM. "Looking forward to seeing you. I'm here early and already having a drink at the table. Tell the hostess that the reservation is under Chad. Drive safely. See you soon." Ughh... I had to go! One of my bottom lines with Alice was that I couldn't cancel last minute or flake on plans. Why did I have to be such a stand-up citizen? *Dude—I miss the old days of being a selfish, ghosting A-hole.*

Also, what the-? Chad was early? And communication with respect? I was in utter shock, since the last date I'd had was twenty minutes late. It was at the Soho Warehouse downtown with that ponytailed sound guy who jokingly wanted to get his dick sucked after dinner. His comment, not mine! And the one before that was this CAA agent who never even showed! Some real Hollywood catches right there. *NOT!*

Who was this incredible man? I was becoming a little nervous that this might be a good date. I had worn my red backless maxi dress from Reformation that I'd gotten at a sample sale downtown. It felt sexy but understated. But what if I was too dressy? Not dressy enough? Crap, I was starting to feel nauseated. The nerves of dating were starting to make me feel all squirrelly. I wanted to run! A physical reaction started to overtake my body. My palms started to sweat. My pits started to stink. Did I forget to put on deodorant? I smelled my underarm, and yep, I smelled badly. *I better do my backup plan for smelly pits.* Time to lather on my famous Jamaican lotion to mask the stench. I know, you're wondering what that lotion is. It's this amazing stuff I've been buying for years from the Melrose flea market. This guy makes it in his bathtub. Doesn't sound very sanitary, but trust me, the smell is hypnotic. It's like catnip for men. It's that good, because everywhere I go, I get compliments. I mean, EVERYWHERE. Compliments from men and women. Let's hope this Chad guy likes it. Not that I should care, but I definitely don't want to smell like nervous BO.

Great, already Chad seems like an unknown unicorn of perfection in the lackluster, sloth-like world of Hollywood dating. *Fantasy living! This is what dating does to me. Fantastic!*

I finally arrived at Pace. The restaurant was a quaint little wooden house right in the middle of an intersection. Luckily I was only two minutes late, which I hated because I'm always on time, but traffic blows no matter how early you leave. A stunning host with the most gorgeous Afro greeted me at the front door. I was obsessed with her hair. In a complete state of compare and despair, I was coveting her thick, wavy weave, which I could never, ever produce for myself. I was literally staring at the back of her head, trying to figure out what I could say to her about her gorgeous hair without sounding like a crazy woman or unknowingly saying something offensive or culturally appropriating. All I could muster without making her uncomfortable was, "Your hair is stunning." She half turned and said, "Thanks." Then she speedwalked further from me like she heard that compliment every second of the day and was over it.

I was hurrying to keep pace while still thinking about her hair as we rounded the corner to meet my Raya date, Chad. I stopped midstride when I arrived at the table. Because guess who was magically sitting at Chad's table? Not an unknown unicorn with potential, but someone I knew. Intimately. I will give you a thousand dollars if you guess correctly who was claiming to be Chad. With astonishment and dismay, combined with confusion, I saw the one person I would have never pictured at this freaking table. The notorious I-break-your-heart-and-you-break-mine... WEST! And NO, I am not kidding!

I was officially breaking my bottom line! Alice would not be thrilled with this picture when I bookended this date tonight. If you have never heard of bookending dates, it means to call before and after each date to check in and discuss how it went. What was the timeframe of the date, were there any red flags, did you want to see the person again, etc. Really, someone to call you on your bullshit and make sure you're not hopping into bed or marrying your date. *A watchdog kind of person for your addict self!*

There I was, standing in front of the table, trapped by this shocking situation. It wasn't like I technically broke the bottom-line rule. For instance, I hadn't called him or sneakily met up with him to bone at his house, like after my first SLAA meeting. Looking back, I definitely should have turned around and walked out. But did I? Nope! That would have been way too healthy for me to do. Of course, my curiosity got the better of me. Sitting there with a glass of champagne, pretending to be someone named Chad, he was looking damn fine. Almost more delicious looking than that cedar salmon I was craving two minutes ago. *He looked good enough to eat!*

I stood there completely mute. I looked back and forth, thinking that the hostess had taken me to the wrong table. West stood up and smiled devilishly with his perfectly white veneered teeth that looked naturally real. Stepping forward, he apologized, "Roxie, please sit. I'm sorry for lying to you. I used my friend Chad's account. I know it was wrong, but you blocked me. The last few weeks, I haven't heard back from you. I didn't know any other way to get ahold of you, since I couldn't remember where you lived."

Swirling in my head, all I was thinking was—*because you only came to my place once the whole time we were together.* Okay, yes, technically I was with other people, but maybe it was because he was unavailable. Ever think of that, guys? *So, give me a break!* I was a dick but so was he.

The famous words that Alice reminded me of when I was stuck in my fantasy of what West and I were: "Let's get real, Roxie, you two were just completely unavailable assholes pretending that you both wanted more." *Sometimes you have to be snapped back into reality, whether you like it or not. At least, I had to.*

I stated simply, with no dramatics, "Not cool at all, West."

He continued to justify his lie. "I wanted to say I was sorry for everything and happy that you're doing good. I heard through the grapevine that you're dating and then I saw your profile on Raya. I'm seeing someone now, but I wanted to admit my wrong to you. That I have no hard feelings."

I looked at him with massive uncertainty and asked, "Does your new girlfriend know you are here talking to your old girlfriend?"

He smiled his charming I-get-away-with-murder smile. "It's no big deal. She gets it." He took a sip of his champagne. "Please have a seat. I got you a glass of your favorite champagne as an olive branch." Reluctantly, I sat down. I took a sip of my champagne, thinking—*You are starting to feel those addict butterflies. Get up and run!*

Of course, I didn't listen. I was stuck in the vortex of his beautiful eyes. My thighs were officially glued to my seat. He declared proudly, "I wanted to see if we could be friends. It's important to me. You were one of my longest relationships. I care about you."

I cut him off before he completely derailed me from my program. "I don't think it's healthy for either of us to be friends."

He nodded like he was agreeing with my self-care statement, then added, "Well, the other reason I wanted to get you here was to let you know that I got offered a part in the London movie you're doing." My mouth gasped open in a new degree of shock. Stunned into silence. He smiled. "Roxie, here's the kicker. I got cast playing your husband. Hilarious, I know. When my agent told me they agreed on my rate, I wanted to tell you first to see if you were cool with it." My mouth smirked in protest, but once again he cut me off. "Now, hear me out. It's a great part, and you know how good the script is. Maybe Sundance or Oscar worthy? I need this for the next step in my career, and so do you. We can make it work, I promise. No funny business! Come on, give it a shot. I know it wasn't right to use my friend's Raya account, but I haven't talked to you in over a year, since you ran out of my house in tears. And then you blocked me on *all* social media. What was I supposed to do? Wait until the first day of filming?" There was a sadness in his eyes that definitely weakened my conviction. Lastly, West added, "Come on, Rox, we can kill these parts together. I know we can. You know we can." *He just stroked my EGO!*

I felt that rush and power that I hadn't felt in a very long time. I smiled my I-won-and-you-owe-me grin. It felt great! Man, I missed this high. The inner thoughts started to swirl—*I can do this. I can be professional with an ex on set. I have done this before.* Okay, I made the official decision—without my sponsor, I might add. *Whoops!*

I wanted to prove that I could be strong enough and healthy enough not to fall for his charm. I got this. This had to be a GOD's test. I gulped the last of my champagne, stood up, and stated, "It is not my call to say yes or no to you taking this job. It's your decision. I will be professional no matter what you do. I'm happy and don't want any more drama in my life. Thank you for the drink. And never do this again. See ya on set." I walked out, gliding like a champion who just won a prize fight against themselves. My hair swaying and ass bouncing—huge thanks to all the squats Trainer made me do over the weekend!

But as the valet pulled up in my Range Rover, my stomach dropped out. A tornado of regret circulated in my mind—*what did I just agree to? I can't do this! Now I have to tell Alice. And where is this perfect date with Chad that I'm supposed to be enjoying? All the gentlemanly texts he sent? The compliment he gave to me? Arriving early for the date?* It was all a lie. And on top of out, the cedar salmon would have been arriving just about now. Then it smacked me in the face with a lead hammer—there was no perfect mate! I would never find "the one" to complete me. It didn't exist. Maybe that was what God was telling me. *A new rule was necessary.* **Rule 11.5: There is no such thing as a perfect mate.**

All I knew as I pulled out into traffic was to turn to the one thing that always brought me comfort, which wasn't a bag of dicks, chips, or Peanut M&M's. *Even though those things all taste delicious!* It was the simple words of the Third Step Prayer: "God, I offer myself to Thee—to build with me and to do with me as Thou wilt. Relieve me of the bondage of self, that I may better do Thy will. Take away my difficulties, that victory over them may bear witness to those I would help of Thy Power, Thy Love, and Thy Way of life." It simply broke down my ego, my righteousness, and my resentment with West. It slightly muted the fantasy of someone else being the perfect partner for me. I needed to keep my side of the street clean and be of service to others. What I did know was that I couldn't call the shots and tell West not to take the job. That was not my place. I was not his God. And I had to trust in my recovery. That I was healthy enough to make it back from London with my sobriety still intact. I trusted myself. I had done the work. This was just a test I had to pass.

Would I fail or succeed? Could I let go of the fantasy of a "perfect mate"? Would I suit up and show up for my life? Let's see! Only time would tell. Which was scary—giving my life over to the unknown! And doing it ALL ALONE!

CHAPTER THREE

Rule 12: Show up for those
who show up for themselves

CHECKMATE! I WAS DONE. Let's wrap this up. I officially called the shots in my life—I was off Raya! *Now and forever!* That app was too much for me to handle. No peace had come from me being on it. It was constantly triggering my fantasies of meeting an A-list celebrity, only to be rejected by random dudes on a daily swipe. And to top it all off, now I was being stalked by an old qualifier. For the record, a qualifier is a toxic person who literally brought you to your bottom emotionally and is no longer allowed in your life because all they bring is chaos and destruction. The person who robs you of all your serenity and peace. Yes, that person you can't stop obsessing over. And mine was back in full force. That was a hard over-and-out for me. It was too dangerous for my SLAA sobriety, which I'd worked so hard on. And let's just say that Dr. Kath and Alice were not happy about West catfishing me.

On my way home after that fiasco, Alice screamed over FaceTime, "What the actual f-? What was he thinking? Dickhead! I'm so glad you're not seeing him anymore."

Dr. Kath was much subtler in her approach. "Wow, you were definitely blindsided there. I can see how that would make you feel unsafe on the dating app. How are you feeling today? What was it like seeing him?" After dissecting my feelings and thoughts on the whole dating-app situation, I decided to meet potential partners the old-school way. Out in the real world. Not behind a screen, where they could pretend to be anyone they wanted. I decided to make myself available everywhere I went—when I was out running errands, hitting up a restaurant for takeout, even asking my healthy girlfriends if they had any great guys to set me up with. You know—those old-school dating tactics, which were centuries old but actually new for me. When I thought about my experience on the dating apps, I had a huge revelation. I was always trying to be interesting instead of being interested in others. What did that say about me? I needed to stop making it about me! The only way I knew how to do that was by giving to others. I was stagnant in my growth, and I needed to "get out of self." *In other words, I needed to stop being a selfish bitch!*

One thing I did every morning was record myself reading a meditation from the *SLAA Daily Reader* for my sponsees. I sent them off to each lady every morning. It was a good way to ground myself in service and help my girls start their days off right. That particular morning, I had a meeting with my newest sponsee, Eve, the oversexualized flight attendant. We were discussing her Step One. How truly powerless she was over her sex and love addiction. It had taken her a long time to commit, but she was officially a member of this nutty group. Her surrender was much more drawn out and painful than the others', but I was there for her. It was a challenge, as she was literally self-harming with flirting, having one-night stands all over the world, and fighting daily with her ex-husband. Talk about emotionally cutting yourself—she needed a tourniquet, or she was going to bleed out all over her life. Watching her act out was like watching the slow death of someone you love.

Eve just lived for power and control over the opposite sex. I wouldn't know anything about that! *Insert hilarious laughter here!* It was ironic that, before I met her at our Wednesday-night SLAA meeting, I'd always envied the transient lifestyle of a flight attendant. It hit every fantasy for me. Traveling around the world to exotic places and acting out with gorgeous foreign men without any commitment whatsoever. Pure bliss... until you were given a front-row seat to the dark side of that occupation when afflicted with this deadly disease.

Eve was sitting across from me in her denim-on-denim ensemble, which, if you don't know, is famously called a "Canadian tuxedo," AKA jeans and a denim top. Eve was delving into her worst bottoming-out in her addiction and career. The irony is that helping her kept me sober after all my dating disasters. "For fun and for free," Alice loved to remind me. "Just like I did for you. Now take your selfish ass and go be of service to another who is suffering." Shockingly, sometimes it was the only thing that kept me from texting an ex or masturbating in my discomfort. Helping others truly was the last line in staying sober. I guess that is why it's the Twelfth Step.

Eve and I were sitting at the corner table at Urth Caffé. Purple was waiting on us. This was the spot for a lot of her step-work. It was like Purple, Eve, and I were all on a mission to stay sober together. The fucked-up Three Musketeers. Every morning, we had a mini SLAA meeting. News flash for you all—Eve was one of my many doppelgängers in LA. Luckily, she wasn't an actress, but she was Southern and blonde. We looked like sisters—her being the older sister, of course. She was about five years older than me, which was odd at first, since I was her sponsor. But there I was at Urth Caffé, willing to share my experience, strength, and hope in getting her out of the horrific self-inflicted pain of this shameful disease. I had initially given her my notorious fourteen pre-step questions that Alice had given to me. I might add—they were brutal to answer. Usually, sponsees bailed on me before they finished the questions. I can count at least fifteen people who quit our work together in the middle of answering them. They were the most in-depth questions I had ever had to answer. They really made it clear who was ready to surrender their bullshit and do the work needed to get relief. Here are just a few of those questions:

1. What was my "payoff" for acting out?
2. Where did I lose my sense of self?
3. When did I feel like I lost control?
4. How did I use my addiction as a "hit" or "fix"?
5. Where did my disease create insanity?

And on and on....

I was in total shock that Eve finished her questions! The next rule showed up in full force—**Rule 12: Show up for those who show up for themselves.** I was even more taken aback that she showed up ready to read them to me after her overnight flight from Australia. *Badass bitch!*

She sat down looking utterly exhausted. Eve gave Purple a wan smile. "I'm beat. Matcha latte and a blueberry scone, please. Actually, make that two matchas!" Turning quickly to me, she said, "You are not going to believe what happened to me on my trip last night. I got thrown up on, cleaned up pee, and had to help contain a drunk. Good times in first class." *Okay, maybe not the glamorous job I was envisioning!*

Eve pulled out her questions and dove headfirst into the deep end. She rattled off her insanity, especially when she told me about the time she was held against her will in a stranger's apartment in Paris. It was truly terrifying, the situations we put ourselves in. If this didn't keep me sober—nothing would!

"It was psychotic, Roxanne. I was trying to leave this guy I had met on Bumble. That was the third time I had hooked up with him on my layover. He was a sweet guy, so I felt completely comfortable meeting him at his place. But... something seemed off from the start. The hair on my neck stood up when I walked in his door. He was behaving differently. Now, reflecting back, I can see the red flag that something was amiss."

As you know with my own acting out—we addicts ignore those red flags. We paint them green, as in, GO. We only focus on the euphoria of our behaviors. It's GO time.

As Eve was breaking down the red flags, she realized they had started earlier in the week. "He was obsessively texting me on WhatsApp. Asking when I was back in town. Telling me that he missed me and had been thinking about me nonstop since our last date. Which I should have seen as crazy, since we never went on an official date! We would just meet for a drink at a hotel bar and then screw."

I nodded in acknowledgement, because I understood that false intimacy with a stranger.

Eve delicately placed a small piece of scone in her mouth and chewed slowly. Thoughts of self-judgment swirled around in my head—I would never eat like that, especially if it was a carb. I would shove that so fast into my gullet; because, let's be honest, I'm a gluttonous pig with when it comes to pleasure.

As she read her answer to the question of where she felt like she'd lost control, Eve continued to explain the terrifying situation with that stranger abroad. "I found out later that the apartment wasn't even his. It was an Airbnb. And he was married with two young kids, even though I specifically asked him, since I do not believe in crossing that line. The last thing I would ever want to do is break up a family." She was mentally transported back to the deceit. She became pissed and upset that her disease had brought her to the point of no return with her morals. "When I confronted him, at first he denied it. Then he apologized, followed by professing his undying love for me." She paused as the flashbacks physically affected her right before my eyes. Her face turned pale. I thought she might pass out at the table. The thought popped into my mind, Maybe I should move the yummy scone, so it doesn't get smashed? See, told you, I'm a pig! She breathed through the painful memories of her past. "I wanted to puke as he kept waxing on and on about his devotion. He kept repeating that he was madly in love with me. I kept screaming at him, 'Stop! You don't even know me. You should be ashamed. I mean, your poor children and wife. How dare you be so dishonest.'"

Shaking her head, she vaguely recalled getting up and putting on her clothes. "That's when he snapped. He grabbed my phone and purse. He ran into the closet naked and put my stuff in the safe deposit box. He set a code and turned around with a crazed look in his eye. My mind shook with fear. Survival instincts kicked in. He told me I wasn't going anywhere. That we were soulmates and we belonged together. I was truly scared, Roxanne." She added, teary eyed, "He had my passport, my ID, my phone, and my money, and no one knew where I was or who I was with. I thought I was going to die. I mean, no one would find me. Or my body! I was in this foreign country and no one could account for my whereabouts. Not even my coworkers!" She pulled out her sunglasses from her non-designer purse—which I loved, by the way. As the tears rolled down her cheeks, she put on her glasses to cover the emotion, coming to the conclusion, "That was my bottom. I knew I needed help. I never wanted to put myself in those dangerous situations again. My life had spiraled out of control. It was insanity, the lengths I would go to in order to get laid." She finished her answer about insanity with this realization: "There I was in the city of love, and I have never been in love. And my last partner was a crazy, obsessed, married man who was about to murder me. How ironic and sad is that?"

I handed her a Kleenex from my bag—I carried a small pouch of them, since I had a

I had my own breakdowns to take care of. *I don't think you realize how many times I have been stuck with snot and tears running down my face and nothing to wipe them with. Gross!*

"Eve, I completely hear you and have been there myself. A lot of our bottoms happen in dangerous situations. I'm so glad you made it to the SLAA rooms. And you now can see that there is a different way to live your life. Your God definitely helped you get out of that place." I quickly added, "I've never been in love either. You're not the only one." As we wrapped up her in-depth writing, I read our daily meditation for the day. It fit perfectly, stating, "It's hard to deal with all the ups and downs of a sex and love addict's love life. A whirlwind romance, intense passion, basically a rollercoaster ride is much preferred over the boring drudgery of our day-to-day life. It takes time to change lifelong patterns. It takes time to heal."

I ended our coffee session with my experience. "Eve, it will take time to heal the trauma we've caused in our bodies and change our patterns of behavior. But this morning, you did the work. And that's what it's going to take. You spent the last twenty-plus years acting out to get your hit from men. It will take work to change those patterns. Trust me, I have been there, done that. There's nothing you can tell me that I haven't seen, heard, or done."

Eve reached across the table, pulling me in for a big awkward-as-fuck hug. Now, listen, I'm not a hugger. I'm not your typical Southern belle like Eve, who's from Birmingham, Alabama. I hate hugs! They make me uncomfortable, but Dr. Kath had given me instructions to hug others back when they hugged me. "You need to lean into that intimacy, Roxanne. Especially with your fellow women in the SLAA program."

So that was what I was doing when Eve abruptly hugged me. I closed my eyes and breathed, even though my skin crawled. I kept telling my body to relax and let go of the tension.

"Thank you so much, Roxanne. I'm so grateful for you," she stated, while still holding me at a very awkward angle.

I started repeating to myself—*Relax, Roxie. You are safe. It's okay to accept love and affection.* Even being sober for over a year in SLAA didn't mean I didn't still have work to do on my intimacy issues. Just so you are aware, intimacy stands for Into-Me-See. And I was not fully sure how to let someone see into me. *A work in progress over here!*

Tension erupted from my shoulders when Eve finally released me from her death grip of intimacy. I quickly grabbed my purse and coffee, while throwing a thank-you over my shoulder to Purple. Halfway out of my seat, I told Eve, "I'll email you the next part of the step-work. Like I said, it's a brutal four-part series for Step One."

Eve replied, standing up hesitantly, "Oh, okay. Thanks again, Roxanne. I hope you have a good day."

I hollered back before she could hug me again, "You got it. No prob!" Speedwalking to my car, I climbed into the driver's seat, and a huge sigh of relief escaped my mouth. Wow, intimacy was still difficult for me to handle, even with another woman. I started up the engine and headed to my first appointment of the day, a callback for a recurring guest star on an ABC pilot that was shooting after I got back from London. Oh joy, television-pilot season. My favorite season as an actress! *Insert eye roll.*

At the beginning of every year, not only does this self-involved industry flood our minds with the hopes of booking a life-changing job, but the all-important awards season is also in full swing! Compare and despair in full effect! The whole obsession of awards season makes me sick to my stomach. Oscars. Emmys. Golden Globes. Grammys. BAFTAs. Critics Choice. SAG Awards. A bunch of overexposed celebrities parade around for a series of high-profile events in borrowed dresses and designer jewels, giving each other praise and trophies while smiling for paparazzi and dutifully sharing which designer they're wearing. It's often a popularity contest. High school all over again, where the inner-1% circle is nearly impossible to break into. Let's just say I truly hate January through March. *Not the best way to start a new year, I'm aware.*

As I drove over to the Disney-ABC lot to perform for a potential killer paycheck, I was doing my best to miss all the Golden Globes traffic. Insider information: The Golden Globes are notorious for being a popularity contest, where actors and their team of agents, publicists, lawyers, financial advisors, trainers, makeup artists, stylists, etc., campaign for the award. It's all about money and campaigning. While the world is under the illusion that the GGs are about the craft of acting, it's actually "All About the Benjamins" ... even just to get nominated.

As I got over my rage and frustration with Hollywood politics, I pulled into the studio lot in my blacked-out, rimmed Range Rover, actually feeling like a baller. There is something quite wonderful about pulling onto a lot. Being one of the rarified few allowed in as if it was the holy grail. As I handed over my ID and was ushered onto the lot, I felt the surge of false materialistic pride returning, which, incidentally, was not spiritually sober of me. Speaking of not being healthy, I let my fantasies linger a little too long on the hot parking valet.

EXT. STUDIO PARKING LOT—DAY

ROXANNE pulls up in her Range Rover, looking like the typical Hollywood C-list actress. Her nails are done. Her hair is perfectly curled. She wears the standard audition outfit: tank top, jeans, and those notorious nude Jimmy Choo heels, with her chicken cutlets tucked firmly into her 34A bra.

She swaggers out of the driver's-side door in front of the parking attendant with some

kind of generic boss-bitch song playing in
the background. (Come on—you always need
background music, even when you can't afford
it.)

Roxanne throws her keys to the attendant
and trips on the curb. She breaks her fall
by grabbing onto his shoulder, and her body
swings around his legs like a stripper pole.
Not the best dismount before the big callback.

                    ROXANNE
          Bet that was the most awkward
          lap-dance you NEVER asked
          for.

VALET, twenty-eight and built like a brick
shithouse, catches her with one hand. Roxanne
notices his ripped torso under his tight-
fitting guard T-shirt.

                    ROXANNE
          Wow… you're…

                    VALET
          I know. I get that a lot.

                    ROXANNE
          You look like the guy from
          The Bear.

                    VALET
          I was his body double in
          Shameless.

                    ROXANNE
          You're shitting me.

                    VALET
          Yeah. They needed a bigger
          cock.

She blushes. She wants him. Right there, right
then. Screw the life-changing job. She'd
rather screw him.

> VALET
> You're cute. Want to have a
> quickie?

> ROXANNE
> Yes—yes, I do.

She hasn't let go of him yet. Her body wants to jump him right there. He oozes animal magnetism, and she has an itch that needs to be scratched.

Roxanne gets that familiar rush until… she sees his wedding ring.

> ROXANNE
> Send your wife my apologies.

Confused and vulnerable, she starts to cry.

> SMASH TO BLACK

FOCUS, ROXIE. I refused to linger any longer on the hot valet, and I marched toward my audition. Clearly, I was a hot mess. Internally, I was the least secure individual. But going into that callback with any form of fake self-confidence was better than nothing. I felt uncoordinated and vulnerable 95% of the time. I don't think non-addicts understand what it's like the first couple of years in sobriety. You're like an adult-sized sensitive toddler walking around trying to function in the world. Let's just say—I felt physically naked twenty-four hours a day. Every day. I was always vulnerable. Anything or anyone could knock me down or make me cry. Even Eve's hug at Urth Caffé was still vibrating my insides.

As I signed in at the producer's building, all the big names were there. Mostly the same ladies you've seen on TV for the last twenty years—*the Jessicas, the Jennifers, and the Katies.* Right at the top of the page was—you guessed it—Coolgirl! What was in the air? Reunion week? First West, and now Coolgirl? What the actual heck was my God trying to tell me?

I had a mini panic attack trying not to look around the waiting room to see if she was still there. As I tried to act nonchalant sitting in a chair, I peeked up from my audition sides and saw she was not in the room. *Phew*, I could feel my heartbeat slow down. Listen, I would have loved to confront her on the pain she caused me, but an audition waiting room was not the ideal location for truth-telling. Also, I was fully aware of my part in the debacle of that botched threesome. My side of the street definitely needed some serious street cleaning. After a much-needed deep dive with Alice and Dr. Kath, I realized I had not stuck to my instincts. Instead, I'd let her pursue me when I was wholeheartedly against the threesome. Yet again, my need to people-please had reared its helpful head. Hopefully, in a perfect world, we could be friends again. But a showdown was very hard for me, especially when it was with someone I cared about. Luckily, I didn't have to do that today. I looked down at my sides to refocus on the character's objective for the scene I was reading. I repeated in my head the first sentence, which always helped me get into the character.

Suddenly, a roaring laugh escaped through the cracks of the casting director's door. I heard it. Worse than that, I recognized it. My breath caught in my throat. It was getting louder and louder. Closer and closer! The doorknob turned and the ultimate bohemian goddess sashayed out. Talk about getting hit by a two-by-four. The one and only Coolgirl, with all of her sexual allure, threw air kisses to the assistant like they were BFFs. That was her superpower, and she did it so beautifully. She made you feel like there was no one else more important than you. All the while, she was just playing that role to get what she needed. Still wasn't sure who she truly was underneath her mask. Pure manipulation at its finest, and I knew this because I perfected my own tricky ways years ago. I just wasn't allowed to do it anymore. And yes, it made me green with jealousy at times. And an even bigger yes, I whole-heartedly missed her captivating attention that once was directed toward me. Wow, it made me sick to my stomach to admit—*I'm still addicted to the seduction of the unavailable.*

Coolgirl's eyes locked onto mine. I tried to smile, but I don't think my lips moved an inch. She walked right up to me, acting as if nothing had occurred the last time we saw each other. "Hi, chica! Kick ass in the room. They are so nice. I worked with them before, they're great." A dramatic pause as she flipped her perfectly wavy mane-like Afro over her shoulder and continued, "I'm so glad we ran into each other. I've been meaning to tell you. It's just been so crazy busy, you know? Can you meet me after? I need to call Superstar, but I'll be out front waiting."

I quickly answered, "Sure!" Her energy was so confident and infectious that she was already moving to the door tapping on her phone. Bulldozed once again by our toxic patterns. I turned away and gave my signature eye roll, just as my name was being called to go into the room. The most frustrating part for me was that I knew she'd killed that audition, because, like I told you before, she was a badass at our craft. She transformed so easily and could memorize ten pages of dialogue like it was nothing. *Compare and despair was festering right on the surface!*

I hated actors who had photographic memories. I always wanted to stab them in the brain through their ear canal. I know, kind of fucked-up and definitely morbid. But it was hard being dyslexic in this business. It was just one more way I felt less than. I literally had to record the other characters' dialogue on Voice Memos to practice saying my own lines out loud. I listened to the recordings repeatedly till I had to go in for the audition. I mean, if you were a fly on the wall at my house, I would look like a crazy person talking to a recorder, repeating the line over and over again. It was beyond exhausting work for me, but like I said, I loved playing make-believe for my career, and I couldn't picture doing anything else with my life. Learning disability—*SCREW YOU!*

My mind was cursing her brilliance as I walked in the door to read for an Academy Award-winning director. No pressure, right? It's like you want to piss your pants at the same time, while trying not to let your voice crack with overwhelming nerves. One of the amazing side effects of my SLAA program was that it had helped me remember the director's lack of importance. Sure, they decided my fate, but let's be honest, they were as screwed up as all of us. They just had more money and power. I had enough evidence in SLAA for that statement to ring true. It had helped me *rightsize them.* They were flawed humans who put their pants on in the morning, got zits, farted, and took their after-coffee shits! Even with this very real observation, the entertainment industry can still make or break your spirit on any given day. That's why you often see someone at their height of fame getting a divorce, being a drunk, or going to rehab. You think—*What the f-, they had it all. Why are they blowing up their lives?* Because we all believe this silly fantasy that if we get what we want, we will be complete. We'll live happily ever after. I'm here to remind you that this is another big fat lie we tell ourselves. It's all a bunch of crap.

So, there I was, about to read for this life-changing part, and I had managed to get Coolgirl out of my head. I stated my name and agency, and I dove into the work. They had me read it twice with redirects. And... it went pretty well. I made them laugh when I wanted them to laugh, I was emotionally present, and I think the casting assistant teared up when I got to the emotional climax. Okay, it didn't go pretty well—it went great. No one answered their texts or asked for their lunch during my audition. That was a win in itself. I felt decent with most of my acting choices. They thanked me and I walked out. It had only been five minutes in that room, but I felt like I had climbed Mount Everest. The irony was that, even though I felt terrific about the audition, in order to keep myself sane, I had to magically let go of the results and have amnesia. Honestly, this is the only healthy way to participate in the magnitude and torture of auditions; otherwise, I would spend every waking moment waiting for the phone to ring, enmeshed in either the fantasy of getting the job or the misery of not getting it. My secret to immediately forgetting about a life-changing potential job is to throw away my sides in the nearest trash and try to get on with my life. Easier said than done, believe me. But the good news that day was that all I was thinking about was my ex-best-friend waiting for me outside to rehash our failed threesome. *FUN!*

I spotted her after my eyes adjusted to the blasting California sun. She was across the parking lot on her phone, talking so loudly that the entire lot could hear. "I nailed that shit. They would be lucky to have me. Yes, I did that mantra you taught me right before. I know, babe, it always works for you, and you are the shit!" *Insert annoying high-pitched giggle here.* "Okay, Superstar, I got to go. Love ya, baby." She hung up and turned to me. "What's up, girl? Been a long time."

My one-word reply: "Yep."

We stared at each other, waiting for the other to crack. She squinted her catlike eyes and looked around. "Let's go take a squat on that bench." It wasn't a question, more like a statement. Of course, my ass dutifully followed her without hesitation. We both sat down, and when I turned to look at the end of the bench, there was a statue of Mickey Mouse stupidly grinning at me. *Awkward having this conversation about seeing my friend's wet vagina during a horrible threesome while sitting next to this iconic mouse.*

I pivoted my train of thought and cut to the chase. "Let's discuss the naked elephant in the room."

We both broke out in roaring laughter. That's when I saw it. The subtle changes in her. She'd definitely gotten thinner, and her eyes were a tad sunken in. Plus, it looked like she'd gotten some more filler injected in her lips. As I was deciphering the subtle changes, she started in on her problems with Superstar. I was taken aback by her redirect of the conversation. I'd thought we were going to rehash Throw-up-on-her-married-boyfriend's-face Gate. *That's a nope!*

She purged her life dilemma. "I'm living in Malibu with Superstar on the down low because he's still married. I met his kids in London on set, but NOW his wife is traveling with him to shoot the remake of his first blockbuster movie! Can you believe that?" She gestured erratically with her hands as I was about to say—*Well, yes, why wouldn't she go with him? They are married.* But I never got the chance. She continued her rant, "Yes, I know I can't stop them being together, because she is his producing partner. But man, I'm lonely. I sit on the beach almost every day, trying to do work on myself. I write in my journal and do my mantras. I even started meditating. I was thinking maybe I should come to one of your meetings. Do you think I can find a sponsor to take me through the steps so I'm okay when he's gone working? Do you know anyone who would work with me?"

I watched her in complete disbelief. First of all, that's not how the program works. You don't stay in relationships with unavailable people. Second, she never said she was sorry about Vagina Gate! *Okay, my unrealistic expectation of her taking accountability might have bitten me in the ass.*

I took a big inhale and trusted that my God had me. I turned to my old best friend and said, with every ounce of compassion I could muster, "I'm sorry you're lonely. You should definitely come to an SLAA meeting. But I can't think of anyone who comes to mind to sponsor you for your situation. Maybe you'll find someone when you start going?" I cleared my throat to prepare to clean my side of the street, even though every ounce of me wanted her to apologize first. I said, "I do want to talk about that night at Hotel Bel-Air. First, I'm sorry for throwing up on your man and running out and not cleaning up my vomit. I was embarrassed and ashamed. Second, I never should have said yes to joining you both in the bedroom. I was uncomfortable and didn't know how to honor my feelings in that situation. I wish I could go back and change the whole thing." There, I did it! I made my first amends, like my sponsor taught me during my Tenth Step work. And look—I didn't die! *Hooray.*

But here is the messed up thing about saying you're sorry. Did she take accountability for her part? NO! She just responded, "Thank you, that means a lot." Then Coolgirl hugged me, stood up, and grabbed her Gucci fanny pack. "I've got to run, but let me know when you go to your next meeting. I'll join you." Then she blew out of there just like she had blown into my life.

Have you ever had a friend who did you dirty, but you were happy to see them and wanted to make up and forgive them, but once they left the conversation, there was a horrible pit in your stomach? That was exactly how I felt after this exchange. I wanted to say all these things that replayed in my mind. I wanted to tell her how badly she'd hurt me. That I'd even had to do the AA fourteen-day resentment prayer to let go of our friendship. Alice started making me pray for all these good things to happen for her. I hated it! I didn't want her to be happy. I wanted her to be just as miserable as I was. After our conversation, I realized I had another layer of work to do around letting go of our relationship. She was never going to take accountability for her side. Man, I hated when other people had this much power over me and my feelings. I had to let go of my ego. I needed to PAUSE and understand that GOD was in the pause, as Alice liked to remind me.

That was when it happened. My phone rang. The name "Tattoogirl" appeared on my screen, AKA divorced, hot-shot stylist-to-the-stars who dated all those lame douches on Instagram. You remember her, right? Married to the rocker dude whom she never loved, or even liked? Had a young son but couldn't seem to get her act together to take care of him, including introducing him to every guy, which was usually a new one every month that she was allegedly #lobstersoulmates with. Yeah, her! I know, Dr. Kath wanted me to stop judging her, but man, she was lying to herself all the time. Yep, my character defects were still there—I was still judgy as hell.

But good lord, all the old "act out" homies were making grand entrances today.

"Hello?" I answered with half-excitement and half-wariness of more drama coming my way, acting as if I didn't know who it was.

She laughed and called me on my game. "Girl, don't act like you don't know it's me. I'm in your hood and would love to see you. I know it's been a while, but I miss my friend. You around? Want to meet for a quick lunch before I head back to Milk Studios?"

Milk Studios was right down the street from my house so it would be a conveniently quick getaway for me if things went south. I had to stay on my toes with this one—she was crafty. I told her, "I'm leaving the Disney-ABC lot now and should be there in twenty minutes. Meet you at In-N-Out Burger? PMS-ing and need some red meat."

She replied, "I'm a vegan now, since I started dating Annoying Chef. But I can get just fries. See ya then." All I heard was "blah, blah, blah." This girl would never learn. Today was just getting weirder and weirder with these chicks. God was definitely telling me something. Not exactly sure what that something was. All would come to light soon—I was sure of that.

Walking into In-N-Out at lunchtime was an insane act of treason on my part, but I was desperate for some ground beef. I always got a Double-Double burger, Animal Style and Protein Style. I really wished I could get Animal Style light fries, but my diet wouldn't allow me.

Listen, every Californian resident will know exactly what I just ordered, and I know I should tell you all what that order means, but I am kind of an asshole, remember? And I think it is much more exciting for you to go online and find the secret menu for In-N-Out. Come on, don't roll your eyes at me. It will be fun. Pick up your computer and type that in! I will wait right here for you—no rush!

I saw Tattoogirl's BMW pull into the lot, but it was so dang crowded it took her fifteen minutes to get a parking spot, so I bit the bullet and ordered my burger and her Animal Style light cheese fries with a Neapolitan shake. Freaking bitch, ordering all that deliciousness in front of me, and WTF, when did she become vegan? Must be a new guy—she was always doing that, adapting or changing for a dude. I never understood doing that for a man. I had never changed myself for anyone. Maybe that was my problem—food for thought?

As I dug into my juicy burger, she plopped down across from me in her full-blown photo-shoot-stylist look of head-to-toe black, with her huge black Hermès purse to make it clear to the world that she was rich and successful. I get it, I would show it all off too. "Thank you, Roxie. I'm starving. How much do I owe you?" She barely took a breath before shoving fries in her mouth.

I pulled out the receipt and smiled. "Four ninety-five plus tax."

She looked at me like I had lost my mind. I laughed at my hilariousness of being paid back. This was a friend who had styled me for free on the red-carpet innumerable times without charging me her normal rate of $5,000.

News flash: Did you know that every star gets paid by designers to wear their dresses? It took me years in this business to understand this concept, especially when you see an A-list star wearing the ugliest frock on the red carpet at their premiere or the Oscars. It's because that bitch got paid anywhere between $100,000 and $250,000 to wear that piece of crap. On top of that Hollywood secret, the stylist will make $50,000 to $100,000 for putting them in the godawful design. It's all a money-making machine over here in La La Land. Don't get it twisted. Everything is about the dollar.

As Tattoogirl wiped the cheese off her chin and sucked down her shake, my mouth watered. I was still hungry even though I'd finished my burger. Damn, I missed my bread on my burgers. No carbs for this size 4 actress. I know, absurd, but those designer dresses only come in sample sizes.

She started in on her drama. "I did it again. I made the same mistake with the same man all over again. I got back with Fuckface. That is pretty desperate, right? They should put my picture under the definition of desperate."

"I hear ya—been there and done that with NYC," I replied with an eye roll of annoyance.

She rolled her big brown eyes back at me like she had heard it all before and then some.

I asked bluntly, "Really? Do you need me to go through this with you. Again? I mean, I can repeat myself if you want me to, but aren't you tired of hearing it from me? Did you call Dr. Kath like I said to?"

"I haven't gotten my alimony check yet, and you know I can't afford therapy, with Jay's soccer and karate classes. I promise I will when I get paid." She continued her line of excuses, "Plus my ex is a money-grubbing whore. I mean, pay me already, asshole."

I wanted to laugh in her face, which was hard for me not to do. I don't do bullshit well with her. But my girl was on her way to shoot a *Glamour* cover with an A-list ingénue, getting paid the big bucks, plus that purse she carried cost at least $20,000. She could afford therapy for $275 an hour. Let's get real, lady, don't lie to a professional liar.

Pointing to her ridiculously beautiful bag, I said, "Sell that on the RealReal or Poshmark—you could make a shit-load! Just like all your celebrity clients."

Tattoogirl's mouth was agape, like I'd just told her to sell her son. She cut me off, "Hell no, I earned this bag. Do you know how many times I had to give my husband blowjobs in airplane bathrooms, tour buses, and concert halls?" She looked at it with equal parts pride and disgust. "I hated that man, and he had the tiniest penis. I got bruises that turned into scars on my knees for this bag and the two other Hermès I raked in. I will be buried with them. Fuck that!"

She clutched her beloved Hermès tightly to her chest like I was going to steal it from her. "I moved in with Fuckface a couple weeks ago. We got into a fight last night and he kicked me out, which now sucks since all my clothes are there and I have to get to this Glamour shoot, but luckily, baby boy is with his asshole father and not at the house. I was hoping to stay with you for a couple nights till I figure out my shit—is that okay?" She looked at me with her brown puppy-dog eyes. "Look, I know I've been a bad friend and not available, but I am trying to change that. Please?"

I looked at her with empathy and compassion, which was a new behavior for me, but it was much easier for me to forgive when someone took responsibility for their actions. "Of course you can stay with me. But no drama, cool?"

The biggest smile formed on her face, and in that moment, I saw my friend for the first time in years. She was still in there. "Thank you, Roxie. I promise to behave. It will only be a couple nights. I better run. Thanks for the fries. Maybe swing by the shoot later?"

I grabbed my bag. "Sure. Text me and I'll walk over to steal a good fruit shake."

I forgot to tell you the best part of doing a photoshoot or set job—all the free food at the crafty table. Especially when it's a big job, like *Glamour* or *Vogue*, because they have really yummy treats, like a sushi bar or a smoothie truck or a coffee truck. You get the idea. So, I would definitely bring my appetite and a large purse to stock up. I had no qualms with freeloading off someone else's job. It's part of this business!

As I was driving my still-hungry ass home, I got a call from another friend, Glamgirl—you know, my married friend whose husband, the former NBA player, was the sex addict and who'd just had her second child. I was officially calling this day "Fucked-Up Friends Day," since they were all coming out of the woodwork. I was planning to head to her place in a couple days to support her recovery from childbirth. She was struggling with her postpartum body and her saggy breast-feeding boobs. *Her words, not mine.*

It was crazy seeing all my friends become mothers. Or starting to think of having a family, or getting pregnant, or freezing their eggs. My doctor actually mentioned it to me the other day, that it was something I should consider. Ugh, sounded like a hormonal nightmare, but these ovaries were starting to get old. I probably wouldn't be able to get pregnant, with all my bad karma of unsafe sex since the age of thirteen. But that was just my fear, as Dr. Kath liked to remind me. "**Fear** is just False Evidence Appearing Real. It's all negative fantasy that is playing out in your head." Easier said than done, right? Letting go of future tripping and being okay with the fear of the unknown. Fucked-Up Friend Day had proven to be a good day to stay in the present and not go into fantasy, by practicing my Twelfth Step for the ladies in my life. I was finally feeling like I was of service to other people, who were finally showing up for themselves. Listen, I knew I couldn't fix Tattoogirl, Eve, or even Coolgirl. I got it. But it was nice to try to be an example of possible change, which was what I hoped was happening and not them triggering me into my old behaviors. *There they are again—my fears.*

It was time to do some meditation. If Tattoogirl was staying with me and had broken up with the worst dude ever, Fuckface, I knew I needed to get centered before I had her stay here. The Eleventh Step is one of the most important steps in the program. Actually, the last three steps, Ten, Eleven and Twelve, are the ones that keep any addict sober.

Step Ten in SLAA: "Continued to take personal inventory, and when we were wrong promptly admitted it." This meant keeping my side of the street clean, or more easily said, having accountability for my actions.

Step Eleven: "Sought through prayer and meditation to improve our conscious contact with a Power greater than ourselves, praying only for knowledge of God's will for us and the power to carry that out." The hardest out of any step was meditation—I couldn't sit still.

Lastly—the one I was practicing very well, I might add—was Step Twelve: "Having had a spiritual awakening as the result of these steps, we tried to carry this message to sex and love addicts and to practice these principles in all areas of our lives." This meant giving back the freedom of choice to those still acting out.

For me, Step Eleven was the bitch of all freaking steps! Alice wanted me to do at least one minute of meditation in my car before I got out to go somewhere. And even for that minute, it was hard for me to be still and clear my mind. So, there I was in my driveway, forcing myself to sit there and "just be."

Come on, you try it. Count to a minute so you can see how hard it is—this is tough!

After a grueling minute of just being, I grabbed my bags and jumped out of the car. As I unlocked my 1920s door, my phone beeped.

Don't you hate when that happens, when you have to set down all your bags to look at your phone, and in those couple seconds, you feel like you are missing something so important—which is crazy, right? I grabbed my Amazon packages at my door—luckily, no one had stolen them, even though they were just my extra shampoo and various stuff to take to London in a couple weeks. Yes, I was an over-planner. I had already started packing for my trip. I was always nervous I wouldn't have everything I needed, especially when traveling overseas. I was juggling all my things when Dog tripped me coming into my kitchen. I hit the wall and went down like a load of bricks. *Great! Maybe two trips to the car next time, Roxanne! Always in a rush to get done.*

I called my pup a bunch of names, even though it was not really his fault, but I was kind of hangry at that point, and hoped this was Tattoogirl telling me it was time to come get some free food to stock up my fridge. Hot damn, it was her on the text: "Get here now. About to lose my it on this young actress! And Fuckface is blowing me up with mean messages. Over and out."

I texted back with my one finger (yes, I was one of those texters), "Girl, keep it together. You are on the job. Be there in ten mins. Need to walk Dog. Over and out."

That was our thing at the end of texts, which I had very much missed the last couple of months. I quickly walked Dog and picked up his two nugget-sized shits. If you are the asshole who doesn't pick up your dog's poop, we can't be friends. Ever. Actually, I have wished many of you dead. I think it is one of the most selfish acts, and this is coming from an addict who has lied, cheated, and stolen. So, pick up your dog's poop, you lazy ass!

I quickly ran to set and got there just when the metaphorical shit hit the fan. I walked into Armageddon, with Tattoogirl screaming at the new it girl of a hit HBO series with the whole crew standing around watching. What was going on? It felt like I was in a movie where the lead was having a mental breakdown for the whole world to see. Tattoogirl was literally picking up designer clothes and throwing them at It Girl, hitting her in the face. Screaming, "You entitled cunt! How dare you treat people who work for a living like this? Who do you think you are? You are a naive twat and will be replaced in a year after your drug addiction takes you out of the game. You, you little bitch."

My mouth was wide open in shock. But I had to give it to this young actress, Tattoogirl might have been lean and too skinny and fierce-looking with her tattoo-sleeved arms, but the actress was not backing down. She was in Tattoogirl's face, pointing her finger and yelling back.

All I could make out was the catty name-calling. "You old hag. You suck at your job. Your style is horrible. Fuck you too."

You get the gist, right? Tattoogirl was definitely getting fired from this job. She looked like she was having a nervous breakdown. I ran over to her and pulled her back from punching It Girl in the face. The actress's assistant grabbed the girl and dragged her into the changing room to help me defuse the situation. As I grabbed ahold of my friend's face to snap her back into reality, she looked at me with crazy-person eyes.

"Girl, what the actual hell? You've got to calm down. You don't want to get blackballed or, worse, sued by her cutthroat lawyers."

She turned to the hallway. "That little bitch was trashing all the clothes and yelling at my crew—I just lost it. Then Fuckface started harassing me with text after text. saying I'm ugly and old and a washed-up single mother. That I have to get my stuff out of his place before he throws it all in the trash. I'm just over all this bullshit. I've had enough. I quit."

I said quickly under my breath, "Yeah, I don't think that is going to be a problem. You're probably fired anyway, just saying."

She shook me off. "I don't care. My life sucks. I hate myself. But I am not going to let that girl talk to me or my team like that."

At that point, the shoot editor for the magazine came in and looked at me like I was Tattoogirl's handler. "I'm sorry. But she has to leave. I have security here to help her collect her things."

"Thank you. I will handle it." I turned to my bottoming-out friend. "It's time to go, girl. Let your assistant take over. Where are your things?" We grabbed her stuff and were walked out by security, which totally sucked for me, because five feet away with its windows open was the Niche smoothie truck. *Ughh, I wanted to cry! I loved that smoothie truck.*

My mouth was watering for that Green Goddess smoothie, with eighteen super greens, banana, vegan protein, agave, and coconut milk, topped with bee pollen. Sounds a little nasty when I write it all out, but trust me, it's refreshing, and all the things this starving actress needed to get through the friend drama on this shoot. But instead of enjoying my favorite drink, I turned to my friend who was in crisis and reluctantly walked her to my house, as tears streamed down her cheeks. Let me be clear, I'd only seen Tattoogirl cry once, over a random, unavailable dude. Her tiger mom taught her to be a hard worker. Her motto: "Always work hard. Put your head down, and never let them break you." With her immigrant background, Tattoogirl had done just that. She was the most sought-after stylist in the biz. Her reputation was impeccable. But the tables had turned. It was official, this girl had hit bottom. She was broken, and there was nothing I could do to stop the pain for her, except be there to listen.

The words started spilling out very quickly, like she was drunk with grief. "I hate my life. I hate men. I hate Fuckface and wish I could leave him. But I have never been without a guy. He is the one who made me really look at my life and make a change. Yes, I cheated on my husband with him. I never told anyone that. It was my secret. I know I should have told you. Sorry that I lied. But now he's been treating me like trash, almost like I'm disposable. I don't get it!" Tears were now pouring down her face like a waterfall of sadness and heartbreak. "We had so many good orgasms together, which made me realize that my ex was not sexually fulfilling me. I needed real romance. I needed twin-flames passion. I needed to feel like a woman. He gave me that. He saved me. And now it's over! It can't be over. I don't want to feel like this. I can't live like this. Help me!"

My poor friend! I grabbed her hand and walked her into my spare bedroom, sitting her on the edge of the daybed. She was now weeping uncontrollably. I took off her booties and socks like she was my toddler having a total meltdown. I tucked her into bed and turned off the lights, telling her in my gentlest, most motherly tone, which I never knew I had, "Let it all out. It's going to be okay. You will be okay, I promise. Let that pain out."

I sat in the dark and rubbed her back while she mourned her relationship and her job, which would be all over TMZ the following day. But we don't future-trip, remember? The quote from Scarlett O'Hara in *Gone with the Wind* bubbled into my head: "Oh, I can't think about this now! I'll go crazy if I do! I'll think about it tomorrow."

As I hummed softly to her, rubbing her head and back, she slowly quieted down and fell asleep. I pulled the duvet over her shoulders and snuck out the door. I stopped abruptly and thought to myself in shock, *I could be a mother*. I did have the loving-compassion gene that I'd always thought I was missing.

I realized then how far I had come in my journey by being there for those who were willing to walk through their pain, hopefully to come out on the other side and see the light. I would be there as best as I could for all of my girlfriends and give to them what I had received from others in the program, but only if they were willing to do the work and change. For me, my rock bottom had become the solid foundation on which I was able to rebuild my life, because there were really only two options: Make progress or make excuses.

Either you meet yourself in the mirror or the mirror will break you—it's dealer's choice. Choose wisely, my friend.

CHAPTER FOUR

Rule 13: Don't bother changing anyone—
that shit never works in your favor.

I HAD WANTED TO control and manipulate others to serve my will for my entire life. But I'd learned in sobriety that I was in control of jack shit. Despite being intelligent, educated, and psychologically aware, I had always heard my soft addict voices whispering into my ear that I needed to return to painful relationships to prove my value. Yet, by doing the work, I was able to ignore the voices, putting one foot in front of the other and walking past my old ways. I didn't hear those seductive voices in my head as loudly anymore, but all of those demoralizing and abandoning actions still replayed in my mind—*Call him, you'll feel better. See him, and it will all be good. You can have sex with him; it's no big deal. BULLSHIT!*

The voices were softer and less demanding now because I had changed. I read this quote from Lighthouse Recovery Institute that beautifully states the process of getting and staying sober: "First, we stay sober because we have to, then we stay sober because we are willing to, finally we stay sober because we want to." I truly believed I was in between the *willing to* and *want to* section of my sobriety. I found a lot of joy being healthy in my sex and love addiction. My story had definitely been littered with broken pieces, ugly truths, and horrible choices, but I was filled with the possibility of a major comeback, grace in my heart, and peace in my soul. And the best part was that I didn't have to try to change myself or anyone else ever again. It wasn't my job. That brings us to the fabulous **Rule 13: Don't bother changing anyone—that shit never works in your favor.**

My job was to show up for those still suffering and surround them with an image of hope and serenity. Which is what I was doing with my three girlfriends, Tattoogirl, Coolgirl, and Glamgirl, whose crib I was on my way over to so that I could talk her off a ledge about ending her marriage, especially since she'd just had a baby boy two weeks before. I even went bearing her favorite gifts: a box of Thin Mints Girl Scout cookies and a bottle of red wine.

I was working triple friendship duty with these sex-and-love-addict ladies. Whether they knew it or not, they all suffered from aspects of this disease. And they were all in some kind of toxic relationship they could not get out of. They were pulling me in all different directions, like a Gumby doll who was stretched as far as possible by its limbs but always bounced back. Yes, the metaphor was clear. I was indeed Gumby. You could stretch me, pull me, and twist me, but you couldn't break me. And believe me, these ladies were working my last nerve as they tried to pull me in their three directions: Glamgirl with her husband and his addiction, Tattoogirl recently dumped by Fuckface and living with me, and Coolgirl hitting a meeting with me to look for a sponsor who would support her still seeing Superstar as his sidepiece. *Good luck with that one.* It felt like I was the ringmaster in a relationship circus over here, and all the while, I was trying to: a.) get to my therapy session with Dr. Kath; b.) be alert, available, and present at my weekly check-in meeting with Alice, who was obsessed with her wedding; and c.) pack for my upcoming shoot, where I would be playing the wife of my toxic, hot ex, West. My life sounded like a long-running soap opera. Tune in at three to catch the latest drama starring the one and only... Roxanne.

Seriously, my life was far more interesting than the recycled, regurgitated crap I'd been busy auditioning for lately. Anyway, sorry, just going off because in the last few days, I'd truly had to audition for the stupidest pilots ever written! *THE WORST!* They were all remakes of old shows and knockoffs of CSI. I literally had to say the same dialogue for four different roles in four different shows. It was hair-pullingly irritating. I felt like a robot! No emotion, no variety! I mean, nothing original was coming out of my mouth. Pure and absolute bullshit lines.

Look, sometimes my job is exhaustingly unfulfilling. I'm sure everyone's jobs have their downsides, and I am normally not that picky with my roles. If you look me up, you'll recognize me in a number of prostitute and girlfriend roles. Sure, I've starred in shows and films as well, but if someone needs a hooker, streetwalker, working girl, tart, or trollop, they put me on the list to call in.

INT. EXPENSIVE HOTEL BAR SET—NIGHT

ROXIE, wearing cleavage to her belly button and a mini skirt that nearly exposes her vagina, sits at the bar nursing a martini. An OLD ACTOR approaches.

                    OLD ACTOR
          Buy you a drink?

                    ROXIE
          I already have one.

                    OLD ACTOR
          How much for the night? And
          call me Daddy.

                    ROXIE
          You can't afford me, Daddy.

DIRECTOR (Off Screen)
CUT!

DIRECTOR, 20s, a nepo baby straight out of
Northwestern, rushes onto set and squeaks in
a voice betraying his inexperience.

DIRECTOR
Roxie, I need more
authenticity.

ROXIE
Then you need different
lines. This is completely
unbelievable.

DIRECTOR
Listen, sweetheart, just ooze
more sex. If I don't want to
fuck you, the scene won't
work.

He looks at his AD, who winks at him. Clearly,
they will be sleeping together later.

ROXIE
You can't "sweetheart" me.
This is post #MeToo. I want
to feel safe as a woman and
seen as a viable actress.

DIRECTOR
There are twenty other girls
I could pull up right now
on Tinder who could bring
authenticity to these lines.
Just push out your tits, suck
in your belly, and hit your
mark. Think you can do that,
sweetheart?

Roxie smiles daggers at the director. She
needs the job to pay her mortgage.

ROXIE
Tits. Belly. Mark. Got it.

Here's the thing you've got to understand: Through being healthy, I now honored myself and my talent more, so these crappy shows were not doing it for me anymore. You know what I mean? I had grown as a woman and now felt like I needed to grow in my work as well. It was hard to phone in something that brought no meaning or purpose to my life.

My life was already so full of helping my friends, working with my sponsor, going to meetings, learning my lines for the movie with my acting coach, Allan, and taking my sponsees through their twelve steps of the Sex and Love Addicts Anonymous program. I had two sponsees at this time: Sara, the sweetest PR girl and my longest sponsee; and Eve, my newest addition, the flight attendant in her first step of withdrawal. Reality check: So far, since being in recovery, I'd officially had fifteen sponsees, but all the rest had bailed out on the program and never come back. That's how high the turnover rate was in the rooms. It was a revolving door of reluctant addicts who were looking for a quick fix to heal their pain and relationship dramas.

Luckily, both of my girls seemed serious in their decision to get better. Eve was on her Step One, and was doing pretty well not breaking her bottom line of sleeping with strangers on layovers. She even started doing EMDR with Dr. Kath to work on the traumatic hostage situation in Paris that she'd revealed during our step-work. She was really trying to heal and move through her sexual trauma. Sara still loved that dickhead who cheated on her with the girls who wore glitter lotion in his bed—remember that story? Sara had been waffling back and forth with getting back together with him. I wasn't sure if I was going to fire her or stick around, waiting for when it went south with them again. It was a hard call, since we had been working together for so long. It already felt like a lifetime of knowing her. That's what happens with this inner-child/ addiction recovery work. You get close to someone very quickly. You meet all the dark shadows of their past and present behaviors. And when they go back once more to what was destroying them, it can be a hard pill to stand there and swallow. Mercifully, I could turn that over and not try to control Sara's situation. The choice was hers, which would then inform my decision. That's the beauty of letting things play out without trying to move the players in your favor. The old "let go and let God."

Good news though: I'd heard that Eve would be in London when I was shooting there—should be fun to go to an SLAA meeting while in town. Yippee, much-needed out-of-town support! Since I knew I would probably lose my shit having a love scene with West. I would need all the grounding in reality to keep me sane. And having my newcomer sponsee with me would definitely keep me more in line, since you never want to be the example of bad behavior around them. That was the whole point of having a sponsee, to walk them through the steps and be the example of sobriety. Newcomers are a great reminder of where you were and how badly you don't want to go back there. They are a cautionary example of how crazy life used to be and the pain that followed. The intensity of chasing that first-love high is not worth the crash afterward. Thank God for the constant reminders, because a part of me still confuses intensity with intimacy.

I had dropped off my ridiculously expensive dry cleaning, which I tried never to do because I was so penny-pinching cheap. I usually just sprayed the pits and crotches on my clothes with perfume until they were so smelly of sweat and floral/woody notes that I was then forced to spend the money on dry cleaning them. I would then continue to complain and curse myself for buying clothes that required dry cleaning in the first place. It was definitely a vicious cycle of self-loathing. I get that.

I pulled up to Glamgirl's obscenely monstrous house in Studio City. You know the kind, the new construction that looks like it's straight out of Cape Cod. You know, the kind of house found on *Big Brother* or *The Bachelor*, or the kind where all those reality stars on *Vanderpump Rules* live? Yep, there was my judgmental character defect flaring up once more. But screw it, I was hangry again! Before every job on camera, I started on a goddamn nine-day cleanse. That particular day was the dreaded third day, which made me literally want to eat trash off the street, that's how hungry I was. The price of vanity never escaped me. My need to starve myself so I looked my best on camera had to be another trauma-induced pattern I needed to break.

I jumped out of my ride, kind of feeling like a baller as I imagined living in this mansion instead of my two-bedroom shack. But reality hit me as soon as Glamgirl opened her front door. Where was her postpartum pooch? That bitch was wearing skinny jeans. Are you freaking kidding me here? She was one of those girls who never had to diet and was a size 2, even after just giving birth to her son—her second baby!

Man, sometimes life is really not fair. Plus, on top of that, she was the sweetest person ever—almost too caring, you know? I looked at her and thought, *No, you can't be that giving, it's just not normal.* I didn't know if I trusted it. Because I didn't have a sweet bone in my body. I would cut you to get my way or my needs met. But we were friends. And she and I were polar opposites! She was the quintessential people-pleasing codependent, and I was the sex and love addict with narcissistic tendencies. Listen, don't you judge me—everyone on this planet has narcissistic tendencies. Here is a short list, so you can see that you have some of the same things I do:

Universal Narcissistic Tendencies

1. Selfish—come on, we are all a little self-involved

2. Arrogant—many people think of themselves as being the SHIT!

3. Need for admiration—hello? Attention whores are everywhere, especially in Los Angeles

4. Fantasies about power and success—okay, really? That's what the entire social media world is founded on. The fantasy and make-believe of being successful and powerful! IMAGE!!!!!

Okay, I will stop now. I just went off on a bit of a tangent. Everyone has their issues, and Glamgirl and I were both gluttons for punishment, just on opposite ends of the spectrum. She was definitely the ebony to my ivory. She was drop-dead gorgeous, with a perpetual perfect tan. I could go into a tanning bed for a solid three months and never come close to her color. My fair ass was too pasty white. If I didn't put on my favorite self-tanner, Vita Liberata, you would literally be able to see my veins. I swear by the natural look of this tanner, which never streaks or looks too orange. I should be their spokesperson—I think I've bought at least two dozen bottles since I found out about it from my hair girl. It's on Amazon for $39. You can thank me later, all you pale-white girls!

As I handed Glamgirl her "welcome to the world, baby boy" gift of booze and carbs, I stared at her overinflated tits. "Wow, you get a boob job on the birthing table after you pushed him out?"

She hit me on the arm. "My milk has come in, you pervert. And I refuse to breastfeed because I don't want saggy tits and fucked-up nipples like my mom. She told me at a very young age that my dad broke up with her over her breastfeeding tits.

So, after birth, she taught me how to wrap them up and wear three sports bras."

I stared in shock at her candor. I had never heard Glamgirl talk so openly about her mother. I knew they had a complex relationship, but this was another level that was very telling to me. Glamgirl was always smiling, but in that moment, I saw the pain in her eyes. Did she want to breastfeed her baby? Was her vanity taking over? Her fear of her mother's judgment? Or losing her husband's affections? She spun around dramatically and said in a high-pitched 180 of glee, "Let's go in the backyard. I need to get away from these kids."

I followed her outside to the pool, which was gated off so her children wouldn't drown. We both grabbed a lounge chair, and I stretched out to relax for what felt like the first time in days. She cut to the chase, frustratedly. "Girl, I mean, is that normal, for his sponsor to say it's okay to look at porn online? I mean, that was our deal, and he did it again." She sipped her bubble water, which I'd declined because bubble water made me burp really loud. *I must be a very gassy person.* Back to her dilemma with her husband's sex addiction problem. "Can you believe this bullshit, Rox? His sponsor congratulated him on coming clean with his actions, BUT he did not come clean; I caught him red-handed." She let out a burp. *Hell yeah, I'm not the only one.* "He got caught! And his sponsor congratulated him."

I looked longingly over at her tan body and then at my pasty-white legs and tried to explain. "I think his sponsor does not want to shame him more. He wants him to make the right decision and come clean when he screws up. But I get it, I would be annoyed too. It sucks to be with an addict. I feel bad for whoever I get with next." I drank my lemon water as I talked because that was the only thing I could drink before a shoot on this freaking cleanse. It was hard following an actress's diet, especially at thirty years old. Things are not the same as in your twenties. Listen, I know it gets worse for women in their forties, but I am not there yet, so let me just complain about my stretch marks and this cellulite forming. Yes, I have the coveted thigh gap, but news flash, cellulite forms on thin legs too.

"Look, Glamgirl, I'm like a freaking toddler in maturity. A baby! I pity the poor dude who will have to deal with me, if there is even one coming. God only knows at this point. Did I tell you I got off Raya? It was just too triggering."

She sat up extremely quickly for a lady who just squeezed out another baby—good for her ab strength. "GIRL, you are hot. You will find someone. You could go out now and find a man." Then she lay back down, and it got really quiet. I was thinking, *I don't just want any man. I want a partner and a teammate.*

Suddenly, the quiet broke as she screamed, and my heart stopped. I thought we were about to get attacked. She jumped up like a crazy person, yelling, "OMG! It's a bee! It's a bee. Kill it."

I yelled back just as loudly, "No, we need them. Don't kill it. They are almost extinct. If they die, we die. I just read a whole article about it." Wait! I know! Who was this person who now cared about bees? I was shocked myself when I said those words. I'd been so selfish and self-seeking, and suddenly I cared about a little bee. I mentally patted myself on the back. I was evolving. I mean, clearly I was getting better, with all of the inner-child work I was doing with Dr. Kath.

Meanwhile, Glamgirl was hopping back and forth with her too-flat stomach and perfectly shaped, size-C boobs bouncing, trying to avoid the tiny bee, and then it happened. Her nipples started to leak milk through her string bikini, and I lost it. I couldn't stop laughing at her. She looked down and fell to the ground, cracking up. "No one tells you how hard it is to dry up the milk. Even not breastfeeding, my milk won't stop. I feel like a cow. I want my tits back." Holding her breasts and trying to use pressure to stop the flow of milk, she sat back down. "TMI—technically, I have breastfed, just not my baby. Hubby loves to drink from my nipples. Weird, right? Mommy issues, probably." She rolled her eyes and grabbed her towel, holding it to her breasts to stop the lactation.

While I was sitting there, watching my friend who had just brought another soul into this life and thinking about what a miracle it was, it hit me what a sorrow it must be for her to have to deal with her husband's unwillingness to let go of his toxic disease and his disconnection from his family with the fantasy of porn. And she couldn't fix him. She had her own issues, which Dr. Kath tried to point out, like her workaholism and her obsession with perfection in her past three marriages, which pointed to her love addiction. Glamgirl had gone with me to a couple meetings and really liked the fantasy and intrigue meeting. But she was not a regular and would not commit—*cough, cough, issues?* And now with her family "complete"—since last year all she had been obsessing about was getting pregnant again, like that would fix their relationship or something.

I asked simply, with no ulterior motive, "You call Dr. Kath yet? To talk about your part in the marriage?"

She turned to me with slight annoyance. "Roxie, girl, I just had a baby. Give me a minute. I will call her. I know you're trying to help. But at this moment, with no red-carpet events or a foreseeable job, I'm struggling, yes. I could talk to someone. But it's just easier for me to block out the bad in my life when I'm busy and traveling all the time. It's when I slowdown that I start feeling the feelings. So, my schedule is always packed, and I have so much responsibility, especially taking care of the bills, since I am always the breadwinner. Now, I'm just trying to keep baby boy alive." She added quickly, placing blame elsewhere, "Plus, he needs therapy, not me. He's the one addicted to porn. Why do I have to look at my stuff?"

"I get it, but this stuff is always going to come up. You can't keep busy to not feel. You know I know that, right? There is something in you that has made you get married three other times, and let's not forget that you cheated on a lot of your boyfriends too. Plus, you keep picking other addicts, a pattern that might not be working for you anymore. You know?" Honesty was the only way I could authentically be with my friends, even one who just had a baby and was going through postpartum.

She looked at me with a sad smile. "You're right. I will call her. I promise." She turned and looked at her beautiful backyard. I watched her see that you can have everything and still feel empty. She said very softly, "It would be nice to talk to someone other than you. I will call her today. I'm lucky to have you." She reached over and hugged me, which made me want to pull away. I told you; I'm the least Southern girl you will ever meet. I hate hugs—they make me feel so uncomfortable. And she knows this, so what did this little bitch do? She hugged me harder and started kissing my cheeks. "I love you, Roxanne! So much. You are one of my besties," she said on repeat, purposely trying to make me squirm. *Ughhh. Friendship intimacy. Gross!*

I was pushing her away, and all she kept doing was hold on tighter. I wanted to kill her, screaming, "Let go of me! Stop touching me." She was cracking herself up and couldn't help but laugh. We looked hilarious because I was pulling back so hard that she ended up on top of my lounge chair, and we fell to the ground while she was still trying to kiss me.

"Get off me, bitch. I hate you." I finally broke free, smiling at the sweet playfulness of our friendship. Then I looked down and saw that her breastmilk had stained my silk top.

She grinned in apology. "My bad."

I looked at her. "You're paying for my dry cleaning, you cow. Moo."

As I walked to my car, I waved bye to my girl, since I was leaving for London in a couple days. I prayed she would call Dr. Kath or try to get to the Saturday-morning 9:30 a.m. love addict meeting. I knew I had no control over that, but I also knew it would help her deal with her own issues, which might then help her marriage.

I then stopped into Whole Foods to grab a quick bite before picking up Coolgirl for the SLAA meeting. I was browsing the salad bar, adding as much protein as I could get, since it was my one meal of the day on my cleanse. I reached for the garbanzo beans to put on top of my arugula, and a hand grabbed the serving spoon at the exact same time. I looked up and my heart stopped. The hand belonged to a guy who looked so familiar. Did I sleep with him? How did I know him? Friend of an ex's? He looked at me with his widow's-peak dark hair, 6'2" height, and scruffy face. And his eyes, they were the kindest, most sincere eyes I had ever seen.

"Sorry, but were you trying to steal my beans?" he said. "I was here first. These are my beans." He broke out into a huge grin, making himself chuckle.

"Ummm, I was here first. These are my beans!" I smiled back.

"Good to see you. It's been a couple years, right?" His smile was magnetic.

Of course I knew him. But my mind was blank. No idea who this handsome older man was. I grinned sheepishly. "Sorry, I can't remember where we met. Refresh my memory." I quickly added, "I am very old now—aged a lot over the last two years."

He drew back. "Wow. I guess I'm not very memorable. That's got to hurt."

I stopped him as he backed away. "Look, I just have a lot going—"

"Just kidding, we only met once in a Saturday acting class.

You came in and then left to go shoot a series. Nice to meet you again—I don't remember your name. I'm Mr. Handsome."

"Roxanne. Nice to meet you again too, Mr. Handsome."

That's when a girl walked up to him and asked if he was ready to go. *Shit. Shit. Double shit.*

I smiled. "Have a great night. Enjoy your beans." I turned and speedwalked to the register with my salad, kicking myself that all the good ones were already taken. That's what happens when you're a recovering addict getting your life together at thirty. You missed the boat to hook up with the normal guys. *Damn it all to hell! Just my luck!*

I started my Rover and quickly realized—I forgot to buy dressing. There was no way I was going back into that grocery store. Dry salad it was.

Coolgirl was, of course, running late! She texted that she was stuck at blah, blah, blah—her MO. I texted her back, "I will meet you there." I gave her the address, and I wanted to add, "Girl, you have a problem with tardiness. It's a huge character flaw—get it together." But of course, I didn't. As a recovering addict, I was not allowed to call others out on their character defects. Keeping my side of the street clean. I held my boundary of taking care of myself and not waiting for her, instead telling her to get her own ride there.

I pulled into the parking lot next to the church and ran into the church's daycare room to help set up the chairs and greet the newcomers at the door, since this was an SLAA newcomer meeting. One of the ways I'd kept my sobriety after my slip was that I now held a commitment position at a couple of meetings. That's when you take a role in running the meeting for half of the year. Since there's no one authority in our program, we elect new people to positions to keep the meetings running. I was the women's newcomer greeter at Wednesday meetings and the treasurer at the Monday 10 a.m. women's meeting. The main reason to take a commitment is that it forces you to show up and get your ass in the seats, because the room is counting on you.

Standing at the door welcoming all the fellows, I felt a sense of purpose and responsibility, which was good for a disconnected addict like me. Then I saw her—Coolgirl had freaking shown up. It was a miracle. A shock! She must have truly been in a lot of pain to get her ass here. Coolgirl was wearing a wide-brimmed hat and sunglasses, even though the sun was setting. I whispered into her ear when she hugged me hello, "No one cares who you are. It's okay to be seen." It's so funny when actors come into the room, like anyone cares who they are. We are all just in pain and needing some relief. But I got it. I'd been in this room for my first meeting, and I remembered how overwhelming and vulnerable I felt, especially if someone recognized me from television. Yes, it was absurd, since I was so C-list and no one knew my name, but ego can play mad tricks on your importance level. Like the world revolves around you.

As the meeting started, I could tell that Coolgirl was barely paying attention, but I reminded myself that she was here, and that was a great step. It was not my job to entertain her in this room. She was not my responsibility to fix. As I kept repeating this in my head, the signs of recovery brought me back into focus (I'm paraphrasing here): #5, we learn to love ourselves, take responsibility for ourselves, and take care of ourselves and our needs before others. I had to remind myself that I was not her keeper, and it was not my job to help her to "get it." I was here for me and to get centered, which I definitely needed to do before I headed out of town to work with the old hottie ex. My goal this week was to hit a meeting a day in order to stay healthy in all my affairs.

Newcomer shares were starting, which were always my favorite because it was a great reminder for me of what the pain of using looked like. I mean, no one came into the SLAA rooms because their life was "kind of" unmanageable and a little in the shits. No, they crawled into the rooms because they were usually at the end of their rope and out of other options. So, when they asked who would like to start and share, to my astonishment and dismay, Coolgirl raised her hand. *WOW! I guess people can still surprise me. I did not see that one coming.*

She was still wearing her sunglasses, which was a little ridiculous, but she spoke with such heartbreak and trauma that I was moved to completely listen to my friend's past.

"I keep flashing to my first love. I was a freshman in high school, and he was my art teacher." My heart plummeted right there when she said those words. She continued, "I was madly in love with him, and when I was in class, I would uncross my legs so he could see my Tuesday panties, even though it was Thursday. I used to tease him so much. He would resist me and resist me, but I finally made it happen with him when I was a sophomore and ran into him at the movies after my parents dropped me off. I stalked him and made him fall in love with me. I knew it was wrong, but he was my soulmate, and I needed him. Long story short, he was arrested and fired from his job. I was called the school whore. I dropped out and got my GED after my junior year. Now, I find myself with another man who has age and power over me. I just love him so much. It's hard to be in an open relationship, but I don't want to let him go. I know damn well that we are meant to be together and that God brought him to me to make all my dreams come true." The two-minute timer went off, which meant she had one more minute to wrap up her share.

That's how it works in the twelve-step rooms. You can't let an addict share longer than three minutes, or it would just be an attention-seeking jumbled mess. We are so self-involved, even three minutes can be too long. Believe me, there are some shares when you just want to shove your fingers in your ears. The same people dealing with the same problem, meeting after meeting. Sometimes I just wanted to yell, "Then do something different, asshole!" *But that would not be VERY recovered of me.*

Coolgirl continued preaching that her situation was a great thing—*insert eye roll here.* "I need him in my life. He can help me so much, and I can't screw up my career again with letting things slip through my fingers. I need this to happen. I have messed up so many opportunities in the past with my attitude and not being willing to just go with the situation. Like the studio movie I bailed on because I couldn't get out of bed. I believe this is the right situation for me—I just need to learn how to navigate this new kind of relationship where I don't have as much or any power over the other person. I tend to pick men who want to take care of me, but this time it is to the extreme. He is a GOD in people's eyes." In that moment, I had a huge wave of sadness that she was actually stuck in this fantasy she had created in her mind. She truly believed she needed him to succeed. A tear formed in my eye for the little girl inside of me who was once there too. She continued on her purge, "I love him, or I guess I love how he makes me feel. I mean, he chose me out of all his options around the world. Yes, he's married and has another girlfriend. So was my teacher. But it's not the same. This is an open relationship." Her one minute was up. She turned to me with a downcast smile, then turned back to the room of other addicts. "Thanks for listening. Oh, and I need a sponsor. One who can help me, but the caveat is that I will not leave the relationship. Thanks!"

I peered across the room to the old-timers, who were all just slightly shaking their heads. I got it. She sounded crazy. But she was here, and I was not judging her. At least, I was trying not to.

As we stood up to leave the meeting, an old-timer, Barbara, whom I loved—that lesbian lady I'd heard at the Malibu retreat my first year—walked up to us. She was the one who was almost like me, except she was gay, white-haired, and seventy. She introduced herself to Coolgirl. "I'm Barbara. I was a sexual-assault survivor too. And I was in a situation like that with a prince in the Middle East when I was younger. He had a harem of ladies. I understand being scared and not wanting to leave. But nothing real can come from someone who is with two other people. He is never going to be yours, I'm sorry to say. Call me if you ever want to really work the program. I would sponsor you once you're ready to get out of your *situationship*." Barbara turned to me. "Hey, Roxanne. Good to see you. I truly mean it."

Barbara picked up her cane and walked away. Coolgirl turned to me with so much outrage, I was blindsided by it. "What was that old lady talking about? I am not a sexual-assault survivor, and did she not hear my share? I am not leaving my man."

I squared up to her with all the sincerity I could muster—it was hard for me to have the empathy gene when all I wanted to do was shake the hell out of her and snap her back into the reality of her current situation, but that never worked. "Coolgirl, you were what, fifteen or sixteen years old?"

"I was sixteen, a couple of weeks after my birthday. So?" She recoiled while swinging her dark curly hair with major attitude.

"Okay, you had just turned sixteen. But how old was he? At least twenty-eight or twenty-nine? I think that is illegal in all fifty states. You were a minor. He should have known better," I responded carefully.

Now it was on, and she was in total defense mode. I could see it all over her face. "What the fuck, Roxie? He did not do anything—I did. This was exactly how it went down. I was the aggressor, not him. I ran into him at the movies. He was on a date with some stupid-looking blonde girl. I smiled at him when we both got our tickets. We were in the same theater and across the aisle from each other. We kept making eyes with each other. So, I decided to be bold and brave, and got up off my seat and looked to him to follow me out into the hallway. My heart was pounding; I was so nervous. I waited in the hallway around the corner near the bathrooms in case someone saw us, so we could move into the bathroom and not get in trouble. I took off my sweater and pushed up my bra and tits. He saw me and started walking my way. I turned on as much fake sassiness as I could muster, and he was hook, line, and sinker. I grabbed his hand and pulled him down to me and kissed him. He matched my intensity then pulled away and said, 'I knew you were trouble.' I smiled and giggled, and said, 'I knew you wanted to find out.' I walked past him and felt my power over this older man."

I stared at her, unsure of what I was feeling—mostly disappointment, some anger, and a great deal of frustration that nothing was sinking in. She pressed on, oblivious to my sorrow about her situation.

"That is how it went down, Roxie. I did it all to him and teased him. After that, we were together every chance we got. It wasn't his fault, it was mine. I wanted it. I loved him. Then the principal found out and he got fired. It was a nightmare after that. I don't want to talk about it." Coolgirl was so worked up by this point, I could tell she was about to totally lose it on me if I didn't tread lightly. She finished her thoughts, "Anyway, that's not why I am here. I don't even know why I mentioned that. I just need to get out of this pain when Superstar is out of town or with another of his girls. I need some tools like you guys talk about to be more self-sufficient when he's gone. That's what I need. To be okay when he is gone. Nothing else is a problem."

My heart broke for her. Nothing I could say would change her into seeing the truth that I saw. She would have to do this work herself. I could see on her face that she had completely shut down. Empathy flowed through me. "I understand, girl. I'm not trying to make you upset at all. I just see things differently after doing this work. Stuff that happened to me when I was sixteen looks different now in my adulthood. That's all. It's just my perspective. Didn't mean to make you feel bad. I'm glad you came tonight. I hope you come again. Give it another chance. Maybe you will find the right sponsor, who knows." I hugged her goodbye quickly as she got in the Porsche that Superstar had bought her.

In my car, I did something I had not done in a year. I started to cry. Fat teardrops of heartbreak fell from my eyes. I mourned for my own loss of innocence. For her loss of wholesomeness when she was just sixteen. Now, for her loss of self-worth with this very rich, powerful man. I cried for my friend to find herself. I cried for the pain she must have felt all these years, holding that much trauma in her body and not even knowing that she was doing more damage internally. I cried for the unnecessary envy I had been carrying around since we became friends. That I'd always compared myself to her and never felt like I measured up. Such a waste of self-harm that I did to myself too. The tears kept flowing all the way over the 405 South to the 10 East.

When I pulled into my driveway, a sick feeling came over me. My intuition was ringing when I opened my front door. I immediately saw Tattoogirl's bags packed by the front door. I set down my black Chanel Caviar Quilted Medium Double Flap purse with my keys, and yelled, "Tattoogirl, are you leaving? I thought you were staying till Saturday, when you had to pick up your son?"

She emerged from the guestroom with her bag of make-up. She was all dolled up and looked high as a kite. I knew she was sober in AA, but something was off. I just wasn't sure what it was.

She smiled like the cat who got the canary. "We are back together. Isn't that great! I'm so happy. I'll be out of your hair in no time. Thank you so much for letting me stay. You are a great friend, Roxie."

I had no words. I stared at her in complete confusion. This was a girl who had said horrible things last night about Fuckface with a capital F. That he pushed her in their last fight and she fell; that he called her fat in front of her son; that he was emotionally abusive, calling her every name in the book and DMing a bunch of other girls on Instagram in front of her. That's just naming a few of the abusive things he had done to her. That she felt like a piece of crap around him. That she hated herself when she looked in the mirror. That she lost her seven years of sobriety in AA with him! *I was about to lose it. Were these women out of their minds? Was I the only one grounded in reality at this point?!*

"NO, you are not going back to him. I won't let you!" I said, with as much parental authority as I could muster. She started laughing at me as I picked up her bag and dragged it past her back into the hallway.

She grabbed it from me with a giggle, and said, "Rox, are you nuts? I have to go. He's waiting for me."

I grabbed the bag again. "NO! He is a horrible man. I will not let you do this to yourself again."

Her face turned. "It is not your call. Now give me my stuff." I held on as she pulled the bag back, and we were literally playing tug-of-war with her Louis Vuitton duffle bag. The leather strap was in danger of breaking, we were both pulling so aggressively. But I didn't give a damn about this $2,500 designer bag.

"You're going to break my bag, bitch. Let go or I will call the cops, Roxanne. Let go, you crazy bitch."

I screamed at the top of my lungs, pulling the strap as hard as I could and finally breaking it, "FUCK you, Tattoogirl!

You are not going back to him—he is a horrible person. Do you understand? He is bad news. You deserve better, my friend." I held the strap of her bag in my hand like I had lost the turkey wishbone game, which my family did every Thanksgiving.

Tattoogirl turned away, and I knew she knew I was right. But when she turned back, she said, "I know you are worried about me. Especially after everything I told you last night, but I did exaggerate some of it. I'm a big girl, Roxie. I am going. I love him. You just don't get our connection."

By then, I had lost it. I was not letting her destroy herself. I had to say something—those thoughts kept whirling through my mind. I had to save one friend, at least. In that moment, it hit me. I was holding on so tight to that bag strap and wanting it to be different that I would never win this war. I let go of the strap and it fell to the floor in defeat.

I looked her straight in the eyes. "He is going to kill you. Don't you get it? He does not love you when he abuses you. He just wants to control you. It's not love. It's obsession. I'm scared for you, my friend. I am scared that I will never see you again."

She stared right back at me, but this time it was filled with hatred. "Fuck you, Roxie. You think you're better than me, but you are a whore too. Now you're supposedly recovered or some bullshit like that. But you are just a self-righteous little bitch. You don't know anything about Fuckface's and my relationship. I don't need this."

She walked out with her one-strapped bag dangling from her shoulder. I watched her struggling to get into her car. She threw the car into drive—without putting on her seatbelt, I might add. Wow, talk about a metaphor for her life right now. Going a hundred miles an hour with no safety harness. I turned away from the window and sank to the floor against the door, like in every movie I had ever seen when a breakup happens, but this time it was in real life. My flat butt hit the cold wooden floorboards with a thud, my tailbone throbbing. I reached up and grabbed my chest, trying to stop the pain from overtaking me.

My heart was truly broken all over again. The tears didn't flow softly down my cheeks this time; the floodgates opened as my friend drove away to a horrible man and there was nothing more I could say or do to stop it. I sat there sobbing.

I was sobbing for all four women circling around in my life who wanted the same thing. I was sobbing that they were all going about it the wrong way. I was sobbing that Tattoogirl, Glamgirl, Coolgirl, and even my sponsee, Eve, all wanted to be enough to be truly loved just as they were. They were searching for this false sense of connection with another in the most unavailable way, since they themselves were scared of connection and commitment. They were not unique or special in their disease.

Looking for a fictitious form of love, Eve acted out with strangers in exotic lands. Coolgirl wanted to be a floating-free-love bohemian sidepiece. Glamgirl truly wouldn't look at her broken relationship and take ownership of her side of the street. And lastly, Tattoogirl was drowning in her attraction to an unavailable, toxic man. I hoped that me being healthy would be an example for them all—obviously as best as I could, because I was not their savior. I was trying my best to help them by doing my Twelfth Step, being of service, but I felt like I was failing epically. I had given myself the unattainable task of fixing another in their sex and love addiction, which I knew was my own addiction acting out.

This addiction is cunning, baffling, powerful, and very convincing. Only a person themselves can beat this disease. If my friends were unwilling to change, it was not my job to force them. A very wise newcomer shared the other day, "Never deny anyone else their process or their pain in their journey."

Pain is personal, just like change is personal. We don't try to change people.

It doesn't work well... I prayed for the courage to persist in my own surrender of others. If there was pain, let me accept it now, get on with it, and get through with it.

CHAPTER FIVE

Rule 14: Feelings aren't facts. Let yourself feel them anyway, they're just information—they won't kill you!

REMEMBER THE FEAR ACRONYM, right? *False Evidence Appearing Real?* Well, at this point, I was packing my third suitcase to go shoot the movie in London, and all I was feeling was overwhelming amounts of fear arising in my mind and body. And it felt real. Overwhelmingly real. It felt really real.

After the breakup with Tattoogirl in my living room, I had been having trouble sleeping. So, to purge my demons, I sat down on my couch and wrote the FEAR acronym on several dozen Post-its. I put them everywhere: On my mirrors, on every door, front and back, both on and in the refrigerator, on the TV, inside the pages of the books I was reading, all over my script pages, and even above my toilet paper roll in the bathroom. You get the idea. At this juncture, I was even thinking about tattooing it on my body in a font like Blackletter or Old English to remind myself that my fear and anxiety were NOT freaking real! Extreme, I know! *I won't, don't worry—I'm too vain to mark myself up permanently. Then again, never say never, right?*

Those feelings of loss and anxiety were almost paralyzing me. Dr. Kath's words of wisdom looped in my head: "Roxie, did you know anxiety is fear of the future? You are trying to control the future, which is completely impossible. No one can control anything in the future, past, or present. Life is all about going with the flow. Surrender to life's feelings. Anxiety is just a false sense of control. Grab your bag of ice or dunk your face in your bowl of ice water to calm your nervous system."

Ughhh, dialectical behavior therapy (DBT) skills aside, no one on this planet has ever died over a feeling, right? Unless they truly believed it would kill them. When I was going through nine months of withdrawal from my sex and love addiction, I thought I was going to die over my feelings of pain, and when you think about it, I did kind of spiritually die, right? A new ME was actually born. But the point is that I made it to the other side; I grew from my pain and my fear of my feelings.

Rule 14: Feelings aren't facts. Let yourself feel them anyway, they're just information—they won't kill you! Even experiencing and knowing the truth that we grow by going through our feelings of pain and discomfort, still did not make it any easier to actually enjoy the process of feeling my feelings. That never gets easier for me. As I said before, addicts only want to feel one emotion, and that is the glorious feeling of euphoria. It's intoxicating. But the problem with euphoria was that I never got to feel it anymore. I knew that when I started to feel the first signs of euphoria, I needed to run away as fast as I could because that emotion was not to be trusted. It was fleeting, like the taste of a piece of Juicy Fruit gum. Am I right? I mean, I love the flavor of that gum so much, but it lasts approximately three minutes before it goes away. Then you're just chewing a bland, diluted piece of rubber. At that point, I just swallowed that crap.

Yep, I am one of those women who can't walk and chew gum. I have probably swallowed thousands of pieces of gum in my lifetime, and contrary to old wives' tales, my stomach is not full of gum. It does not take seven years for one piece to digest. I would be dead if that were true. Google even agreed with me and said that gum, though not properly digested, absolutely passes through the body just like any other piece of food. Ha!

Putting a new piece of gum in my mouth, I realized how far I had come with my feelings. When I felt overwhelming fear, I didn't sit in it like I used to. Since the good-old-fashioned DBT skills were not relieving my troubles, I picked my ass up and drove myself across town to sit in Dr. Kath's office to analyze it in order to hopefully release its fake power over my anxious nervous system. That's where I was, in her tiny cement office building chewing frantically with my leg bouncing up and down, listening to bohemian bells playing from her 1990s boombox behind the couch. I had called her early in the morning when I was having difficulty getting out of bed to finish packing to leave on the red eye to London. She told me she would squeeze me in after her last session.

I had an abundance of gratitude for my blue-tip-haired, flowy-skirted therapist, who came to my rescue when I had exhausted every other option. Including, in no particular order, attending an SLAA meeting, outreach-calling other fellows, DBT jumping jacks, a thirty-second ice-bowl face bath, a cold shower, calling Alice, prayers, and of course, the dreaded meditation, at which I completely and utterly sucked. As I told you, I was the worst meditator in history. I had trouble sitting still for the one minute before getting out of my car, which Alice told me to at least attempt to get me into the habit of meditation. I was a fidgeter. A mover. I hated being still and present. It made me uncomfortable to sit in that space, and I hated feeling uncomfortable.

How did those nutty yogi people who meditated an hour a day do it? To me, that was just plain overachievement at its finest. Give all of us who are struggling over here a break. No one should be without thoughts for an hour, come on! That was just pure insanity, as I saw it, completely indulgent. Remember when everyone read that Elizabeth Gilbert book, *Eat*

Pray Love? It's all anyone could talk about. Every woman over the age of twenty wanted to take a year off from her life and follow the three revelatory directions. Not me. Sure, I could eat with the best of them, and we all know how well I could love. But pray? Sit silently for eight hours a day on a mat, meditating on my innermost thoughts. No thank you. All I would hear would be a pack of wild, crazy neanderthals arguing in my head.

FYI—Elizabeth Gilbert is one of us. After the success of her bestselling novel, she came to realize she was struggling with the same disease of sex and love addiction—constantly searching for someone outside herself to feel whole. She even opened up about it in her latest memoir.

When I sat down in front of Dr. Kath for our last session before flying out for my shoot, she asked me to close my eyes and think of my most painful memories and those feelings attached to them.

"Huh? Seriously? We're doing this activity again, Doc? Didn't we do this when I was first sober?" I said in a very confused, annoyed, childlike voice. Yep, sometimes I could be a big baby when I wanted to be.

She smiled her therapist smirk. "Humor me, please."

Jeez, okay, so I closed my eyes and thought. This was a hard one to do again, and I've already gone through a lot of painful memories with you guys. Do you really want to hear more at this point? *I'm so hurt and sad because this happened to me... blah, blah, blah.* It seemed, even for me, so self-indulgent. I was over my self already too.

But in all honesty, as my eyes were closed, I accepted that I'd had a lot more painful moments since my year of sobriety had passed. The fact was, I was rawer and more open to my painful feelings. Remember *The First Wives Club*—which, incidentally, is one of my all-time favorite movies—when Goldie Hawn drunkenly yells, "You think that because I'm a movie star I don't have feelings. Well, you're wrong. I'm an actress. I've got all of them!" I love when Goldie Hawn wears her tacky purple sweater and screams at her besties, Diane Keaton and Bette Midler. Despite her successful career as an actress, she is really just a tsunami of feelings in the body of an alcoholic struggling to get sober. Sound familiar? Except for the movie-star part, right? Don't worry, I'm not saying I'm a movie star. I have just been there, with my addiction to sex and love and toxic relationships.

That's what I wanted to do when Dr. Kath asked me to talk about my painful memories and those feelings. I wanted to dramatically refuse her paid-for expertise like a whiny toddler by throwing my hands up and saying, "I have all the feelings. Too many feelings! It's all too much. I'm an actress. I feel them all." Then throw my water glass or espresso at someone dramatically, turn, and stomp away.

Instead, I dug in and closed my eyes again. But I drew a blank. I was completely and utterly empty. I opened my eyes suddenly and frustration overcame me as I blurted out, "When I am being truly touched by the good and bad situations in my life, it is at times beyond heart-wrenching for me. Like a knife is stabbing me internally. I get physically sick to my stomach when I feel intense love for someone; also, when I feel sadness and disappointment, like I have with Tattoogirl."

I paused dramatically to regroup. "I don't understand how others have gone through their lives feeling this much. And I just started at the age of thirty. How do others survive this? It is mind-bending, the truth of emotions going in and out of us at all moments of the day. I'm overcome with so many feelings that sometimes I don't know how to move forward."

I put my hands over my face and talked through my fingers, trying to grasp the tornado of thoughts swirling through my mind. "I have felt many made-up emotions as an actress and can emote those very successfully, but to feel the real version of them as just me, it's excruciating. My point is that painful moments happen all the time. If I see one of those Sarah McLachlan ASPCA adoption commercials on TV, I bawl my eyes out. If I see a homeless woman shivering in the cold, I feel my heart truly ache. If I see a dad playing with his daughter, I get tears in my eyes with the love I see between them. It's all painful. And now, with Tattoogirl officially out of my life, I feel like I'm bleeding internally and am unable to put a tourniquet on the wound."

Dr. Kath rubbed her forehead, and I wondered if she had a headache like me. She breathed in deeply. "I understand. True emotions are very hard for addicts to handle once sober from their addiction of choice. There is a need, also, for us to feel needed by another person, using our codependency to fix them, thinking that if we make ourselves needed or 'indispensable' to them, we will be 'safe.' But instead, we're setting ourselves up for heartache, clinging to the fantasy of saving them. Just like no one could save you, Roxanne, you can't save her. That leaves you with unrequited emotions and feelings."

Yes, thank you, Dr. Kath once again, who just stated it perfectly and to the point. I felt my codependency in not saving her from her addict. I had truly lost the battle of savior, and those feelings were unbearable. I saw Tattoogirl getting sucked back into her disease with Fuckface, and I was powerless to help her crawl her way out of it. I was making this about me and not about her. My feelings of failure. My feelings of inadequacy as a healthy, sober woman in the SLAA program. My need to save others like I was saved—but the only difference was that I'd been ready to be saved and helped. Not everyone is. And that was not my burden to bear. My feelings of "not enough" did not ring true here.

I got off the couch when the timer went off, and I did something I had never done before in my life. I walked over to Dr. Kath and bear-hugged her. *Yes, you heard that right. I ini-*

tiated a hug. Me. The anti-hugger. I actually enveloped her in my arms and squeezed her. I said, "Thank you for all you have helped me with. I don't know if I would have gotten through this year without you." I pulled back, and I swear I saw slight confusion and a tear form in her eye. She looked like she was at a loss for words.

Then I freaked out. "Was I not supposed to hug you? Is that inappropriate for therapist–client relationships?" My feelings of inadequacy arose all over again. Damn, these feelings were no joke. The thought of me screwing up and doing something wrong in our relationship almost negated all of the work we had just done. I pulled back like I was waiting to get spanked, and not in a sexual way.

"No, a hug is okay, Roxanne. You are okay. You will be okay." I breathed a sigh of relief. She finished the session with this unbelievably kind gesture: "WhatsApp me if you are in crisis while overseas. I will make myself available." I grinned back, feeling twelve years old all over again, and quickly hugged her again and walked out before the tears of gratitude started to flow.

Man, how was I going to manage these raw emotions when I was out of the country? Maybe I shouldn't have taken this job? Maybe I wasn't ready? All I knew while getting my ass home and dropping off Dog at my pet sitter was that it was too late to back out now, so I'd better suit up and show up for this commitment. Mama needed to bring home the bacon. There was no backup man to pay my mortgage anymore. No sugar-daddy app for me. Apparently, I was over the hill at age thirty.

The next day, as I was sipping my free bottled water in the back of the black town car that picked me up to drive my fancy ass to the airport, my phone rang. It was an unknown number from back home in Atlanta. Who would be calling me at 10:00 p.m. on a Monday night?

I hesitantly answered the call. "Helllllo?"

A frantic voice on the other end spoke in a whisper. "Roxie, please don't hang up. It's me, ATL. I can't talk long, but please hear me out. I know you didn't want me to call you anymore and that you blocked me. Which kind of hurt, I have to say."

I rolled my eyes at the sorrow in his voice. I mean, come on. It had been over a year since that rejected proposal. I know that probably sounds harsh, but bear with me. He was now married to a lovely lady and had a baby girl. I knew that because my mom told me after running into him at Target, so naturally I broke down and stalked them on Instagram. I sound like a crazy ex-girlfriend, but really, I was happy for him that he was free from my web of deceit.

"What's up, ATL?" I responded with as much warmth as I could muster.

He whispered, "I wat ___ou bk ___ad I dp___ t."

He was so quiet I couldn't make out anything he said. "I can't hear you. Can you please talk louder?" I was almost yelling into my phone.

"Hold on a sec." I heard all this rustling in the background and heavy breathing. What the hell was he doing? I waited patiently for him to come back on the phone, which we all know is not one of my virtues. *UGHH, PATIENCE!*

"Sorry about that. I had to switch closets," he said proudly.

Huh? Closets? That's when the doomsday feeling came over me. "What's up? I have to go in five minutes. I'm pulling up to the airport."

He quickly asked, "To visit your mom?"

"No, to work on location," I said, not wanting to be too specific.

"Oh. Okay. So, I am calling to tell you that I have been thinking a lot lately about what went wrong with us. That the reason you cheated was because I was never around. No wonder you were unhappy with us. I would be too. So, I came up with a plan—how about we both move to a new city together and start anew? I know that it's sudden and your job is in LA, but you can do it in New York too, right? We could buy an apartment there and start a new life. Refresh."

What the hell? This was the second time he had done this to me. The first was right before he married his wife and had a baby. I tried to put myself in his shoes and understand how he was feeling. Was he scared? Was he living in the past? Did he assign magical qualities to me? Was he trying to win the love of an unavailable person? This was clearly a sheer act of desperation. All of my tools from SLAA raced into my mind. I was not going to get mad at him or hang up on him like I normally would have done. I understood that this man was obviously struggling with his reality. How could I "be of service" and help him move on?

That's when it hit me. I would become Dr. Kath to his ass. I would play the role of his therapist, since I knew he had never attended therapy. I would trick him into seeing the light of the situation.

"Listen, that is very sweet of you to think of us so fondly. But can I ask you, what's going on? I heard you were happily married to a great girl. Are you okay?" I said in the soothing voice of someone who had their shit together, which you all know I didn't.

He hesitated for a minute, but I could hear his breathing, so I knew he was still there. He finally said, "Yes, I do love her, but I just feel like you and I are soulmates and meant to be."

I sighed. "I don't know if I believe in soulmates. But, what we had was special, but our time is over. People come in and out of our lives for many reasons. I was blessed to be with such a kind man like you for ten years. But it's over between us. We have both changed. You are a father now. I saw your little girl. She is so beautiful—you all make such a lovely family."

I heard a crack in his voice, and he said softly, "Thank you, I just miss you tons. I miss us. And she's pregnant again. I don't know if I'm ready to have another."

I knew it! I am a genius at reading people now! Maybe I should have been a therapist—obviously, I had a gift. *That would definitely be a plot twist you all didn't see coming. Okay, take it down a notch, Rox, but I was so happy ATL's breakdown wasn't about me.* He just didn't want to adult up into his responsibility as a father. He was having conflicted feelings about that commitment. I got it, I would be wanting to escape reality too. "Listen, I get it. It's hard being a parent. But from what I can see in your social media photos, you're a wonderful dad. Your life looks so beautiful, so full. You don't really want to be with me. I'm unstable and have a career that makes it impossible for us to be in the same town. You're just scared, but I know in my heart you are in the right relationship with the right woman." I stopped to see what he was going to say.

Silence. Pure and deafening silence. I continued, "Why don't you just talk to her about your fears? I'm sure your wife is feeling them too. Maybe it would help you both calm your anxiety and feelings of responsibility. She is your partner for life now. Not me. You guys need to lean on each other like we used to do."

I heard him breathe a sigh of relief. "You're right, Roxie. I do need to lean on her, like we used to do with our troubles with our parents. I can do that. Thank you! I will."

"Great! Well, I have to run. Just pulling up to the airport. Good luck, and congrats again on the new baby." I jumped off the phone before he could say another thing. That's when I realized how much tension I'd just been holding, and I let out a huge sigh of relief, laid my head back, and closed my eyes.

That's when I felt it. A wave of pride washed over me. I had just helped the man I had once destroyed. I'd just made living amends to the guy I cheated on a handful of times. I'd just saved his marriage, instead of using his confusion as an ego-building activity for my own self-indulgence. And it hit me. An emotional rush of forgiveness for myself. I'd just made the best Ninth Step amends to ATL. *Wow, good job, ME!*

"Nice job talking that guy off a ledge," the town-car driver called back to me. I opened my eyes. "Thank you. He was just scared. Glad I could help him see the truth."

I thought about the dichotomy between my two most emotional cab rides. This was a night-and-day difference from the time when I was in my addiction of cheating, bawling my eyes out to the cabby in New York after my affair with NYC went south, when he punched a wall and broke his hand because I would not have bloody sex with him. No, not the British-slang bloody, the really *bloody*, like menstrual bloody sex with him, because I was cramping. That was a terrible situation, and the poor cab driver had to listen to my story of woe the whole hour and a half to JFK. Holy crap, this recovery really worked. I was on cloud nine with the action of service for another suffering human being.

I jumped out of the town car with a skip in my step and gave the driver $20, even though I knew the tip was included. I just felt like shouting "YIPPEE!!" and twirling in the slightly rainy drop-off terminal. But I didn't want to look like a crazy person, on some kind of upper drug. Instead, I put my hat on because my hair was greasy. Personally, I believe any hat can pull an okay outfit together. In my full-black-head-to-toe ensemble, I walked with a slight swagger in my step to the first-class line to check my monstrous amount of luggage.

Just so you're aware, I requested that the movie's production coordinator, the poor individual who has to deal with all actors' demands, book me on my favorite airline. The swanky rockstar airline Virgin Atlantic Upper Class. If you ever get a chance to fly first class, book this airline. I am obsessed with their service, and the best part is those little cubicles of privacy. When I sat down in those flatbed seats, I felt like the world was my oyster for ten and a half hours, I was a queen! I sipped my champagne and asked for multiple refills. And I ate whatever I wanted. Like it didn't even count, because we were all out of commission from the people in our lives and living in this magical fantasy palace in the air.

My real gluttony started before the flight, though. I immediately started to order ridiculously free food in the impressively appointed first-class lounge. We are talking spinach empanada chimichurri, mushroom miso ramen, Beyond Burger with guacamole, and lastly, miso donuts with a cheese plate. I know, I was on a diet, but I was in travel mode, so I was officially off the dieting clock. I could eat normal food again, but just a small bite of each. I sound like such an asshole, with all the starving humans in the world. I wished they were with me, sharing this delicious food. Believe me, I was never this wasteful and was by far one of the thriftiest women you will ever meet. But something in me had taken over, and I was all of a sudden a spoiled, privileged aristocrat dining in the first-class lounge. I was out of control. My egotism character defect had taken over. I was a god for the time being, from the moment I stepped into the lounge until we landed back on the ground in England and reality hit that no one was waiting on me hand and foot. *Forgive me—all will be back to normal after I land. So please grin and bear this environment with me.*

I left the first-class lounge and sauntered to the front of the line to board the plane, half from fullness on those lounge appetizers and the other half tired as shit since it was 11:30 p.m. I mean, I was usually in bed by 9:30. After my glass of champagne, I was already half in the bag. I was feeling all cool and fancy since I got to board first and didn't have to wait in line with the coach passengers. That's when I looked around the gate and realized all these passengers could be in my SLAA program. It seems like everyone has a look-alike in the rooms. Any one of them could be my fellow. It really puts things into perspective for me and my ego. I was no better or worse just because I had a free first-class ticket. The reality was a curse and a blessing at the same time.

As you guys know, I loved one-upping others. But sobriety hit me square in the jaw. We were all just humans wanting to connect and get to our assigned seats to get this flight over with. We were all freaking tired at midnight.

That morning, I'd read in the SLAA daily meditations book: "The love addiction doesn't discriminate. People in the rooms are from all different levels of society and ages. We are not people who would normally mix. But we can't afford to let personal differences get in the way of recovery. We practice tolerance and create a safe space for recovery. We don't fight about religious or political beliefs. We stay focused on our primary purpose—to carry the message of recovery to the addict who still suffers." That's when my whole body shifted. I released this deep belief that if I had more, I was more. The truth would set me free.

Gratitude shifted over me as I sat in my roomy seat, and instead of it being a validation of my worth, I realized it was just a goddamn roomy seat that I would be occupying for the next ten hours. It meant nothing more than that. My feelings of superiority evaporated like a fine mist. I put on my eye mask and drifted off to sleep before the plane took off. No fancy meal. No glass of champagne. No bullshit bougieness that gave me an inflated ego high.

Memories came flooding back as I nodded in and out of sleep. That's when the past always came full force into focus. Long-embedded dormant memories rose to the surface, and I realized that my acting out had been a lot worse than I'd ever realized. I'd completely forgotten about my almost-arrest, when I was thrown off a flight a couple of years ago. This is how it went down: I was coming back from a trip to Atlanta. ATL wanted to move to LA and buy a house—it was the first time he'd brought up moving to my city. The problem was, I was half living with West at the time and starting to see NYC too. So, my plate was full of indiscretions, and the last thing

I needed was for my primary relationship to move to town. To say I was anxious and stressed coming back on that night flight was an understatement. I could not breathe. I felt like my chest was tight and I might have a heart attack. I had to think of a good lie by the time I landed to make sure ATL did not buy his flight and put his house up for sale. But nothing was coming to me. No lie I was trying to spin sounded likely to work in my favor.

So, what does a sex and love addict do when they are stressed and feeling unbearably uncomfortable?

Yep, I bet you're guessing something to do with sex, obviously. No, I did not have a one-night stand with a stranger on a plane. That was Eve—she could tell you a bunch of those kinds of stories. Instead, I put in headphones and turned on porn on my iPad. I then proceeded to watch two girls, and a guy dress up in cheerleading uniforms and do it in a locker room. Right in the middle of a nighttime flight on Delta business class. So, clearly, you can imagine that there was no first-class cubical to hide what I was viewing. Since Debbie doing Dallas and Donna was not relieving my angst, I kicked it up a notch with my acting out. I masturbated under my blanket right there. Yep, you heard me right. I unapologetically masturbated on a plane. I quietly let go of my built-up tension, since that was the behavior I did when I was anxious as a kid with my lover, teddy bear. Why would I not use this coping mechanism on the dark airplane with no one next to me and a blanket to hide my actions?

Well, for one, silly addict Roxanne, it was illegal. Yep. It was against the law. I get that, especially now that I am seeing things more clearly with sober eyes. Second, the old lady behind me figured out what I was doing and buzzed the flight attendant. Then I saw her get up and walk to the front of the plane as I was using a facial wipe on my pussy. I saw her pointing back toward me and whispering in the female flight attendant's ear.

The disgusted look I received from both of them paralyzed me into knowing that I'd just gotten caught red-handed, or more like wet-handed. I sank into my seat, trying to hide my face with my airplane blanket—hoping in the back of my mind that they washed these things, especially with what I'd just done beneath mine. No one needs my female juices on them. *How nasty of me!*

I started praying to some kind of god—since at that time I had no concept of something bigger than me—that I was just being paranoid, that they were not talking about me and my fingers. Wrong again. The next thing I saw was an attendant coming right toward me. I turned my head to avoid eye contact, just like a toddler who believes they are not being seen. I heard, "Miss, can you please come with me?"

I ignored her, hoping she would go away.

I heard again, "Miss, please look at me." This time closer to my ear. Then I felt a tap on my shoulder after I did not comply, which is not the best look on an airplane, because you can't run or hide. I didn't have any idea what I was truly thinking. "Miss, you need to come with me now. We have a big problem."

I turned to her and said very softly, "I'm sorry. It's all fine. I understand." Then I turned away again.

Suddenly, the sternest voice erupted from her tight, lined orange-red lips, which was possibly the worst shade of lipstick for her pasty complexion. "No, everything is not fine. Get up now, before we have to remove you from your seat."

That made me move pretty fast. I did the walk of shame to the front of the plane, then proceeded to be lectured about my regretful behavior. "It is against the law to watch pornography on an airplane. You are going to be charged when we land with public indecency and indecent exposure for masturbating in public, which in California can be a misdemeanor or felony. What were you thinking?"

I started to breathe heavily, and the tears started to roll down my cheeks as they kept threatening to take me to the airport police when we landed, but I did my best acting job ever.

I could have won that shiny gold Emmy. I was crying and making up a story: "My boyfriend of ten years just cheated on me. I'm so lonely and feeling so nasty and inadequate in my skin. You guys are completely right—I screwed up and I need help. I called my therapist before I got on this flight because for the last two days I have been so low, I was going to jump off the bridge in my hometown. It's just been a really bad week for me, and now I am going to jail." The snot and sobs were flowing because the only real thing in that sentence that brought emotions was my fear of jail time. I kept going. "He was with my cousin at our house. I caught them having sex..." Blah, blah, blah. You get it already—I was pulling out every storyline I have ever acted in a Lifetime movie. I was committed to the tale of a single woman's woe.

Okay, not only could I have won an Emmy for acting, but I was starting to think I could get one for writing.

INT. ROXANNE'S APARTMENT—NIGHT

ROXANNE enters her apartment, taking off her waitressing apron. It's been a long night and an even longer shift, and all she wants to do is pop open a bottle of cabernet and cuddle with her boyfriend.

                    ROXANNE
                  (calls out)
        I'm home! Mean Boss let me off
        early.

No response. She pulls off her mini dress, grabs the wine and two glasses, and walks down the hallway, still chatting in her bra and panties.

> ROXANNE
> Remember Executive Producer? That douche tipped me a hundred bucks. Brunch is on me tomorrow. Wanna check out that new place on—

She stops when she opens the bedroom door and sees…

INT. ROXANNE'S BEDROOM—CONTINUOUS

BOYFRIEND'S bare ass is bobbing and weaving as he screws COUSIN. Roxanne drops the wine and glasses in shock.

> ROXANNE
> Cousin, you bitch.

> COUSIN
> Obviously, you can't keep your man happy, you twat waffle.

> ROXANNE
> I'm going to kill you.

They grab pillows and start beating each other. As if on cue, the pillows burst, and feathers fly everywhere.

We stay on BOYFRIEND, a voyeur in his own fantasy as he watches the two semi-naked women going all MMA.

Okay, maybe not an Emmy, but definitely a solid episode of *The Real Housewives of Beverly Hills*. Luckily, my audience was a bunch of female and gay flight attendants, so they took great pity on me and let me go with just a slap on my wrist. The worst part was that the person who took the most pity on me was the bitch who narced on me. That old lady actually gave me a long hug. It made me really uncomfortable to hug a stranger, especially for that long, but the relief of not getting in trouble let me lean into her soft, wrinkly skin.

When I got off the plane that dreaded night, I mouthed the words *thank you* to all the attendants, then ran down the jetway to get out of there as soon as possible in case they changed their minds. Waiting at the luggage terminal, I was convinced they were still coming to get me. I was even debating whether to just leave my luggage, since LAX has the longest wait time to get your checked bags. I cursed the workers in the back running the luggage machines. I hated them every time I landed and had to wait for at least forty-five minutes. Tip for you travelers to Los Angeles: NEVER CHECK YOUR LUGGAGE! Pack light! I promise, you will thank me. Especially if your luggage is lost! It's the worst ever dealing with them at the counter to report that your life's most important material items have disappeared somewhere over Missoula, Montana.

I did not leave my luggage at that terminal. I just hid behind a pole, waiting for my red leather Bric suitcase to make its way down the belt. When it did, I rushed to grab it and hoist it up as fast as I could, which made me rip the handle off the suitcase. The night was just getting better and better. I got into my Uber and breathed a sigh of relief. I then googled it on my phone and discovered that watching porn and masturbating in public were indeed both misdemeanors, and possibly felonies. In either case, a misdemeanor conviction was punishable by up to 364 days in jail and a $1,000 fine. Felony convictions carried a sentence of up to three years in jail and a $10,000 fine. *Wow, I dodged a bullet with that one!*

I sat back in this stranger's Civic four-door, which smelled like cheap musky cologne and bean burritos. I closed my eyes, thanking my God, whoever he was. In that moment of addict behavior, I turned to God without realizing he always had me. He always took care of me, in good times and bad. I just needed to believe that when I was not in crisis. But as you know, that realization and that bottom was fleeting—my end-of-the-line behavior got much darker and crazier two years later. I wish that was my moment of *aha!* I was a low-bottom addict, as you all know.

My lowest was still to come.

So, I'd blacked out that felony behavior from my mind. But now, in the luxury of first class, it reared its ugly head as I was once again left with feelings of shame, loneliness, and anxiety, trapped on a plane in the middle of the night. It almost felt like coming full circle. I had that addict thought that it would be so easy to get away with doing those behaviors now, since I was in a cubby and could hide my iPad under my blanket. No one would know. I could make these feelings of anxiety go away with a couple flicks of the "man in the boat" or the "bean," or however you like to refer to your clitoris. A part of me wanted to prove I could get away with it. My addict wanted to feel that release and high. Should I? Could I? Would that be considered acting out, even though it's not one of my bottom-line behaviors? Who would know? It could be my little secret. It would not hurt a soul.

Sucked back into reality, I pulled off my face mask, the shame and guilt of my thoughts overtaking me—and the grief for me as a lost addict, even now, after all the work I had done. I still did not want to feel my feelings completely. Why? Why did it always have to be so hard for someone like me to just be in the discomfort of their emotions? Why was I always looking for an easier way out?

It was so embarrassing that I never told a soul about my night on that plane, not even Alice, when I was doing my Fourth Step. Then why was I trying to reinvent that high/low and experience that all over again? To what end? To prove that I was able to get away with it this time? How egotistical of someone to test the rules of society just because they have something to prove.

BRIANNE DAVIS

Well, I was not going to do it. I would not try to soothe my feelings away. I would not use my clitoris to numb out my emotions. I would sit in the face of anxiety, pain, and fear with a big fat "I can take it, bring it on" attitude. *I'm a big girl. I can face my emotions head on!*

Kindness and empathy overcame me as we got closer to landing in London and the flight attendant who resembled Masturbation Gate served me my orange juice and croissant. For me, the fact that I'd blocked something so completely traumatic from my memory told me that I still had a lot of work to do on myself. That I still had a lot of blind spots in my mind that I needed to process.

Over my delicious gruyere omelet and fruit parfait on the last leg of this transformational first-class flight, I had gone through the whole gamut of my feelings about myself, my past blocked memory, the shame of acting out, and my loss of Tattoogirl's friendship. I went through all the feelings a human being could have, and I was still alive. I was still breathing. I was not dead. I really could make it through the worst beliefs about myself and others, then come out on the other side unbroken.

Feelings would not kill me. I was refusing to let the scared-addict voice win this battle. I would not go down without a fight, because feelings weren't facts. Feelings were always meant to be felt. To flow through us. Not to get stuck and dictate our behaviors and patterns of survival. And I was always responsible for how I acted, no matter how I felt.

CHAPTER SIX

Rule 15: Learn humility before God humbles you.

"I PACKED GOD INTO my suitcase."

"I know why I am here."

"I am a worker among workers."

"I am here to do my job and then go home to my reality."

"Set life is not real life."

I put these "facts" on yellow Post-its all over my suite to remind myself of the realities for the next couple weeks. I then proceeded to say these quotes aloud on speakerphone to Alice, with whom I had required check-ins on our international WhatsApp thread. Another preemptive tactic to protect myself from my old addict self, rearing her ugly head on set.

Once I finished talking to Alice, I frantically put on my makeup, trying to get ready while battling terrible jet lag. I was scheduled to attend our table read of the movie script. The email specifically said, "You're invited if you wish to attend the table read tomorrow afternoon at 4 p.m. at the production office." Which was the first bullshit lie of the entertainment business. Though they can't officially make you, you don't have a "choice" to attend. If you do not show up, you will immediately be labeled as difficult and not a team player. If you decide to bail, you might even get fired. But contractually, they can't force you under the rules of SAG-AFTRA, our union.

I forgot to explain what a table read is. I just figured the two-word name "table read" might be self-explanatory, because I am an asshole and have been in this business too long to realize it's not everyday lingo for non-Hollywood folks.

A table read is where all of the actors, producers, writers, and the director sit around a table in their name-tag-assigned seats with their respective character names stated. Then we all say hello in the classic Hollywood greetings—*air kisses, I'm so excited to work with you, even though I am lying and heard you were a dickhead*—then we all buckle down and read the entire script out loud.

I detest table reads. I always feel like I have to perform my character perfectly while sitting in a plastic chair in a stuffy fluorescent-light conference room. It doesn't matter if you are Zendaya, no one looks good in fluorescent light. And don't get me started on trying to make someone laugh or cry. Especially if you're trying to make everyone in the room laugh at your cheesy joke in a sitcom script. You're pretty much doomed to fail from the start. The worst is acting out a love scene. Imagine this: You're sitting across from your fake lover, saying passionate words while everyone is checking their phones or drinking their coffee, and you both are acting out this love-making scene with each other. It's awkward as hell. It's beyond nerve-racking to perform this way in front of your peers. You are judged no matter how you play it—overacted, underacted, blasé, etc. There is no way to get around the discomfort and judgment of the initial read-through.

There is also always the fear of getting canned after the table read. As actors, we have all heard the horror stories of an actor booking an amazing role then sucking at the table read and getting recast just afterward. It's humiliating to think that someone, whether the producers, studio, or director, decided you sucked a big fat nut so badly that they'd rather not take a chance on you in the part. I have never met an actor who has not felt this way, even the A-list stars. Maybe the only person I can imagine not caring would be Daniel Day-Lewis—he probably would not even show up. The only people who enjoy those table reads are the director and writer. Everyone else wishes they were somewhere else, doing anything else, especially when the first assistant director decides to read every single line of direction/action in the script. It's beyond boring, and you are so hangry by the time you're done, but you can't eat that granola bar because it would make "too much noise" and be disturbing to the other performers. So, you freaking starve and sit quietly, imagining you're in a restaurant ten miles away, eating a steak and having a nice bottle of wine.

No matter how prepared you are, the nerves are always there. That's why I had a check-in with Alice before heading to the production office for those dreaded two hours and then attend a wardrobe fitting afterward. Extra support was always needed for me during those pre-production days, because I always felt extra vulnerable and unstable. Plus, this bitch was tired! I had barely slept, and I felt like I had been on a bender for days with no food or water. Jet lag blows!

Poor Alice had to be up at 6:00 a.m. LA time to jump on the call with me. The time difference for her was true commitment to being my sponsor and now friend. We had literally scheduled a check-in call every day while I was there to keep me on the right track and accountable, which you know I needed, since I was a slippery addict.

Let's just call it an accountability call from this moment forward. I was trying not to be too obsessed with my appearance, since I did have in the back of my mind that I would see West—plus, we most likely would be sitting next to each other as we were playing husband and wife. I had already pre-planned NOT to wear my signature scent, because it was West's favorite lotion. He had told me that every time he smelled my scent, it drove him wild. And I had no interest in that happening. I was there to work, nothing else. Look, I admit that it took every ounce of me not to slather my whole body in my signature lotion just to drive him nuts and make him think of the last time we were together, when he was pounding the hell out of me against his living room wall. But I was healthy and sober, so I would not do that to him or myself. There would be no sex whatsoever. See how balanced I was? I was clearly a pro at this.

All good intentions aside, I was still dressing hot as shit. In my defense, I would anyway—it's just my style. I was wearing my all-black tight pants and black backless bodysuit, finished off with my knee-high lace-up black leather boots and my black leather baseball hat. I couldn't help it, I knew I looked good in this minimalist outfit. I felt like a fierce assassin in a *Matrix*-style film. Like I could destroy another human being with my badass glare.

I headed out still on the phone with Alice, reciting the Serenity Prayer to her in the back of a very fun London black cab. I felt all international and well-traveled. The cabby looked at me like I had serious problems since I had just said the Serenity Prayer. The Serenity Prayer recap for you non-twelve-steppers: "God, grant me the serenity to accept the things I cannot change, the courage to change the things I can, and the wisdom to know the difference."

Alice's last direction before I disconnected the phone call was, "Roxie, please define for me the specifics of the Serenity Prayer." I quickly tried to rack my brain while side-eyeing the driver. "What I cannot change is how West is going to act or how the table read goes. The courage to change the things I can is my attitude with the whole situation and how I handle my side of the street. Lastly, that I do know the difference between what I can and cannot change and that I can only control myself and no one else in that room."

She said, "Great. Good job. Text me after to check in. I have to get in the shower for parent-teacher conferences today. God help me. I needed that reminder, too. Love you, girl. Trust that you are enough and you are exactly where God wants you. You got this."

"Thanks, lady! Love you too," I replied as I hung up. Then, getting my compact out to retouch my lips, I saw the cabby still looking at me. I said bluntly, "I am sober but not from drugs, so relax. It's sex and love." He looked taken aback by my comment, then got a weird, perverted look on his face.

You know, that's a sneaky problem with this addiction, gross individuals who find it sexy that a woman like me is addicted to sex. It's not hot, dude. It's gross to use other people for your own pleasure, I wanted to scream at him. I hated that about being in this fellowship of SLAA, but again, it saved my life, and I was a sex and love addict, so I guess I needed to wear it with a badge of honor and maybe not mention it to strangers—or more specifically, random cab drivers. Next plan: I would wake up earlier and finish my call with Alice in the privacy of my hotel room. You live and you learn sometimes in these new situations.

I pulled up to Studios Leavesden in London to meet with everyone on the shoot. To say I was nervous would be an enormous understatement. I was petrified, overwhelmed, and shaking. I had not been on location since before I got sober, and especially not with my ex-boyfriend. But here I was, showing up for my life and my job. I was just a worker. I was not special. I was not unique. I was there to do a job, then go home. Despite being armed with these manifestos, I still stepped into the table-read room feeling like it was the first day of school all over again. I smiled at the first person in front of me. "Hey, I'm Roxanne, playing the wife."

He said, "Nice to meet you. I'm the second AD, Sean."

Sean moved out of the way after we shook hands, and I saw... NYC? I did a double-take. *WHAT THE FUCK WAS HE DOING HERE?* I was utterly confused and looked around the room like I was on a bad acid trip. I was speechless! Bewildered! And kind of pissed off. NYC was standing right in front of me, smiling like the cat who ate the canary. He had a huge sinister grin! "Hi, Roxie. How's ATL?"

I breathed in the biggest breath and tried to play off that I was cool as a cucumber and not at all floored that he was right in front of me. "Hey, NYC. He's great! Are you PA-ing movies now?"

He shook his head cockily. "No, I'm playing West's best friend in the movie. He's a great guy—I'm sure you know that and everything. We had beers the last two nights to establish our lifelong friendship."

My face dropped. I couldn't even begin to respond. I was seething. What did they talk about the last two nights over beers? I mean, I had slept with both of them, and I was not seen in the best light by either of them. I had cheated on both of them. I had lied to both of them, although I was fairly certain they had both lied to me—West, for sure. And now, I was going to be stuck on this job with not one but TWO of my acting-out ex-boyfriends. All these thoughts were spiraling in my head as NYC gloated in front of me. He added, "Oh, and by the way, I did get tested. Thanks for not giving me any sexually transmitted diseases. I appreciate that you picked somewhat clean individuals to fuck all at once."

Damn, I was just bitch-slammed in the face by that remark.

My cat claws came flaring out fast. "You're very welcome. I do have good taste... sometimes." As I looked him up and down, thinking of all the times he bent me over, a wave of nausea washed over me with repulsion.

My lucky day—at that moment, West walked up to join us. "Hey, set family! So happy we all know each other so well already. This is going to be a fun shoot. Shit, Roxie, I forgot to tell you at our dinner date the other night that NYC was in the movie, my bad."

I looked back and forth between these two egotistical, pretty-boy actors and smiled my "I will mess you up, and you won't see me coming" smile, deciding right then and there that I would not be played. As the director walked in behind us, I turned to them. "Can't wait to start shooting. And I am also glad you did not get any transmitted diseases, since West was sleeping my girlfriend and I was sleeping with him. Good job, West!" I then turned to West. "No problem not telling me about NYC, Chad. I couldn't give two shits—a job's a job. It'll be over before I know it." I swiveled around on my four-inch-heeled boots and took my assigned seat at the head of the table.

West sat down next to me after he went around the room with his charming swagger, introducing himself to everyone. I usually did that too as one of the leads of the movie, but at this point I wanted to scream and run away from this sticky situation. Instead, I opted for just sitting my ass in my assigned chair before I forcibly broke my contract and quit this job and got sued by the producers. That was the wisest choice at this juncture, to suit up and show up as an adult.

Surprisingly, the table read went pretty dang well, especially for this cynic. Many folks laughed at my lines and got teary eyed when West and I had our heartbreaking scene. It was quite refreshing to have a real acting job that I was getting paid for. It had been so long that I'd forgotten how fulfilling my job could be. I was almost on cloud nine, except for the fact that NYC was still cast in the movie. I am not going to lie to you and say he sucked, because he was actually damn great. He was a very talented actor. I had to give him that— very method-type, which could be a little freaky at times, but bravo to him and I guess to me for picking a guy with some redeeming attributes.

I said goodbye to everyone except the Two Stooges and walked my ass to the wardrobe room. Here is where I loved to create my character. I became the part when I started to mold and pick the wardrobe for her. The shoes for my character were usually the most important aspect to bring her to life. This sad mom of two young kids with an alcoholic husband, played by West, needed to have the right tennis shoes and flats to bring her into existence for me. I personally would never be caught in flats. I hated flats. I always needed a heel to pull off the slightly exaggerated 5'8" height on my resume. I needed those extra inches. And it made me feel more powerful as a woman to wear heels. It was something a man could never do, just like giving birth—not that I knew firsthand what that felt like, but I had given birth on camera a dozen times. So, there was that—I had skillfully demonstrated a handful of mock labor pains to add to my life experience.

As I was finishing my fitting, West popped his head in the room, charming the pants off the wardrobe girls, one of whom I expected was sleeping with the married director. West was so good at being captivating to the opposite sex, that I got slightly irritated, with a touch of admiration. He definitely knew how to play the game of life.

"Roxie, you have a moment to chat after you're done with your fitting? To discuss our scene tomorrow?"

I smirked. "Sure. We'll be done in five."

I headed back behind the curtain, but the douchebag did not leave my fitting room. Instead, he stood there all cocky-like and flirted with the pretty but naive wardrobe assistant, whom I adored already. Poor girl, she was going to be eaten alive in this business by these attention-seeking actors. *I would know, being one of them myself and having destroyed far too many crew members with my validating flirtation. We actors can be brutal in our pursuit of attention.* I took off the horrible nude strapless bra—I hate all bras, by the way. You can understand why when you barely have a full A cup. The need for a bra seems silly, especially one with underwiring that digs into your ribcage. I threw my bralette back on and stalked out of the room with so much confidence that I felt like J. Lo with my abs all tight from the nine-day cleanse.

I pulled my tight T-shirt over my head, not caring if West saw my banging body. "Thanks, ladies. Love the options for her. Let me know which one the director picks, so I can mentally prepare with that look in mind." I turned to West with a no-nonsense business-like approach. "You ready?"

He grinned. "Totes. Let's go."

We walked out together into the sunlight. He turned sharply and I almost ran into him. "Whoa, what's up?" I said, my hands raised to protect me from actually touching his ripped chest. I would have to touch it tomorrow in our love scene, so I was waiting as long as I could before that dreaded doomsday arrived.

West laughed at my hands still raised in front of me. "Relax, Rox. I'm not going to touch you. I just wanted us to have a real conversation about tomorrow so we're both on the same page. I know things between us are prickly and awkward, but as you saw in there during the reading, these two roles were made for us. Combative lovers who lose it all in the end. I think the best way to tackle this is to bring all of the antics, passion, hatred, and disappointment of our own relationship into these parts. Wouldn't you agree?"

SHIT! BALLS! "I don't know, West. That's not usually how I work," I replied, unsure.

Inside information for you non-actors out there: Some thespians use their own personal experiences to fill in the moments in scenes, some become the characters during the shoot, and some actors just use their imagination. I was in the latter category. I strictly played make-believe in my head. I tended to phone it in when I tried to substitute my real life in the lines. *Maybe because I had never fully felt my real emotions? Or I didn't know how to play real life even in real life? Or I only knew how to be a real human in make-believe?* These revelations rang really true, wow.

West leaned closer to make his point, and I smelled his natural scent, which I could literally bathe in. I reluctantly breathed in that hypnotic aroma; my pheromones couldn't help themselves.

"Rox, this could be what we both need to heal and to finally let go of each other." *WTF? Wait, has he not let go of me?* A small tingle in my vagina started to pulse. He continued, "Plus, we both need this for our careers to get back on track. You saw the reaction in there—this could be a statue kind of reward. I know you've practiced your speech in the mirror just as much as I've practiced mine." Also inside information: All actors have the fantasy of receiving an award in one of the two top accolades, the Emmy or the Oscar, and have practiced their acceptance speech in a mirror. That's just the way we narcissists operate.

INT. ROXANNE'S BATHROOM—DAY

ROXIE, wearing a hair mask, a face mask, and a fluffy pink bathrobe, holds her can of hairspray like an award and beams into the mirror.

ROXANNE
Wow. This is so unexpected. And it's so heavy.

She holds onto the hairspray with both hands.

ROXANNE
Is this real gold? Ha. But seriously, folks. I am shocked. I mean, this was so unexpected. I am in a category with the titans of my field. Meryl, you were as always, phenomenal, and Viola, I

saw your film four times. You
were a revelation. Emma, my
sister, my peer, it is such an
honor to be in this category
with you, and Gaga... I mean, I
worship you, sister.

She starts to cry, smudging the face mask.

                    ROXANNE
          This is a dream for a poor girl
          from the South who thought her
          options were teaching Pilates
          and working at Hooters for the
          rest of her life.

She laughs along with the fake audience,
incorporating the joke.

                    ROXANNE
          KIDDING.   I   could   never
          get   hired   at   Hooters.   But
          seriously, folks, this trophy
          is for anyone who has ever had a
          dream. For anyone who doesn't
          take no for an answer. For
          anyone who... TWENTY SECONDS? I
          was just getting to the good
          part. Okay. This is to the
          eight-year-old me who wanted
          more than anything in the
          world to become an actress.
          We did it, kid. We did it!

She starts to leave "the stage" and then
rushes back.

                    ROXANNE
          Oh, and thanks to Alice and
          Dr. Kath. Thank you!

She holds up the trophy in victory and bows
to the applause.

                              SMASH TO BLACK

"Okay, I may have practiced my speech already. And I see your point. I will do my best to put my all into it. But please respect my boundaries on set and off set."

He smiled like he had already won an award. As my car pulled up, I set my ground rules. "The pussy is off-limits! I am talking during and after the scene, West. You can touch the tits but not the vagina."

He nodded in agreement as I was getting my butt into the car. As he was about to shut my door, he added, "Cool. I got you. But is it off-limits before?" Laughing, he closed the car door and banged on the window, tossing in the last remark, "My body is all yours. Whenever you like it."

Then the car moved off, and as my mouth dropped open, I saw him giggling hysterically like he was the funniest guy in the whole world. Oh no! I was in trouble. I was getting triggered. *I needed a SLAA meeting fast.*

Luckily, Eve was officially in town on her layover. It was like God shone a beacon of hope on me with the gift of showing up as a sponsor for this newcomer. How fated was it that she was in the same city, at the same time as me? That's when you can truly say, "God had my back. A total God shot," which is a saying in the rooms when it is blatantly clear that God is everywhere. You just have to get silent to hear him.

I met her at 7:00 p.m. at St John's Church in Waterloo, near our hotel. Also, another God shot, I was shooting in a city that had the second biggest SLAA community. London had just as many meetings as Los Angeles—about five to eight meetings a day. If you go anywhere else in the world—like Vancouver, where I shoot a lot—there's only one, and it'll be at like 4:00 p.m. on a Sunday!

I almost believe it should be a city requirement to provide SLAA meetings for their twenty-one-years-and-older residents. Because the true foundation of SLAA meetings is the fear of intimacy and self-worth, making the sex aspect of the disease such a small amount of the program—it's the "behavior," not the "symptom." It's very clear every time I'm in a meeting that self-love is the most talked-about goal.

The stunning Eve walked toward me, and all anyone else would see when they looked at her was a very put-together, strong, determined woman. You would have no idea she was literally dying of pain inside and that she was struggling.

"Hey, lady!" I said. "So glad you're in town. I needed a meeting badly."

"Me too. I had one of my ex-stranger qualifiers on my flight. He cornered me in the galley and tried to make plans with me. I said no, of course. But he kept pressing the call button on his seat, and I felt like I was being stalked at work. And in my work, there is nowhere to hide. I guess it's my fault for hooking up with my customers. Karma is a bitch."

I agreed wholeheartedly. "Yep, karma will bite you in the ass."

We walked into the room. It was a big mixed meeting (both men and women)—always a blessing to be surrounded by males and females to really have an understanding of the opposite sex. I could feel that both Eve and I needed a reality check on the male perspective, as we were both predators of men. We sat our addict asses down in the metal seats, and we both breathed a sigh of relief. Then simultaneously giggled for having the same reaction. We were two kindred spirits, that was for damn sure. It was speaker night, which I loved, since it was nice to be quiet and just listen to another addict share their experience, strength, and hope for twenty minutes. Also, it was quite lovely to hear all the readings—like "Characteristics of Sex and Love Addiction," "The Twelve Steps," and "Signs of Recovery"—in a British accent. It definitely made SLAA sound a lot posher, making it feel like the best secret club you could possibly belong to.

The older gentleman who spoke hit on a lot of things I needed to be reminded of. He stated very clearly, "This process of increasing awareness led eventually to a final surrender of the whole addictive pattern, and I was launched into withdrawal and sexual and emotional sobriety."

His sponsor had demanded that he "cycle down" from acting out for sixty days, which seemed like a temporary surrender to him. He added, "For the newcomer, to 'cycle down' means no contact with qualifiers, while avoiding unsafe places and unsafe people. It excludes spending significant time with anyone who disrespects my values and program." CHECKMATE! I needed to hear that bit about anyone who disrespected my values. Cough, cough, West! And most definitely NYC!

He continued, "After a while, with patience and my daily spiritual practices of meditation and prayers, the feelings of loneliness and despair dissipated. I was humbled by God's grace. After six years of sobriety, I am no longer drawn to inappropriate people, places, or things, and this new way of living and thinking is awesome. Abstinence has heightened my awareness to all aspects of my life and brings me hope and humility everywhere I go. Thank you, and keep coming back. It works if you work it."

Amen, my fellow brother. I was definitely brought to my knees once again. Sometimes after you've been sober for a bit, you think you have it all together. But now, faced with the dread of working with not just one but two of my ex-boyfriends, I was humbled by the misery caused by my disease. **Rule 15: Learn humility before God humbles you.** And I was truly being humbled. Not only did I feel a shift of surrender in my attraction to West, but I also felt an acceptance of the situation with this job. But to make matters worse... tomorrow was D-Day—the dreaded love scene!

After we all held hands in a large circle and said the Serenity Prayer, which is how every twelve-step meeting ends,

Eve grabbed me by the shoulders and gave me the biggest hug. "Man, I needed that. I feel so much lighter. I was ready to jump out of the plane today, and now, I feel okay."

I replied with an equally grateful hug. "Me too."

As we walked out, I asked her, "When do you head back to the States again?"

"Tomorrow. Want to go grab a drink or something?"

I shook my head. "I really wish I could, but I have a five a.m call on set tomorrow. It was so great to see you and have a safe trip back. See you back home in a couple weeks."

Then I was all alone again. I headed back to my hotel because I needed to get myself plucked, shaved, and scrubbed for the following day's sex scene. If you can imagine going on a first date with a stranger and primping for the evening, you feel like you have to look your best and be perfect. Well, it's a thousand times more intense when you have to do a love scene on camera. Every hair has to be in place, you need to self-tan your whole body, you have to shave every little hair, especially if you do not believe in waxing anything. I was never interested in having hot, burning wax brushed on my labia then my pubic hairs ripped off while spread-eagling it to an esthetician. Man, that poor lady gets the inside view of a lot of females. Not a job I would ever do—you could not pay me enough. I feel the same way about giving pedicures. *Yuck, but God bless you if you like feet. I hate them.*

I was in my hotel room prepping for the big day—Naked Day, as it was mostly called in the profession by the crew. I'd brought all the supplies from home that I needed to get my ass in top form for the camera. I shaved, exfoliated, and slathered my body in tanner while wearing a sheet mask on my face. Jet lag hit me fast, and I looked nuts walking around my room naked except for a face mask, reciting my dialogue for tomorrow's scenes. It was going to be a big day for me; I had three scenes, and my eyes were barely staying open. I'm sure it was a pretty sight for all to see. I was trying to dry my body with a hair dryer before I crawled into bed to be up at the crack of dawn, and it was already 10:30 p.m. I was royally screwed! I was still feeling sticky—this was taking too long. I made a drastic decision that I would later regret, but I needed my beauty sleep. "F- this. I'm going to sleep. I don't care if I have orange streaks down my legs." I dove into the bed, and the jet lag was so intense that I was out cold immediately.

Hitting me like a dump truck, the alarm blared at 4:00 a.m. I struggled to get to the set, but I made it right at my 5:30 a.m. call time and quickly grabbed set breakfast. Which included everything you can imagine eating, and it was free—the best part. Usually, I chowed down, but this time I just grabbed an apple and a double shot of espresso, since I would be mostly undressed, performing simulated sexual acts with a man who seriously had the best body I'd ever laid eyes on. This is coming from an actress who has seen a lot of naked male A-list celebrities. I had to look semi-decent to even compete with West's twelve-pack abs. *Talk about humility at the most primal level!*

I jumped into the hair and makeup trailer, got beautified by their magic skills, and then got chewed out by the head of makeup for not letting my tanner dry properly before I fell asleep. Yep, I had orange streaks down the front of my left leg! She had to hand-paint concealer and body makeup all over my legs to make them match. I think she literally wanted to murder me. *My bad!*

I got to my trailer, changing carefully with the makeup girl assisting me since she had to help me get dressed in a nude thong and pasties—not much to change into. She essentially had to babysit me so I wouldn't ruin the body paint they'd just applied for the last hour; there was no trust at all with these ladies. You might like to know—some actors, I'd say 90% of them, get fake abs painted onto their stomach. Yes, they literally will brush shadows to give the illusion of a six pack and... yes, guilty as charged. I admit that I have had them airbrushed on. It's genius. So never compare yourself to any actor on screen; we are honestly painted, pulled, and tucked to look like that. Reality is rarely presented on camera. It's all an aspirational fantasy of what the audience wants to see.

I was ready to rock this scene! I was wearing my black robe, waiting in my trailer for the 2nd AD to come get me to go to set to shoot. *Insert impatient fingers drumming here.* Because I was still waiting and it had been almost an hour, and I couldn't lie down and ruin my hair and makeup. I was just sitting in an uncomfortable swivel chair, repeating my dialogue over and over again in my head so I wouldn't forget it. This is what it really looks like to be an actress. A lot of waiting, obsessing, and self-doubt before getting to really do my job, which was to act like I was madly in love and in the throes of passion with another actor, whom I hated at this point. Not so glamorous, right? It's all smoke and mirrors!

Once I was called to set, everything got hot. Like, third-degree-burns hot. The sexual tension filled the entire set. We were both so in the zone and listening to the director that I realized it made the situation much more intense and erotic that no words were even exchanged. All the built-up tension was not released as we got into bed to start the scene. As soon as the director yelled, "Action," our chemistry exploded on camera. I couldn't contain how unprepared I was for this moment. Every other love scene I had ever done was always very technical—a "your hand goes there and mine goes here" kind of situation.

Putting it very bluntly, I had never, ever been turned on when shooting any love scene! But this one... this one was orgasmic! An out-of-this-world explosion! I even started to forget that the whole crew was standing around eating their bowls of chili from crafty, just staring at us on the monitors while we simulated sex. If I were into voyeurism, this would have been the ultimate experience, but I am not.

I was usually very focused and used technique in my sex scenes, but for this one, we were in it to win it with our realism. Our eyes were on the prize to do the best we could in these husband-and-wife roles while kind of getting off on each other's animal magnetism.

After each take with West in bed, I forced myself to step off to the side of the set and pray to my God. "I am in big trouble here, and I know it. I am starting to go into fantasy of what our relationship was and all the good times. Please help."

Listen, I know I was in recovery for this crap, but this was very, very hard. I told you before that I was "in love with being in love." I tended to get caught up in the hypnotic intensity of sexual and romantic encounters or relationships. I grew up with such a warped view of what a healthy relationship looks like that I made up my own criteria, which were based on the notion of obsessive romanticism with West. Obsessive romanticism in a relationship looks very off-balance. One or both parties in the relationship become obsessed with each other, putting each other in a magical light that they are your "everything." West was the one guy whom I put on a pedestal. He was like that Arabian stallion that no one could tame or catch. There was always a huge push-and-pull dynamic between us, until it became very unstable and toxic. I had to get out. And here I was, hiding off set behind the grip lights, breathing and praying for the will to get through this without losing my way. I was trying to stay rooted in the reality of this situation. I whispered, "I am humbly asking you, God, to guide me. This is not real. This is a scene in a movie, and I am just doing a job."

West then came over and grabbed me by the waist as I was bent over praying to my God. Yep, that just happened, him behind me once again.

"Hey, baby, wow, that was intense. Are you okay?" he said with a look of concern on his face, which made me think of a sweet puppy, not the wolf he truly was.

"Yeah, I just was not expecting that to happen between us. I've never had a love scene like that before. I feel a little overwhelmed at the moment, that's all." I knew what I had just done. I had revealed myself to him. I had let my guard down. The problem with being healthy and authentic was that it was hard to turn it off, even when I was with a qualifier or someone I should have had my guard up with. But I was kind of spilling my soul a bit. I felt vulnerable like a little girl all of a sudden.

He smiled sweetly, the smile that used to make me melt, even when I was screwing around behind his back. That smile was everything to me, but like I said, he was a very unavailable man. He leaned into me and put his forehead to my forehead. "I know. I felt it too. We are so good together. I know you feel the same way. Will you have dinner with me tonight after we get off?"

My healthy brain was yelling in one ear, "DANGER. DANGER. No! He is not good for you; he is not capable of being the partner you need." Then the addict brain was gently saying, "But you have done the work and changed. Maybe he has changed too, with all that time apart. Maybe you both can make it work together in a healthy way."

He stared at me with those big eyes and added, "I have missed you. We can make this work. Please, let's try."

Checkmate! I felt my resolve weaken. I was hooked. I felt it. I was going down with this ship. "All right let's meet afterward. Text me when you're off."

I was scared. But I was also very, very joyful all of a sudden. Like the clouds had parted after a rainstorm and there was a new, fresh possibility to be had.

That's how it felt even as we finished up shooting the rest of the day. We didn't talk about getting together again, but we were both catching each other's eye during the day, even with NYC in a scene, which was beyond awkward. I mean, I had slept with both these guys. I still wanted West. And I was grossed out by the thought of letting NYC even touch me. He repulsed me completely. Why would I be with such an asshole like him? It really goes to show how lost in my addiction I'd been.

You ever had that happen to you? When you look back on a past relationship and it smacks you squarely in the face? Like, WTF did I see in that person? Like the veil of fantasy is lifted, and you see the real person behind the magical qualities you assigned them? *Come on, I know you have experienced that kind of revelation before too. It's disturbing, to say the least.*

Here is the growth: I freaking made it through the day, working with them both in a scene, and I did not create outside drama. I kept it professional! I was so proud of myself as I headed out to my car, waiting to drive me to the hotel. Did I mention that the whole cast was staying at the same hotel? It's usually like that for location shoots. It gets to be a little much, since everyone knows what everyone else is doing. But hey, it's part of the deal. I texted Alice, "Had a great first day shooting. No drama! Proud of myself, even though the sex scene was a little intense, but I got through it. Going to eat and then bed. Call you in the AM to check in. xo, Roxie."

Okay, okay, okay, I know what you're thinking right now: Why did you not tell her about meeting West tonight?! In my defense, I honestly just didn't know what it meant yet, and I wanted to see for myself. I figured I could handle it. I was a big girl who had her act together. It wasn't a big deal—relax! I got this.

I heard the ding of her response, but it wasn't her. It was West, and I got that butterflies feeling that I should be listening to my inner voice saying RUN. Run as fast as you can for the hills, away from this toxic, gorgeous man who broke your heart! But did I listen? NO! Instead, I looked at his text: "Hey,

I'm in Room 705. Let's eat in my room so no one can see us, cool? Or do you want to eat downstairs in the hotel? Your call, of course. I will do whatever. I'm just exhausted and don't want to have to make small talk with anyone except you."

Everything he just wrote was honestly how I felt, too. I didn't want the whole crew to know we were having dinner together, and I especially didn't want NYC finding out—not that I cared about him, but still. I typed back, "I agree. Let's keep this on the DL. I'm starving. Can you please order me the burger, medium rare, with sweet potato fries? Be there in five minutes. Just wrapped. On my way back to the hotel."

He typed back right away: "Cool. Will do. See you soon. Cheers."

As I was about to knock on his door, it swung open. Before I had a chance to speak, he grabbed me by my jacket collar and pulled me into the room, shutting the door with his foot. He looked deep into my eyes and said, "Let's do this for real. I need you now."

I was so off-balance and thinking, What about my burger? But as soon as his lips touched mine, I was a goner. *Toast!* All sense of sobriety and reality was gone. I was in the throes of passion with this man I had craved since the moment I met him. But this time it felt different between us. It felt like we were on equal ground with our relationship. I felt like we were really seeing each other and connected.

As I pulled off his T-shirt over his head like I had done a million other times, he stopped me. "I missed us."

And my heart just felt like it beat out of my chest. We really were meant to be. We just needed space and time to heal our issues. I replied, "Me too."

I pulled off my black maxi dress over my head and had no underwear on, since I always changed my nude thongs three times during sex scenes. Believe me, it was necessary with how nerve-racking they are and how sweaty you get in the sheets.

No one needs stinky panties, at least not me. Anyway, I was commando, and he literally growled, going down on his knees and kissing my pussy. He muttered, "I wanted to do this on set today so badly. Could you feel how hard I was?"

I breathed out a sigh. "Yes."

He then said, "Tell me you want me too. Say it, Roxie." I was panting as he licked my thigh and clitoris.

"I want you."

He pulled me down to the floor and pulled out his dick so fast I couldn't see straight. He entered me with a grunt, stating, "Sorry, I couldn't wait anymore. Today was torture for me."

There we were on the dark-green carpet in the entryway of his hotel room, making love like we had never done before. It felt magical, like I had never experienced with anyone else. As he was entering me, I was repeating the word *God* in my mind over and over again. Chanting God's name with ecstasy and gratitude for all the work I had put in for my recovery. All the healing I had done in therapy and in the SLAA rooms. This was my reward, to connect and be intimate with the man I was truly meant to be with. I was so warm with gratitude and about to COME HARD. The wash of intensity overcame me, and I was sent to the heavens with release. *It should be mentioned that I had barely ever come with a man inside of me, only by finger banging. So, this moment was everything. I felt so alive and a part of West.*

He pulled out of me after he came too. It was like a movie moment for sure. I turned to him and asked with a sultry smile, "Where's my burger, sir? And you better have gotten cheese on it."

He cracked up so loud. "Roxie, you are hilarious, you know that? We just had the best sex ever and you're thinking about a medium-rare burger? You are always thinking about food. I've never met a girl like you." Then he sat up with his twelve-pack abs on full display. "I'm sorry, I forgot to order. I was texting with my agent. I'll order for you now." He got up ass-naked, and it was a great sight. "You still want fries? Glass of wine?"

I lay back down in heaven, wondering who else had screwed on this nasty carpet. I probably had foot jam on my ass. "Yes, please. Both would be lovely."

He walked into the living room of his suite, and I heard him on the hotel phone ordering. I was smiling ear to ear. I couldn't wait to tell Alice how much we had grown and how grateful I was to her for her patience.

I was searching for my phone on the floor somewhere. I grabbed it and picked it up. But it wasn't my phone—it was his. I was about to put it down when the screen popped up: a text from NYC. I opened it and looked at it in confusion and then disbelief.

"You fuck her yet? You better not, dude. I don't want to have to buy you another round and pay that $200."

Then another text popped up. "You didn't even make it fair. You both looked like horny teenagers today. I would never have made that bet knowing you had a sex scene today."

Then another text. "Kidding. Hope you drilled her good. See you at the bar in an hour?"

I dropped his phone. I was lost. Blank. Crushed. How could I have been so stupid? I knew better. Then it hit me: I knew nothing. I was not to be trusted. I heard West go into the bathroom and yell out, "Order is in. I have to take a shower badly. Join me if you want. Should not be long for the food."

I said quickly, "Okay, thanks." Not really meaning it but wanting to get out of this room. I picked myself up and untangled my dress, throwing it over my head. I set his phone down on the table next to his script, then wrote on his cover, "Congratulations. Enjoy your $200 and beer."

I walked out. I walked down the hallway and pressed the up button to go to my room on the twelfth floor. As the doors opened, I saw myself in the elevator mirror, all flushed and hollow. I really saw myself. I did not have the luxury to go back to my past. I couldn't handle the unavailable person. As I looked at myself, I said, "Dear God, pray over my heart. Please keep me humble and remove hate from my soul." I closed my eyes, and the last thought that raged in my head before I hit the twelfth floor was: Humble yourself or life will do it for you.

I opened my eyes and saw the cold hard truth. If you do not learn the lessons of the past, they will ultimately humble your ass.

CHAPTER SEVEN

Rule 16: Enjoy the Dark Night of the Soul

"TRUE SURRENDER OF OUR sex and love addiction meant not only being willing to take ourselves out of the painful situation at hand. It meant, most importantly, being ready to be free of our whole life strategy of obsession with and pursuit of love and sex"—quoted from the SLAA basic textbook, which I was feverishly reading under my covers before dawn after a long night of painful grief for the addict who still suffered inside of me. I had read this book hundreds of times, and every time, I got another nugget of wisdom I'd never retained earlier.

I had heard of this dreaded moment in one's life: the Dark Night of the Soul. I spent last night obsessively looking on my computer and researching for two and a half hours how one could get through, survive, and thrive after such a soul-stirring shit show of a night, AKA the bet that NYC and West made. How disgusting of them to bet on my sexuality for their revenge. I'd immediately blocked West's number and canceled our WhatsApp connection. But I was determined to get on the other side of this situation in one piece. At least as much as I could since I had to still finish the rest of the shoot with those dickheads.

According to Google, the concept of the "Dark Night of the Soul" comes from the Roman Catholics and is described as a spiritual crisis in the journey toward union with God. While this crisis is usually temporary, it may endure for a long time.

FUCK ME. I needed to be healed by tomorrow at 7:00 a.m.

I searched for a different definition, but they all pretty much kept coming back to the same meaning: A dark night of the soul is both the most painful and the best possible, most transformative thing anyone can (and will) experience at some point in their life. And in simple terms, it's a spiritual crisis, ego death, existential crisis... whatever you want to call it.

FUCK ME again.

The Dark Night of the Soul Experience:

- Intense feelings of sadness, frustration, hopeless-ness, meaninglessness, and confusion—a sense of homesickness for a place that never was. *Awe-some!*

- You will uncontrollably cry, feel empty, and feel abandoned all at once. *Good times!*

- Leads to a spiritual death where everything is lost, and all seems like darkness. *Crawling on the floor in so much pain that you want to physically die... which leads to your REBIRTH!*

FUCK ME—a third time!

Rule 16: Enjoy the Dark Night of the Soul.

I made one last furtive search and found this pearl of wis-dom (and here's the kicker for my impatience): You don't have to "do" anything to get through this Dark Night of the Soul. All will be "done unto you." You just have to surrender to the mo-ment and let it unfold naturally in its own time. *Wonderful.* I closed my computer and slid deeper under my covers, hiding from the world.

In a movie, the Dark Night of the Soul is the worst position the protagonist finds herself in. It's when the character believes that everything is lost. Usually, a character is alone. In *Bridesmaids*, Kristen Wiig's character breaks up with her best friend, her love interest, and her fuck buddy all within minutes. She finds herself all alone.

I could relate. Big time.

But in the movies, after going through the Dark Night of the Soul, the hero somehow receives the encouragement and advice that helps her get through the rest of the film. Where was my encouragement? I was too ashamed to call Alice... yet. So, I was searching for it in the pages of the SLAA book.

My mind was trying to make sense of this happening, especially since I had done so much work on myself. Hadn't I been here before? Hadn't I gone through enough suffering? I'd always thought I had already endured my soul-destroying Dark Night throughout those agonizingly long nine months of withdrawal during my first year. Or maybe I'd been restored to sanity by passing through that spiritual redecoration of one's inner being. What a joke it was on good old me, right? I was now humbly on my knees, begging this power greater than myself to restore my ass to a new spiritual solution. I had thrown up my white flag, crying uncle to this terrifying night of acting out, even though I'd been subconsciously carrying out my doom. This was a spiritual disease for me, and the only way out of my soul-crushing curled-into-a-ball-wanting-to-die state of being was a spiritual solution.

I knew that. But it's still hard to pick up the phone and admit defeat, especially to your sponsor. Especially to your sponsor whom you pointedly DID NOT TELL that you were going into the belly of the beast, because you thought, "I've got this. I don't need you. I'm fine." *Yep, I was feeling major guilt and shame.* So instead of calling Alice, I ordered breakfast from room service and lay in my huge king-size bed and read the

SLAA book under the covers. *Sometimes you have to go back to the basics to figure the shit out.*

Luckily, I had the day off to recover, and I didn't shoot until the next day. But my scenes were with that asshole gambler-of-my-body-and-emotions, West. And the real kicker, NYC was also in the scenes, since it was a party in the script. *Good times. NOT!* So here I was trying everything I could to quickly get through the realization of where I went wrong in my sobriety, so that I could be "all healed" by the following day. *You're laughing at me, right?* The probability of that happening was slim to none. I got that, but at least I was looking at my shitty ways and trying to be better.

How could I move past this experience and grow from it, never repeating this delusion again? That was the million-dollar question. I had no clue, but I was in so much agony from this betrayal that I was willing to do some digging and figure it out. Also, I needed to get my butt to a meeting ASAP. Unfortunately, Eve had already headed back to the States, so I didn't have her to be my support—plus, it's hard to lean on your sponsee, especially a newbie. That would not be fair to her. I kept reminding myself that slips can happen; it only matters what you do afterward, but man, this shame spiral was tricky. Shame can take you down to the lowest of the low with your self-worth. I was battling my shame, and until I got it under control, I was not getting in the shower or putting on makeup. I needed to sit with it in a dark room and really look at where I made my wrong turn.

Supposedly, when you get down on your proverbial knees to admit defeat—admitting that you are powerless over acting out with these behaviors of sex and love addiction—you are already choosing to turn your will over to your Higher Power. To be completely honest, I'd never really felt that before. In the past, I'd still felt like I had some control over my actions. That if I just kept getting on my knees and pretending to turn all my crap over, God would reward me with what I truly desired. I saw it clearly now: I was always trying to get my will back. I was playing liar, liar with my God. I just never truly trusted that I was taken care of, fibbing to myself that this time with West would be different. That he had changed because I had changed. When in all actuality, we were still acting out the same scenario, just in a different location. It was all physical once again. Our pheromones were just stimulating each other's. Nothing was of substance. We'd never even had a real conversation about our mistakes in the past. There was no communication of our rights and wrongs, and how we were going to do it differently this time. No commitment to us! That was definitely where I'd lost my footing in my serenity. I was once again blinded by lust. Not love. Not honesty. Not trust. Damn it, none of the requirements on my dating plan for future men in my life that Alice and I had painstakingly laminated. I'd just thrown all those out the window. I had ignored every red flag furiously waving in my face. One of the questions Dr. Kath used to ask was, "Did you not see the red flags?" I told her one time to be funny, "I thought it was a carnival."

My head was now peeking out from under the white 1000-thread-count sheets. My shame had let up a tad—I felt like I could at least look at the room without crumbling in humiliation. That was when I realized I had to call Alice. There was only so long I could put off the inevitable. I was dreading this conversation. I was mortified that I had not even made it a full day of working with him without succumbing to his charm and foolery. Weakness in one's resolve was one of the qualities I detested most. But I had to admit to myself that I was human, and I couldn't always strong-will my way through my own love obsession. I was truly powerless over my attraction to this man.

My vagina had a mind of her own, and that bitch was not to be trusted.

I reluctantly picked up my iPhone and made a WhatsApp video call to Alice. I hated video chats, especially when I had no makeup on. Welcome to the craziness of me—no one in my life had seen me without makeup, even Alice, who knew all the bad stuff I'd done in my life. I was still so vain, because right before I hit her number to make the call, my first thought was that I probably looked like hell and should put on some sunglasses to hide my face. Or maybe hang up really quickly and at least add foundation and concealer under my dark-circle raccoon eyes. Maybe some blush, eyeliner, and mascara, at least?

"No, Roxanne," I said aloud in my room. "You are fine just as you are. Stop it!"

Plus, she needed to see my face to look into my eyes when I broke the news to her on my slip. I held the phone in my hands and closed my eyes to build up my courage. Letting go of my ego, I hit send. Then I looked into the tiny lens and smiled. It rang about four times, and I was about to hang up when Alice answered during her workout at the gym. It was 9:00 p.m. in Los Angeles and she had just finished a workout, which was hilarious to me since she was one of those girls who never had to. But since her wedding was around the corner, I'd hooked her up with Trainer, to kick her ass hard.

Trainer was also giving her a sweet discount since Alice was a schoolteacher. Also, Trainer promised not to take it easy on her. It was my own deviant behavior to get pleasure out of other people's pain. Even though this kind of pain was good for Alice. She was one of those skinny-fat people; so thin but no muscle mass at all. Like chicken arms. I know, I'm a horrible friend but it was kind of fun torturing her.

Alice answered completely out of breath and looking like she was dying. I couldn't help but chuckle that she was in as much pain as me. Man, I was a sadistic bitch sometimes, but at least I knew it. And I was working on that dark side of myself.

"Hi, lady. Sorry, I just got done with Trainer. Man, he is brutal. I can't feel my arms right now. And he would not let me take a water break—does he do that with you?" She added quickly with winded breath, "So rude."

I replied, "Yep, he is a beast. But your ass is going to look great on your wedding day. You will thank me then." I sighed very loudly and she instinctively uttered, "Oh no. What happened?"

"How do you know something happened? Are you a witch?"

"No, I can just tell when something happens. Your face looks like a puckered asshole. So, spill it, please."

I sighed again all dramatic. "I screwed up last night."

I wished I could have stopped talking right then, but she waited, making me say the words aloud. "I had sex with West. But the worst part was that I thought it was a real connection. I mean, we both beautifully orgasmed together like we were in sync. But right afterward, he got a text, and I thought it was my phone. I looked at it and it turns out I'm a major fool. He and NYC had a bet to see who could sleep with me first." I was hysterical as I relived the entire experience to Alice.

Alice listened intently with a small nod of her head. She waited for me to calm down, then said gently, "Roxie, I'm not surprised you lost your time with West. You are literally like an alcoholic hanging out at a bar, trying not to drink. It was really only a matter of time. Give yourself a break."

Now I was annoyed. "What the f-? You're my freaking sponsor. You are not supposed to let me get in these situations. Why didn't you tell me? I needed you." *Okay, I know that sounds a lot like I was blaming her, and I probably was a tad. Trying to take some self-hatred off my back, but I thought I could handle this job situation. Really, I had truly thought I was going to make it out unscathed, but boy, was I wrong. Dead wrong.*

She calmly rebuffed my attack. "Roxanne, first of all, you are a grown-ass woman and can make your own decisions. I am not your keeper. My only job as your sponsor is to take you through the steps and be the voice of the program. Second, I did in fact mention to you after he tricked you on Raya that maybe it might not be the best situation to get yourself into. Third, I recall very clearly that you said you had already signed your contract, and you needed the money to pay your bills. There was no way I was going to force you to quit that job. It's not my place to tell you what to do. Also, I don't recall you mentioning ANYTHING about going to West's hotel room for dinner. Had you given me a heads-up, I would have been able to advise you absofuckinglutely not to go." Holy crap! She just dropped the mic on me and handed me my ass. I broke down in tears. "Fine. I was wrong. I really messed up. Now I have to go work with both of them, and I'm completely lost and having a crisis of faith."

"No, you are not. You just had a slip. You know what to do to get out of it. You get dressed. You find out what meetings are happening today and get to as many as you can. You be of service to other people. You show up for your fellow addicts. And then you go to work and take accountability for your part of the transgression. Then you do your job. Go home to your hotel and start all over again, until it is time to pack your bags to come back to LA. You have the tools." She ended with a sharp look that said, I dare you to dismiss my direction.

We were both silently staring at each other. She was not going to give me anymore, I could see that. I replied reluctantly, since I was a very, very stubborn addict at times, "You're right. I will." I hated admitting sometimes that others know more than me, but it was getting easier. The more I practiced, the more I could let go of my will and the tightness in my chest when admitting defeat.

Alice was definitely happy that the emotional standoff was not as long as they used to be. She cheerfully ended the call with a thrilled but annoying, "Great. Text me later to check in.

I have to go. I gave my word that I would be on time for dinner tonight, but you got this. You have the tools—use them."

I hung up with a grunt of irritation that even my sponsor could not fix me during this period of my Dark Night of the Soul transformation. This moment of shedding the old self was mine and mine alone. I knew all of this intellectually, but I still wanted to be saved from the heartache and pain that was arising from this triggering experience. It was like all that I thought was true was erased. The sobriety I thought I'd earned had not saved me from myself. I had lost my focus and had put on my old rose-colored glasses with West. Everything I had worked for over the last almost two years felt flushed down the toilet. *You ever have moments like that? Where you've truly screwed up your life, and it's almost like you subconsciously knew you were but still went ahead and believed the lie you were telling yourself?*

That's how I was truly feeling as I wormed my way out from under my sheets and hit the nasty green carpet on all fours like a dog. I proceeded on my hands and knees and crawled my way into the bathroom to get myself together for a day of SLAA meetings. It was the only thing I knew that could help me in this moment. I had to go. I had to let go of the poor-me victim state and go be in a room of fellow addicts who loved me despite my behavior.

Eckhart Tolle discusses the importance of the Dark Night in detail on his website: "The 'dark night of the soul' is a term that goes back a long time... It is a term used to describe what one could call a collapse of a perceived meaning in life... an eruption into your life of a deep sense of meaninglessness... Nothing makes sense anymore; there's no purpose to anything. Sometimes it's triggered by some external event."

When I read this, it struck me so deeply that I was jolted by the false sense of security I'd felt with my sobriety and that I'd still been holding onto a belief, especially after seeing West at Pace and learning that we were playing husband and wife. The belief that the purpose of this job was that we were supposed to be together. That this was God's plan all along. That the sole purpose for me to get healthy was to make it work with the one man who was truly unavailable to me, whom I was always trying to get to love me. That all those horrible online dates had led me to my one true "soulmate." My "twin flame." The man with whom I was supposed to make it work.

Boy, was I dead wrong. Every man I had ever been with was unavailable. Why? Because I'd been unavailable even to myself and still was in some sense. Last night really hit the nail in the coffin. As I brushed my teeth and looked at the five meetings that were taking place all over London, I formed a game plan: I was going to try to make it to every one of them. I was going to play to win, snatching victory from the jaws of defeat. *Okay, I had no idea why I was using idioms at this point—it was probably a combination of jet lag, withdrawal, and utter surrender on my part.*

The last thing I read before I applied my routine thick brown eyeliner to balance out my dark circles was this by Tolle: "What dies is the egoic sense of self... You are meant to arrive at a place of conceptual meaninglessness. Or one could say a state of ignorance—where things lose the meaning that you had given them, which was all conditioned and cultural and so on."

A huge snort blurted out of my nose, because here I was applying my mask of vanity and egotism to go try to find my true sense of self. Seemed counterintuitive at this point, but it was the only thing getting me out the door: perfectly applying my foundation, concealer, blush, bronzer, lipliner, mascara, and my warrior-painted eyes. For the last accessory to my uniform of marathon meetings, I threw on my black fisherman cap, and I was out the door, determined to get my serenity and peace back once and for all. *Or die trying!*

Sitting in those five different meetings was a trip, for sure. The first two were mixed meetings. One was really big—over sixty-five fellows—and the other one was only eight people. In London, you have to have a certain amount of sobriety in the program to be able to share during the meeting. I think it was to force newcomers to just listen, be present, and hear the experience, strength, and hope. Not really sure I agree with that, since it has always helped me to hear both newcomers who are struggling as well as old-timers who carry the message of healing and hope. But I was just another fellow, so it was not my business how they ran their meetings in this country. The loveliest thing about going to both of those meetings back-to-back was the different environments and personalities I ran into. A young actress I had seen in a huge blockbuster was in the big meeting, sharing that she was struggling with her co-star. They'd had an affair and he was married. She was struggling with still going to work with him, where they used to act out, while keeping it professional. I so needed to hear that, since it was pretty much exactly what I was going through. Then an older gentleman spoke about not letting his ex-wife go and that she'd just gotten a restraining order against him for following her around. He had believed he was just trying to win her back. But now he saw that he had a huge problem with codependency and letting go of the past in order to move on with his life. This also reminded me of West tricking me into dinner with him and how I had to move on from the past. That I had my own form of codependency rearing its ugly head.

My Codependency Patterns (Especially with West):

- A pattern of avoiding conflict—*YEP*

- My self-worth depends on what others think about me—*OF COURSE*

- My mood reflects how others feel, rather than my own emotions—*TYPICAL*

- Doing things I don't really want to do, simply to make others happy—*THAT'S WHY I'M IN THIS MESS*

- Overwhelming fears of rejection or abandonment—*HOLY SHIT, THE MAIN ISSUES*

- A deep-seated need for approval from others—*THAT'S A GIVEN, LOOK AT MY PROFESSION*

Good lord, it felt like I could never catch a break with my addiction to other people. Especially that hot-as-fuck man.

The best part of this journey in the program was that there was no judgment, and just because our stories were not alike, I could learn from other people's stories, and they could learn from mine. They say in the rooms, "Look for the similarities, not our differences."

My three-minute shares were all over the place. I can't remember exactly what I said in the meetings, since they all kind of blended together by the end of the day. That's what happens when you hit a bunch in one day, which I had never done before, but I'd needed to do it to get out of myself and the dark hotel room. The following is a summary from the meetings, but you can go ahead and imagine that I was sitting in either a metal chair or a couch in a church, office building, or hospital conference room. That's pretty much the standard environment for twelve-step meetings, as you probably know from all the movies and television shows that reenact the scenario. Here is the overall dialogue of my shares, in no particular order. Brace yourself, folks, for this babbling mess out of my mouth:

"Hi. My name is Roxanne, and I'm a sex and love addict."

"I believe my role in this life is to heal myself completely."

(*I HAVE MY SHIT TOGETHER HERE.*)

"So, my Dark Night of the Soul happened last night. It sucked to be pulled back into a relationship I had already grieved and thought I had moved on from. Now here I am in this country, trying to be a better example of what happens when a horrible person is faced with themselves—they make a choice and shift as a person for the better. I hope I can be that person again after my slip."

(*MY EMOTION IS RISING, BUT I'M TRYING TO HOLD IT TOGETHER.*)

"But who really knows, right? Only my God knows. I am trying to listen to his voice as much as I can, but sometimes my addict voice is louder. When I lost my time with West— Sorry, no names. I forgot. When I lost my time with him, it was like God gave me a chance to make a different choice and I did not take it. I took the road I always traveled. I really wanted to try to make these not-so-healthy relationships work. Why do we do that to ourselves? Trying to prove we are worth these people's love and attention, when they are so obviously wrong for us. To try to be powerful enough to change them? NOOOOO!!!"

(*I'M STARTING TO LOSE MY SHIT AS MY ANGER AT MYSELF IS BOILING OVER.*) "It's hard to believe. I'm back in the insanity of my disease again. Now, did I slip as far as I have in the past? No, my sponsor pointed that out to me. I only crashed for a short while, and I didn't go down with the sinking ship. It felt like a Titanic moment, but I survived. I was Rose on that flotation, shivering and barely alive, but I did not sink."

(*NOW I'M OFFICIALLY BAWLING.*)

"I see now that I have to be diligent with myself. I have to see even the small red flags that people are showing me. This is a real life lesson for me, and I learned it big time while crashing hard last night and getting my ass back up and to these meetings. I am proud of myself."

Then the three-minute buzzer beeped. My time was up.

I was always mentally exhausted after just one meeting, so after five meetings, I was dead tired. Talk about wanting to bail at the midway point—even I was over hearing my own voice. But I did it. I forced myself to dive into the program to relieve me of my addict self. To get closer to my God. To feel the Dark Night of the Soul and grow from it, to not wallow in the self-pity I was stuck in earlier.

I walked back to the hotel with a lighter step; albeit, mentally drained by a day full of sex and love addict shares. Also, my ass hurt from sitting in those chairs, but that's what happens when you have a bony, flat ass. Luckily, I had just picked up the best-smelling fish-and-chips dinner at Golden Union Fish Bar, just up the block from my last meeting.

I was in a happy food fantasy as I made my way back to my hotel, holding the smelly, greasy bag. As I walked through the lobby, I kept my head down, not wanting to see any of my cast or crew. I was going to go up to my room and sit on my king-size bed and devour my meal with overwhelming ecstasy. Food was my life, especially when you took away the sex and intrigue with men. I ordered the cod and chips plate, obviously the large portion with the homemade tartar sauce, which was a pretty good deal for £13.95. After I gorged—since I deserved some kind of comfort after the toll the last forty-eight hours had taken on my nervous system—I crawled my dog-tired butt into my huge bubble filled bathtub to soak the day off of me. I scrubbed my legs, feet, and face with exfoliation. It almost felt like a baptism to cleanse myself of all traces of West and the taint that I let him leave on me. I dragged my body into the smooth, cool sheets, and my last thought before my head hit the pillow was that tomorrow was going to be different. I was going to bring God with me to work this time. I realized I'd left him in the hotel room on my first day of naked shooting. I realized I did not have to do this alone. I was not solo on this journey; I would be protected. God would be with me to face the lions tomorrow on set. *This sheep has her flock to safeguard her.*

I woke to the blasting alarm clock, and I felt different. I felt lighter. I felt like my anger and resentment had lessened. As I dressed in my all-black uniform to face the day, I was reminded that I would most definitely make it out of this job with my self-love intact. I looked in the mirror, telling myself, "You are loved. You are enough. You will be okay."

Walking into the hair and makeup trailer, the fear started to rise in my chest. I knew I was going to see both of the douchey exes in about 2.6 seconds. As I was taking my first step up the steps, I said the words echoing in my head from Alice, "My Universe has me," then I opened the door — they were both right there in my face. *COME ON!* The only chair open was the one right between them. I would literally be sandwiched between two assholes during our entire makeup application. *You have got to be shitting me? GOD, I do not think this is funny or even a tad humorous.*

Sometimes, I still truly believe that the Universe has a very sick sense of humor. It's like God loves to test me and see if I have really surrendered. I feel like he's a teacher giving his students a pop quiz to have them prove they listened, did their homework, and learned something. That's how I've felt about my God my whole life. Always waiting to see if I was going to screw up AGAIN. Alice told me that it was not true, that I didn't have a vindictive God/Higher Power/Universe. That was just an old belief of mine. But she does believe that the Universe either gives us benchmarks to move us forward in our growth or creates another situation where we have to re-live the pain again till we learn the lesson. Always asking—Are you ready to evolve yet?

I was sure done with my lessons of unavailability with other humans, and especially myself. I didn't want to have another Dark Night of the Soul. I didn't want to feel that over-whelming, shameful grief of withdrawal from an unhealthy situation that I had once again put myself in.

As my behind hit the chair, both of them said at the exact same time, "Hello, Roxie. How was your day off?" I looked at them with my resting bitch face (RBF)—hey, I was still human when I got played. That bitchy side of me still had not gone away, even though I had a God and was trying to be a better human. *No way—my RBF was always ready to play!*

I replied, "Hello to you both. I hope you could sleep well the last couple of nights with a clear conscience."

NYC looked at me with pure delight. "I slept great. Best sleep I've gotten in ages. You too, right, West?"

West looked at me and then at NYC, and for a brief moment, I saw a glimpse of regret in his eyes, but it floated away just as fast as it had come. Then he said with a huge grin, "Best sleep ever."

Part of me wanted to kill them both.

DISSOLVE TO:
INT. MAKEUP ROOM—DAY

NYC and West sit in a row getting their makeup done. Roxie enters wearing a long black leather trench coat.

> ROXIE
> Hey, makeup artists One, Two,
> and Three. Director wants to
> see you. Immediately.

The trio of makeup artists leave. Roxie LOCKS the door. It makes a loud CLICK.

> NYC
> What the hell, Roxie?

> ROXIE
> Sit down, dick face.

She pulls out a Hattori Hanzō sword, à la Quentin Tarantino's "Bride" in *Kill Bill*.

                    ROXIE
          Only one of us is going to
          leave this trailer alive, and
          fun fact, it's not going to
          be either of you.

With the prowess of an action star and Jedi Master, she runs up the wall, does a backflip, and on her way down, DECAPITATES both NYC and West in one slice.

She looks at both of their heads on the floor.

                    ROXIE
          Sweet dreams, motherfuckers.

                              BLACKOUT

But instead of homicide, a wave of acceptance flooded over me like a warm waterfall, and I knew it was God guiding my way. It had to be him guarding me to have these feelings of calm and stability in this intense situation. "I'm happy for you both. I had a bit of a hard time with the jet lag, but I'm feeling much clearer-headed. Clarity is the key to one's happiness, that's for sure."

I could tell they were both taken aback by my demeanor, but NYC looked a touch disappointed. He had obviously wanted to cause me some pain for my past indiscretions. *I get it, believe me!* I would want to literally "cut a bitch" for what I did to him a couple years ago on that fated day with ATL. I would feel the exact same way if the shoe were on the other foot. I was not denying my terrible past behavior, but I also knew I couldn't hold onto this resentment for what they had just done to me. Resentments are the key ingredient in the recipe for acting out, at its finest.

As I sat between them, sandwiching me in the tight space like an Oreo cookie—*which, for your information, is one of my favorite treats*—I came to realize that I was truly okay. I had learned a lot from the last forty-eight hours. I felt like I had grown from my Dark Night and had released some old shame and feelings. I saw that I couldn't change the past damage I had done to either of these men.

I could only do better from here on out.

When I finally wrapped in the makeup chair, I saw NYC walking out of his trailer to go to crafty for more black coffee. I yelled at him across the studio lot, "Hey, NYC, wait up. You going to get coffee?"

He turned to me. "Huh? Yeah, why?"

There was so much Brooklyn attitude and Connecticut snobbery oozing out of him that I wanted to abort my mission. But I knew I had amends to make, so I stopped right in front of him with as much kindness as I could muster. "Can I join you? Would love to talk for a second if you're free?"

He contemplated whether to allow my company, then decided, "Why the hell not. Sure."

I smiled. "Thank you. It will only be a minute of your time." We took a few steps, and then I turned to him. "I just wanted to say that I'm sorry about what happened in my driveway and back at your Airbnb when we were dating. I know I was not a good person then, and I was in a lot of pain, but that's no excuse to hurt you or anyone else. I'm truly sorry."

He just stared at me. Nothing. No emotion. Total blank.

I continued cleaning up my side of the street, as they say in the rooms—a tad reluctantly, I might add, since he did just do me wrong, but there was nothing I could do about that now. I quietly added, "Also, I am aware of the bet you and West had working with me. I totally get why you guys felt the way you did, even if it's unkind in my eyes to wish me pain and harm. But like I said, it's not my job to judge you both."

He literally laughed in my face. "The bet? It was a joke, when we were drunk. I would not sleep with you ever again. You disgust me. I had no idea West would bone you. He's a moron and is already screwing the wardrobe assistant, so the joke is truly on you. Good luck with that!" He walked off chuckling.

WOW! Didn't expect that attack. This was one of those moments where I could have completely shut down and gone into fight. But I held my tongue.

He truly hated my guts. He looked like the Devil as he drank his cup of black coffee to fill his black soul—even though he was entitled to his feelings. I normally would have lashed back at him and let him have it, but I didn't. I hated when people didn't like me. I mean, probably everyone does not enjoy someone hating them, but I used to act like I couldn't give two shits if someone liked me or not.

Somebody once said to me, "Being overly independent is a defense mechanism from constantly being let down." And I promise you that when they said that to me, I felt it in my soul. I hated not being liked, but it also made me fearless; almost to the point of avoidance.

This one time, on a USO tour for the troops, a bunch of us television actors were going to support and hang out with the soldiers in Iraq. Another well-known actress, who was on a very popular preteen show, was on the panel as well. Every time I went near her and tried to talk with her, she would turn and walk away. I was so taken aback, thinking all these crazy thoughts like, Did I do something wrong? Say something to hurt her? Am I just annoying? Or am I just being sensitive and about to start my period?

Hallmark Star was on the tour with me at the time, and she advised me to go and ask her and to apologize if I had done something. Taking her advice, I walked up to the actress after we finished dinner in the mess tent, away from the other travelers so as not to start gossip or drama. I smiled at her and said, "Hey,

TeenSoap, did I do something that upset you? I'm just feeling like I did, but if not, cool. Was just feeling some weird vibes."

She told me blatantly, "I just don't like you."

I looked at her with so much "fuck you too" that it formed into an actual smile, and I said back, "No problem. You don't have to like me. That's fine. Let's just ignore each other the next couple of days." I turned, walking back to our table to act all cool and unaffected, but I was truly crushed on the inside.

Still to this day, I can't stand to see her name and face, but I tend to run into her every year or so at an audition or red-carpet event. We both just turn a blind eye to each other. But deep down, I still just want to be liked and loved like everyone else. I think we all do.

So, witnessing NYC's deep-seated disdain was not so shocking, but it still stung, not going to lie. I stepped forward to the crafty espresso machine and began to make my much-needed double shot. I felt someone over my shoulder, probably waiting for their turn to use it too, since it was only 7:30 a.m. I looked over and saw the one person I didn't want to see. Yep, you guessed it, West. He did this shitty half-hearted smirk like he was feeling bad for me. I just turned back to my shot, waiting impatiently and praying for it to be done brewing. It felt like it was taking forever. I almost just walked away without it, but I was determined to get some caffeine in me as soon as possible.

West was still behind me—I could smell his body cologne. "Roxanne, you okay?"

I didn't turn around this time, instead calling over my shoulder, "I'm cool." Still staring at the machine like it was my only lifeline.

West said, "I had no idea you would see my texts. I didn't want that to happen."

Holy cow, that was what he had to say? Now I was pissed. The espresso machine beeped just as my blood started to boil.

I grabbed the cup, and it splashed and burned my hand. "Fuck, that hurts! Damn!"

West jumped to the conclusion that I was referring to him and his lies. "I know, Roxie. I'm sorry I hurt you. It was a joke. It went too far. I get it. I'm sorry."

I turned to him with the same disgust that I was sure NYC had for me. "Relax, dude! I just burned my hand with the coffee. But yes, you did hurt me, but I have done a lot of thinking and looking back. I'm glad it went down and that I saw those texts, because the fantasies I had of us being good for each other or having a decent relationship all flew out the window. So, thank you kindly for the clarity." I grabbed a wet napkin and held it to my hand as I turned away. Then I called back over my other shoulder, "Tell Wardrobe Assistant I said good luck—she's going to need it."

That was it! That was the last moment West and I talked outside of our scripted dialogue for the rest of the shoot. I managed to make it through those nine days with my serenity and peace intact only because I set a schedule for myself. When I wasn't shooting, I was at meetings, working with my sponsees, or working on my lines for the next day. The following weekend, I took it even a step further to protect myself: I stayed at another hotel and had spa days both Saturday and Sunday. I treated myself to as much pampering as you can imagine. Giving tons of self-love to my body, my mind, and soul.

The last day of working on the film was with both of them, and I felt nothing. No anger, no hurt. It was all gone. I was free. I was alone but not lonely. I was disconnected from all the drama as I watched West hook up with Wardrobe Assistant and NYC screwing my stand-in. A stand-in is the person who takes the place of an actor to help the camera department light the set, as well as tweak their blocking, composition, framing, and focus. They are usually the same build, height, and coloring as the lead. *Yes, he was screwing the fake me. Good times!* I literally felt like I was surrounded by a bunch of sex and love addicts acting out. Normally, I would have been envious of the flirtation and getting high off the attention while on set, but again, I was fully grounded in reality. I had no illusions of grandeur. That Dark Night of the Soul had truly changed my mentality.

As I headed to the airport, I thought back to my Dark Night. More revelations came into light about the significance that night had held for me. I realized what a gift I'd been given. A Dark Night of the Soul's true purpose is to purge us, releasing all that is unhealed and unnecessary in our lives. Letting go of all that is in the way of us achieving our highest good, and bringing us closer to our true divine self. Although the Dark Night of the Soul is not something we would ever wish upon anyone, even ourselves, it is the most transformational experience this life has to offer.

Imagine your SOUL is saying to you at this moment in time, "You know, I've looked through your memories and found little bits of lessons not yet learned and wounds not yet healed. All of which are holding you back. So, we're going to do a thorough cleanse of whatever we can so that you can move forward into a better life."

Then your wise SOUL continues to explain, "By the way, we have some good news and some bad news. The good news is that the Dark Night will not actually kill you. The bad news, however, is that at times it might make you wish you were dead."

Everyone—I mean, *everyone*—will go through the Dark Night of the Soul at one time or another, and at one level or another. In fact, we all go through it at least a couple times in our lives. Many say that the Dark Night of the Soul is one of the world's best-kept secrets. Nobody talks about it or even knows anything about it.

I hope you enjoy your Dark Night of the Soul and ride the waves of uncertainty and pain, because all will be rewarded on the other side; most importantly, clarity of self. It truly is a blessing in disguise. And one of the most profound nights of my life.

CHAPTER EIGHT

Rule 17: Getting dumped sucks— nevertheless, embrace the change!

ARE YOU BEYOND CONFUSED at this point? I mean, why is a single lady like me talking about getting dumped? Your brain might be spinning trying to figure out if I was having a secret affair or something. I wasn't. Also, I am not talking about a toxic breakup with a dude; I am talking about handling a healthy breakup. But both would apply for this rule, for sure.

"Sometimes good things fall apart so better things can fall together"—a quote by the talented but extremely troubled Marilyn Monroe. I always loved those sage words, even from a very addicted individual like Ms. Monroe. She was a sad, poor, empty soul who had both everything and nothing at the same time. That was one of my major fears if I didn't stay diligent with my recovery. That I would end up drowning in my own loneliness after another failed toxic relationship. While getting older and older, trapped in my own pursuit of fantasy, in this ageist business that hates any woman over forty. Ironically, Marilyn Monroe died when she was thirty-six, just before Hollywood would have considered her geriatric. Whenever a new documentary or movie came out about Marilyn Monroe's life, I felt like I was watching myself. It was a reminder to get help whenever I was feeling even a little off from reality.

I always watched the original blonde bombshell with an equal amount of enchantment and sadness. It hurt me to my core that she had no programs like SLAA during the 1950s and 1960s, and that nothing could stop her from destroying herself. I easily could have turned out that way. I grew up watching her films, and I was obsessed with one film in particular. I could quote it word for word. Any idea which one?

Gentlemen Prefer Blondes is about two women who are looking for the perfect male to complete them or for them to conquer. Sounds about right for a budding love addict to watch at the age of eleven, right? Even as a prepubescent, all signs were pointing to YES for having unrealistic expectations of the opposite sex.

But enough about the movies—back to my real life. After I got back from London, the first thing I had to deal with was the worst jet lag I had ever experienced in my life. I was dead. Literally and figuratively totes spent. Probably the exhaustion was exacerbated by the emotional exorcism of my old self, creating the new *ME*. That was definitely taxing to one's physical well-being. I spent four days holed up in my house with my pup, loving on him and resting. I needed to allow myself time to slowly creep back into my reality with tons of self-care. For example, I probably did about ten sheet masks on my face to rehydrate my worn-out skin from traveling and all that makeup. Yep, every actress has about a dozen or so products on her face at one time. Got to say though, since TikTok, eight-part nighttime skin routines are now the norm. Man, when I was a teen, I was lucky if I even washed my face and put on moisturizer. The obsession with perfect skin started for me as soon as my face appeared on that camera. I have plucked, filler-ed, scrubbed, and buffed my way toward that unrealistic vision of female perfection. On top of that full-blown reset and glow up, I did a nice three-day cleanse with Glowing Green smoothie from Kimberly Snyder to really clean out my system. I medi-tated twice a day for twenty minutes. I really honored myself when I came back, making sure not to rush back into the mad-ness of getting the next job, having to show up for this/that event. I just cocooned myself in my home, only listening to SLAA meetings on Zoom.

Makes you want to throw up, right? Sounds so healthy and stable. The Brady Bunch of boring, I get it. I'm bored even telling you about my homebody activities of self-care. I sound like a very balanced individual—which I was not. I was learn-ing new tools to help myself be more sane, but not completely normal. So don't worry your little heads.

I was still an incredibly flawed work in progress.

After those couple days of recharging my life force, it seemed things had started to reveal themselves in my life. Definite shifts were coming since my Dark Night of the Soul. That moment was like an enormous earthquake. We're talking an 8.5. And soon after an earthquake comes... that's right, the aftershocks. There was a series of signs telling me I needed to reexamine once again what was *off* in my universe to allow me to get in the space for that slip. It was a nasty wake-up call. It was certainly time to re-group and revisit all areas of my life. *ONCE AGAIN!*

Got to tell you, it was not always enjoyable to be this aware. A part of me missed the old days when I did not care and was blind to my own humanity. Now, I was in tune with myself, so much so that I couldn't ignore that nagging voice telling me that something was amiss. That intuitive voice tell-ing me it was time to move forward or be stuck where I was. That was precisely what I was doing as I emerged from my cocoon to participate in the world.

The first stop on my tour of *What the Fuck Needs to Shift* was to visit my favorite individual, Alice. We met at our usual spot, AKA her living room on the bohemian rugs before her wood-burning fireplace, of which I was totally jealous since there weren't many of them left in the city of Los Angeles.

I loved me a sexy-smelling fireplace, which was equally romantic and dangerous. It made me think of that fantasy of living in a log cabin in the middle of nowhere, when a stranger shows up stranded in a snowstorm. We both are invariably— due to inclement weather and sudden lack of cell service— holed up alone in a log cabin. Stuck in the woods with no communication with the outside world and only enough food and water to survive. Admittedly, we realize that we can't stand each other, and the fighting becomes unbearable. We are silent for days but also sneaking forbidden looks whenever we have to bathe in the sink. Then the lights suddenly go out on the third night, and the heat from the fire is our only warmth. So, we have to sit close and use our body heat to keep warm. Then it happens: He accidentally brushes my nipple when he turns, and it is officially on. It is every Hallmark movie before the PG rating shifts to R.

INT. HALLMARK CABIN IN THE WOODS—NIGHT

ROXIE and BROCK are strangers who are stranded together due to inclement weather and sudden lack of cell service. He is a carpenter, well versed in wood and building, while she is a real estate developer, out of her element.

                    ROXIE
          I'm scared.

                    BROCK
          I'll throw another log on the
          fire.

The wood crackles with heat. Roxie and Brock's chemistry crackles as well, but neither will admit it. The weather is freezing outside,

but the cabin is so hot that Roxie wears
panties and a see-through T-shirt, while Brock
wears long johns and no shirt, his six-pack
illuminated by the fire.

                    BROCK
          Do you want some more wine,
          Rox?

                    ROXIE
          Just a smidge, but you know I
          hate you, Brock.

                    BROCK
          I hate you too, Roxie. There
          is nothing in the world that
          could change my mind.

Suddenly, the lights go out. Brock and Roxie
instinctively grab each other and start having
animalistic sex. In the throes of passion…

                    BROCK
          I love you, Roxie.

                    ROXIE
          I love you too, Brock.

Okay, maybe a fireplace would be a bad idea for me. Probably not a good idea for me to buy a house with a wood-burning fireplace in Big Bear anytime soon. *I got off on a tad of a
tangent there. My bad!*

Back to reality and my check-in with Alice—not roman-
ticizing the wood-smelling fireplace anymore, damn it. "I
just feel stuck with my progress in the program," I explained,
mid-sentence to her, as she finished setting down her nasty
green tea.

Alice replied, "I get it. I felt like that after the first couple
years. Like I had done the steps, worked with sponsees, etc.
Now what?"

I looked at her with love. "This dating thing is hard enough. I need to try something new, I think. But I don't know what. You?"

She bowed her head and hesitated for a moment before gently advising, "Maybe it's time to shake things up and get a new sponsor, start working the steps with them? I had to do that with my sponsor after my seventh year in the program. I'd gotten what she was offering and needed something different."

I looked at her, immediately heartbroken. "Wait! Are you breaking up with me?"

She roared a deep guttural laugh. "No, Roxie, I am just trying to help you look for the next step in your growth. It's okay if I don't sponsor you anymore. We are more like friends now anyway. It would make sense, if you think about it."

I sat there in silence with an enormous sense of loss. Oh my gosh, I'd never thought this day would come. "I thought we would be going to meetings together till we were old and gray with too much arthritis in our bodies and vaginas to act out."

She giggled at my nastiness. "I love you, girl. We can still do that, but now I can just be your friend and fellow. I think it's the perfect situation. Plus, you need more time than I'm available for. I have a lot of stuff going on with the wedding and my own fears. It would be nice to share with you. To be honest, I feel at times like I don't tell you things going on with me and I put on a front because I want you to think I have my crap all together. But gosh, I don't."

Man, a new realization of our relationship had just opened my eyes. This whole time, I had thought we shared everything with each other when in fact, she had been with-holding from me. I didn't want that in the slightest; I wanted an equal friendship with her. "Alice, I did not know that. You can tell me anything. I could never think less of you. Hell, you know all the shameful, horrible things I've done in my addiction. There is no way you can make me think anything but greatness about you. You are my tribe. I need you."

She hugged me with so much force it knocked me over, and we fell back on the floor with her on top of me. I said stiffly, "Awkward, much? Too much intimacy—get off me. And you are not my type. I want to be close but not THAT close."

She hit me, rolling off on her side. "Okay, so it's settled. I dumped your ass?"

I flicked her off in protest but reluctantly agreed. "Yep. I've been broken up with once again." My heart did break a little after I said it aloud. I'd never had a healthy breakup like this. Even though she was still in my life, change is always hard in any relationship.

Rule 17: Getting dumped sucks—nevertheless, embrace the change!

"Oh good," Alice said, "because I'm struggling over here. I need to vent. I'm freaking scared to get married and it not working out, like my parents' marriage. I'm scared he will not be truly available, or even worse, change after we get married. I'm scared I have this fantasy in my head that I'm holding onto that I need everything to be perfect. Or that it will mean God really does not want me to be happy. I'm scared the other shoe will drop if I'm not perfectly on my game. I feel weak. I'm about to lose my shit. I feel like I'm about to have a massive anxiety attack planning this wedding. Help!"

Alice was starting to hyperventilate, and I knew I had to help her before she had a full-blown panic attack. "Jumping jacks! Ten fast jumping jacks, quickly. Right now!"

I ran into the kitchen and looked for a paper bag like I had seen in the movies, but then I remembered Dr. Kath telling me that the best thing for a panic attack is a bowl of ice water to dunk your face in. Not finding any ice in the freezer, I tried to emulate what I had seen them do in airplane demonstrations.

I grabbed her an old brown Vons shopping bag, which was way too big, but it was the only option. I told her to breathe in and out to calm down. I gently patted her head like my mother used to do when I was sick, which always gave me a lot of comfort. But Alice suddenly grabbed my hand and pulled it away.

"Stop, Roxie. My hair is greasy."

I was taken aback by her bluntness, a side of her I had never seen before. "Oh. Okay. Sorry."

She quickly apologized. "No, I'm sorry. I'm just feeling very vulnerable and kind of prickly right now. I want to crawl out of my skin."

I could easily identify. "Gotcha. I've felt that way too. It will be okay. You are just having feelings. Like my old sponsor, Alice, would tell me. You might know her—she's pretty cool, though a bit of a bridezilla..."

She laughed. Her breath started to regulate as I continued, "Anyway, this chick Alice would tell me, 'You can get through this, just one foot in front of the other, one day at a time, or even one minute at a time. You got this. You have been through worse.'"

I smiled warmly at her, and she looked back at me, and then it hit me: We were going to be friends for life. This was not a horrible breakup that I would be knocked down by. This was another beautiful ending that was a transition from one form of connection to another. I was being dumped but at the same time promoted to another position in her life. She was not going anywhere. I could be her rock now, like she had been mine for the last two years. As we hugged goodbye, it felt more intimate. Which meant scarier for a woman who was afraid of real intimacy.

I drove away from her home in Studio City to the other side of the hill, singing "All My Friends" by Counting Crows, belting out my sorrows around letting go of my attachment to the old relationship, and I just really wanted to get home and kiss my dog for comfort. Mostly because of the feelings that were arising about the end of this stable kind of relationship. The swift abandonment leading to the sudden change in our dynamic began to overwhelm me. The tears started to spring from my eyeballs.

I abruptly pulled off to the side of the road on Laurel Canyon, threw my car into park, and bent my head over in my lap. Grabbing my chest as a touch of pain started to emerge. I actually sat there for what felt like forever, holding onto my heart. Then the words escaped from my mouth, "Ouch, that hurts."

I allowed the tears of letting go to overtake me. Holding my heart and swiping my eyes, I sat in that fetal position and allowed myself the grace to feel my feelings. Those feelings of loss were usually pushed down and masked by a penis or flirting with the drive-through guy, but I sat in them and felt the discomfort. I literally held myself and tried to vibrate self-love into my heart. I breathed in and out. This moment was why I was afraid of change and usually stayed in relationships long after they were over. It was why I refused to look at the reality of the situation at hand. This pain I was feeling right now scared the utter crap out of me. I would constantly hold onto people to keep from feeling this kind of moment. Because, man, change fucking hurts. Hurts like a son of a bitch. I believe this "letting go" pain is what we addicts are always running from when we don't want to feel.

But I knew better and would do better.

The pain finally subsided, and the truth was revealed. A wave of determination washed over me to proactively move forward with finding a new sponsor and starting down a new path. You know—that moment we all have in our lives when it hits us: I'm going to be okay. I can get through this. I breathed and realized I was taken care of, even when it looked like the worst thing had just happened—not that I'd made Alice my

God, but she was my guide. Losing her in that position gave me small pangs of anxiety, but I had been through worse losses. Even though she was my compass in this journey, she was not filling that role anymore. On top of that loss, I had to freaking start dating again in this god-awful town. Thoughts of How? Who? Where? Why? When? swirled in my brain. Then my words of wisdom to Alice came back to haunt me—I can get through this, just one foot in front of the other, one day at a time, or even one minute at a time. You got this. You have been through worse. Look at that inner wisdom!

I smirked to myself as I lifted my head, and then the answer appeared from the universe. Right in front of my car was a beautiful yellow butterfly fluttering her colorful wings, giving me the strength to move forward one step at a time.

"Thank you," I said out loud, staring at the graceful dance of her wings in front of my windshield. As soon as she appeared, she flew away. Grinning, I put my car into drive and wiped my eyes. "I get it. Thanks for the beautiful message. I needed that badly." Memories of my caterpillar/butterfly-quote mug from my first year of sobriety flooded me with gratitude: "Just when the caterpillar thought the world was over, she became a butterfly." Witnessing the butterfly was another God shot. Reminder: That's when God puts something blatantly obvious smack-dab in front of you to hammer it in, hoping you finally receive his message.

I was clearly being reminded that I had been through much worse and had grown from it for the better. I could get through this shift in my relationship with Alice. As I pulled into my driveway, guess whose car was parked on the street in front of my cul-de-sac? Tattoogirl's. As I hesitantly got out of my car, she got out of hers. She was decked out in all her finest wares, with a floor-length black leather coat to make a very dramatic impact. But I could immediately see the visible chinks in her armor. There were mascara streaks down her face, and she was a hot mess—and I mean that in the kindest way. She looked like she had gained some weight and seemed kind of out of it.

"Hey," I said, as I grabbed my purse and walked toward her. "Good to see you. It's been a while."

She said sheepishly, "I know. I was a total ass last time we saw each other. I've been wanting to call you and apologize for being a shitty friend this past year. And that night I left was one of the worst I have ever had. I'm sorry."

I nodded and accepted her apology. "Thanks. That was really hard for me too." We stood in silence as I tried to let go of my stubbornness of being right. "Listen, I should have just let you go. It's not my business what you do with your life. And it was wrong of me to hold onto your bag. I felt really horrible about that, too. Can I please pay for the repair?"

She nodded vigorously. "Hell yeah, that shit is expensive. That's why I'm here. It was two grand!"

I blanched, doing a quick mental inventory of how the hell I was going to come up with $2,000 that quickly, when she started to giggle.

"I'm kidding! I sold it. I couldn't look at it anymore without thinking about our fight. Plus, I needed the money for tuition and getting a new place. Douchebag ex-husband still has not settled the divorce. I hate him." She stepped forward and I saw something different in my friend. She looked so hollow, even more so than the last time I saw her. "You mind if I come in? Baby boy is with the dad, and I don't want to be alone at our new place."

Dog was going ballistic at the front window—I always thought he was going to break the glass. He was probably dying to go out and wanting to pee on the floors. "Yeah, come on in. I need to get him out."

As soon as I opened the door, my shitty dog went straight to Tattoogirl and ditched giving his mom love. Man, getting rejected even sucks when it's your own dog whom you feed, bathe, and take care of. *What a dick!* I abruptly got on the ground to try to make him give me the love I deserved, like the needy girl I was. But he just jumped into Tattoogirl's arms and licked her face. I was now on all fours, looking up at both of them with disdain.

I slowly stood up as Dog jumped down from Tattoogirl's arms and ran past me to the back door in the kitchen to go out. I yelled at him with humor, "You're a dick, Dog. I am going to send you to the glue factory."

Here's a little insight: Tattoogirl was obsessed with dogs. Like, she would get on the floor and let any dog lick her face. Gross, right? That's a big HELL NO, for me over here! I only let MY dog do that in my mouth. But she had no fear or boundaries when it came to a pup walking down the street with its owner. She would literally run across the street to see a puppy or throw her car into park, jump out to scratch a dog's ears, which was sweet at times, when you weren't in a hurry. But also, kind of nuts too! Got to love her for her childlike obsession with dogs.

She set her stuff down on the kitchen counter like old times as I grabbed us some glasses of water. "So how has it been?" I asked casually, as I didn't want to dig too deep and get into her business. Trying to stay out of other people's drama was hard work, especially since my whole job thrived on theatrics.

She dropped her head. "He broke up with me again. I just don't want to be alone. I hate my new place—it's so lonely there. I feel like I'm always picking the worst guys for me. I don't know why I do that."

I smiled at her. "Yeah, you do. Bunch of dicks, just like my dog. They say when you keep picking the wrong people to date, it's like you're painting the red warning flags into white. We ignore the signs that they're not good for us. You think you do that?"

She looked at me like I was a moronic asshole who had just asked if the sky was blue. "Of course I do that. Duh! It just feels like me against the world right now. I'm tired, and I feel like I have lost my ability to make good choices and have no control over myself. I say no, then I do yes."

She leaned down and put her chin on the counter, staring off into space. She looked tired and worn. I had never seen my girl looking so empty. I knew I had to make her feel better. "Look, Tattoogirl, I feel like I was always doing that with all the guys I was seeing. And I was lying too. I was trying to soothe something in me, wanting someone to please make me feel better. Almost pushing others to the limit to fix me. I was exhausted, too." I paused, then added some other thoughts that popped into my head. "I always felt like I was trying to upgrade to my next partner. Like the person was never enough, no matter what they did or did not do."

"Exactly! That's what I was just saying to my assistant about why I got divorced." Her response was the most animated I had seen yet. She put her head down again, talking into the counter. "Will I ever find enough love?"

I sat down next to her, replying with brutal honesty. "Hell, if I know. I just started to see things clearly. Who knows? But I know what I was doing was killing me, so I'd rather try to find real connection than keep doing the same thing expecting different results."

She stated abruptly, "Getting dumped sucks!"

I let out a blubber. "Yeah, it fucking does. Sucks badly. My sponsor just broke up with me too. It sucks. Now I need to go find another one fast before I slip again."

She looked up at me. "What happened?"

I reluctantly admitted, "I slept with West on location. It was bad."

She gave me a fast hug, because she knew I was allergic to affection. "Sorry, friend, both of those sound harsh."

I stood up with determination. "That's why we are going to a meeting. We both need it. Addicts hate connection, and that is what we get in the rooms, plus my bond with my God has wavered. I need a recharge. Join me?"

She hated the twelve-step rooms with so much passion that I could see in her face how she was scrambling to find a way out. But I was not taking no for an answer. "You are coming. We both need some clarity."

As I was forcing my friend to join me, I got a text out of the blue from Glamgirl. *I'm telling you, when it rains, it pours, people.* Her text read, "Girl, I'm filing for divorce, dumping his lying ass. He is on the apps again, talking to another girl. I am lost about what to do."

I texted her back, "Where ya at? I can swing by your house and pick you up if you're at home. My friend Tattoogirl and I are going to a meeting near you. Join?"

She replied in a matter of seconds. "Yes. I have to get out of this house. I'm about to lose it."

Ironically and hilariously, my two friends and I were all dealing with some sort of breakup situation. I just knew, very simply, that the best way to get out of suffering was to be of service to others. In terms of service, I would be driving all of our broken love-addict butts to the meeting, which always helped me when I was hurting and heartbroken from loss. Even if neither of them were ready or willing to admit to their love-addicted ways, I would hold that space for them. There is a saying in the rooms that we show the way without any expectations: "If you don't want what I have, I don't have to give it to you."

All I knew was that I desperately needed a meeting; with or without them, I was going. Meetings were sometimes the bridge to being seen and getting more connected to the world. Without them, I often fall back into myself and my addiction.

I picked up a still very angry Glamgirl and drove down the 101, I felt like I'd been thrust into the *Twilight Zone* of bitter, enraged women. They were both going off on their partners— *Screw him. He sucks. You deserve better. You don't need him, divorce his ass. He said what?* And on and on. A big piece of me wanted to point out their roles in the matter, but I was fully aware that this would have been a truly idiotic move on my part. They didn't want to hear it. They weren't ready to listen to it. I needed to bite my tongue, stay in my lane, and just drive my car.

I truly believe there are two sides to every bad relationship. I believe we all play a factor in every situation. We all act out our parts, and the only way to change the dynamic of any relationship is to look closely at our side and make amends to alter the future partnership. Honestly, some people are not supposed to stay in your life forever—they come and go to teach us lessons— so even if it is a horrible coupling, there are always benefits to take away from that toxic relationship. Instead, Tattoogirl and Glamgirl were both feeding off of each other's outrage, and I didn't have a death wish. I would never step into that lion's den. The claws were out, the teeth were bared, and I didn't want to get scratched or bit. I was more than content to simply be the chauffeur. *The very quiet chauffeur.*

We walked into the meeting and took our seats in the back since Glamgirl refused to sit up front. I think she was afraid to be recognized. I get it, especially since she was way more famous than I was. Tattoogirl couldn't give two shits. She immediately started to look around the room, then leaned into Glamgirl and said in a hushed voice, "He's cute."

Man, you couldn't stop an addict even if you tried; they were shifty. I shook my head in astonishment. "Lady, keep it in your pants." Thankfully, after her side-eye look toward me, the meeting started. And this group's topic from the *SLAA Daily Reader* was, shockingly—*not making this shit up*— RECONCILIATION. Can you believe it? I freaking couldn't. I burst out laughing, and everyone looked at me like I was a nutjob.

A brief sample of the reading: "Reconciliation can be a difficult subject for sex and love addicts in recovery. Sober addicts wonder if they are going back to their disease behaviors if they reconcile with their past partner or friendships. There needs to be a lot of soul searching before you go back to that old relationship. Were the foundations of the relationship basically good? Was it an equal partnership? Did the relationship give you room to grow as a person? Was it just that our disease got in the way and messed everything up? Or was the relationship fatally flawed and toxic?"

I was in shock with that reading. It pointed out to me that my disease had gotten in the way of my relationship with Alice, and I would ensure that the next sponsor–sponsee relationship would be different. The bigger revelation was that West and I had never grown with each other; in fact, none of my relationships had been foundations for growth. I had to start anew with this healthy dating. I had to get back up on that horse. Looking at both Glamgirl and Tattoogirl as they listened to others share about their successes and struggles, I could see their eyes glazing over.

Ugh, another waste of my time.

See, I'd still made it about me, damn it. I needed to realize that taking someone to a meeting meant I couldn't place a single expectation on them. That wasn't fair to either of us.

I once read this cool quote from an unknown source on Pinterest: "Someone asked me, 'Who hurt you?' I replied, 'My own expectations.'"

Genius, right? Pretty straightforward where most of our letdowns and pain come from. *From us!* And yes, I love Pinterest! I'm a regular browser of the app when on the toilet when that burrito hits. And especially when waiting to be called into an audition room—it sometimes helps the nerves subside to focus on the year's trending haircuts because you hate your hair, or those Freebird boots you're coveting and can't afford. You get it—it's a great tool to distract yourself. Thank you, inventors of Pinterest, and to the millions of subscribers for posting on their personal boards. Bravo for creating another way to disconnect from our mundane lives. Another way of not staying with our feelings while living in our reality. *Sarcasm at its best! I'm guilty just as much as the next person.*

The meeting was still going on when I was snapped back into the present by the voice of Tattoogirl. I had no idea what others had said, but she started her share by saying, "I have my shit together in most areas of my life. I am a strong, powerful woman. That is what I talk about when I go to fashion events—being a feminist. But really, I am obsessed and addicted to men on Instagram. I know, I should probably not date all these douches, but I love the attention. I can't stop going back to the worst one. I found out last night at an art show that he was with another girl. I saw them at the show, and he hugged her. We got in a huge fight in front of his fans and friends. I'm so embarrassed that I let him get to me again and treat me so badly. I was also embarrassed that I made a scene. I am just so tired of the back-and-forth. I know we don't have a great relationship, and we bring out the worst in each other, but I can't stop wanting him. What is wrong with me? I feel so lost that I feel like I might die either way, whether I go back or don't go back." She added at the end of her very powerful share, "It's so strange to me, too, that a lot of you say you're grateful sex and love addicts. I don't want to be here. I don't want to be a sex and love addict." The alarm went off; her time was done. The leader asked if there were any more newcomers who wanted to share. And wouldn't you know it, Glamgirl raised her hand.

Jackpot! Bullseye! We got my homegirls opening up.

Glamgirl opened her mouth, and a barrage of emotions came tumbling out all at once. "It's difficult for me to be here, to really look at my marriage and see the mess I've made of my life. I tend to just put a pretty filter over it and smile through the discomfort. I tend to plan a job or say yes when things are really bad, so I don't have to physically be at home to deal with the truth of our relationship. Then I just smooth it over by blaming my husband and not myself. It's exactly what my mom did when she was married to my father. He was very unavailable, and she wore a perfectly plastered smile across her face, and not a hair out of place. She was an expert on the disguise of the perfect wife and the misnomer that it's always the man's fault. Now, with my husband being dishonest again, I'm reeling with anger and self-blame. I'm all over the place. I obviously struggle to forgive my husband for his cheating, but now I feel like I'm starting to struggle to forgive myself for turning a blind eye. Also, I have a secret that no one knows. I have cheated on him too. I cheated in revenge, so I feel like I can get away with it. I have not told a soul until now. I rented a male prostitute when I was working in Vegas last year. After everything I went through with my husband, I wanted to see how it felt."

The timer went off. She stopped suddenly and looked at me in confusion. I said, "You still have one minute."

She turned back to the small room of fellow addicts and continued to build up more courage as she added, "Now I think I'm filing for divorce from him for his secrets, but can I do that if I have one? It is my secret. It was my secret. I guess it's no longer a secret. I can't believe I just shared it. But I have to tell you, it was the best five hundred dollars I have ever spent. I got fucked every way possible by this male escort.

I probably came about three times. And they were three excellent orgasms. Seriously, it was the best gift I've ever given myself. I have his number in my phone as 'The Cleaner.' Hubby still has never found out, so screw him."

The timer went off as hands flew up for her to stop talking. That can happen when you trigger others; that's the thing with SLAA meetings, you can't be too descriptive about your acting out. *Whoops, my bad for not telling her!* I leaned over and whispered in her ear, "Too graphic, girl. We can't say any sexual details."

She replied, "That's the stupidest freaking thing I have ever heard. It's a meeting about sex and love. But OKAY. Whatever."

I reminded myself that she was in pain and this was her first time, and to cut her some slack.

Got to tell you, that meeting had exhausted me. I happily dropped Glamgirl off at her house and was on my way back to my pad with Tattoogirl. As I made it down Laurel Canyon, Tattoogirl started crying in the front seat while fixing her makeup using the visor mirror. "You are such an inspiration to me, Roxanne. I see how much you have changed and you seem more at peace with yourself. I want that, but I don't know how to get there. I'm trying my best, but I'm not as strong as you are."

I reached over and placed my hand on her knee. "You are girl. You are a very strong, capable woman. You are talented and have been through some stuff, but you made it to the other side. Don't let this asshole take you down. It's not even about him. It's about loving yourself, lady."

She broke down even more while applying her red lipliner. "But I don't love myself. I have never loved myself. Even when I was a little girl, I hated being me. I wanted to be like my sisters. They were so much better, and my mom paid more attention to them."

She shared more details, many of which I had not heard before in our ten years of friendship. "My mom was cruel to me. She told me I looked just like my father and would give me a hard time, saying, 'Don't be like that jerk. He is worthless and a loser.' I feel now like I have become him. Yes, I'm more driven, but I am an addict just like him and screwed up my marriage and now career. And the guy I love just broke up with me for the hundredth time. I can't do this anymore. I feel like I can't take another heartache."

She wiped her eyes as I pulled into the driveway. "I really don't want to die over this guy. But it feels like I am. I'm scared to be alone, Rox. I can't be alone."

I held her hand to give her strength. "You are alone even when you're with him. He was never really there, because he's also broken and unavailable just like you. Being in a relationship like that is more painful than being physically alone. I promise."

She climbed down from my Range Rover, grabbed her purse, and started heading to her car. "I don't know, Rox. I don't think I'm as strong as you, but I'm glad I came to the meeting. I really dig Glamgirl, too. We should all hang out."

I smiled and waved bye. "We should. She's a supportive woman—I adore her. Drive safely. Text me when you get home."

I walked into the dark house with Dog barking at my heels. I picked him up and gave him so much unconditional love. I said aloud to the empty kitchen, "I am grateful for this safe space. I am grateful for my healing and my sobriety. I am grateful to let go of all that no longer serves me."

I grabbed a couple slices of pepperoni, string cheese, and some crackers for a makeshift meal. Don't judge, I didn't have time for dinner and was starving. I ate my mini pizza crackers and made my way into my bathroom to start a bath and soak the day off. As I pulled my maxi dress over my head and climbed into the hot water to submerge my lingering sadness over parting ways with Alice, the phone beeped on the toilet across the room.

Figuring it was just the text message from Tattoogirl saying she got home safely, I ignored it to enjoy my time alone to recharge. As the bubbles burst in the tub, I felt my body relax, thoughts of the last fourteen hours playing over in my head. Clarity emerged—that our ideas are so limited by our perception of ourselves, our circumstances, and the world. The nature of the situation lives beyond our ego and our fears. It is only in surrendering our idea of "the breakup," and the way we believe things ought to be, that we begin to glimpse the way things actually are and start living in that reality.

Toweling off, I applied my Jamaican lotion, then looked down at Dog and realized I had forgotten to take him out. Sometimes I am so self-involved. Grabbing my robe and the leash, I took off into the dark to let my baby relieve himself. I know, not the safest move to walk around in a robe in a city like Los Angeles, but I could be idiotic at times. Thankfully, nothing happened as I got back to my house and locked all the doors with gusto. I gave Dog his treat, and just as I'd made my way back to my bedroom, I remembered that my phone was still sitting on the edge of the toilet.

I grabbed my iPhone with half-closed lids, since the heat from the bath and jet lag were still making me beyond exhausted. I looked down at the four missed texts. Three were from Tattoogirl and one was from Glamgirl, but they were not what I'd expected.

Tattoogirl's texts:

"I'm sorry, Roxie. I'm not like you."

"I can't be alone. I'm headed over to Fuckface's house."

"Please don't be disappointed in me."

Glamgirl's text:

"You won't believe it, Rox. When I got home, he had roses covering the whole house and a private chef cooking us a delicious dinner. There was even a new diamond ring since I threw my ring in the toilet. He pulled out all the stops to say he was sorry for his indiscretion. The best part, the kids are with our in-laws for the whole night. I mean, come on. He is so sorry. I believe him this time. Thanks again for taking me to the meeting. It's not my thing. But proud of you. Love you, girl. Got to go. He just started the hot tub. Nite, nite."

I hung my head in defeat once again. After crawling under my sheets with Dog, I turned on my bedside lamp and stared at the phone. Hovering my fingers over the keys, I was stumped about how to respond.

As I lay there looking up at the swirling ceiling fan, these quotes came back from my last Pinterest search on the toilet. I have no idea who wrote them, so sorry if you're not getting credit, but I looked and could not find the authors. But they are true geniuses, so I typed the words into one group text thread.

"Stop looking for happiness in the same place you lost it."

"Be strong enough to let go and wise enough to wait for what you deserve."

"Because you will not heal by going back to what broke you."

As I hit send, a little prayer came into my head to help them let go of their toxic heartbreakers. I turned off my lamp, drowning myself in darkness, and gently hugged my pup, hoping my friends would be released from their breakup scenarios once and for all, to finally embrace their real changes. To meet their true selves. Change is scary, especially when it is good for us.

But if nothing ever changed, there'd be no butterflies. We'd all still be caterpillars. Butterflies are not called butterflies overnight—they have to undergo tons of changes to acquire the name.

So don't be afraid to embrace your change.

CHAPTER NINE

Rule 18: Hell will come even if you are not calling.

GOD CAME BLARING INTO my head this morning, "Buckle up, Roxanne. Things are about to get bumpy. Hell is upon you." I felt a strange feeling. You know that feeling when you know something is wrong, but you have no idea what it is? That niggling itch in the bottom of your stomach that says something is amiss, but you can't put your finger on it. It was one of those kinds of feelings. Some say your intuition knows when the shit is about to hit the proverbial fan.

And my intuition was spot-on.

Like most addicts, I usually ignored those tiny warnings in my body. So, I initially ignored it. The morning was uneventful. I went to the bathroom and let my pup out to release his bladder as well. I hit my espresso machine to churn out a double shot of morning love. I looked at my little book of quotes and read, "The devil doesn't come to you with his red face and horns, he comes to you disguised as everything you've ever wanted," by the enlightened Oscar Auliq-Ice.

Looking back, if I had gotten everything I had ever wanted, I would definitely be my version of Satan, which would include being a horrible, selfish human being. It simply means that when evil is upon you, it won't look like evil; it will always disguise itself as the good you want and need, and you won't see the truth until the damage is already done. Other quotes similar to this one that I enjoy using as inspiration when my vanity or ego wants to run the show: "The devil won't show his horns until they've stabbed you," and "The devil hides himself in sheep's clothing." But I digress.

To recap: pooped, walked, had my coffee, read. Just another typical Tuesday.

Then all hell broke loose when I picked up my phone after taking a big gulp of my coffee and saw the twelve missed phone calls and thirty-six unread messages. What the fuck had happened? I opened my phone as fast as I could, after three tries to get my lock code entered correctly. That's when I saw it. I read the article headline that a number of loved ones had sent me — "Double murder! In Echo Park! A man and a woman! Stabbed and strangled!"

As I scanned the article, trying to put the pieces of the puzzle together, my heart quickly broke in half: "Police are investigating a Romeo and Juliet murder-suicide between a couple in Echo Park. Famous stylist to the stars found dead with her estranged boyfriend this early morning at their home."

It was Tattoogirl. I couldn't speak.

I dropped to the ground. I was paralyzed with shock. I felt numb even when Dog climbed into my lap. I looked down at him, his puppy-dog brown eyes staring back up at me, and I lost it. I was flooded with a barrage of feelings. Guilt. Shame. Sadness. Loss. Anger, and Emptiness. I heard my phone ringing beside me, but could not move my hand to pick it up. I was stuck in that position, crying with a depth of pain I'd never thought I could experience. I wanted to hurt someone just as badly as I was hurting. I found myself screaming out to my God with so much anger. *Fuck you! Why couldn't you stop her from going back to him? Why couldn't you help her like you helped me? She has a son! Why couldn't I save her? Why couldn't she just listen to me? Why??*

As I screamed out to the Universe, Dog got scared and ran into the other room to hide under the bed. Meanwhile, I curled up into a little ball and cried my soul out. I lay there for at least an hour, the phone beeping and ringing in the background. It was almost like I was physically stuck in that position and could not move even if I had wanted to. I just wanted her back. I wanted to hug her and reassure her that she could get through this breakup. I wish I could have chained her up in my guest bedroom and kept her there till she got better. I wish I had done a ton of things differently. Even thinking this, I realized none of that would have made a difference. You can't save someone if they don't want to be saved. Intellectually, I knew this, but emotionally, I was going into myself to place blame. I just wanted my friend back. And she was never coming back.

That's when the doorbell rang. I barely heard it over the thoughts spinning in my head. It was only Dog's bark that snapped me back into the present. As I pulled myself up off the kitchen floor, I asked who was at the door.

"It's the police. We need to talk to you."

"Can I see your badge and ask what this is about?" Even though I already knew, I had seen too many *Dateline* episodes not to do my due diligence for my own safety. I was broken, not idiotic. After they showed the badge through the chained door, they said it was about my friend's murder. I opened the door to two young officers and suddenly felt like I was acting in a TV show.

If you knew how many cop shows I've guest-starred on, you would understand why this feeling that I was on set came over me. I guess it was my way of dissociating from the pain of losing my dear friend, especially to this disease. Any minute, I felt like they were going to call "cut" and have the police make a better entrance into the scene. Or the director would tell me to stop "ugly crying" and start to "pretty cry"—*yes, that's a thing*. I even found myself looking around to get touched up by my makeup person. I realize that I sound like I was losing it. I know that; I probably was. Especially because I tended to dissociate when the going got tough. And this situation was a minefield of bombs waiting to go off. Disconnection was the only tool I could pull out of my proverbial toolbox to deal with my friend's death. It was my only means for survival.

I had an out-of-body experience when they started to question me. Let's call the youngest gentleman Officer #1, like on a crime show. Officer #1 had a crew cut and looked like a military extra straight out of Central Casting.

"When was the last time you saw her?" he asked.

I replied nervously even though I'd done nothing wrong, "Last night around 9:30 p.m., after we went to a meeting with our friend Glamgirl."

"Do you have this Glamgirl's address?" Officer #2 was a tad chubby and looked like a wrestler. I gave him the address, which I will not share with you in order to protect Glamgirl. Then Officer #2 continued his line of questioning. "What was this meeting? And can you share that address too?"

I took a big breath, waiting for them to give me that look that all men had when I told them about my addiction. "We were at a SLAA meeting in the Valley. The church is off Noble. I will have to get the address from the website."

He looked at me blankly. "What is SLAA?"

Here we go. "It's a twelve-step program for sex and love addicts; it's called Sex and Love Addicts Anonymous, or SLAA. I took both Glamgirl and Tattoogirl because they were dealing with bad breakups. Obviously, it didn't help Tattoogirl." Tears started to form in my eyes as I felt the pain of my loss and failure. Self-blame is automatic when you're a codependent playing-God love addict. It was really the only option I was used to when I felt like I had failed a loved one. And I had indeed failed: I could not save her from herself. I was heartbroken as big fat tears poured down my face.

Officer #1 handed me a tissue from his pocket, kind of sweet and gross at the same time. Then he asked for some details about her behavior the night before.

"I don't know, she seemed tired and like she was willing to give him up. She had just moved to a new apartment with her son, since she was going through a bad divorce. She seemed ready to leave him and move on. But I could tell she was still struggling a little. That's why I made her go to the meeting with me. But I got a text from her last night, right when I was going to bed. I should have called her to stop her. But I was so tired with jet lag. I... I failed. I failed to stop her." There, I said it aloud, but it didn't make me feel any better or assuage any of my guilt. Instead, I hung my head in defeat and cried harder.

Officer #2 asked to see my phone. I handed it to him. As I waited, I wiped the boogers coming out of my nose and tried to hold it together.

He handed me back my phone. "Thank you. If we have any more questions, we will call."

As they were getting up, I bluntly asked, "How did she die? Did she suffer?" They looked at each other, not sure whether to tell me or not. I begged them, "Please. I have to know. We were friends for over ten years; her poor son." I wept as I stared at them, pleading with them to tell me.

Officer #1 cleared his throat. "No, she did not suffer. She shot herself in the head. It was quick and painless—they are pretty sure of that."

I gasped. "Oh my god. I thought he killed her."

I looked at them, wanting them to explain more. Officer #1 continued, "No, she killed him. There were strangle marks on her neck and cuts on her knuckles and elbows, so we figured there was a fight between them. But she shot him and then shot herself. That's what the forensics are telling us."

Rule 18: Hell will come even if you are not calling.

At a loss for words, I nodded that I understood and I felt my knees get wobbly underneath me. Officer #2 grabbed my elbow to steady me. "Are you going to be okay? Can you call someone to come be with you? It might be a good idea to have family around."

"My family lives in Atlanta. But I will call my sponsor," I said, not remembering in the moment that Alice was technically no longer my sponsor.

They nodded and turned to walk back to their police cruiser. Officer #1 turned around and asked me one more question. "Did she tell you who the father was?"

"Huh? What do you mean?"

He looked at Officer #2 and sighed with a *Shit, I just let the cat out of the bag.*

"Wait. She was pregnant?"

He hung his head. "Regrettably, yes. Looks like she was fourteen weeks pregnant. She didn't tell you?"

Another wave of sadness consumed me. That poor baby would never see the light of his mother's love. I looked at them like I'd had enough truth for a lifetime. "Thank you for telling me. I'll reach out if I remember anything else."

As I shut the door, a flash of our last fight overtook me—when she drove away, going back to that horrible guy she could not let go of. And it had killed her. Her qualifier had literally killed her. She went mad over his unavailability and mental abuse.

"Sometimes we think we've been away from our toxic qualifier for so long that we can handle it again, or that they've changed, but we don't need to go back to relationships that caused us pain." Little did I realize the foreshadowing of that ironic statement in that dreaded morning meditation reading.

If only she could have read it.

If only, what if, and should have haunted me as I trudged back into my bedroom, shut all the curtains, and turned off all the lights. Crawling under my covers and throwing them over my head, I buried my sorrow in my pillow for the next week.

The ringing question in my head: How do you come back from the death of another sex and love addict?

Have you ever watched someone slowly kill themselves? I have. Over the last two years, I'd had a front-row seat to what this disease does to a person, watching Tattoogirl literally dying right in front of my eyes, and there was nothing I could do to stop it. When she actually passed, it was she who had caused all that pain. She was the one who murdered him, then took her own life. And I was so angry. As I was mourning her, I was also cursing her. *THIS DISEASE IS A DEADLY KILLER. WHY DID YOU NOT LISTEN TO ME?*

Whether you surrender or not, you either kill your old sense of self, or you literally die. The murder-suicide situation was not necessary at all. The fantasy I'd had with murder-suicide love, like in *Romeo and Juliet,* had woken me up. The fantasy bubble had finally been popped. She had lost herself in him, and he in her. They had officially tortured each other to death, and there was nothing I could do to stop that wreck from happening.

Not that it was about me at all, but my God had definitely proved to me that my idea of passionate, all-encompassing love was false; it was a movie script that was never going to have a happy ending. That twin-flames fantasy I'd had as a young girl was forever crushed, and I was forever grateful for that.

I know, it's wrong to be grateful for a death, but in my program, we try to find any little gratitude with big, horrible circumstances. It is sometimes the only way to get through a tragedy and stay sober. If not, you would easily find me back in a dirty hotel room with a dude I hated but wanted to angry-fuck. You know what I mean? Gratitude was the only way out for me. And prayer, of course, with lots of therapy.

After a week of the most painful mourning, I picked myself up and headed back to Dr. Kath's office across town. As I walked into her waiting room, Doppelgänger was there. AGAIN. But she looked different. Not exactly sure what it was, but if I had to guess, it would seem to be that she had a new nose and a matching pair of new tits, perky Cs. Good for her, if it made her happy. I had no desire to get my tiny boobs done, but I have had a nose job. Yep, admitting it right here in these pages of truth. Believe me, I needed it—my beak was too wide for the good old television roles. I was told a number of times to fix it. There was one occasion when I was shooting a guest-star role on a Western TV show and the flamboyant gay make-up artist took one look at my nose and told me, "Fix that nose, girl, or you will barely work in this town." And I did a year later. I saved up $7,000 and bought myself a new nose. It was a lot for a poor guest-star actress.

But it was worth it.

Okay, I can feel you judging me for succumbing to the film industry pressure, but I genuinely had always hated my nose and wanted it fixed.

Looks like old Doppelgänger got herself a little refresh. That's what happens to us ladies when we're reaching the age of thirty. We want to get ahead of those terrible HD televisions. Luckily, Doppelgänger's looked really natural. I wanted to praise her, but I also didn't want her to feel uncomfortable that I'd noticed the snip and lift. What to do? What would I want to hear?

"Good to see you. You look great. How have you been?" I said with a subtle grin.

She looked at me with the most joyful expression, which warmed my cold, dark heart since my friend's death. "Thank you so much. I have been using a new dermatologist and eating vegan. It has changed my whole being. I feel like a new woman."

The reaction I wanted to give her would not have been appropriate for my sobriety, like, "Bullshit, girl. Be honest. I see those new perky tits and nose." But instead, I just smiled back and nodded in agreement. Sometimes it's better to keep your mouth shut and not say anything at all.

Dr. Kath opened the door for me to enter her office. She had gotten a new haircut, it was shorter, a bob like mine. It felt a little *Single White Female*, not going to lie, but she was pulling it off. I told her as I planted my butt on her couch, "Like the new cut. Suits you."

"Thanks. The pink tips really dried out the ends; it was the only option." She lowered her eyes. "How are you doing? I'm so glad you're here."

I shook my head, no words coming out as I felt the emotion rising once more. It came in waves. After the initial shock had worn off, I'd spent the first two days crying nonstop. Then it subsided and it descended into sweeps of sadness and disbelief. That's why I'd dragged my ass here and planned to attend a meeting down the street right after. I knew if I didn't stay diligent with myself, I would find a way to justify ruining my life with an ex or even a brief hook-up with West again—not sure my self-esteem could handle another rejection by him. Anyone else, I would be fine with, but not him. He was my kryptonite. Everything else was a blur, but of that I was very certain.

I started to babble, "Screw it. Who cares, we all die anyway, right? I mean, I was starting to feel that way, lying in my bed for a week. Thought I'd better get my ass into your room pronto."

Dr. Kath agreed with me. "Good move on your part; that's a strong testament to your sobriety and willingness. Loss is very hard to process, especially under your circumstances. It could take even the sanest person down. How are your outreach calls?"

Outreach calls are when you call a bunch of people in your program to talk about your feelings, and they help you. It's a part of Step Twelve, giving back and using the program to help you understand that you're not alone in your pain. They are the most difficult calls for me to do. To call a stranger and tell them your problems and feelings over the phone. *Awkward*! I would rather drown in my sorrows or act out than call a stranger. But I know—this is one of the ways we connect and stay sober.

I kept babbling, "I called my old sponsor, Alice, and that was really it. I just have not felt like talking to anyone. Now I know I have to get back out into the world and learn to function again. I know I have to keep up with my sponsees, and Alice's wedding is around the corner. Honestly, another part of me doesn't want to do this anymore. Doesn't want to freaking deal with anything anymore. Doesn't want to live anymore— not that I want to commit suicide, I just feel empty at times, like, what's the point of living? Food doesn't even taste good to me anymore. I mean, I ate my favorite sushi rolls—they just tasted like cardboard. Then I tried to make some strawberry cupcakes like I had for my tenth birthday party, but after I baked them, I wasn't hungry and threw them away. I think I've lost five pounds for sure."

Dr. Kath reassured me, "That is a very normal reaction to the death of a loved one. You are not alone in those thoughts and feelings of 'What is the point of this life?' I hear it every day, so please don't go into the darkness of those thoughts. They will pass. But we should really buckle down with our sessions and you going to meetings. You need to reach out and stay connected, Roxanne. It's imperative to your health and sanity."

"I know. I was feeling that. I'm meeting my sponsee Eve after this, then hitting a meeting at four, but I know I should come in a couple times at least to see you. I know I need help. This pain..."

I stopped talking as the loss of my friend overwhelmed me in a rush once again. "I really miss her. I wish I could have saved her. A part of me feels like I failed her. And I know it's not my problem to fix another person, but I can't help but replay every conversation we had about her relationship with Fuckface; what I could have done differently. I know that's not healthy. That's why I called to see you."

Dr. Kath waited till I was done feeling my emotions of failure and pain. She held that space for me as I grieved. I really appreciated her handing me the box of tissues after I lifted the cover of her wicker tissue box and it was empty. Why would anyone need a cover for their Kleenexes? I didn't even own Kleenex anymore. I just used a roll of toilet paper, and not even the good toilet paper—I used the Scott's septic-tank kind since the pipes are old in my house. Plus, they are $15,000 to fix—no thank you!

Also—and I realize I'm on a tangent, but I just have to say—I hate soft quilted toilet paper. You know what I mean? Yes, it's soft, but it does not feel like it gets the job done. A doctor once asked me if I was a hard wiper. Funny, right? I answered her proudly, "I am a rough wiper." She said, "Yeah, that's not good for the skin around your anus."

"Gotcha, lady. Thanks for the tip," I replied with a thumbs-up. Appreciated her concern for my butthole, but all was good so far, and I'd never had a problem with my wiping techniques.

Off topic, my bad—just needed to put some levity in the situation. I was blowing my nose into my tissue when Dr. Kath cleared her voice with a cough. "You will feel better, Roxanne. You have been holding in a lot of your pain for a long time. We need to figure out a way for you to feel your feelings whenever they need to come out. The suppression of them is where the trauma stays in your body. That's where your addiction lives." She smiled at me, and I smiled back, feeling thirteen all over again.

"Let's do another exercise, shall we?"

Ugh. I did not love her exercises, I have to say. Once, I almost left and never came back when she made me put a crystal on my chakras and hum with her. Seriously, I almost leapt off the couch and ran out. But I kept telling myself to trust the process. Shockingly, the next day, my energy felt a huge shift. I was not so heavy anymore.

"Hit me with it, Doc," I said with as much gusto as I could muster after crying for ten minutes.

"Close your eyes and place your hands on your heart."

I smiled tightly with discomfort—no shocker there, I'm sure. I did as she asked.

She continued when I was in that position, "Let's speak to our higher self. Let's ask it what secrets you are hiding from yourself."

I opened my eyes and looked at her in uncertainty. "Dr. Kath, how can I tell you the secret I won't tell myself if I don't know it?"

She looked at me. "Trust, Roxanne, you got this. Please close your eyes."

She had been talking to me a lot about trust and trusting myself and not being so controlling and calculated. *Funny, right? Me? Calculated? HAHA.* Annoyed, I closed my eyes.

She started her weird sound machines and spritzed her chakras spray around my body.

I was stumped and tried to rack my brain for a secret I had never told myself. I seriously had no earthly idea if I had a secret hidden from me. She could probably see the tension in my face as my eyes were pinched together—well, at least as much as they could move, since I'd recently had Botox.

She stated very calmly, "Don't try to force the answer, Roxanne. Let it come to you. Try to clear your mind."

I relaxed my expression and felt my whole body let go. No idea I'd had that much stress in my shoulders. I cleared my mind as Dr. Kath's earthy voice gently instructed, "Let your thoughts flow in and out of your consciousness. When something pops in and feels right to share, just say it out loud. Let it go. I will start the drumming to help you clear your mind."

Not opening my eyes, I just nodded. Then the drumming began, and it was a bit intoxicating, even though this shit made me laugh.

It took me a good fifteen minutes to silence my brain. It was busy having a silent debate about when this was going to be over and if my big secret was that, in addition to mourning my friend, I was wondering if that hot dog stand nearby opened by 11:00 a.m.? *I loved their chili cheese dog with sweet potato fries. My mouth started to water as the drumming intensified.*

I stopped thinking about the hot dog and focused on Dr. Kath as she started moving around the room, drumming. My senses were on high alert. My mind was trying to make sense of all the thumping. That was when my inner child's secrets that I had stuck deep inside of me came out. I opened my mouth and from some unknown place the words sprang out, "Even with all this work on myself, I probably will screw it up by not ever fully loving myself."

The big guns then came into my consciousness, as I blurted out, "The true secret I feel is that I will never be cured of this. That deep down, I don't want to be."

Tears slid down my cheeks as she played her bowls on the table in front of me. The hypnotic sound calmed my heartbeat down.

I felt myself lighten. Dr. Kath stopped drumming.

"Great work, Roxanne. We are almost done with our session. You can open your eyes. Here's some alkaline water and tissues for you."

I drank a huge gulp of the water, which tasted just like normal water but whatever. I wiped my eyes, certain that I had black smudges all over. I had never learned not to wear eye makeup to therapy. You would think, knowing how many times I've cried my eyes out, I would come prepared at least with makeup-remover wipes, especially since I was meeting Eve afterward.

Dr. Kath snapped me back into the present. "I thought you really did some great work. I had a couple of thoughts sink into my consciousness when you were in the trance-like state. Would you like me to share?"

She was so kind. She would let me call the shots on whether I wanted to go deeper with her input or not. I had never heard of a therapist who did that. I'd always pictured someone telling me straight out what was wrong with me. *Even though she'd done that too.* But it seemed that with her body work, she was more considerate. "Of course, that's why I pay you the big bucks."

She smirked, which made me warm inside. I always got a hit of joy when I made her smile or laugh. I liked it when I accomplished the impossible. She was a hard nut to crack, very professional, and kept her boundaries around the therapist and client relationship, which I loved to try to break with my sarcastic remarks. Not until these last few months had I been able to get more information about her. I'd just found out she was in a serious commitment with a fella, and they were now engaged. *I felt like I had officially made it, now that I was in the inner world of Dr. Kath.*

The timer for the session went off, and she said quickly, "We can go over your time a tad today, if that's okay with your schedule." *The hot dog would have to wait.* I nodded, excited to hear how she thought I did. I hoped I got an A+ today, even though I was not in school—it would be nice for her to at least give me a gold star sticker, right?

Continuing her analysis, not realizing I was thinking about a cool-looking glitter star sticker, she slowly explained,

"I really want to share with you some insight into what I experienced today with your session. The truth is that the secret you won't tell others is usually something you're ashamed of or that you believe might weaken your position. What you just said to me about not wanting to really be sober and cured of this disease... The secret you don't tell yourself, Roxanne, is that you are fundamentally okay, and when you understand that, you might not need to be doing all the things you do that are creating conflict in your life. It's really that simple. You're okay just as you are. That's the real secret you are withholding from yourself."

I sat there confused and thought, SHIT, that is probably very true. We addicts are addicted to the drama and hardship of our lives, that is for damn sure. We can't let go of our narrative, and we replay the same scenarios over and over again. I mean, if you ever go to a twelve-step meeting, nine times out of ten you will hear an addict complain about the same thing over and over again, *ME included. It can be quite exhausting.*

Dr. Kath stood up from her leather chair, which always indicated that our session was officially done. I stood and when I bent over to grab my purse, my jeans button popped. *Great. Was it a metaphor? Was I holding everything in too tightly and needed to let it go? Or was I looking into it too hard? Maybe I was just fat.* As I turned around, Dr. Kath said, "Hey, it happens to the best of us in those skinny jeans. And remember, you are okay just as you are. Jeans fitting or not!"

I laughed with a sarcastic, self-deprecating exhale as I got on my hands and knees to retrieve the button from my obviously too-small pants.

As I got back up, Dr. Kath touched my arm and looked me dead in the eyes. "Roxanne, you will get through this time of loss. It's the circle of life, whether now or in your eighties. And your friend who passed, the secret she was keeping from herself was also that she was okay just as she was. If she'd only let herself know that, she would still be with us today. There's nothing you could have said or done differently. I truly hope you hear me."

A small, sad realization overcame me. I nodded my head and said softly, "Thank you."

I headed into the elevator, wiping my raccoon-stained eyes, and pressed the down button. As I waited patiently, and trying to clean off any makeup under my eyes, the elevator door opened, and my worst nightmare was standing right in front of me. Nope, not West. I literally was facing Mr. Handsome. The guy from Whole Foods! The tall one who said I was stealing his garbanzo beans at the salad bar just before that hot girl walked up to him? You remember him, right? Too good looking but oh so nice, like literally, he did not even know how good looking he was. Yeah, HIM!

Thoughts of me cursing God were playing in my mind. *Really, God? You had to do this now? I look like hell. Maybe this IS Hell? Damn sure feels like it.*

He didn't look from his phone and I quickly walked in and turned around to face the front of the elevator, praying for it to move faster than the speed of light to the ground floor.

I tried to hang my head and not make eye contact, even though he was right next to me. I could hear him shifting and bending at the knees to try to make eye contact with me.

Nope, I was not falling for it. He was too cute and obviously in a relationship with Whole Foods Girl, so I kept looking down and tried to hide my face even more with my hair. I felt like an ostrich hiding its head in the sand, thinking no one could see it. Yes, I was like a child pretending she was invisible. I could feel him getting closer to me; every time he bent lower to catch my eye, I also bent lower. It started to make me giggle.

He finally said in an echo, "Hello, down there... there... there..."

I looked up in confusion since he was talking to the floor. He was smiling a big toothy grin. I couldn't help myself, and I lost it. I started laughing so hard, I think snot started coming out of my nose. Could I look any more disgusting? I had decided that this was officially hell on earth.

He looked at me. "What? I thought we were looking for the devil down there, since clearly you don't want to be stuck with me in this elevator. I just figured we should say hello, no?"

Crap, he was funny *and* clever, a dangerous combination for an unavailable man. I looked at his too-handsome face. "My apologies. I'm having a really rough week." The honesty began to pour out of me. "My friend just passed away, and I was just at my therapist's office telling her these secrets and crying my eyes out. I look like hell, and I have mascara all over and was just shocked to see you standing there. I thought you probably did not remember me or that you forgot who I was."

What gibberish was babbling out of my mouth? I didn't even know this person. I felt really stupid. *Overshare much, Roxie?*

"I am sorry for your loss," he said. "I know how you feel. I had a friend pass last month falling off a ladder. I'm still brokenhearted about it."

I looked at him with a newfound respect. Here was a guy, who understood and had not tried to fix me. Or made a joke because of the awkward intimacy we'd just experienced. "Thank you for sharing that. It means a lot."

The elevator landed on the lobby floor, and we filed out. I started to walk toward the parking lot and felt him still looking at me.

I turned back, and he said, "I really am sorry. Hang in there."

I smiled and nodded because if I said any more, I might cry all over again. He stated, "It will get easier. I promise you that. The grief bag will get lighter, but it never really goes away."

I turned and walked to my car. He yelled from across the lot, "And I think you look great with or without mascara smeared on your face."

I laughed and yelled, "Sure."

Despite my hellacious day, I stood there for a moment and imagined a different scenario in that elevator.

INT. ELEVATOR—DAY

ROXIE—makeup, hair, and outfit on point, steps into the elevator. She looks terrific. If there were a fan nearby, it would blow her hair; that is how on top of the world she feels.

                    MR. HANDSOME (O.S.)
          Hold the door, please.

Roxie searches for the voice down the hall and dutifully holds the door open. Suddenly, MR. HANDSOME enters the elevator. He wears a freshly pressed tuxedo and hands her a rose.

                    MR. HANDSOME
          I thought that was you. You
          stole my beans.

                    ROXANNE
          I'm sure you enjoyed your
          enchilada with Whole Foods
          Girl.

                    MR. HANDSOME
          That was my sister. I'm single
          and have waited until I was
          emotionally mature enough to
          be in an adult relationship.

Roxanne smells the rose, unsure of what to say. Could this perfection be real?

                    MR. HANDSOME
          I'll be honest, I'd love to
          take you right here, right
          now, but I think we should
          take it slow. Let me wine you
          and dine you. Let's really get

```
        to know each other as friends
        and then take the leap.

He holds out his hand, which is both ruggedly
strong and sensually soft.

                    ROXIE
        I'd love that.

Roxie holds his hand, and they giggle like
school children who have discovered their
first crush.
```

I laughed, imagining such a scenario instead of my awkward raccoon-eyes meet-cute and climbed into my car feeling a little lighter in my thoughts. I was grateful for the past hour of connection with Dr. Kath and the bonus of running into Mr. Handsome.

Completely forgetting the hot dog stand at the bottom floor of Dr. Kath's building, I decided it was my turn to give back, to be of service to another, which was the only way out of my own hell. I drove over to Coral Tree Café on Ventura Blvd to meet Eve, while doing a botched job on the concealer under my eyes. I was trying to hide the puffiness from crying.

As I applied the powder and blush to give myself a brighter demeanor, I spotted an officer looking at me from the other lane. *Shit, was it against the law to apply makeup while driving? I started to pray, Please don't give me a ticket. Please, it's the last thing I need.*

Clearly, the universe was not on my side today, as the officer pulled me over. I rolled down the window. "Hey, sorry about that, officer. I was in a hurry."

He cut me off. "Young lady, I'm going to give you a warning. You cannot be applying makeup while driving. It's actually worse than texting. Please stop before you kill someone."

As soon as he said "kill," I completely lost it. I apologized through tears, "I'm so sorry. I just got out of therapy, and one of my best friends just murdered her boyfriend, then herself last week. I know it's dangerous, and I promise I won't do it again. I'm just trying to pull myself together at this point and make it through this day."

He scrutinized me with major concern, like I might need to go to the psych ward. "The murder-suicide over in Echo Park?"

I nodded; I had been doing that a lot today when I couldn't get the words out. He leaned in and said a little too closely, "Yeah, that was a brutal crime. Sounds like she went loco on his ass. Did he cheat on her?"

I was in shock but didn't want to yell at a cop for his callousness. I just looked at him with a blank stare. "Yes, and many more things. He was the devil incarnate."

He stepped back from my window. "Wow, poor girl. Well, I'll let you go with a warning this time. No more makeup. Plus, you don't even need it."

I nodded and said, "Thanks."

He leaned in again. "You married?"

I was incredibly uncomfortable and officially a liar as I said, "Yep. Thanks, officer. No makeup, got it!" *These are the times you tell a little white lie!*

All I could think of as I drove into the restaurant parking lot was that I wanted to get this day over with already. I was going to meet up with Eve and then go home. No meeting for me. I couldn't take any more of this rollercoaster of a day. I needed to crawl under my duvet and never come out. *Checkmate, this day, I am done!*

Eve had been in her own disease of withdrawal, which could be brutal. She had only been checking in by text, so I thought it was probably a good idea to meet face-to-face this week. Plus, I loved the Cobb salad at Coral Tree; their green goddess dressing was, hands down, the best in Los Angeles.

I saw Eve sitting in the corner, waving me over. "Sorry, I already ordered. I tried to wait, but I was starving."

I beamed proudly at my new foodie twin soul. "I get it. You sound like me. You need anything else while I'm up ordering?"

She shook her head, and as I walked to the counter to order my latte and salad, guess who was there?

Lo and behold, Hallmark Star was standing in front of me with her two sons. I hadn't seen her in ages—I barely recognized her. I tapped her on the shoulder. "Hey. How are you? It's been way too long."

She looked at me with a sad smile. "Hey. Good to see you too. I heard about your friend through the grapevine. I'm sorry for your loss."

"Thank you." I stood there awkwardly. Our breakup was kind of weird, just so you know. We were really good friends, and then she decided to marry that guy I was not a fan of, and it all fell apart. It took me a long time to let go of her as one of my confidantes, but with no remorse. "Your sons are beautiful. Congratulations on being a mom; it was always something you wanted. I'm very happy for you."

Hallmark Star responded, "Yeah. Some of us care about others and don't want to be obsessed with their career. I'm lucky, for sure."

Whoa. Major dig. It was clear where her frustration was coming from—her career had stalled, and she was stuck doing Hallmark conventions, as anyone could see on the old Facebook. *Not that I looked anymore. Never on a lonely night did I stalk old friends. Can you hear the sarcasm?*

Even though she was obviously over this impromptu reunion, I was not bitter at all. I truly wanted what was best for her. Keeping my own bitchy tone in check, I rebuffed her daggers: "I hear you. This career can be brutal, especially with kids. I'm glad I'm waiting to have them until I am truly ready, if I ever am. Who knows, right? Only God."

Okay, so I made a little dig back. *Come on, I'm only human.* I knew she hated God and was not spiritual. And I knew she was a couple years older than me, which was freaking her out. Her eggs had been getting old, and she didn't want a geriatric pregnancy. So, Hallmark Star married the next rich guy she dated and made him get her pregnant. Not a life I would envision for myself, but to each their own, right?

She was up next to order, but first replied with, "Right. Well, good to see you."

I walked over to the other counter to order my food and drink, throwing back, "Good to see you too."

Man, I was starting to regret this day out in the real world. Why did LA have to be so small? I mean, it was a big city, but you could run into anyone no matter where you went. It was always annoying—but it was *extremely* annoying when I was living a double life in my addiction, or even a triple life some of the time. It was a difficult time for me to go out into the world with the men in Los Angeles and New York City. And I would inevitably run into someone I knew or who knew me.

One time, when I was dating NYC, we were in Brooklyn, and he forced me to see an awful play. *I feel like I'm the only actress who hates musical theater. It always makes me want to take a screwdriver to my eardrums. Sorry, but it's the truth.*

When we were walking out of the show, we ran into the paparazzi out front. They recognized me, which hardly ever happened. Good news—I was looking great in my Donna Karan black turtleneck dress with my fake-fur Nicholas K jacket. I mean, I looked hot. I was ready to get my picture taken. Bad news—NYC, who was not very well known but worked a ton, grabbed my hand and hijacked my photo.

First, I was pissed at him for robbing me of my single press photo on WireImage that my agents could use for PR. Second, I panicked and took it out on him because I did not want West to see it, or even worse, ATL. Lastly, he did not look that great. He'd lost a bunch of weight for this Off-Broadway play where he was playing a drug addict—those dang method actors for you. *Ew... Not a good shot. It was a waste.*

Anyway, long story short, it was hard to hide in both of those big cities. Truthfully, I should not have been surprised that I ran into Mr. Handsome and Hallmark Star, but I was.

I made my way over to Eve, and she asked, "Who was that? She was obviously not a fan of yours."

"An old friend who was over me and we lost touch." I didn't want to bring Eve into my drama. This was her time for a sponsor–sponsee check-in. We sponsors, have to check ourselves at the door when we're being of service. It's not about us anymore. That is the whole meaning of giving back and giving to others. It isn't about you and your failed friendships from the past.

"How's it going? How's it going with your withdrawal?" I asked her, just as the young male waiter dropped off her pancakes and bacon. Man, I was so jealous of her metabolism. Skinny bitch! She dug her fork into those delicious blueberry pancakes and cut off a piece.

I was staring at her with such envy that she stopped midbite and asked, "What's wrong? Do I have something on my face? What? You're freaking me out."

"Chill, lady. I'm just drooling over your pancakes. Go ahead."

"You want some?"

"Nope," I said, as my salad was placed in front of me. I closed my eyes for a moment and pretended it was bacon.

She started describing her experience. "This withdrawal feels like I'm stuck in my own personal hell. I feel like I'm drowning. Sometimes I feel like my skin is burning, and I want to peel myself out of it. You know?"

I responded, "I hear you. I used to want to unzip my skin and crawl out of it. It's the worst feeling ever."

She continued, "I have all these fears coming up about never getting out of it. Never being with someone again, never feeling pretty, or using my feminine wiles. That I'm going to dry up like an old hag. My sexuality is going to wither away for good. I'm freaking out over here. And I miss dick. But not the man. Just the penis. I thought I would want to be in bed with a stranger, like I've always done. But now I see that I really want to take time off and not be with anyone. I have been sexually active with men since the age of fifteen. I need a break from guys. But I miss the dick. And I want to masturbate so badly. Why do I have to take a break from that, too? This is too hard. I know the time alone is good for me. I need time to just be me. I'm just not sure how long I can go without being with some-one, because I still enjoy casual sex."

I broke it down as best as I could, the way Alice had bro-ken it down for me. "We don't have to know everything now. What's good is that you are taking the time to date yourself. You are your own person, and you fill yourself. I'm not saying you can never have casual sex again. I'm not saying you won't masturbate again. We're creating space in your nervous sys-tem for feelings to come up, so that you don't sexualize your feelings anymore. We're giving you time to just be in your skin, uncomfortable and alone, and see what is revealed. We just have to see what boundaries you can have around casual sex, too. Or who knows, you might never be able to have ca-sual sex or even want to. We won't know till we really look at what this new Eve needs in her life and what she needs to stay healthy. So please be patient with yourself."

She breathed a sigh of relief, like she had been holding on to the worry. That was it, right there! That was the whole enchilada. Carrying the message to other sex and love addicts still willing to surrender their pain. That was the whole rea-son for being sober—I could help others even when I was still drowning in myself.

I had the tools.

Before we parted ways, I shared a quote I'd heard the oth-er day: "Your worst battle is between what you know and what you feel. It takes risk and removing yourself from the known to finally tend to those feelings. And yes, it's a battle, but one you can always find a way to win."

As I was driving home after that long day of hell and revelations, I realized I was still trying to find a way to outmaneuver life on life's terms and win in this journey. *What was that about? Survival? Control? Fear of the unknown? Fear of death? Who knows.*

Armed with this knowledge, I was willing to let the old strategy die. I could not fight myself anymore, at least not in the way I had been. I surrendered. My way had proven to be ineffective. There was no hope of winning. Life will drag you through hell to see if you have enough guts to still believe in heaven.

In fact, as I drove up the 405 in rush-hour traffic, I came to understand that there was nothing to do but surrender.

Sometimes we all need to experience loss, to drop the old paradigm of winning and losing in order to turn our attention to the truth in our lives.

From the insightful T.D. Jakes, I share this final revelation from this very shitty day: "Come hell or high water, you will never take me back to the place I was before. I have been through too much to let life whoop me again. My faith is stronger than it's ever been, my mind is more tenacious than it's ever been, my soul is more absolute."

CHAPTER TEN

Rule 19: Keep peeling the onion of your soul.

THE ABOVE IS A cheesy but very effective saying we addicts like to use to explain all the trauma that literally is being extracted from our bodies and minds. You will hear many people in the rooms say they are peeling the layers of their onion— getting down to their true core self. We are peeling away all the masks, facades, and personas we use to function in the world. We are becoming raw and exposed. And that shit is mad scary, but growth demands a temporary surrender of all security. These layers we cover ourselves with are our invisible security blankets.

Honestly, even non-addicts have them. Another term is the "shell" we wear out into the world to protect ourselves. But as with any addiction, we can't function properly in society when we wear our shields. They help us hide, which in turn develops into secrets and lies.

A very vicious cycle.

So instead of the old system of survival, I was peeling off the next layer of my onion to get to the center of my being. For your information, it was not a very pleasant experience. It was kind of like the pain of withdrawal but different.

You cry a lot in both experiences, ironically, just like when you actually peel or chop a real onion. During withdrawal, you usually don't have a Higher Power or God relationship yet. Once you are sober for a period of time, you deepen that connection to your God, but you're still in ridiculous amounts of pain. Yet, there is a clarity to what you are doing. There is a knowing that you will come out on the other side of this new growth with a whole new perspective. But in the withdrawal process, the addict is always surrounded by the unknown and so much damn drama because your life is usually falling to pieces around you. No one is like, "Hey, let's give this a try for the hell of it." You're usually at the bottom of a deep well of overwhelming hardships in the situation you've created in your world. You're on your knees and have tried everything you could think of to climb out of it, only to find out that your way of thinking is never going to fix your problem. You are never going to get out. EVER! Your way of thinking got you in this mess in the first place.

And the way to start healing is to shed: people, places, and things.

Look, the onion-peeling process is usually a forever process, as you continually learn to let go of another layer of your mask. You have no idea when you will reach the core, so you keep peeling and peeling. *This process never seems to end; it just moves through you more quickly and with less discomfort.*

The ultimate goal for this excruciating task: We were willing to be available not to the next lover or new fantasy, but to whatever might happen next within ourselves. We were now in a committed relationship to ourselves and our growth.

To be honest with you all, I thought I was already done with all this growth shit. Man, was I dead wrong! The death of Tattoogirl helped me hit my knees once again and allowed me to go to the next level of self-love and acceptance.

After hell week, I had all these crazy fantasy thoughts of multiple ways I could get out of myself. For example, the fantasy of calling someone to fuck away my discomfort, going shopping to get a whole new wardrobe to make myself feel better, flirting with a guy to get a sense of worth, or getting a new procedure on my body to improve my looks. It's like I was transferring my fear of loss to my outside being.

I started to have these feelings that everything that was wrong with me was on the outside. I even went back on Instagram to obsess over other actresses' lives, which was a big red flag for me, as you all know.

While searching the mind-numbing, consumer-obsessed worldwide web for new shoes that I had to buy (*hilarious*), this quote from none other than Academy Award-winning actress Emma Stone popped up on my screen: "I can't think of any better representation of beauty than someone who is unafraid to be herself."

Mic drop.

This God shot hit me: I really didn't want to alter my appearance. I really didn't want to be afraid of myself anymore. I recommitted to peeling my soul to get to the next layer of my growth.

But before all of the onion peeling, I was on my way to help Alice with final preparations for her wedding the following weekend. Alice and I had easily transformed our sponsor–sponsee relationship into a true friendship. I was worried when we parted ways after my London slip that we were not going to make it as friends. But man, was I wrong. God had bigger plans for us. It was a truly beautiful and equal friendship. I loved being able to help her just like she had helped me. I was still without a sponsor, but I trusted that the Universe had my back in that area as well, turning my fear into faith. *I know, I sound a little too twelve-steppie, makes me cringe too sometimes. But those steps saved my life, so give 'em a break.*

We met at her favorite vintage shop in Topanga, a small town off the beaten path above Malibu, called Hidden Treasures. I wasn't really a vintage girl like Alice, but I loved helping her find little nuggets of recycled clothes and house decorations. This trip, she was specifically looking for old suitcases to fill with wildflowers for the centerpieces on the tables at the reception.

Okay, not exactly my style, but to each their own. I was sure it would be a magical, bohemian, fairy-like atmosphere. She was into that mystical world. I thought she might even play D&D with her fiancé. That's the acronym for Dungeons & Dragons, for those of you who weren't super nerds in middle school and clearly didn't get laid until college. *Sorry... not sorry. Despite my sobriety, I could still be a judgmental jerk sometimes.*

While Alice favored slightly odorous thrift stores, I felt a lot more comfortable in major department stores, especially my faves, T.J. Maxx and HomeGoods. Seriously, once you walk into that candy store of tchotchkes, home furnishings, and quirky decorations, it is nearly impossible to leave without buying something. Even Dog likes it there because there are so many fun toys for him. Also, don't tell Alice, but I'd gotten her the most badass side table made of reclaimed wood from the Burbank HomeGoods. It had strips of different-colored wood with a Moroccan motif. It was absolutely gorgeous, and I was giving it to her and Charlie as their wedding gift.

She would have no clue since there was only one at the store and it said *Made in India* on the bottom. It didn't look like a manufactured table at all. It was the find of the century, but SHHHH... It's our little secret, our little white lie.

Yes, I know, I was not supposed to do secrets, but this one was fun and harmless, completely for my enjoyment. I just knew she would fall in love with this table, which was a steal at the bargain-basement price of $49.99.

We were going through piles of old junk in the back of the thrift store as I told her all the things I had been realizing this past week through my grief.

Alice asked me, while shifting through boxes of smelly old books, "What are the five traits you value most in yourself?"

"Bossy," I said, with the aren't-I-clever smile I do when I'm talking out of my ass.

She looked at me with her not-so-funny school-teacher face. "I'm serious, Roxanne."

"I don't know. I never thought about my traits I like."

As I picked up an old-world globe and showed it to her, she gleefully hollered at my find for her centerpiece vision. Laughing at her hilarious reaction to a tattered globe, I said, "I like how organized I am, and I feel very responsible now as a human."

"Okay, see, you have so many wonderful traits. That's why I'm your friend. I think you should come up with a couple more to have on Post-it notes around your house, for when you're feeling blue or in fear about your self-worth. You can look at them and they'll remind you what a great catch you are and that you deserve a balanced, equal relationship with all the people in your life."

"I thought you weren't my sponsor anymore. That is a very sponsor thing to say," I joked.

"Old habits die hard, plus I know you have a lot of amazing traits, Rox. I just want you to acknowledge them," she insisted.

I started to think about that as she clutched her new globe and moved on to the crocheted pillows, most likely handmade by some weed-smoking hippy.

I called after her, "Well, I do like that I am creative, humble, and courageous since I have really done this work. I like how fair and forgiving I've become. And I think now I'm more compassionate, which was not in my DNA when I started."

"See, you are a very brave, determined, and empathic human being, Roxie. You will get to the next level of your emotional sobriety. Now you just have to lean into trust," she added, smiling up at me like I was the best thing in the whole world. That just warmed my heart right then and there.

I couldn't help myself as I blurted out, "I love you, Alice. Do you know that? You are my true savior. You are a blessing to me. I am so happy for you and Charlie, and I'm wishing you nothing but true happiness and love."

Tears started to fill her eyes as she put down the globe and medieval trinkets in her arms. She rushed me with such love that I ran and hid behind the rack of old rocker T-shirts, teasing her, "Stop, Alice, you know I hate hugs."

She laughed and charged at me again, and we played cat and mouse, laughing like two little schoolgirls in this musty old vintage shop.

She kept coming after me. "Come here. I just want to give you some love."

I squealed like a pig. "Seriously, stop it right now. You are freaking me out. You look possessed."

Of course, she did not listen to me at all. I stopped abruptly and turned around to face her with my arms out and hands up. "Enough, lady. I'm out of breath. Stop chasing me."

Alice giggled at the ridiculousness of my affection phobia. "I will stop chasing you if you let me hug you for thirty seconds without pulling away, deal?"

"Fine. Let's get this over with."

She walked over to me like the cat who had finally caught the mouse. As she wrapped me in a bear hug, I was literally stiff as a board with my arms down by my sides. I didn't mind hugs every once in a while, but these lingering, overly affectionate hugs were somewhat painful for me.

I mean, I literally felt pain in my chest. Like it was too much love, and my heart was not equipped to withstand that amount of connection. It was a problem that I was very aware of, and I'd been trying for years to lean into other people giving me hugs. But still to this day, I pull away pretty quickly when someone I love wants to show me affection. My body still stiffens up, and all I try to do is remind myself to surrender and relax, that I am okay. Which feels more difficult than climbing Mount Everest.

It's getting to a point where I might even have to hire a cuddle expert. Yes, it's a thing, and I know people who swear by them. Okay, I realize that sounds even worse than a loved one hugging you. But I need to start working on my ability to hold affection without it turning sexual or my skin wanting to burn off. Because I still can't do a hug normally.

But in that moment, I was trying with Alice. I really was just trying to relax my body and let her love me.

So, there we were in the middle of this store, holding a bear hug for thirty seconds. Alice was actually counting to thirty. Very slowly, I might add. As she was getting to twenty-six, I shouted, "Come on, hurry this up. Everyone is looking at us." I wanted this to be over already.

She responded with so much glee, "I don't care. Let them look. Twenty-seven, twenty-eight, twenty-nine..."

As she finally let the number thirty slip out of her mouth, I gently pushed her away. "Yuck. Gross. Now I have Alice cooties."

She grinned proudly from ear to ear. "Lucky you. Everyone wants some Alice cooties." Turning her back on me, she returned to her globe and crappy trinkets, collecting them and head to the register.

"How are you doing with the wedding and everything?" I asked.

Letting out a deep sigh, she came clean with her feelings about this new stage she was entering. "I could not sleep last night. All these fears were coming up."

"Like what?"

"It makes no sense, but there I was, lying next to the man I want to marry and be with for the rest of my life. And all I wanted to do was run. For no reason. Nothing happened that should make me want to run, you know? No red flags or anything."

I nodded. "Yep. I mean, you were just giving me a hug because you love me, and all I wanted to do was run. I get it."

"Charlie is such a great guy, so available to me. But I'm not used to that. All the men in my life have either left or were never available. My father was always cheating on my mother. So, the main male figure in my life had another family on the side." She sat down on an old rocking chair toward the front of the store. "The fears last night were so overwhelming, I actually could not breathe for a second. I sat on the kitchen floor with ice in my hands to calm my nervous system and prayed for the fear to go away. It helped, but I still felt uneasy this morning. I almost canceled our meeting, but I forced myself to show up for my life."

"I'm glad you did. What were the main fears? We can talk it out."

She laughed. "Look at you, all recovered and wise. Giving me advice now. Someone put on her big-girl sponsor panties." She looked away toward the parking lot, which made me follow her eye line to see that nothing was there. We both just sat there in the front of the smelly store, she in her rocking chair and me on a wooden stump.

Then she finally spilled it. "What if I can't do this marriage thing? What if I can't be a good wife? What if I can't be sober and married? That is a whole other ballgame than being single and dating as a sex and love addict. I don't know if I have it in me to make this work and to be healthy. I mean, what if my expectations are too high and unrealistic? I tend to expect too much of people, which then hurts me in the long run. I'm not as stable as I think I am."

She looked at me and confessed, "I was at school the other day and started to have a mini panic attack while I was grading papers and the kids were taking their tests. I had to excuse myself and run into the bathroom to do jumping jacks and box-breathing exercises."

BECOMING MY OWN F-ING SOULMATE

Slight interruption—for those of you who don't know what box-breathing exercises are, I highly recommend them. It's a four-step breathing exercise to calm and center yourself. Step 1: Breathe in, counting to four slowly. Feel the air enter your lungs. Step 2: Hold your breath for four seconds. Step 3: Exhale slowly for four seconds. Step 4: Hold your breath for four seconds. Keep repeating steps one through four until you feel centered. Okay, back to Alice, who was still processing.

"I mean, that's nuts, right? I should be happy and looking forward to walking down the aisle to the man I love. Instead, I'm paralyzed with fear."

I thought to myself after she had finished her confession, *I'm actually not really sure what to say.* I took a deep breath and told myself, *Let God do the talking, not you, Roxie.*

Then the words started to flow from my mouth without me even knowing what I was going to say. "No, it's not nuts at all. It actually makes perfect sense to me when you tell me about all the unknowns of entering into this union with Charlie. I would probably be doing the same thing, or worse, for that matter. But I do know this. Whenever I'm in fear of an event, Dr. Kath points out to me very clearly that it's just a day in my life. It's just a party or event that will last four hours max. It will be over before I know it. And when I keep that in mind, it takes away the pressure for it to go perfectly, or for me to have all the answers about the magnitude of the occasion. Really helps me to rightsize it."

She looked at me. "You're right. It's really just a fancy party, and I love parties. When I put it in that context, the anxiety leaves my body. Thanks, Roxie. So helpful." She got up to go purchase her stuff, calling over her shoulder, "I think I should maybe go see Dr. Kath since she's helped you so much. Can you text me her info?"

I sat there on my stump with at least three wood splinters going straight into my butt. "Yep. Will do it now." I was suddenly filled with a strong sense of purpose. That small moment just revealed to me how much I had grown and made me more excited to see what the next layer of my development would bring.

As I drove down the mountain on Topanga Blvd to hit the 101, Coolgirl gave me a ring. It had been a minute since we'd talked. I was happy to see her name pop up on my screen. "Yo, what's up, lady?" I said into the hands-free speaker.

She was in crisis—shocker, I know. Her response was a whisper, "Girl, I am at his house so can't talk loud. Where you at? Want to meet me?"

"I can't, I'm on my way to therapy," I spoke through crumbs falling out of my mouth as I shoved Goldfish crackers in my mouth to sooth my growling belly.

"I am freaking out over here. Can you talk now?" She was about to lose it.

"Sure. I have a thirty-three-minute drive." Luckily, I was feeling back in my body again after devouring those crackers. Hopefully, I would get through this traffic and therapy without getting hangry.

Coolgirl asked, "Can I FaceTime you right now? I'm in his closet. And need to see your face."

"Girl, I'm driving, but sure, you can see me, but I can't look at you." She called me on FaceTime, her beautiful lioness curls bouncing into the frame. "You look great, even if shit has hit the fan. What's going on?"

"Thanks. I needed that. I have to be quiet. He's resting before he does the talk show circuit today. I am freaking out. Last night, I was at his birthday dinner with his family."

"Fun."

"No, it was the opposite of fun. It was a disaster. I think he's going to break up with me. I'm so scared. The dinner was with his wife, kids, and his other girlfriend, and I kind of lost it on him."

I was preparing myself to be nonjudgmental of the self-inflicted pain she was causing. "Oh no. That sounds like a recipe for disaster."

She went on to tell me all the details that unfolded. She clearly did not understand her addiction to pain. Her past relationships had always included love with a high dose of agony, torture, and emotional suffering.

Much of the love-addiction literature describes how our nervous systems get addicted to discomfort in relationships. As addicts, we have become accustomed to pain. Pain is the main characteristic of our romantic involvements and even many of our desired sexual pursuits. Some of us even equate pain with love, so that in the absence of love we would at least be comforted by the presence of pain.

I listened with the intent not of fixing her but of being of service in my Twelfth Step.

She plowed into the drama. "I have fallen in love; we are soulmates. It's been almost a year. We're working together, and I don't think his wife is happy about it anymore—that's why they started producing his movies together. I think she thinks I'm moving into her territory. She was so rude to me last night at his birthday dinner. Normally we're cool, but not last night. His other girlfriend, who is a totally vapid model, was there too."

I interrupted her monologue of woe with some humor. "Wow, that's a full house."

Not appreciating my humor, she told me, "Stop, Roxie. I'm being serious." And she continued to recap the drama. "I tried to act cool, but I felt a little odd. I don't even want to admit this, but it felt like I was a side piece, especially when they took a family photo with his kids. I stood on the sidelines with Dumb Dumb Model, looking like a fool. I don't hate Dumb Dumb at all, and I see why she likes Superstar too. He is charming and so sweet, but she is dumb as dirt. I can't even have a conversation with her. The whole night was so uncomfortable and painful. I felt like I did not belong, which is the first time he's made me feel that way."

I interrupted again, "Girl, no one makes you feel any type of way. That is just a very unusual situation to be in. Anyone would feel uneasy in that scenario."

"Yes, thank you for understanding. I didn't know what to do, so I went into the bathroom in the pool house and sat on the toilet and watched positive affirmations on TikTok. Then I started watching all these videos about celebs who have gotten buccal fat removal."

"Hang on there," I interrupted. "Buccal what?"

"You know, when they suck the fat out of your cheek. It's like an instant face lift without the downtime. Bella Hadid did it, and Zoë Kravitz, and Chrissy Teigen, and Dumb Dumb." She was silent for a minute, and then the real issue came up. "I mean, Dumb Dumb is me ten years ago. I feel... old."

"Again," I repeated, "no one can make you feel that way but you. And you are not old. Stop it, lady. Focus. So what happened next?"

"Okay, so I stayed in there for maybe ten minutes, trying to pull myself together. But I heard something in the other room when I walked out of the bathroom."

In my head, all I was thinking was, *OH NO, it is never a good idea to follow a sound in another room. Here we go...*

As I took my exit to Balboa Blvd, she continued, "I walked out and looked in the guest room, and there was Superstar kissing Dumb Dumb. My stomach started to churn. Like I'd floated out of my body. I said to them, "I'm so sorry." They both looked at me like I was rudely interrupting. I closed the door and just stood there for a second, thinking that he would come out to talk to me, but he didn't. I'm so naive. I thought he would chase me down and beg my forgiveness. But no, I saw him twenty minutes later out in the backyard near the fire pit with everyone, and he barely even acknowledged me."

Trying to be as sensitive as I could to her messed-up relationship with this man, I said, "I'm so sorry. That must have been hard to see."

"It was. Look, I know he is with other women, but I have not actually seen it. It hurt so badly. I know I should have left, but I didn't; instead, I stayed and got drunk with his son. I sang songs and tried to get his attention. I have no idea what happened last night. I must have blacked out. But right now, I'm in his room with him and I can't remember anything."

I didn't know what to say to her at this point. And when we don't know, we don't say anything. I stayed quiet. I couldn't fix her in this.

She went on, "Sometimes I regret losing myself in Superstar and his world. I know there are parts of it that are a blessing and that I'm grateful, but the other part is that I always feel less than and, underneath it all, kind of disposable to him. Like, at any minute, he could discard me and let me go. I'm always on edge."

Then she added this nugget about her lack of self-worth: "I hate how replaceable I really am, how he doesn't really need me as much as I need him. It's not a great feeling, that's for sure. I detest it, actually. But I feel stuck and need his connections in the business, so what do I do? I stay, right? Or should I grab my stuff and go? I'm just so confused. I don't know what to do. Tell me what to do, please."

Oh no, not this again. I did not want to get in the middle of someone else's bad relationship, as I did with Tattoogirl and Fuckface's. The old me would have said something along the lines of, *Coolgirl, you can't be scared of your own shadow; that is where the growth lives. Tattoogirl was scared of the darkness of letting go instead of walking through to get to the light. Look what happened to her! (Morbid, I know.)*

Unfortunately, we all saw how it ended when I stuck my nose in too deep—very badly. I had learned my lesson there. She needed more support.

Then an answer came out of nowhere. "Call Dr. Kath! I think you need to talk to a professional about this. Let me give you her number. I'll tell her when I see her that you're going to be calling her in a crisis. That you need to get in ASAP."

She whispered, "Oh my gosh, thank you. I will. Text me her number. I just don't know what to do. I feel so stuck."

As I pulled into the parking lot, I said quickly, "I've got to jam, just pulled in. I don't want to be late."

"Thank you, Roxanne, and sorry about your friend dying. I meant to call, but I have been in my own shit." A sadness swept over me as I saw how similar her situation was to Tattoogirl's. "Thanks. I appreciate that. I'll text you Dr. Kath's number right now. Hang in there."

As I texted, I walked to the stairs—no elevator for me this time. I didn't want to run into another soul. My social anorexia side was flaring up; that's when I liked to self-isolate and completely shut down emotionally. It was another side of the coin of this addiction—another way to disconnect.

As I was in my own world, I tripped on the curb but caught myself just as my ankle twisted in my 3½ -inch rag & bone booties. Awesome! "SHIT, that hurts. Another God shot that I need to get out of myself?" I said out loud to no one in particular. I staggered up the stairs, favoring my right foot.

Man, this building and I were not friends. I always felt it was doomsday walking into her office. Maybe I should start doing virtual sessions with her instead?

As I hobbled into the waiting room, I was relieved to see it was empty. Luckily, Doppelgänger wasn't there. I couldn't do small talk. I was spent. I was empty. I needed to refill myself. Which is why I was here—therapy had become a massage for my soul. A way I could self-heal.

As I hobbled into the room, Dr. Kath asked, "What happened to you?"

I replied with my sarcastic self, "You know, just in my own crap, not in reality!"

She gave me the official nod that I was calling myself on my own messiness. Then she hit me with a new challenge. "It's time to cover your mirrors."

WTF? What was this woman saying to me? Was she being figurative or literal? I was not in the mood to play mind games, especially after hearing Coolgirl whine for half an hour on the 101

"It's time to dig deeper inside," she said matter-of-factly.

Whew. She was talking figuratively, good. I needed my mirrors. From my tiny magnifying mirror to my full-length mirror in the hall. Mirrors were my happy place.

But she wasn't finished.

Dr. Kath had decided to force me to put my money where my mouth was. She was challenging me to take it to the next level. I mean, it felt extreme to me as she told me very clearly, "I have been thinking about you this last week. I think you are ready to go to the next level. We need to dig deeper inside."

I paused while maneuvering my underwear out of my crotch—sitting on this couch always gave me a wedgie.

"Wait. I'm confused. What do you mean by 'dig deeper'? And what does this have to do with mirrors?"

"Listen, Roxanne, you are forever going to be peeling your layers of facade that you wear; it is now time to shed another layer. We need to be shaking it off once and for all."

"Okay, I can see that. And I know I need to go deeper within myself. But I'm not sure how we do that." Her enthusiasm was getting me pumped about the next actions I could take to be a better me.

"I want you to cover up your mirrors, Roxanne! We need to let go of that outside validation."

Insert a record scratch! "HUH?"

"That's right, young lady. You need to get rid of all the mirrors in your house. We are going to work on not relying on your outside appearance for self-fulfillment. You are ready. Trust."

I was starting to sweat under my arms—and more uncomfortably, my crotch. To say I was about to have a panic attack would be a gigantic understatement. I used my shoulder to scratch my chin to see if I remembered to put on deodorant this morning, because I was sweating like a beast.

"Yeah, I don't think I will be able to do that. I'm an actress and have to always be aware of my appearance. I have to look my best. I mean, what if I have food in my teeth or my hair is all over the place?"

"You've got this," Dr. Kath assured me.

I was starting to hyperventilate as I continued to spiral. "No. I don't. I don't 'got this.' Come on, Dr. Kath, I have fine hair and a big cowlick. I have to be able to put on my makeup. What if an eyelash gets in my eye? Or I have a zit that needs to be popped and then lacquered with cover-up?" I was moments away from a full meltdown.

"Okay, calm down. Breathe in and breathe out. Let's talk it through."

I nodded nervously, but I was not liking this layer of the onion peel. I was not liking it one bit.

"I understand," Dr. Kath continued, "but I feel that it's important to your growth not to rely on your looks for any type of purpose to feed your ego and sense of self. I think it will be very healing for you, Roxanne. You've never had to honor yourself with what is on the inside. Please just consider this assignment," she said with a clear, direct voice, which was actually helping me calm down and change my feelings abruptly.

I looked at her with annoyance, because I knew she was right. I had never not relied on my looks. I'd never pictured myself not looking like I do. It was my job to look a certain way. But how could she possibly expect me to be able to not have mirrors around my house? Also, Dr. Kath knew I was a very competitive person and that if she challenged me to do an exercise, I would do what she asked just to prove her wrong. I hated authority sometimes! Okay, really all the time. How would I survive without a mirror?

INT. ROXANNE'S BATHROOM—DAY

Roxanne puts on her makeup. She likes what she sees. Suddenly, JUSTUS VON LIEBIG, a stern man in a black suit, stares at her from the other side of the mirror.

                    ROXANNE
WHAT THE FUCK? WHO ARE YOU?

                    JUSTUS
I could be asking you the same
thing, beautiful young lady.

                    ROXANNE
Okay, first of all… thank
you for the "young" and the
"beautiful." Second of all,
who the hell are you?

                    JUSTUS
Justus von Liebig, at your
service. I created the mirror
you are looking into.

                    ROXANNE
What the fuck?

                    JUSTUS
Since fuck seems to be your
favorite word, yes, I fucking
did.

                    ROXANNE
How…

JUSTUS

Glad you asked. I invented a
chemical means of applying
silver to glass so that—

ROXANNE

No, I mean… why are you here?

JUSTUS

Pleading my case. I mean,
obviously, you can't stop
looking in mirrors. They
are the world's greatest
invention, thank you very
much.

ROXANNE

Right? I mean, what did people
even do before mirrors?

JUSTUS

They used primitive means. A
puddle. Ha. The most infamous
story is that of Narcissus,
the Greek god, whose obsession
with his own reflection led to
his doom. People are obsessed
with themselves—they love
admiring their reflection. So…
I made it easier for them.
You're welcome.

ROXANNE

Wait. Did you just call me a
narcissist?

JUSTUS

If the Louboutin fits.

SMASH TO BLACK

"I am not a narcissist."

"I'm not saying you are, Roxanne, but remember, as
I explained before, a lot of people have narcissistic tenden-

cies. The most important thing is that I think it will be a good experiment for you. I suggest you cover the mirrors in your house and car for at least a week. You can keep a compact mirror to check your teeth, if you need to. Also, I think it might be the best time to try not to wear any eyeliner."

My mouth hung open in disbelief. This demon lady had been trying for almost three years to get me to not wear eyeliner. Damn her for throwing it into this assignment. She smiled her bohemian-beaded-boss-bitch smile, knowing that she had just gotten through to me.

I swayed my head with a sarcastic grunt and said bitterly through clenched teeth, "Fine. I will try it, but if I hate it, I am not going to go the whole week, deal?"

She stared at me with her prestigious righteousness. "This is for your growth, Roxanne, not mine. So, it's up to you to do the work. If you don't want to do the whole week, that's your call. But I think it will be eye-opening for you."

I replied quickly, "Fine. I'll start tomorrow." Adding silently, *I will prove you wrong. I will be the same amount of vain after this assignment as before.*

Damn her!

As I walked out of the session, feeling angry for putting myself through this hot mess of self-improvement, I looked down at my phone and saw several missed calls from Coolgirl.

I texted her, "Call you in 30 minutes when driving home. I've got to eat. Hangry! Also, was just told I have to break up with my mirrors for a week."

A thumbs-up emoji was her response.

I walked into the hot dog stand and ordered a fat dog with chili cheese and diced onions on top. Plus, a side of sweet potato fries. I needed this. I sat in the corner booth by myself. I couldn't tell you guys the last time I had done a lunch date by myself. When I first started this SLAA work, I literally only dated myself. I would go to fancy restaurants and movies solo. But this past year, I had done none of those things.

I sat in silence, alone with my thoughts, eating this delicious hot dog. As the nacho cheese dribbled down my chin, I felt a sense of peace. I realized I could do this assignment with the mirrors. That it might actually be very freeing if I gave it a true shot. Why not? What did I have to lose? Why couldn't I just look inside myself for my worth? Why did I have to check myself out every time I passed a reflective surface?

That's pretty narcissistic, right? To admit out loud? That I seriously could not stop looking at myself? But I had been doing it my whole life, as far back as I could remember.

My favorite activity while growing up was to blast my music in my room so I would not have to listen to my parents argue. To drown out the noise, I would sing and dance in front of the mirror, talking to an imaginary person. Telling them what I really felt about them. I would act out scenes in my mirror. I would talk to myself in the mirror. I would tell that bitch girl or bully or even my parents how I really felt about them. I would make all my fantasies and dreams come true in THAT MIRROR.

I still do it today—I just use my huge hallway mirror now.

Also, I had my first kiss in my mirror. I used to act out kissing the boy I liked with the mirror when I was ten. Then I upgraded my acting skills by reenacting the death scene in *Romeo and Juliet* with that goddamn mirror. I mean, that mirror saw things I've never done with anyone.

Now that I think about it, the whole time, I was just looking at myself. I was always mirroring what I wanted with other people. I had been acting with mirrors all my life. Like I said before, I could put a bag over any man's face, no matter who he was. It only mattered how he made me feel and what I wanted to see.

How freaking crazy to go through life interacting and not really connecting with a living soul?

As I shoved the last bit of chili dog into my mouth, a homeless man walked by, talking to himself. It hit me: I was just like him. Not saying this guy was one, but his behavior was very similar to that of a schizophrenic man I'd seen on my street sometimes arguing with himself. I mean, I did that all the time. Was I really any different?

Did I really hate reality that much? I was certainly always contemplating my past—what if, could have, should have. If my mind was on the future, it was about control and what I could do. So, when I was in the mirror, I was acting out every scenario I desired and wished to be true instead of being in the moment and being present in the NOW.

I needed to stop. I needed to stop looking in that literal and figurative mirror for the answers to see myself. I needed to be okay in the unknown space within myself. Instead of the outside version of me.

I decided to take Dr. Kath's direction as soon as I got home. I wouldn't even wait twenty-four hours. I would cover all the mirrors. I would commit myself to trying another way. I would be present to how I feel, more than how I look.

I felt a new sense of self-awareness. I felt a tremendous amount of relief knowing that I could do something about it. That it was possible for me to change with an easy-enough exercise. That it wouldn't kill me. I could do this. I didn't have to be so vain anymore.

Picking up my trash and walking over to the front door, I looked at my reflection in the glass pane to fix my hair. *What the...?* I'd just caught myself. Damn it! This was going to be a lot harder than I'd thought. I was fairly sure I would need to stare at the ground all week in order not to look up and be tempted by the reflections around me.

Luckily, it rarely rained, so there would be no puddles to reflect my image.

I climbed into Black Stallion and hit the call button for Coolgirl. As the phone rang, I kind of hoped she wouldn't answer. I was tempted to hang up—seriously, I was not in the mood to listen to other people's problems. Maybe I was PMSing? About to bleed? You know, a lady's monthly friend? *Attractive!*

No such luck. She answered out of breath and sounding relieved that I'd called back. I had to keep my word now, which sucked for a noncommittal woman like me.

"So glad you called me back. I booked a session with Dr. Kath tomorrow," Coolgirl informed me. "I'm working out right now but need to talk. I'm spinning out. I left Superstar's house. He has not called. I don't know what to do."

She needed to calm down. He was allowed to have a life without her. I mean, technically he had a whole family. "Girl, I don't know what you should do. I'm on the next level over here with Dr. Kath—I can't have any mirrors for the next week. I can not even relate to relationship problems at this moment," I grumbled.

Coolgirl gasped at the horror of my reality. "WWWWhat? Is she crazy? How in the world will you even go out of your house? Maybe I shouldn't see her, then? Will she do the same to me?"

I calmed her vanity down. "Girl, relax, we are not the same people. It took me a year to get to this level. She will have a different kind of session with you. Chill, homie."

"Amen, so glad. I was about to cancel. I really needed to talk to her today, but she was booked. It's just, I'm starting to think about us getting married and having a child. I'm almost forty, and I saw a little boy at an audition and felt my heart pound in my chest. I feel like I need to be a mom now. But Superstar said he is never going to leave his wife. I get that.

But I think I'm going to start freezing my eggs like a lot of my friends are doing, so I don't put pressure on myself."

I was taken aback by this new admission from her. "Good for you. Take care of your future and make sure that's what you want to do. I have a lot of other friends who have done it too."

"Awesome! That's what I'm going to do. I don't need to tell Superstar, right? I mean, it might freak him out," she said, extremely relieved. I could hear it in her voice.

"Nope, you're good. It does not even involve him, no need to share," I replied, with a sudden urgency to use the bathroom. Should have gone after therapy. You live and you learn.

"Great." She rattled on, "Also, I made an appointment with Dr. Dermatology on Rodeo about a buccal face lift. I mean, Miley's is still holding up. I think it will shave off a couple years, right?"

I wanted so badly to talk to her about her self-esteem issues. I mean, I was about to cover my mirrors, and she was considering a cosmetic procedure that would make her rely even more on hers. Yet, I couldn't even think straight, as I was focusing so hard on whether to pull over, or see if I could hold it until I got to my own private, clean toilet. Squeezing my legs together, I realized an accident was about to happen. "Girl, got to go. I have to pull over at this gas station to pee. About to burst. Bye, call me after tomorrow."

I rammed my car into the parking spot in front of the gas station, threw it into park, and rushed inside to ask for the key to the ladies' room.

DAMN IT!

God, you have got to be kidding me here. Guess who was at the counter paying for his gas. Mr. Handsome. Of course, I looked like hell, but we were on the other side of town. What were the odds? One in a million? One in a billion?

This was starting to feel a little kismet with a touch of stalker on both our parts.

He turned around and flashed his too-charming grin at me. "Hey, you!"

"Hey back. I don't have time for this. I have to pee." Okay, yes, I was rude, but I really had to freaking pee. As the attendant handed me the key, I yelled over my shoulder, "Good day to you." Like I had suddenly become a character in *Downton Abbey*.

I raced into the nasty stall, trying not to look at the mirror directly in front of the toilet. I pulled down my skinny jeans and let out a huge sigh as my bladder emptied. Seriously, the best feeling ever!

I zipped up and washed my hands. I kept my eyes down and didn't look in the dirty, scratched-up and graffiti-covered mirror. I looked at the door. I was hoping Mr. Handsome left already. Then, I heard a knock on the door. I yelled, "Someone is in here."

There was another knock, then another, and I spouted, "Ugh," as I accidentally looked in the mirror and yanked open the door to face the asshole who was hurrying me.

Who do you think was standing there with his shit-eating grin? Yep, Mr. Handsome. I looked like a hot mess and that motherfucker looked like he had just stepped out of *Vogue*. I couldn't even reprimand myself for going straight into judging our outer appearances. Instead, I glared at him and said, "You did that on purpose."

"NO, honestly, I just had to pee really badly. Good day to you." And he hustled into the bathroom.

Just before he shut the door, I said, "Stop following me. Not interested."

I was turning to go when he called through the door, "You sure about that?"

OH MY GOD, WE WERE FLIRTING. WHAT WAS HAP-PENING? I told myself he was not in my dating plan since he was in the entertainment business. He was an actor. Clearly, actors were not good for me. Besides, despite his charm and humor and wit, I was not interested in dating anyone right this moment.

I climbed back into my car as he was coming out of the restroom. I waved bye and he returned the gesture. Maybe it wasn't flirting. Maybe we were just two friendly people. Two good-looking friendly people. Two good-looking friendly people with potential chemistry. *STOP IT, ROXIE, now is not the time.* I would not fall for another pretty face and charming personality.

After getting home, I immediately got down to business.

I pulled out the black garbage bags and tape. I made my way around my house and frantically covered all surfaces that I could see my reflection in. Dr. Kath did allow me one tiny compact to check my teeth—so nice of her, right?

Now here I was, feeling accomplished with my commitment but also freaking tired. I was officially unable to see my reflection in anything in my house; I had even taped up the chrome on my oven. Extreme, I get it. But I was willing to do what it takes.

I was just so addicted to seeing myself and having that fantasy in the mirror of what I longed to happen, instead of living life on life's terms. I knew it was not going to be forever; it was just an assignment. I could do this. I was already starting to feel like I was about to embark on a deeper withdrawal from my false self. *I would be getting closer to the core*, as Dr. Kath told me.

Also, I knew my eyebrows were going to suffer, but this was a price I was willing to pay. I needed to do this.

A commitment to my *felix culpa*—you know, *the happy fall*. It's the famous theological concept where you reframe your failures. You look at the fortunate consequences of an unfortunate event, consequences that never would have been possible without the unfortunate event in the first place. My bottom in my sex and love addiction turned into the resurrection of my true self.

The soul-onion-peeling process has only one goal in mind—to get you back to your core being. Your innermost self.

Most of us run so far away during a period of survival that we forget to come back home to ourselves. Return home to yourself.

I am safe now. You are safe now.

CHAPTER ELEVEN

Rule 20: EGO never wins—
it tries to get everything for NOTHING.

I HAD SUCCESSFULLY MANAGED three full days of blissful abandonment of my own reflection. I had let go of all vanity—okay, I still wore some makeup, but come on! I only had a small compact to apply my concealer and foundation, but holy moly, I had let go of my eyeliner, plus mascara! Can you believe it? I actually did not put on any of my warrior paint for an audition! It was wild.

I had never truly thought I could go twenty-four hours, let alone three days; I felt like a baller.

You have to understand, I was a vain motherfucker. I loved perfecting my appearance. It was part of my ritual of acting out and getting much-needed attention for my disease.

Mirrors used to be my happy place—playing make-believe in my mirror, fantasizing about who I would have a certain date with, or how we would end up in bed together, and various other romantic obsessions. Even now, after being without a lover or partner, I still rely very heavily on the validation of my looks to fulfill me.

I know this might not make sense to many people—you might be rolling your eyes at this ridiculous exercise that Dr. Kath handed to me—but you have to really understand the world I live in. Looks mean everything in Hollywood. Well, let's actually be honest, looks mean everything in this so-cial-media-obsessed, filtered world. And now with AI, it's only making beauty standards unattainable. I saw a filter the other day that makes you perfectly made-up through artificial intel-ligence, so no one could ever see your flaws. And another filter that instantly takes ten years off your face. Remember a few years ago when the closest thing to this was a feature on Snap-chat that allowed you to (badly) switch faces with someone? It was all so innocent and fun. Now, it's downright repulsive. AI is literally changing our online presence and warping our own minds as to what we actually look like. Ironically, mirrors have become a form of truth tellers. They reflect back the flaws and imperfections. But for me, the mirror still heavily represented my fantasy addict self. They made me disconnect from my in-ternal world and only focus on my outer shell.

And yes, being a Hollywood actress, for god's sake, makes everything revolve around those petty vanity traits. You want it all. All the accolades for little actual work, because when you base it on outside vanity, not much is built on the inside.

Rule 20: EGO never wins—it tries to get every-thing for NOTHING.

For better or for worse.

For example, here is the day-to-day life on set for an actor: We are treated like gods the moment we arrive to set. People do our hair and makeup and dress us up like their own little dolls. They carefully hand-select our wardrobe and mold it per-fectly to our bodies. They ask if we want water or coffee every ten minutes. Then they follow us around all day like our own personal watchdogs, walking us to our chairs after a take on camera, because we are not to be trusted—we might get lost.

Our chairs have our names on them, and no one else is supposed to sit in them. Assistants ask if we're hungry, then go make us a sandwich. It's a narcissist's dream job.

Look, as I'm saying all this, it seems all glamorous—and trust me, I love the attention—but the reason actors are treated so phenomenally on set is that we spend 260 days a year auditioning, enduring innumerable soul-sucking callbacks, maybes, almost, and then the very rare; YOU GOT IT! A part of me thinks we deserve all the pampering for the early struggle of rejection. We deprive ourselves of carbs, obsessively work out when we're tired, schmooze when we're exhausted, and have forty-odd jobs to pay rent. When we finally book a job, we get that ridiculous royal treatment.

The only problem with this theory is that my ego loved the treatment on set. I loved the limelight, the adoration, the constant ego stroking. My ego told me, hell yes—Bring it on! This is the payoff for the hell we put up with the rest of the year. I earned this! Get me my damn sandwich.

So, when I had to give up the mirror—which, in the last few months, I had been religiously using to study my new wrinkles and flaws—it was hard. I mean, constantly judging my looks was simply another form of self-punishment.

Letting that mirror go became another form of withdrawal for me.

Still, I was walking through this mirror challenge with flying colors. I'd committed once again to bettering my inner self rather than the outside. I was open to the possibilities of who I might actually find in there.

Proudly, I walked out of my house, strutting like the stud I was on my way to meet Coolgirl for her monthly wax. Yep, you heard me correctly. Not my choice of meeting place. Don't worry, I wasn't going to watch her get it done, just meeting her there to grab a tea afterward.

As I climbed into my beloved Rover, I looked at my reflection in my car window. *UGH, I'm an egotistical freak!*

I ran back into the house to get my dark sunglasses; it was much harder to see myself in my black aviators. Sure, it was a hack, but I was doing anything I could to battle this vanity disease.

Fun fact: It was surprisingly freeing not to be so obsessed with my looks. It now felt like every time I looked around me, I saw other people obsessed with their own reflections. Plus, don't even get me started on the whole selfie generation, which I've gone into great detail about before.

I felt like God had held a larger mirror up, showing me how empty it was to be all about oneself. The deeper lesson was that it doesn't matter in the end. Looks fade, but self-love doesn't.

Remember that scene in *Barbie* where Margot Robbie sits with the old lady on the bench? *Incidentally, the woman is ninety-two-year-old Academy Award-winning costume designer Ann Roth, but I digress.* Margot Robbie, who is the epitome of beauty, stares at this old, wrinkled woman devoid of makeup and pretense, and says with earnest awe, "You are so beautiful." To which the woman giddily responds, "I know."

I've thought a lot about that scene and the message Greta Gerwig was trying to get to all women: Barbie, as we know her, is not the template of beauty.

All women are beautiful.

It was truly a whole different take on peeling this onion to my core self. I started to really base my existence on a much deeper level than surface-level beauty. It blew my mind how doing this one little action had completely shifted my perspective.

I wished I had done this earlier, which was always a regret/judgment feeling when I went deeper within myself. I longed to be healed earlier in my life, but that was another way to shame myself for simply not knowing. I did not have a strong enough sense of self-worth to do it before. For as long as I can remember, my looks were the only currency I had to offer the world.

Not true anymore, you fine folks. I had discovered many more traits I was proud of and that my God had filled me with and brought to my attention.

One of them was being there for others, which is why I was on my way to meet Coolgirl. She was still struggling with Superstar. I truly wished she could let him go, but it was not my call. That was her battle to fight.

I was supposed to meet her at a coffee place in Beverly Hills, La Provence. I got there early, of course, because I was always early to everything, while she was always late—a very bad combination for a healthy friendship. One of us was always annoyed with the other, which was usually me. I hated waiting.

She texted me that she was still at her waxing place, *Brazilian Honey Waxing*, and that I should walk over and keep her company since the waxer was running behind.

Lovely, not exactly what I had in mind for my viewing activity this afternoon. I'd already seen that vagina once, during our botched Vagina Gate threesome. And once was definitely enough for me.

I got to the office, and she texted that she was in Room 4. I knocked and walked in. There she was, spread-eagled. Thank God, she was facing away from me this time. *Hallelujah!* The Russian lady was prepping the wax.

For your inquiring minds, I've never been waxed. *No thank you!* I do not need hot molten slime lathered on my labia by an older woman to then have it be unceremoniously ripped off. I can just shave that myself, no biggie.

Really, if you think about it, guys do not care as long as they're getting some action. Let's be serious, ladies, they couldn't give two shits if you have a Brazilian or opt for au naturel. *Sex is sex.*

Some twisted sicko wanted his lady to look like a young, pure pussy. *Again, a big pedophilia hell no; I will pass.*

Coolgirl was getting it all ripped off, and the entire time, she was screaming and cursing out Superstar's real name. I would have had the decency to scream out a few other A-lister names to hide Superstar's identity, but she was laser-focused on her momentary hatred of him. Hopefully, Russian Waxer didn't make the connection; then again, she probably couldn't give two shits and had definitely heard it all AND seen it all. I felt like I was in a surreal Fellini film, and I could not stop laughing.

Man, this shit was funny to witness.

"Why would you want to do that to yourself?" I asked, fully aware that her bush was being torn bare for her man's enjoyment.

She replied between screams, "It makes me feel good with how much he loves it." SCREAMS "I love that he gets turned on." SCREAMS "And I can see from your judgmental expression that you don't approve, but I like to turn my man on, Roxie." SCREAMS, "It's okay to do things to please your partner."

SCREAMS.

She then looked at me and frowned. "Are you not wearing makeup? Wow, hell has frozen over."

"Uh, thank you very much for the hell remark. You have seen me without makeup before. Now, can you please get dressed so we can go get some tea?"

I stepped out of the labia-ripping room, saying the Serenity Prayer under my breath. "God, grant me the serenity to accept the things I cannot change, the courage to change the things I can, and the wisdom to know the difference."

She was working my last nerve, and I was feeling triggered by her response to getting waxed and her comment about my makeup-free look. I suddenly felt a little self-conscious. Mostly because her beautiful, dark skin never needed makeup and she looked stunning even on no sleep. It also triggered me that she'd never done these sorts of things before she was with him. A part of me believed she was compromising too much for this relationship. I never could understand why women do these ridiculous things for a man. Was that my ego being judgmental? Probably, but at least I was self-aware enough to know it.

I knew I needed to have compassion. I did. It was just really hard sometimes.

As we walked over to the French coffee shop, she was adjusting her leggings, and I giggled. She shot me a look. "You have always worn makeup, even when training with my brother. He actually asked me about it the other day. I was just surprised when I saw you, but I love that you are au naturel."

I had to change the subject, because all I wanted to do was run into the nearest alley and apply my eyeliner. The pull was that strong. So instead, I asked her, "How was therapy with Dr. Kath?"

She gave a dramatic sigh. "We talked a lot about the relationship and why I wanted to be in it. I told her I believed that my guardian angels brought him to me to make my wishes and desires come true. He's teaching me how to love in a different way, that it's not all monogamous partnerships. That there can be many forms of connection and love partnerships in this universe."

I was going to tread lightly here after all that had happened with Tattoogirl, but it was still my job to speak the truth; albeit, in a much softer, gentler way. No one reacts well when they are ambushed and accused in this disease. I had tried it my way, and I'd failed miserably.

I chose my words carefully. "Huh? I'm sorry, but I'm confused by you lately. Please help me understand. I truly want to support you. But the last time we talked about this, a year ago, you were wanting a family and a man to come home to. Do you even have that now?"

She turned to me. "This is exactly why I didn't want to talk to you about this. We have different ideas of what a partnership can look like and what our journeys are in this lifetime, Roxie."

I took a deep breath and tried to hold it together and not lash out at her. "Coolgirl, I'm sorry if you think I'm judging you—I am not. I just remember very clearly that before you got involved with Superstar, you wanted something else."

She looked at me like I was an idiot. "My Universe has me, like yours has you. You and I have totally different takes on when God brings something into our lives. For example, you always say it's a test that you need to choose a different path in life, but I believe God shows me what I am needing in my life. He wants me with Superstar. I truly believe that. I believe that all of my three marriages brought me closer to this life I'm having right now. To someone on my level, someone whom I envisioned for my life, and someone to bring my creativity to the forefront to share with the whole world. No other past partner has done those things for me. This union is meant to be. And I'm sorry if you cannot accept that."

"I can accept it, friend. But I'm allowed to ask questions without you being defensive, aren't I?"

"Yes, of course you are, Roxie. I can hear the disapproval in your tone."

I thought about that as we got to the shop. "I have one more question. As your friend and because I love you, I have to ask it. Why are you so unhappy? If it is truly what your God wants, why is it making you question so much?"

She looked at me with uncertainty. "I honestly don't know. That's why I needed to go see Dr. Kath. And funnily enough, she asked me the same thing. She told me it might be good to go to some meetings with you."

"You should. All I know is that when I was unhappy and in a confusing place, I had to surrender. Surrender does not mean giving up; it's the moment you realize it is more painful to hold on than to let go."

I saw the way she was looking at me, her wheels turning as she tried to figure out a way to deny what I'd just said. So, I continued, "Surrender means it's a death of our own identity, the end of an old idea, allowing our perspective to widen so we can understand what we were avoiding. Everything else is just noise for our addict to run wild, I believe."

She shrugged. "I will think about it."

We grabbed our tea lattes and sat, immediately changing the subject since she had closed down and was not willing to discuss her relationship anymore. I started to tell her about my upcoming callback for a huge movie. "She is a great character, broken but humorous. So excited to meet the director. I'm kind of nervous though. I loved his last war movie." She had been shifting the entire time I was talking, and finally it was so distracting, I stopped my story and stared at her. "Girl, you got ants in your pants? What's up?"

She groaned in frustration. "My pussy itches so badly. I hate getting waxed. This crap is uncomfortable. It kind of burns after, too." I giggled, and she said, "Stop! You're so cruel."

"Not as cruel as you are to your puss. Ripping hot wax off it. I feel bad for her." I blow a kiss over my shoulder to her and her poor vagina.

An hour later, I pulled up to Warner Bros. Studios. I had a callback for the lead role in a huge studio movie. I was scared out of my mind. My nerves were in full-blown panic at the enormity of this opportunity. I was about to do what I always did before heading into a meeting or audition: fix my face. Just as I pulled the visor down, I stopped myself and said aloud, "Roxanne, you are fine just as you are. No need to focus on your appearance. Just go in and be yourself. Let them see the real you."

I walked into the huge production offices, which were the size of four of my houses put together. I signed in at the lobby with all the other blonde girls my age who were there for the same role. I tried to calm my breath and tell myself that this was my part. I had prepared. I had rehearsed. I was ready. It was my role to lose. Not theirs! Then I saw her. Damn—Doppelgänger! She was like my little stalker. Always around for every opportunity!

You ever have someone like Doppelgänger in your life? Someone who always happens to show up in your big life moments. It felt like I'd had Doppelgänger situations a lot in my life. In high school, there was one who wanted the same guy, and in grade school, another one wanted the same award as me. She's that person who is kind of like your nemesis, even though you like them as a human being. *But still wish they would get lost.*

Well, that was who just walked in the door to my callback. Doppelgänger waved across the room at me, and I waved back. I tried to block her out as I ran the lines in my head—don't worry, I wasn't one of those actors who said them out loud for the whole room to hear. Or one of those people who mouthed the words and acted out the action in their seats. It's a doozy to watch. Not going to lie, it was hard for me not to roll my eyes and make fun of them. Because again, it was none of my business how others prepared for their job interviews. I probably didn't do it myself because I was afraid to look stupid or ridiculous in front of others. Good for them for not caring! As I was feeling jealous of their freedom, my name was called.

Suddenly, I was thrown as I spiraled over others not caring, and me, caring too much. I was jealous of their ease, their self-awareness, their comfort with themselves. Who was I to compete in that arena? I tried to tamp down my nerves and push away the fear as I strutted in as confidently as I could, my nerves going crazy. But my hands were literally sweating. I could not show my fear in case they saw my terrified self and didn't want to give me the part—saw that I was not able to perform under pressure. I think that's why auditions are held. They are more terrifying than actually doing the part on the real shoot.

I nodded to the bigwigs on the couch and took my mark.

The reader across from me started to say his lines, and I accidentally caught my naked reflection in a mirror in the corner. I froze. Yep, full-on paralysis. No words came out. I just stood there and stared at the reader. Out of the corner of my eye, I saw the casting director look at the A-list producer/ director on the other couch.

It was a fight-or-flight moment, and as much as every instinct in my body wanted to flee the room, I knew I was a fighter. I got myself together by saying very loudly in my head, *Roxanne, don't fuck up, you got this.* Then the words started to stumble out of my mouth. I genuinely did not know if it was the best audition I'd ever given or the worst, but I did it.

As I hit the last sentence, I breathed a huge sigh of relief. When I looked up, they were staring at me. The casting director, whom I love and who has always been a huge fan of mine, gave me a half-hearted smile and looked around the room to the team of producers. Then he turned to me with that same slight grin. "Thank you, Roxanne."

I turned and pretty much mumbled, "Thank you," and walked out.

I passed the waiting room and headed straight to my car. I got in the car, and the self-abuse started to seep into every corner of my thoughts. *You are a huge loser, Roxanne. You screwed up another great opportunity. When are you going to give up? You're embarrassing yourself.*

As the self-hatred swirled through my mind, it hit me. I never brought God into the room with me. How could I do my best if I didn't lean back on his presence? I had made it all about me and getting the job—how it would get me to the next level of my career. I was on a never-ending staircase, and each floor meant more opportunity. I hadn't been in the present but rather in the future, as I'd already envisioned the Deadline article about me getting the job.

I had failed myself again. I had been more wrapped up with what the job could bring me than actually just being in the moment. I couldn't enjoy just performing a really well-written part for a captive audience of industry professionals for five minutes. I was more in love with the fantasy of the job than the actual job.

A huge shift in my perspective needed to happen if I was going to stay in this business.

As I sat in my car in the lot of Warner Bros., I asked God to please show me the way, if it was to stay in this profession as an entertainer, and to please help me let go of the glory and egotistical thoughts of what it would mean to me as a person. And if I needed to let go of it, to help me find my new way to be creative and prosperous. I had to let go and truly let God have all of me.

Starting the car, the only thing I could think to do was to call another person in my life and ask about them in order to get out of my own warped thoughts. Alice answered on the first ring.

"What up, homie?" I said. "You excited about your big day this weekend?"

Alice answered with a burst of howls. "No, Roxanne, I am not. I am about to have a nervous breakdown over here. I want to run."

"Okay, lady. I'll come and grab you. Don't panic. Stay put—on my way."

I pulled up to her place, a guesthouse behind a mansion off Beachwood Canyon. I'd already ordered us meatloaf from Joan's on Third, with a chai latte for her and a double shot of espresso for me. I had looked on the SLAA website and found a meeting in an hour at a church nearby.

I abruptly parked the car and texted her, "Get your tush-ie in my car. I got us provisions, and we are headed to the healthy-relationship meeting on Cahuenga."

She typed back, "On my way, thank you, friend."

I had an overwhelming sense of relief that I was okay without that big studio acting job I had just auditioned for. That I was okay without the glitz and glamour, that I was a good friend to my old sponsor in her time of desperate need. That massive sense of worth engulfed me, relieving me of any bondage of self.

My ego couldn't be in charge anymore. Because when I let it run wild, it turned into the death of my true value. Constant vigilance is the price we pay for sobriety. I was truly grateful for the aware person I had become. Even when it could be exhausting to endure.

Alice rolled out of her complex looking like a hot mess. Wow, I had never seen her looking so off before. She was usually so put together, so prim and proper; you would have no idea that this sweet schoolteacher was a sex and love addict. She did lean more toward the love-addict side, but if you saw her, you would be shocked.

Alice was normally in her bohemian maxi dresses from Free People that she found at vintage stores or T.J. Maxx outlets, which I was a huge fan of. It was one of the many reasons we got along so well: our love of a good deal. *Perfect thing to base a friendship on. Retail savings!*

Sometimes, we would do my step-work discussions while browsing the discount section at the T.J. Maxx on Ventura Blvd. We were ideal customers: She had a teacher's salary, and I never knew when I was going to be employed. So, she is usually fashion forward. But right now, she was in mismatched sweatpants and T-shirt, with her long thick hair pulled back into a low pony. She had no makeup on and was frazzled all to hell. My girl was a HOT mess with a capital M.

Out of breath from God-knows-what, she climbed in as I handed her the chai latte and her bag of goodies from Joan's. "Oh my gosh, you are a saint. Roxie, thank you so much for this. I was about to lose it. My mom is staying with us. I'm pretty certain she is trying to make this whole situation about her and making it completely miserable for me, just because she can. I started cleaning our place at five a.m. to get my mind off her behavior and my wedding. She is driving me crazy about the flower arrangements and seating chart. I mean, whose wedding is this, right? I was just about to blow up at her when you called."

She paused for a split second before continuing, "What the heck is different about you? You look so stunning. OMG, you're not wearing eye makeup."

I responded shyly, "Yep, Dr. Kath has gotten her way. She's making me do the mirror test, so I'm going for a week without looking at my own reflection. I'm actually getting used to it."

Alice smiled with pure admiration. "Well, I think you look perfect. Good for you. I wish I had your determination sometimes. When you're asked to do something to better yourself, you always go full force into the unknown. It's very infectious to witness. It's one of the things I admire about you."

"Thank you. Means a lot. But I'm here for you today. How can I help your stress? You know, you can stay with me at my place if you need to get away."

She turned to me like I had just given her a million dollars. "Oh my, gosh darn it, I know how much you hate people in your space. That means everything. I might even take you up on that."

"Well, you would do it for me. Please don't hesitate. I can get over my social anorexia of people in my space. It actually has gotten better for me."

"Oh man, that makes me want to cry. I'm so very proud of you. Listen, I hate to ask, but did you find a new sponsor yet? I feel like I've failed you, or bailed on you—"

"Alice, don't," I said, cutting her off. "I'm glad you fired me, truly. Now we are so much closer, I feel like you're my sister."

That was it, the floodgates opened, and she was officially bawling, which was sweet but a little much for me.

We all know I'm a huge work in progress. But my heart did skip a beat. Progress, not perfection over here.

"So sorry, I don't know what's wrong with me. Everything is making me cry. I'm a mess. Charlie keeps asking what I need from him, and I just get annoyed. Why? That's not fair to him. He's trying to help and I'm being a total bitch." She blew her nose on her sleeve, and I was thinking, *That is nasty, but do not poke the bear when they're upset.*

I reminded myself to be gentle like she always was with me, which was beyond hard because it was so not in my nature. "It's okay. Feel your feelings. You are allowed. Maybe just try to do something nice for Charlie tonight? I mean, I'm just guessing over here since I have never had a healthy relationship in my life, but just a thought."

Wiping her nose on her sleeve again—*yummy*—she said, "Give yourself a break, Roxie. You never had a healthy relationship modeled for you. You are going to be great in your next one. I can see it." Suddenly, she looked like she was going to be sick. She shouted, "Pull over now, I'm going to throw up."

I pulled over to the side of the road off Laurel Canyon, and she opened the door while the car was still moving. It looked like *The Exorcist* as the puke came pouring out, even onto the door handle, I might add. Weirdly, it was a very interesting color of throw-up, all the colors of the rainbow. She kept hurling until she was empty. "Sorry. That came out of nowhere. Of course I get sick right before my wedding, just my luck."

My wheels were turning with possibilities, but all I could focus on was the rainbow of puke on my door. "What did you eat this morning?"

She looked over at the door. "Oh, I had a bag of Skittles for breakfast. I was having a moment."

Alice was also in OA, Overeaters Anonymous, another twelve-step program for addicts who use food to comfort and cope with their emotions. I can now understand how out of control she must have felt. I had an overwhelming sense of compassion for my sister. Then what I truly thought popped out of my mouth: "Are you sure you're not pregnant?"

She looked at me, floored by the absurdity of that statement. "No way, I had my period on time. Wait, what day is it?" She opened her phone to look at her loyal period-tracker app.

My belief: Every woman on the planet should track their period—it can be unbelievably helpful with the mood swings. And obviously, the pregnancy scares.

Good times being a woman!

"Holy crap. Holy crap. Holy crap." She was looking down at the calendar, adding in another "Holy crap" for good measure. "I should be bleeding now. Oh my gosh, what if I'm pregnant? That means I'll be walking down the aisle with child; I am officially the poster child for sex and love addiction." She looked like she was going to start crying again.

"Come on, Alice, you are in a healthy relationship with the man you love. There's nothing wrong with being pregnant and getting married at the same time. I mean, do you want to have a child?"

She hung her head and said softly, "Yes."

"Remember, your wedding day is just a day to show your love to your friends and family, to celebrate. That's it, just a very expensive party. It's your ego that is telling you it has to look a certain way."

I put the car in gear and turned back onto the road on the way to our meeting. "We are going to swing by CVS, pick up a pregnancy test, and then get to our meeting." As I took charge, I added, "Because we've both had a trying day and need to drop back into our reality."

I really felt in the moment of being of service to Alice, being her rock; like I had truly started to let go of my "I" culture, as in, it's all about ME. If you look up EGO in the dictionary, it clearly states, "The 'I' or self—a person as thinking, feeling, and willing, and distinguishing itself from the selves of others and from objects of its thought," which to me then predicts very cleverly that the concept of egoism—conceit and self-importance—serves as the central reference point in all kinship relationships. That "I" can never be the most important anymore, especially in those self-entitled ways.

I knew I had to let go of the concept that everything I encountered was revolving around me.

EXT. MERRY-GO-ROUND—DAY

ROXIE climbs up on a merry-go-round, settling on a black horse. The music starts to play, and she looks at the other riders.

THEY ARE ALL HER. Roxie on a white palomino. Roxie on a spotted horse. Roxie on a stallion.

> ROXIE
> WHAT IS HAPPENING?

> STALLION ROXIE
> It can't all be about you, Roxie.

> SPOTTED ROXIE
> Yeah, Rox. When you let go of your ego, the world does not revolve around you.

The music gets faster. Demonic.

> ROXIE
> My whole life has been about egoism.

PALOMINO ROXIE
When you let that go, imagine
the possibilities.

Roxie tries to look in the merry-go-round
mirror, but the horses are spinning too fast.

STALLION ROXIE
Be of service to others.

SPOTTED ROXIE
Let them see the authentic
you.

ROXIE
How?

PALOMINO ROXIE
When you finally shed your
egoism, you can listen to
others and share yourself.
Then you can begin the process
of loving.

STALLION ROXIE
Take a risk, Roxie. Risk to
love and be loved.

Suddenly, the music stops. Roxie looks around.
The merry-go-round is now filled with friends
and loved ones. Alice is on the white palomino.
Dr. Kath is on the spotted horse. Mr. Handsome
is on the stallion.

SMASH TO BLACK

I ran into the CVS to grab Alice's pregnancy test, since she
was too embarrassed, afraid she might run into someone she
knew. I grabbed her some saltines, ginger candies, and ginger
ale. I was tempted to get her a bag of Skittles, but even I wasn't
that cruel.

I liked to think I was an expert on the needs of pregnant women simply because I had played a pregnant woman

on television and remembered what the character had to eat while she was in her first trimester.

Yes, I was shoving saltines into my mouth the whole season. Still can't stand that cracker unless I have the flu.

My acting jobs have supplied me with random tidbits and facts I use in all areas of my life. I can play the violin, shoot an AK-47, tell you how to kill someone, swing on a stripper pole, and many more interesting things I've learned from the various characters I've played.

As I was impatiently waiting in line with all of my look-world-I'm-pregnant paraphernalia in my arms, a familiar voice rang next to my ear. "I guess congratulations are in order."

"God, no," I said, turning around to face Mr. Handsome again. "How does this keep happening? Are you truly stalking me?"

"How far along are you?" he pressed.

"Huh?" I asked in utter confusion, since the sight of him always had me a tad flustered. "What in god's name are you going on about?"

He pointed at the pregnancy test and provisions. "Your bun in the oven. Pea in the pod. In the family way..."

Laughing uncomfortably, I replied, "Oh no, it's not mine. My friend just threw up Skittles in my car and I think she's pregnant, so I pulled over to grab her some nausea stuff and a test. Thanks for the congratulations, but nope, not knocked up this time." Then I quickly added, "I don't even know if the world needs another little ME."

He gave me that charming look with his twinkly golden eyes. Wait, did I tell you he had golden eyes? They were the most beautiful, mesmerizing color, and when he smiled, they lit up.

"I don't know. Another you, sounds like heaven to me."

"Enough, dude, stop flirting with me. I am not interested. And stop following me all over the city. Good lord, have some game." I couldn't help but laugh as I said it, since the look on his face said he did not believe any of the horseshit coming out of my mouth.

He roared a huge laugh when I turned back around, flicking my hair over my shoulders. "Sure, you want me to stop? Keep telling yourself that."

"I'm not dating right now," I said over my shoulder.

"I never asked you on a date."

I whipped around with attitude. "Why is that?" *Wait? Did I just say that?*

"I mean, I wanted to back at the Whole Foods, and then again in the parking lot, and then again at the gas station, but—"

"But what?" I was red faced. I felt like I was picking an argument when really, I just couldn't stop looking into his gorgeous eyes.

"But you're always yelling at me," he said, laughing.

"Jesus, would you two just get a room already," a gravelly voice said, and we both turned to a woman in her seventies, standing behind Mr. Handsome. Her bright blue eyes were laughing at us.

"Excuse me?" we both said at once.

"You two need to get your crap together. Life is short. You, sir, just ask her out already, and miss, you need to be a little more feminine if you want to catch a man." I looked at her aghast, and Mr. Handsome looked pleased. She added, "Now hurry up, I have a date I'm late for. It's your turn to check out. Good lord, these younger folks."

I moved up to the counter and paid for Alice's purchases. As the cashier was ringing me up, Mr. Handsome sidled up next to me and whispered in my ear, kind of loudly, "How about it?"

Without looking at him, I responded, "How about what?"

"Man, you are not going to make this easy, are you?"

"Nope."

He then said, in a very gentlemanly manner, "Really? Don't you ever give a man a break?"

I turned to him after putting the credit back in my wallet. I stared right at him without saying a word. He stared back. As we both just stared at each other, my ego backed down and a calm washed over me. Almost like something bigger took over. I asked, "Would you like to go on a date with me?"

He smiled very sweetly, almost like a young boy. "Okay. I will go out with you."

It was one of the most innocent moments I'd ever had with the opposite sex. Feeling very vulnerable, I messed it up with my sarcasm: "Well, you call me to make the plans, since I was the one who asked you out." I jotted my number into his phone then bolted out of the store as fast as I could.

I was breathing heavily like a wild animal was chasing me, which scared the crap out of Alice, who had fallen asleep in the car. I was guessing she was probably 100% pregnant, falling asleep that quickly in a bright CVS parking lot. Her head whip-lashed up. "You scared me. What's the matter?"

I was staring at the store, and as Mr. Handsome walked out, I pointed to him. "I just asked that guy out. From my old acting class."

She turned to look out the windshield. "Oh, he is handsome." I silently agreed.

Then he turned and looked right at us, and I shoved her and shouted, "Get down, he might see us." We both slid down in our seats and hid, for some inexplicable reason. I was just feeling very raw and vulnerable.

We heard a knock on my window and a masculine laugh. "Hi, Roxanne and friend. I have your purchases. You left them on the counter when you ran away from me."

I rolled down the window. "Crap."

I sat up, acting like there was nothing weird about us hiding. "Thank you. And I was not racing away from you. I was racing *to* something. We're in a hurry for our meeting."

He asked, "What meeting?"

"None of your business. Now, please hand us her pregnancy test and be on your way."

He ignored me and looked at Alice. "Nice to meet you. I'm Mr. Handsome."

Alice smiled her sweet, innocent teacher smile. "Nice to meet you too. I'm Alice. Roxanne told me all about you."

"She did, did she?" He grinned at me with that irresistible charm.

Alice giggled. "Thanks for bringing our stuff."

I turned to Alice. "Don't be nice to him. He'll get too many ideas."

He laughed. "See you around, Alice. Hope you get the news you're hoping for. And I will see you very soon, Roxanne." He turned and walked to his car.

I muttered under my breath, "Damn, he is too good looking for a man."

Alice added, "Yes, but there is something so kind about his eyes. It's almost like he doesn't know how handsome he is. I like him. A lot!"

I looked at her. "You like everyone, and you're just knocked up and feeling those hormonal feelings. Not the best combination for reading people."

I started the car and pulled out of the lot. "Now, let's get this stick peed on and get to our meeting. Which I now need more than ever, since I have a date coming up with Mr. Charming Pants. Lord, I need to hear some experience, strength, and hope."

As I walked into the handicap stall with Alice in the church bathroom, the irony of attending a sex and love addict meeting right after taking a pregnancy test did not go unnoticed. We were both cracking up at the craziness of this while waiting for the double line to potentially appear.

For three minutes, we stared at the pee stick... until a light-blue double line appeared. We screamed in unison, which scared the crap out of the other ladies in the bathroom. "Sorry, we just found out some news." I hugged Alice tightly as she started to cry. Not sure if it was in fear or excitement.

She was kind of in a daze as we rinsed our hands and she pocketed the test. I turned to her as the door shut behind us. "Are you okay?"

She was still holding the test in her pocket. "I think so. I'm in shock, I guess. I was not expecting this."

"You want me to take you home?"

She looked at me with determination. "Hell no. I fucking need a meeting. I just found out I'm knocked up days before my wedding."

For your information, dear Alice never cusses. So, for her to say the F-bomb, as she usually calls it, she was clearly about to lose it. We walked into the meeting and saw a lot of familiar faces, saying hello to our friends and fellows. It was like my home away from home. I always felt welcome and breathed a huge sigh of relief and serenity.

It was my safe space in this crazy Hollywood world.

We sat and listened to the speaker, Sam—an older married lesbian woman, whom I had always admired and adored—as she talked about all the things I had also been going through. "I was scared to really put myself out there. I did not want to date available people, because then I had to step up and be available. That scared the crap out of me. My ego didn't want to allow me to be rejected. The willingness to really be seen by another was the hardest thing I have ever done. I remember the first time my wife saw me naked without a stitch of make-up, I felt so raw and vulnerable. I felt like I was going to die, that I was going to be dismissed."

As she kept telling her story, I looked over at Alice, who had a dazed look on her face, like she was trying to figure out her whole future. I grabbed her hand and held it. She turned to me and smiled, as I mouthed to her, "You are going to be okay. I am here for you."

She mouthed back, "I love you."

I mouthed back to her, "Love you too." And I saw her shoulders drop and her visibly relax.

We stayed that way through the whole meeting. Just holding each other's hands and listening to our other sober friends share their experience, strength, and hope. Sometimes it's just good to listen. It helps you feel less alone in the unknowns of life on life's terms.

When the meeting came to a close, our hands were sweaty and stuck together. I turned to Alice. "I'm going to ask Sam to be my new sponsor."

"I love her. She would be great with you. I'll wait outside. Need to text Charlie that we're leaving soon."

My heart was pounding and my ego kept telling me to turn around and just text her later about being my sponsor. But something kept telling me to stand in line and wait. Sam had a crowd around her. When it was finally my turn, my hands were sweaty as I thanked her for her share. I gave her a hug and said, "Thank you so much. I needed to hear everything you just said." My voice broke with nerves, but I pushed through. "I was hoping you could be my sponsor. Alice and I have parted ways, and I've been looking for the right person with more time in the program than me. Are you available?"

She studied me closely. "I have five other sponsees right now, but let's talk about it. For me, I can only take you through the steps. I'm not really available for check-in calls every day and all that."

"That's fine. I just need to get back to my step-work and

set a new dating plan. I'm out of the drama and withdrawal, so that can work for me if it works for you."

"Yes. I think we can set up some clear boundaries and see how it goes. Call me tomorrow to set up a time to start the process."

I smiled, so proud of putting myself out there again for true, raw rejection—and, I just realized I did it without my camouflage eye makeup. I mean, I just asked out the hottest guy with no makeup on. Who was this person? Who was I becoming?

I heard this from a fellow in a meeting six months ago, it's filled with so much wisdom: Being vulnerable means allowing all of my defects and all of my fears to be seen by another human being. It means taking a chance on getting hurt by trusting someone else with the reality of who I am. Ego and love cannot exist together.

EGO is a small three-letter word, which can destroy a big twelve-letter word called Relationship.

Now here I was, accepting the true reality of who I was and how I looked. My false self, the EGO, was no longer running the show.

How freeing it felt to want to be the naked, raw, REAL ME!

CHAPTER TWELVE

Am I Ready to LOVE and BE Loved?

WHEN YOU STOP LOOKING, love shows up with no drama and flows so easily you wonder why you were looking so hard for it in the first place. I see that now: True connection does not involve any drama; in fact, it should be easy. I will develop my ability to love and be loved by connecting with people who are capable of love, but am I ready to LOVE and BE loved? Opening my heart to something real was very scary in my life. Sometimes it felt like a monstrous task, and other times it felt like the simplest thing in the world.

"Nothing important is ever impressive," my new sponsor, Sam, informed me, after I shared with her my past failures in multiple areas of my life. She challenged me to truly look at my life now. "How do you feel in this timeframe, compared to yourself this time last year? Let's draw a line down the middle of a page. Let's do your life last year on one side and this year on the other. What do you see?"

I laughed at the exercise she had given me. I opened to a clean sheet of paper in my notebook, drew a line, and started writing all the main plot points of my life before and after. I stared for a moment at the differences on the page in front of me. They looked like two totally different people. "They are completely different. Sometimes, I literally look in the mirror and do not recognize the face staring back at me. If you had told me two years ago, or even six months ago, that I would be this person I am now, I would not have believed you."

"Why is that?"

It weirdly came so easily for me to explain. I didn't make excuses. I didn't place blame. I just... was fully and authentically in my own body and mind—it was pure self-acceptance. "I am just a much nicer, happier person. For one, I don't have a lot of drama in my life. I don't have any people who I would not show up for in the middle of the night and them for me. Also, a huge thing is that I don't wear a lot of makeup anymore. It feels like that literal and figurative mask has been lifted."

"I get it, Roxanne. I felt that way too. And now, when you start dating again, the first things you are going to look at in the relationship with this other flawed human being are: Is there drama? Are they able to show up? Can they keep their word? I think the most important question is: Would I want to be friends with them if sex were not in the equation?"

I nodded. In the past, it would have been their looks, their status, their ability to make me feel better. But she was spot-on. I now saw potential relationships in a whole different light. I looked at Sam. "Is that what you did when you met your wife?"

She grinned. "Yes. And for me, the other important question I asked myself when I started to date her was: Is she doing spiritual work on herself? Does she have her own path to emotional growth?"

Sam and I had met at Aroma Coffee & Tea on Tujunga Ave. It was an eclectic coffee shop with delicious food, where I loved to meet people. All of the tables and decorations were different, and it was a prime Hollywood meet-up spot. When tourists come to LA, they mistakenly go to Rodeo Drive in Beverly Hills or the Hollywood Walk of Fame to see celebrities. But celebrities are just like you and me. They need their coffee in the morning and like to mix food with work. In fact, you can often see an A-list actor at Aroma having coffee with their managers; however, today, most of the customers were a bunch of out-of-work actors like me.

Just for the record, I'd never heard about that movie audition where I sucked royally. I was still hitting myself that I froze—actually froze—before I started. Perhaps not looking in the mirror had made me too authentically me and that scared them. Still, I guessed it was better to hear nothing than a bunch of bad feedback. I stopped my self-hate spiral and smiled back at Sam, who was downing her espresso like water.

"I agree that those aspects in partner are important to me too, Sam. I hope I can find a partner to share that same trust and friendship with."

We sat there for the next thirty minutes coming up with my new dating plan. Sam told me that on the first two dates I simply needed to be light and polite. That I was mostly just interviewing this person for a friendship with me. No trauma bonding. No love bombing. No oversharing about past relationships. I simply needed to ask myself if I enjoyed this two-hour meal with them as a person-to-person connection. That was the simplest way to look at dating for a fantasy addict like me. *That was easy enough, I could do that.*

She advised, "There should not be any pressure to find a perfect match. Too many people are obsessed with future tripping and not living in the pause of this inner work."

"I've never heard that before—living in the pause?"

She explained the concept to me very clearly. "When we pause in our life, we gain access to our inner wisdom. We start to feel connected, nurtured, and cared for by our God, then ourselves, and lastly others. We get off the hamster wheel of life and truly start to live in our authenticity." As I quickly wrote down all her nuggets of wisdom, she continued, "You are going to go into dating with two ears and one mouth."

"What does that mean?" I giggled at all the analogies she kept throwing at me.

"When you're on your dates and living in the pause of your thoughts, you need to really listen to what the other person is telling you, not what you're wanting to hear. The art of listening is truly a wondrous skill for all of us to develop."

She looked at me as if she was about to drop the biggest mic ever. "Inner work is the highest achievement. Dating is just the icing on the cake."

In the past, I would have snickered in her face; yet, I had done all of this tedious inner work, and I was beginning to "get it." Society tells the world, especially women, that life's main purpose is to find our "perfect partner," our "twin flame," or our "soulmate." But the work I had been doing of learning to love myself had enabled me to learn that I was the perfect partner to myself. Everything beyond that was icing on the cake. Love is a necessary tool for life and a gift from God. I believe that the truest form of love is, and I hate even saying this word, but... self-love. If you don't have that, everything else in your life means nothing.

I could see it so clearly. **I AM MY OWN FUCKING SOULMATE.**

I could see how you can have everything your heart desires, but if you don't truly believe you deserve it, you will be forever empty, futilely searching for the mystical unicorn that will complete you.

I am definitive proof of this.

Yes, I did not get everything I wanted in my life as I've told you before, if that had happened, holy crap, I would have been the worst monster. The kind in horror movies that destroys everything in its wake. The bloodsucking, energy-stealing type, which sounds kind of fun but would leave me depleted and finally alone.

Just another empty human being stumbling around this earth, taking from others because they're so incomplete within themselves. Pretty much the worst human being.

Was I ready for love? Sam and Alice thought so.

Even Dr. Kath was astonished by my transformation when I saw her later that day. I think shocked would be a better word. "Roxanne you're glowing. I can see that the exercise has treated you well. How are you feeling?"

I told her, "I'm feeling very free. I'm kind of loving cutting ties to my outside appearance. I never thought it would be possible. I even asked a man out the other day, which would be a BIG NO for a sweet Southern lady like me. It's in our DNA to let men be the aggressors, which is hilarious since I've acted like the man in most relationships. I was living in a fake reality; on the outside, I looked one way, and on the inside, I was completely different." I paused to try to properly explain. "I always believed it was a man's job to do all the work in the relationship, maybe because my father didn't. Who knows? But it doesn't matter. I never would have been able to ask a man out before. I loved being pursued and chased, so for me to step up without any planning and ask this guy out, it was like an out-of-body experience."

She was smiling at me. "Good for you. How did the date go?"

"He's in Sundance right now for work. But we're going out this Sunday. Alice's wedding is tomorrow, so I can't do a Saturday date. I'm kind of nervous, not going to lie. But I'm strangely not obsessing about it either. In the past, I would want to know what I was going to wear, and I'd look him up to see what kind of girl he dreamed about. To mold myself into the perfect date. So that I would be adored and loved."

She listened to me blabbing on and on, which I guess was her job. So, I kept blabbing. "I always put out the image I thought a man would desire most then got what I needed from him. When it became tiresome to play that role, I would lose interest, and drum up intrigue elsewhere while breaking his heart. I was cruel and in a vicious cycle of make-believe."

I added before our session ended, "So with this guy, I haven't done all the normal actions. I have not looked him up, I have not obsessed about Sunday, I have not even picked out what I want to wear. Instead, I've been helping a bunch of my friends, like Alice for her wedding tomorrow. Coolgirl, with her failing relationship. Glamgirl, getting back together with her husband, and even Eve, with her withdrawal process. I've made my life about being there for others, and I have to say, don't ever repeat it to anyone, but I love it. I feel so much more whole. Who would have thought?" I smiled at the revelation of my development. I saw it with new eyes in that moment while talking it out with Dr. Kath.

Dr. Kath looked proudly at me. I could tell she loved her job and helping others too. I felt closer to her and truly loved her in that moment of pulling me out of the darkness and into the light. I told her with unconditional love, "I see why you love what you do. I get it. I always thought you did it for the money, but with how much you have helped me, it must be a very rewarding career."

She looked at me sideways like a confused dog. "Really? You thought I did it for money? That is funny. Money is the least of all reasons for doing this work for thirty years."

I corrected myself. "I know. I just always thought people did things for themselves instead of for the betterment of the world. It's really admirable."

Lastly, I told her while I was grabbing my stuff off the floor and putting my hat on, "I was saved by not being granted all my old hopes and dreams. I know it would have killed me. Life's rejection is God's protection. Self-acceptance and evolution will always save me. So, when Mr. Handsome kept showing up, I was not looking. I was not searching for anyone or anything to complete me. I was feeling complete all by myself. And who knows, the date might be a bust but I'm looking forward to actually finding out."

Twenty-four hours later, as I put on my makeup for Alice's wedding, purposely neglecting the copious amounts of eyeliner, I was feeling pretty good. I was feeling on solid ground. No highs or lows; just very even-keeled. I was taken aback by how easy the mirror challenge had become for me. I mean, over the past week, I'd had no need to constantly look or obsess over that one hair out of place. As I put on my flowery silk dress, applied my blush, and braided my hair into a side braid, per Alice's request, I was happy. I was feeling so content, I couldn't imagine being any happier.

Suddenly, my phone rang. I looked down, and it was my agent, Gail. I answered with uncertainty. "Gail, you butt dialing me? It's Saturday. Or do you just miss me so much that you need to hear my voice?"

"Hi, love. Guess who just booked the lead role in the Warner Bros. movie she auditioned for? The one that will change her career?" Gail said with overwhelming glee.

"Can't be me, since I bombed that audition."

"Roxie, it is you! You got that part!!!"

I was in shock. "Wait?! I got the part. The studio movie part?"

"YES!!!! I wish you would be easier on yourself. You are a very talented actress. Be nice to my girl!!! I don't have the full offer yet for the money and billing, etc., but I should have it by Monday morning."

I replied quickly, "Please, I would do that role for free. Hell, I would pay them."

She laughed. "Yes, I know, but we are not going to tell them that. Just heard from Junie and wanted to tell you ASAP. Congratulations, you deserve it. It's your time. This is what we have been working on for over a decade."

I started to tear up. "Thank you, Gail. You have been with me through some very gloomy times. When I couldn't even get in the room to read for a crappy one-day guest-star role. I'm so grateful for you and your belief in me. I love you tons."

"Aw, sweetie, I love you too. What are you going to do to celebrate?"

I looked into the mirror with serenity. "I'm going to go to one of my best friend's wedding and celebrate her. That sounds like the perfect way to celebrate to me."

I finished up my makeup in under ten minutes, which was a new record, and headed to the bohemian yet fancy venue, Inn of the Seventh Ray. As I snaked over the mountain pass to enjoy this union of love, I had a huge feeling of gratitude for my journey over the past two years. It had been a lot of ups and downs for me, especially with the loss of my friend and the slip with West. But now that I'd gone through it and emerged on the other side, I was seeing all the good that life has to offer. You have to have the dark times to appreciate the light. Just like you have to fully feel the sadness to fully appreciate the joy.

I'm not saying all of that because I booked a huge job, one that could literally change my life. I'd been around the block too many times, with too many successful A-list stars, to see that this shit really doesn't fix you. I think in the back of my mind I was always waiting for the next job, next big paycheck, next big moment to be the thing that made me feel good enough inside. But it never came. Even when I was shooting on my series and in the blockbuster war movie, I was still empty.

A sense of calm and appreciation about booking the role was all I could muster. Don't get me wrong, I was pumped that I got the part, but now I had to deliver. I could feel the false evidence of being real (fear) start to resurface—immediately after that period of serenity. *This addict mind is a tricky one, damn it.*

That's when the surrender came in. I had to trust.

How do you surrender, you ask? Easy! Ask yourself; what does a surrendered person look like? What do you picture a surrendered person's characteristics to be? Calm, going with the flow, trusting, faithful, loving, however you imagine it.

Driving in the beautiful mountains of Malibu, I brought the concept of surrendering to the Universe to the forefront of my mind. What exactly was the fear saying? My fear was that I wouldn't be able to recreate what I did in the audition room, mostly because I'd been in a place of "just being" instead of performing. I reminded myself that I could never reproduce anything in life. Everything was its own new moment—with my art but especially with my life. Surrendering meant that I would stay centered; no future tripping in any arenas of my life.

Walking into the serene, candlelit room, I felt so content and filled with an overwhelming feeling of love. I had never experienced something like that before. It almost made me want to cry. But I held myself back and instead waved excitedly to Charlie, who was standing by the altar while I took my seat.

Suddenly, I felt a tap on my shoulder. Alice's wedding assistant sidled up to me and whispered, "Alice needs to see you." I was taken aback—the wedding was supposed to start in five minutes. I had even thought I was going to be late, with the typical LA traffic. I stood up abruptly, trying not to cause a scene since everyone else was now seated as well. I shimmied between the chairs and people, not wanting to trip like I notoriously tended to do on a daily basis.

Walking quickly with the panicked assistant to the basement, I saw Alice slumped over, sitting in her dress looking miserable. I ran over. "What's wrong?"

She looked up with tears in her eyes. "I don't know if I can do this, Roxie. Major anxiety attack just happened, which is my mother's fault. She got drunk on mimosas and started going off on my cheating father and his young wife. She repeatedly said to me, 'Alice, I hope you are making the right decision and that Charlie is not a complete con-artist asshole like your father.'"

I wanted to find Alice's mother and punch her in her in-sensitive, smug face, but I needed to attend to my friend. I got down on my knees like I was proposing to her myself. "You are not your mother, Alice. You have been emotionally sober in SLAA for almost six years. You have stopped the generational cycle of addiction in your family. You are making sane decisions about your future, not out of fear or obsession. Your mother is just holding on to resentment and revenge. You can't let her baggage destroy everything you've worked for. You have to have compassion for her pain. Think of her as a sick addict who's not in recovery. She doesn't know any better."

Yes, I understand the irony of me telling her to have grace when I'd wanted to go ballistic on the mother just seconds ago. But my priority was being of service to my friend, whom I loved and wanted to help.

I added, "You love Charlie. He is a very stable, good man. You trust him, right? There are no red flags you're ignoring?"

She nodded, and I could already tell she was starting to think more clearly.

I told her, "Don't let your fear of commitment and getting hurt make you run away from all the hard work you've done with intimacy and love. Don't let that old generational curse win." I helped her up off the chair. "You've got this, baby. You can love and be loved. You are ready." She hugged me, then sweetly pushed me out of the room to get to my seat.

As I watched her walk down the aisle to her future, re-fusing to live in her past, I had an overpowering feeling that I could do it too. I could commit to someone maybe, down the road. I could trust, respect, and fully give myself to another human. I'd always thought I could never get married and be with the same person for the rest of my life. That sounded so boring, and the word "forever" terrified me.

But sitting there listening to them say their vows, I was touched by the possibilities, and not the fantasy version either. I wasn't picturing my wedding at all. In fact, I actually couldn't have cared less about a wedding; I was mostly imagining what I would say to my life partner. What he would say to me.

They kissed to finalize their union, and Alice looked over to me and smiled. I blew a kiss back to her. It had become the most perfect evening to celebrate the act of self-love and commitment. Even when the cake fell over and the band was late. All that stuff didn't matter. We danced, and I ate a huge piece of red velvet cake. The details of the flowers, the crappy long speeches, and all the hogwash that goes into a wedding day mean nothing. Personally, I would have been happy with an artisanal cheese plate, a glass of champagne, a slice of cake, and a pretty dress.

I hugged Charlie and Alice goodbye, and she told me she would see me at the SLAA meeting in the morning. Yep, we addicts hit meetings even after one of the most important days of our lives. We need to be grounded in the reality of our sobriety, and nothing brings you back down to earth faster than sitting around a circle in a church with a bunch of other sex and love addicts.

As I made my way home, feeling whole, I got a text message from Mr. Handsome. "Can't wait to see you tomorrow evening. Hope the wedding was fun. Unless you ran off with a groomsman! :)" I laughed out loud. That wouldn't be the first time that had happened.

I wrote back (at a stoplight, of course), "Nope, no groomsman for me. See you at 6pm." That was it. No flirting or intrigue over text. It forms a false sense of intimacy. So don't you do it either. Keep those texts short and sweet!

It was on my new dating plan that Sam and I had put together. "Texting with dates is very dangerous," she informed me. She then advised, "Actually, texting with anyone is not a great idea. I advise you to only text small information, like 'on my way' or 'see you in five min.' Nothing more than that. Because things can be miscommunicated and misread. Honestly, I wish texting would just go away. It's very harmful for our human race. But I'm old school like that."

Man, I loved her. She got right to the point and always tied it back to the health of all human beings on this planet.

When I got home, I pulled into my driveway, and guess who was there? I couldn't believe it. West got out of his car, walking up to me like he was some boy-band member. As I saw him come toward me, all thoughts of him hurting me and being unavailable—all of my anger and resentment toward him—evaporated. I finally felt like the veil of lies had been lifted.

I saw him and felt nothing. Absolutely nothing. It was freeing.

I smiled genuinely. "Hello there. What are you doing here?"

He was taken aback by my sweet tone. Probably not expecting that from me, since I could be a hot head with him. He had always been able to push my buttons and emotionally deregulate me. He said reluctantly, "Sorry to just show up. But can we talk for a moment?"

I normally would have invited him in with open arms, but not this time. I stood there with absolute confidence, which never happened with him. "Yes, what do you want to discuss?"

He looked at my front door. "Can we go in for some privacy?"

I looked at him as kindly as I could. "Yeah, I don't think that would be a good idea. We can talk right here." Wow, having healthy boundaries was quite liberating.

In the past, I would have wanted to please the person who had tortured me, even my girlfriends. But the words Sam had spoken to me about her sobriety with boundary-setting rang in my consciousness: "I started to get my own healthy boundaries and realized that it's better to keep myself safe than to be liked by everyone. I don't have to worry about what other people are thinking of me. What they think is none of my business. I don't live in their brains. I can say no to something that is not good for me."

West shifted back and forth with a nervousness that I had never seen. He muttered, "I've been feeling pretty down these last few months."

"I'm sorry to hear that—"

He cut me off, "Yeah, I started seeing this psychologist guy that my buddy Bradley hooked me up with. I remember you telling me how much your therapist helped you. It's been bizarre to sit there and talk about my feelings. Anyway, I told him what happened with us in London. He said I should really apologize to you for how I treated you on set. With the bet and everything that NYC and I had. I honestly thought it was funny and never thought you would find out."

Can we all agree right now together that this might be the worst apology we've ever heard? I felt bitch slapped in a way, like the joke was still on me.

"Wow, that is a pretty bad apology, West. No need to come over and tell me all of this." I walked past him towards my door and say goodbye forever.

He stopped me. "Wait, yeah, that didn't come out right. I'm not good with these kinds of situations. But, I am sorry for anything I did to upset you. It was definitely not cool of me."

I looked at him with compassion and a bit of sadness. Compassion that this was the closest he would come to a connection with me and taking responsibility for the cheating, lying, and games he played our whole relationship. Then it hit me: I was no better than him. I also felt sadness for all the time we wasted acting out with each other, trying to find love and intimacy, but being incapable of either of those emotions. Especially when intimacy requires seeing into someone. There's a saying, Intimacy = INTO ME SEE. We never got anywhere close to seeing into each other. And there he was, standing at my door. I saw clearly that he was still struggling with his lack of self.

A wave of gratitude washed over me. I never had to be in that place again. I had done the work required to be honest with myself and change. Forgiveness was the last thing my God required of me. Could I truly let go and let God? Could I move forward to find love and intimacy, with no past pain keeping me hostage?

I believe so!

In that awareness, I replied with warmth, "Thank you for saying that. It hurt me, pretty bad. But I'm okay now. I'm actually in a great place."

He looked a tad bummed by my lack of drama. "Great. I'm happy for you."

"Good to close this door finally with you, West. I wish you nothing but the best. Goodbye."

As I turned my back to him again, he asked, "You think we would have worked out if we were nicer to each other?"

I paused with my key dangling in the door. I closed my eyes and breathed. Letting any idea of the fantasy of us being different or the *what-ifs* of the situation blow right in one ear and out the other. I said over my shoulder, "Does it even matter at this point?" I looked at him and shrugged my indifference.

"I guess not. Goodbye, Roxie."

"Goodbye, West. I hope you find what you're looking for." I walked into my house, feeling the weight of that conversation evaporate as soon as the door closed. I locked the door, picked up, Dog, and hugged and kissed him so hard.

I was okay just as I was. I didn't need my fantasy man to show up for me.

I am now my fantasy man.

Going to bed with the feeling of whole, I had never slept so soundly. I woke up at 8:00 a.m. and was excited for the next adventure—the date with Mr. Handsome. But instead of making appointments for my hair, nails, facial, and all the other beauty treatments society tells us ladies we need to trap a man, I got on with my day.

First, I met up with Eve in the morning to go over her step-work before the SLAA meeting, at Urth Caffé, and Purple even waited on us.

As I paid for my double espresso, Purple asked me shyly, "Hey, Roxanne. Are you available to sponsor? I need to get my ass moving in the program. My girlfriend wants to have a baby, and I'm starting to feel squirrelly."

"Maybe, but call me so we can have a real conversation about what you're looking for in a sponsor and what I can provide." She nodded, and I was pleased with my response. Healthy boundaries were starting to feel very natural, and saying NO, was sometimes the best thing for me.

As Eve sat down, we got right to business with her written work. She told me she'd had an eye-opening moment the other day that she wanted to share with me. "I cultivated so many personalities in my disease to fit in and get the attention I desperately needed. Sometimes my lies were so convoluted, I didn't even know I was lying. It especially devastated my emotional well-being and self-image... I truly believed all those lies, and it made me feel isolated and unworthy unless I was wanted and needed by a man."

She explained the irony of her behaviors with this revelation: "I always thought I was okay without a man's attention and that I did not need a man, just his penis. That all those random one-night stands with guys were my birthright to rebel against what society tells women it's not okay to do. That I was taking a stand for all womankind. Boy, was I wrong. I was lying to myself the whole time; because underneath this facade was the deep emptiness inside. This work is mind-blowing."

I was proud of her. "I get it. I had that moment too. Only to realize how scared I was to be the real me and that I deserve to love and to be loved," I added to her truth.

The thing about sponsoring all these brave women is that it makes me braver to look within. Their willingness to go deep allows me to go deeper. Hearing Eve do the work made me want to dig more and get to the core of myself without all the filters I layered on. "Here's the thing, Eve. In the end, really, the only thing that matters is connection, which is love, right? That's all we humans truly want. At least, that's what I believe. So why be scared of it anymore? Why run from that one thing we all crave? I know I'm tired of being terrified."

"I completely agree, Roxie. I'm exhausted, too. I feel wonderful when you and I connect; why can't I let myself do that with a man, too?"

"Let's make a pact to help each other—that we will lean into all the fear that comes up when we're trying to connect with another human being, whether it's a man or a woman. Deal?"

She nodded.

I bravely added with confidence, "Sam told me that connection is the only way through. Not attachment to others. And here's the kicker—if we're not actively connected, then we're not working on our sobriety. Instead, we're working on our relapse. After she said that, I realized I needed to recommit to leaning into God's plan, not mine."

Eve always hated it when I talked about God. She was struggling to connect to her Higher Power. And I totally got it; I still worked to connect with mine too. She sighed. "I will have to trust you on that. That I will find the love for my so-called Higher Power someday, but I'm not going to hold my breath."

I smiled at her stubbornness, seeing myself in her. "I got you. I will hold that for you. I had to surrender my will as well. You will thank me one day."

Come on, you guys know I love to be right. That would definitely be a glorious day for me. She would have her love for her own God, and I would be right—a win-win all around.

I headed home to get myself ready for my date. With my nerves starting to emerge, I sat in my living room with Dog next to me. And I freaking meditated! *I sat in silence with only my thoughts. SCARY MUCH?*

But I had no choice—my nervous system was off. I had tried my DBT skills first to regulate it:

Dunking my face in a bowl of ice water for thirty seconds. *Did it work? Nope.*

Ice cubes in hands and breathing? *Nope.*

Ten fast jumping jacks? *Nope.*

Singing aloud? *Nope.*

Humming? *Nope.*

All my skills failed in that moment to calm my nervous system. That's when I found myself going back to the worst skill of all: Step Eleven—meditation. Pure torture – I always said. I closed my eyes. I breathed in and out for seven counts, held the breath, and then let it out. I repeated this cycle until I felt my whole body relax. As I opened my eyes, I felt better, much calmer. Then I turned to the clock. "Shit, less than an hour."

I stood up, slowly stretched, and got my stinky ass into the shower. I promised myself I would not wear my normal perfectionist mask to this date. I would be myself. I started to put on the minimal amount of makeup and remembered that I still had to call Sam to bookend this date.

Remember when I told you about bookending? The tool we addicts use before dates. I had done it with Alice before and after that blind date travesty that turned out to be West. It's when you call to check in with someone in the program to go over your intentions for the date, then you call them again afterward. It's to make sure you stick to your dating plan and review what occurred, what you could do differently on the next one, and how you truly feel about the person. Really, it's to keep you accountable, since we sex and love addicts are slippery.

On my dating plan, I was supposed to meet my dates at a neutral location. We agreed upon the delicious Clark Street Diner, formerly known as the 101 Coffee Shop. You know it well, from the movie *Swingers*. On my way, I was feeling pretty excited but not in a junkie-want-to-get-high-off-the-fantasy-of-this-hot-guy kind of way.

As I drove over to the restaurant, I made my bookend call to Sam. She answered on the third ring. "You on your way?"

I answered back sarcastically like a smart ass, "No, I canceled on his ass. I can't do it." She was about to go off on me, I could feel it. "Just kidding. I'm pulling in now. Call you after."

Sam breathed a sigh of relief—I'm sure she had dealt with many neurotic addicts over the years. "Good. Hear from you in two hours? Have fun. Remember, all you need to do is ask yourself, 'Do I want to be friends with this guy?'"

He was sitting in a booth in the back of the restaurant when I arrived, and damn, he was a good-looking man. As he smiled, the kindness in his golden eyes lit up the room, and a calm came over my soul. All the nerves and anxiety I was feeling while parking evaporated. I smiled warmly back, and then this weird feeling like I had known him all my life overcame me.

"Hello, so glad you made it," he said, standing up to greet me.

"Me too. I'm starving. What's good here?"

He was taken aback. "You've never been here before?"

I laughed at him. "Yes, of course I have, but it's been ages. I'm an old lady in Los Angeles. I've lived here for over ten years."

He chuckled. "Yeah, okay, you are so old. I got you beat. I've been in LA for over twenty years, so you've got a long way to go, youngster."

We both looked at the menu after connecting eyes a little too long. He said, looking down, "I would recommend the meatloaf and mashed potatoes, or the corned beef."

I found myself studying his face as he browsed the specials of the day on the board.

He had wrinkles around his eyes, and you could tell he'd been through some stuff and come out on the other side. He was neither a perfect-looking man like West nor a boy like ATL. He was worn and kind of weathered, like he worked with his hands. I instantly felt at ease with him and his witty sarcasm. Mostly because there was no maliciousness behind his teasing.

I had never felt this way with a man before. A part of me was concerned, but the other part of me was fascinated by this new feeling. It wasn't the normal high or disinterest. It was something outside of my normal emotional wheel.

And the best part was that I didn't retreat into the fantasy movie in my mind. I WANTED to be present. And I was staying present! *FREAKING MIRACLE!*

A nice rhythm of conversation overtook us. We kept it light and polite, as my sponsor called it, where you do not discuss anything too personal or extreme. It was a nice getting-to-know-you-as-a-real-person chat. Nothing that would create trauma bonding or disillusionment. It was steady. And dare I say it—SAFE!

Funnily enough, our waiter at the diner was a friend of his, who was very cool and down to earth. I saw why it was important to get out in the world on first dates instead of staying in the bedroom. I could already tell I liked this guy as a friend. Not true with the last bunch of online dates.

I usually don't drink but was kind of craving a glass of hard cider. As I ordered one, I asked Mr. Handsome, "You want to split a bottle? This weather is making me want a sip of apple deliciousness."

He replied, with no hesitation, "No, thanks. I'm sober."

"Wow, I don't have to have one if it bothers you."

He gave me his charming no-bullshit smile again, the kind that made my heart skip a beat. "Oh no, go ahead. I got sober a long time ago, when I was nineteen. Been sober for over two decades in AA. It doesn't bother me at all, but thanks for asking."

This relief flooded over me—he got it, he got the twelve-step vibe. Sam had made it very clear that I was not allowed to tell him about my program in SLAA until the fifth date. I smiled. I had this feeling it would be an easier conversation with someone in a twelve-step program than out of it.

Of course, that was if we got to date five. I swear I was not future tripping over here. I just felt a huge sense of relief that I was not alone in my struggles with some kind of -ism.

I looked back at the menu. "I'm going to go for the burger, medium rare, with sweet potato fries. You?"

He looked proud of my choice, not like I needed his validation. "Good choice. I like a girl who enjoys her meat." He caught himself. "Sorry, I don't mean that in a nasty, perverted way, I promise. I just like a girl who eats. Hard to find in this town."

"Please, I hear you. The last guy I dated ordered his steak with no butter or oil. I looked at him like he had a mental illness. Who would do that to a good piece of meat? A cow was sacrificed for you to eat it—don't mess it up by getting stingy about calories. The worst part was that he didn't even finish it. I almost asked if I could eat the rest, but thought it would make me look like a cow myself."

He laughed. "I'm going for the taco special tonight. I love their fish tacos."

The rest of the date was filled with this kind of banter and easy chit-chat. We even shared a slice of banana cream pie, fighting over the last bite as he grabbed the check and paid. I stood up and turned to him, putting on my leather jacket over my tank top and skinny jeans, the LA staple for us actresses. "This was nice. Thank you for a pleasant dinner."

He grabbed his leather jacket. No, we did not plan our matching outfits, but hey, I love a couple who coordinates.

Cheesy, I know, but when I see those old couples who are matching, it makes my heart smile.

He replied, "Yes, this was very nice. Thank you for finally asking me out. I had been waiting for months."

I burst out with a loud guttural laugh. "You were too chickenshit to ask, so obviously one of us had to step it up."

"Yeah, I know. But in my defense, you can be scary sometimes, especially when getting your salad toppings at Whole Foods. You give off the don't-fuck-with-me vibe."

He made me laugh again. "Very true. I can get hangry."

As we were walking out of the busy restaurant, the wait to get a table had grown to an hour, and it was completely crowded at the front door.

Then it happened, so naturally, it took my breath away.

He gently grabbed my hand and navigated us through the crowd. I followed him out like we had been doing it for years.

Not a flirt. A gentle, easy, comfortable hand-holding. It was magic.

We continued to hold hands as we walked down the stairs and through the hordes of hipsters wanting their pie and tables to discuss their upcoming projects.

He looked down at me, since he was 6'2". I looked up at him and he leaned down and kissed me softly on the lips. A very innocent peck. Tingles shot through my body. I had never had a first kiss so sweet and so kind.

We both pulled back, a bit of shock on our faces. *What the hell was that?* But instead of questioning, we smiled and looked away.

He walked me to my car and muttered, "Sorry about that. It just happened—I was not planning it at all." I nodded in agreement. He looked at me again and said, "Thanks for a fun, easy night. I needed it." He turned to walk away.

Then the words popped out of my mouth, "Seriously? What the hell, dude? Aren't you going to ask me out again?"

No idea what had just come over me. I was never like this, and this was the second time I had asked this man out. Honestly, it was like an out-of-body experience.

He turned and had a huge belly laugh. "Well, I was going to wait the appropriate 2.5 days to ask you, but I guess not. You want to go out again?"

I smiled, climbing into my car. "Maybe. I guess you'll have to call me and ask."

He shook his head at my attempt to be all cool and casual after I had already blown that cover. "I will call you tomorrow to set the date. Drive safely. Please text me when you make it home."

I waved back to him. "You too."

As I drove back home alone, I called Sam and left my check-in voicemail. "It went great, very sweet and easy conversation—never had a date like that before. He told me he's been sober for almost twenty years, which is so honorable. Don't worry, I didn't overshare or get into anything too heavy. But he did give me a peck on the lips when we walked out, taking us both by surprise. I asked him out again—it was God, not me. I was not planning it at all. But had a fun time. On my way home alone. Call you in the morning."

As I climbed into bed, still a very sober sex and love addict, Mr. Handsome called. "Made it home safe," he said. "Sorry I acted all cool after our date. I did want to ask you out. I just got nervous. But I would love to take you out again tomorrow night or the next night. Whenever you're free."

I smiled with excitement. "I might be free on Tuesday for a lunch date, if that works for you?"

"Perfect. Well, good night, Roxanne, and I just have to say, that was the best first date I have ever had."

I confessed, "Me too. Good night."

I hung up, rolled over and pulled Dog into my nook. A sense of clarity overtook me.

I still believe that love is a gift—but now I know the truest form of that love is self-acceptance. Without it, nothing else truly lands. You can be surrounded by everything you thought you wanted, yet still feel hollow if you haven't made peace with yourself. I've lived that now. I've seen how believing you deserve love—starting with your own—changes everything.

I was living proof of this. You can have everything and still have nothing if you don't have yourself. I was blessed that God did NOT grant me all my hopes and dreams. It would have definitely killed me.

So, when Mr. Handsome showed up, I was not looking. I was not searching for anyone or anything to complete me. I was complete all by myself.

It was like my Higher Power was clearly guiding me to open myself up and finally say yes to someone who seemed truly available. It was like God was telling me—you are ready to show up as your authentic self to give to another soul.

What they say is very true—when you stop looking, love shows up with no drama and flows easily. True connection does not involve any power dynamics or means of control. It should be easy.

Crazy, how my big fall from grace was actually the thing that saved me. I never thought it was possible that my fear of intimacy and being loved could actually lead me to find a real connection to self and to another person.

My hardships have taught me more lessons than any supposed victory. You know what I mean? Have you had moments in your life when you felt the worst of the worst about yourself? Then you looked back and see that shit was a blessing? *Who knew? Certainly not I!*

Now I was ready to love and be loved. As scary as that sounded, it was also an adventure, as I had both my feet on the ground for the first time. I jumped off the cliff without a net, and wholeheartedly put myself into this relationship. For good or bad, I was ready to feel a full and genuine connection. I was ready for love. Love was a thoughtful, conscious decision I was making. I was not falling in love anymore. Falling is not a choice. Falling is not a conscious decision. Healthy relationships were all I was interested in.

Hold on tight—success or failure is always unknown, but I was willing to try. My heart deserved it. And so does yours.

ROXANNE'S PLAYLIST

Superficial Love - *Ruth B* - Roxanne despises the shallow world of dating. After fighting hard for her sobriety and reclaiming her most authentic self, navigating the LA dating scene feels like torture. Every date feels like a bad casting call: one's performing his trauma monologue, another's selling himself like a used car, and all of them leave her with the same souvenir—the ICK. The men who show up leave her exasperated—each encounter dripping with pretense, facades, and the kind of surface-level charm that makes her skin crawl. She feels trapped in a hellscape where no one seems willing to be honest, vulnerable, or real. Roxanne shows up raw, open, and craving true connection—but instead, she's met with masks. No fake. No facade. No more meaningless attachments.

Roxanne - *Arizona Zervas* - Roxanne drifts back into dangerous daydreams—the old her, the addict her. Back when disconnection felt like freedom, when she could float above life untouched by anyone else's needs. Men weren't heartbreaks or partners then; they were props. Toys for her pleasure. Placeholders for her emptiness. She misses the fantasy of being untouchable—independent, detached, slipping out the door while they were still falling in love with her. It was all ego. All validation. All attention. And God, part of her still craves that high.

Good Cry - *Noah Cyrus* - Roxanne throws herself into the chair across from Dr. Kath. "Dr. Kath, I need a goddamn good cry so bad it might split me open. Dating isn't just disappointing—it's humiliating." Roxanne feels like she's being catapulted back into some pathetic teenage version of myself. It's like, how the hell is she still stuck in these juvenile stages of love when she's supposed to be a grown woman. She feels wasted years drowning in her old toxic shit. The old her? She's gone, buried. But this 'new self? She's a stranger. Confusing as fuck. Some days she hates her more than the addict self I used to be. Healing is supposed to be freeing, but all she feels is lonely as hell. And every failed attempt at dating just gets shoved in her face—like she's too broken, too late, too unworthy. Honestly, she is starting to wonder if this whole 'healthy love' thing is even real, or does she hate that dating makes her feel like she's always playing catch-up, like she's the last one to figure out how to be an actual adult.

July - *Noah Cyrus* - *Her music is my love/hate drug—the perfect soundtrack to Roxanne's addiction to love* Roxanne's mind spirals on the drive, gnawing on West like an old wound that won't close. The push and pull, the venom wrapped in charm—it was never love, just poison dressed as intimacy. Nights stretch hollow with his voice still echoing, those passive-aggressive jabs burrowing under her skin until she questions her own memories. Were they ever real? Or was she just another body he used to feed his ego? The silence is a torment. Why hasn't he called? Where is he? Is he already breaking in that new costar the way he broke her down? The reel plays on repeat, every touch, every lie, every illusion. The traffic on the 405 drags, but the real gridlock is in her head—trapped in the sick comfort of replaying her own destruction. Her favorite form of escapism.

Don't Blame Me - *Taylor Swift* - The moment Roxanne sees West at the blind date, it's like her whole body betrays her—every nerve buzzing, butterflies clawing at her insides, the rush of old feelings flooding back before she can catch her breath. The intensity of their connection slams into her, too big to control, too sharp to ignore. And yet—there it is again. The lie. His mask. Pretending to be someone else, another red flag waving like fire in the night. Still, the attraction won't loosen its grip. It's chemical, electric, a moth-to-the-flame obsession she can't just turn off. This is the song in her veins—dangerous, addictive, impossible to resist. She knows it's false intimacy, but it feels so real her nervous system lights up like a cattle prod. Right or wrong, good or bad, her fantasy has stepped out of her mind and into the room. And now she has to face it.

Hostage - *Billie Eilish* - Roxanne sits across from West at the blind date dinner, her veins alive, crawling under her skin. The hunger is unbearable—she doesn't just want his attention, she wants his soul. Every glance feels like temptation, every word a hook. Should she surrender and let him be cast in the role opposite her in London, let the fantasy consume her again? Or protect herself from the very fire that has burned her before? It's a deadly tug-of-war for a recovering sex and love addict—one part of her desperate to connect, the other fighting to survive. What does she do with the urge to keep him, to trap him, to take him hostage inside her world?

All My Friends - *Counting Crows* - Roxanne opens the door to her circle of friends and sponsees—the women who bring both chaos and comfort, laughter and unwavering support. For the first time, she's able to show up for them with real empathy and balance, more grounded than she's ever been. For once, she's not hiding or performing. She evolved in way she never could before—more honest, more present, more empathetic. These relationships prove to her that she doesn't have to do life alone anymore. She's finally learning that connection with women can be safe, messy, and healing all at the same time. In these connections, she discovers a healthier rhythm, proof that she's found a better way—and brighter days—through the bonds of sisterhood.

Deep Down - *Zhavia Ward* - Roxanne doesn't even know what to feel, watching her friends tumble back into the grip of love and sex addiction. When Tattoogirl walks out of her house, her hand clutching the strap of her designer bag, the weight of reality slams into Roxanne's chest. Something shifts deep inside her soul—grief, loss, a hollow hopelessness. The ache that some people may never find their way out of the darkness. It's a brutal reminder: all she can do is focus on herself, keep working on her own healing, and let others choose their own path. She's not God. She can't drag anyone out if they're not ready to crawl out themselves.

God Only Knows - *(Timbaland remix) by King & Country* - Whenever fear grips Roxanne—false evidence appearing real—she forces herself to hand it over to God. Her higher power, a presence she doesn't fully understand, doesn't always feel, but clings to anyway. Because she knows one brutal truth: her addict mind can't untangle her addict mind. Only God can carve a way through the wreckage when an addict is clawing for change. So she has to surrender—her panic, her spiraling thoughts, the gnawing fear about the London shoot. It's the only lifeline she has. If she doesn't keep turning it over, if she doesn't trust something bigger than herself, she knows the outcome: she'll blow up her sobriety, torch everything she's built, and fall back into the fire she barely crawled out of.

Drowning - *Anna Clendening* - Roxanne is drowning at this table read, barely keeping her head above water. NYC and West both being in the movie feels like her worst nightmare unfolding in real time. The pressure, the ghosts of the past— it's all crashing down on her at once. She knows she needs to call her sponsor, Alice, the second this ends. For now, she's just praying she can make it through without slipping under, without disappearing while nobody notices. Her mind is an ocean, waves of painful memories from past relationships pulling her under.

Drunk Text Me - *Lexi Jayde* - Roxanne is lost in the throes of passion during her love scene with West, and the moment the director calls "cut," she knows she's in trouble. Their chemistry is electric, undeniable—too real. In her head, it's like a song playing on repeat, begging for him to win her back. She imagines West regretting their breakup, aching for what they once had. Every look, every touch on set sends her spiraling into the flood of *what ifs* and *could have beens*, the intensity of their past crashing into her all over again.

Surrender - *Natalie Taylor* - Welcome to the dark night of Roxanne's soul. West just wrecked her—body, mind, and spirit—with that cruel bet with NYC. Her heart feels split wide open, crushed beyond repair. She can't believe she let herself fall for him again, swallowed whole by the same hook, line, and sinker. Now she's stranded in a London hotel room, drowning in her own feelings, forced to face the truth: everything has to change. Her sobriety wasn't as solid as she thought—it was fragile, paper-thin, and West knew exactly how to gaslight and manipulate her back into the fire. On the floor, raw and broken, Roxanne has nothing left but surrender. She cries out, begging her higher power to show up, to carry her through this darkness, because alone, she knows she won't survive.

Hallelujah - *Rufus Wainwright* - Roxanne thought losing Alice as her sponsor was devastating—the way she bent over in her car, heart breaking from the weight of even a healthy goodbye. But this loss cut deeper, a thousand times more brutal. Holy hell—the pain is crushing. Roxanne can't wrap her head around losing Tattoogirl to the grip of fantasy and love addiction. The news hit like a tidal wave, dragging her under with shock and unbearable grief. How is she supposed to keep walking in sobriety when her friend is gone? The truth cuts deep—she can only change herself, never save anyone else. All she has to cling to is her higher power. Hallelujah for the God who can carry her through this gutting, unbearable moment of loss.

Tear Down The House - *The Avett Brothers* - Roxanne is being forced to rip her old life down, brick by brick. After West's lies, the betrayal of her body, Tattoogirl's horrific death, and carrying the weight of Fuckface's dying by her friend's love addictive hands—she can't escape the wreckage. She has to face it all: the grief, the regret, the sorrow that drags her into the darkest corners of death itself. Only by walking through it —can she begin again. Time to tear down the house she grew up in. This devastation isn't just an ending—it's the brutal reset, the raw rebirth she never wanted but desperately needs. This is the turning point for no more and this can never be the same.

Tell the Truth to Yourself - *The Avett Brothers* - Back in Dr. Kath's jungian therapy office, it's time to dig deep again after so much loss. It's time to tell the truth to herself again, to face the inner child work waiting for her. To grieve what's been stripped away, to shed the old skin that no longer belongs, to step out of the past and into the present. She is ready to make amends to herself and anyone else. Telling the truth with reality. Pain helps you do that. The Avett Brothers play like a lifeline—always there for Roxanne in the darkest seasons, a constant soundtrack in her little Los Angeles cottage whenever it's time to do the soul work of starting over.

Love Myself - *Olivia O'Brien* - Roxanne is determined to strip back every layer of her soul until she can finally, fully love herself. Not just the shiny parts—the shadows too, every flaw, every asset. She's committed to loving herself first, before anyone else. She doesn't need to be who she once was, and she doesn't need to mirror anyone around her. All she needs is to stand in the wholeness of her true self. Even the brutal act of stripping away mirrors—so she can't obsess over her reflection, can't hide behind making the outside look better than the inside. Peeling back the layers of her soul is a lifelong journey—one that will never truly end. Still, she's committed to the work, determined to keep moving forward no matter how many layers remain.

Hello My Old Heart - *The Oh Hellos* - Roxanne has found her way back to her old heart. The bricks are gone, the walls dismantled, the armor of eyeliner wiped away. She's softer now, less judgmental, more in tune with her inner child. She's learned how to protect herself without retreating into avoidance, so her heart can finally come home to her—and open to the people she loves most.

We Are Loved - *The Avett Brothers* - Roxanne finally sees that love surrounds her in every corner of her life—because, at last, she truly loves herself. When self-love runs deep, it spills outward: relationships unfold with ease, free of drama, free of broken boundaries, free of explosive fights. What takes their place is communication, understanding, and a steady deepening—of self and of connection. Loving herself makes her a better partner, friend, and human. She knows she is loved—by her higher power, by the people who matter most, and most importantly, by herself. She surrenders to the truth that she is always cared for—because she has finally learned how to care for herself.

AUTHOR'S NOTE

HOLY FUCK—I DID it again. Another book about sex and love addiction. Sometimes I shake my head and think, *Really, Brianne? Why would you willingly drag yourself back into the fire, letting people dissect your life and your mess?*

But here's the truth: this isn't just about me. It never was. This book is for every suffering sex and love addict who still doesn't have a voice that feels real. I was so sick of the dry, preachy literature that never touched the raw nerve of this disease. So, I wrote the book I wish someone had handed me when I was drowning.

This time, it's not only Roxanne's story—it's the stories of all kinds of sex and love addicts. The avoidants who run from intimacy. The anxious attachers who cling for dear life. The sexual anorexics who starve themselves from connection. The fantasy addicts lost in daydreams. The codependents, the narcissistic lovers—the whole messy spectrum. Because addiction doesn't wear just one face. And the more I wrote, the freer I felt to bring truth and imagination together in a way that I hope cracks something open for you, too.

Today, I'm sixteen years sober, and I can finally look in the mirror without flinching. I actually like the woman staring back at me. And the biggest mindfuck? After a lifetime of chasing "the one," I finally figured out that the soulmate I was desperate to find... was me all along.

So, thank you—for daring to open this book, for walking with me through the chaos and the heartbreak, and for maybe even laughing at some of the absurd Hollywood sobriety tales along the way.

Until next time,
Brianne

ACKNOWLEDGEMENTS

TO MY HUSBAND, MARK—my partner not only in life, but in creating art that moves people. Your steady love and belief in me gave me the courage to write these words and share them with the world.

To my son, Davis—you are the mirror that reflects both my wounds and my growth. You push me to heal deeper, to rise higher, and to keep becoming the woman I want you to see. You are my greatest teacher and my greatest joy.

To everyone I hurt in my past, and to everyone who has stood beside me as I stumbled, healed, and rose again—thank you. To the countless souls I've been blessed to help along the way, know this: your courage to trust me with your pain has been one of the greatest honors of my life. In your healing, I found my own.

I am grateful for the darkness that once consumed me, and for the light that continues to guide me. Without both, I would not stand here today. Every shadow, every scar, every lesson has shaped me into the woman holding this book in her hands.

And finally, to the fellowship, the program, and every single person who reminded me that recovery is possible—you saved my life. This book is as much yours as it is mine.

ABOUT THE AUTHOR

BRIANNE DAVIS is a relationship and trauma specialist, author, speaker, podcast host, wife, mom—and unapologetic truth-teller. With more than sixteen years of recovery from sex and love addiction, she has become an authority on breaking toxic cycles, attachment wounds, and the shame that keeps people from experiencing real intimacy.

She is the host of the top-rated *Secret Life Podcast*, where she guides thousands of listeners through raw conversations about addiction, love, mental health, and transformation. Her first book, *Secret Life of a Hollywood Sex & Love Addict*, struck a nerve for its fierce honesty and laugh-out-loud storytelling. Through speaking, writing, and her signature 14-step framework, Brianne offers hard-earned wisdom and practical tools for creating healthy, authentic connections.

Alongside her work as a specialist, Brianne has built a multifaceted Hollywood career. She has starred in films and television shows including *Jarhead*, *Prom Night*, *Lucifer*, and *Six*. Behind the camera, she has directed and produced stories that shine light on hidden struggles.

When she's not working, Brianne can usually be found arranging flowers, tending to her garden, catching up on *Dateline*, curled up with her beloved dog Stella. She lives in

Los Angeles with her husband Mark, and son Davis, where she continues to remind others that the greatest love story begins within.

UP NEXT FROM BRIANNE DAVIS

Secret Life of a Healthy Marriage - *The Follow-Up Novel*
(A continuation of the story,
expanding on the messy, raw,
and redemptive journey of love, recovery,
and self-discovery.)

10 Rules for Staying Married in Hollywood

Okay. I know exactly what you're thinking. One: Seriously, of all people, YOU tied the knot, Roxie? We've seen you through a lot of ups and downs, mostly downs—how did you do it? Two: Weren't you anti-wedding... except for that artisanal cheese plate and cake?

Here's the thing. Yes. Those things are true; however, it is a woman's prerogative to change her mind... especially when she has been through the ringer of the good, the bad, and the ugly. Okay... not so much good or ugly, but I definitely conquered the bad. But doing the work with SLAA gave me the tools to believe, at the ripe old age of thirty-one, that I could have a second act. I could find love—and more importantly, keep it. Relationships are a lot of work, especially when you're not relying on sex as your only connection. So, once you've done the exhausting and rewarding work of slogging through your shit and have found "your person," it is going to take a lot of work, both together and separately, to keep the relationship honest, authentic, and fun. Oh, and of course, passionate... but that's a given. Having climbed the highs of romance and nearly drowned in the lows of addiction, I've come up with, yep, ten more rules to help you stay in a relationship.

Join me on this roller-coaster journey through Hollywood, acting, addiction, and finding and keeping true love.

F-This: My Relationships Are Killing Me!
(The non-fiction companion,
naming the 8 most destructive relationship
types and giving you the tools to finally break free.)

Break the Pattern. Burn the Fantasy. Reclaim Your Sanity.

Yeah, I said it — F-THIS. I'm done watching people destroy themselves in the name of "love." I've seen it up close — the chaos, the gaslighting, the soul-shredding trauma bonds that hijack your nervous system and convince you it's normal.

This book isn't theory. It's battle-tested. These are the same raw, real tools I've used to help clients around the world break free from emotional loops that keep them stuck and sick. If your relationships feel like war zones, addictions, or haunted houses you can't escape — you're not crazy. You're caught in a pattern. And it's time to break it.

We're calling out the 8 most toxic dynamics people normalize:

- The **Stuck Partner** – trapped in a long-term emotional hostage situation

- The **Love Drunk Rebounder** – high on chemistry, low on reality

- The **Soulmate Fantasy Monster** – intense, idealized, and emotionally dangerous

- The **Enmeshed Parent-Child Duo** – where boundaries dissolve into guilt, shame, and control

- The **Love Anorexic** and **Shutdown Master** – afraid to feel, terrified to connect

- The **Partner in Crime Friendship** – loyalty twisted into codependent chaos

- The **Narcissist vs. Codependent** – a toxic power loop that feeds off imbalance

- And **The Low Esteem Self-Sabotager** – the version of *you* that keeps choosing pain over peace

No sugarcoating. No spiritual bypassing. Just the truth — and the tools you need to cut the cord and come home to yourself.

If your relationships are killing you — emotionally, mentally, spiritually — this book is your wake-up call.

Let's burn the fantasy.

Let's face the trauma.

Let's rebuild from truth.

You in?

Thank You!

If this book made you feel seen, slightly attacked, or emotionally called out... you're note alone.

Leaving a **REVIEW** helps other readers find this story—and keeps honest, uncomfortable novels like this alive.

Say what you loved. Say what made you squirm. Say what stuck. Your words matter.

Want more from the **Secret Life** universe? Find bonus content, updates, and behind-the-scenes chaos at:

Websites:
secretlifenovel.com secretlifepodcast.com
briannedavis.com

Social Media:
@secretlifenovel @secretlifepodcast @thebriannedavis